WAITING FOR A ROGUE

By Marie Tremayne

The Reluctant Brides Series
Lady in Waiting
The Viscount Can Wait
Waiting for a Rogue

Waiting for a Rogue

a Rogue

The Reluctant Brides

Marie Tremayne

AVONIMPULSE
An Imprint of HarperCollinsPublishers

Excerpt from *Lady in Waiting* copyright © 2018 by Marie Tremayne.

WAITING FOR A ROGUE. Copyright © 2019 by Marie Tremayne. All rights reserved. Printed in the United States of America. No part of this book may be used or reproduced in any manner whatsoever without written permission except in the case of brief quotations embodied in critical articles and reviews. For information, address HarperCollins Publishers, 195 Broadway, New York, NY 10007.

Digital Edition JULY 2019 ISBN: 978-0-06-274741-9

Print Edition ISBN: 978-0-06-274742-6

Cover design by Patricia Barrow
Cover art by Christine Ruhnke
Cover photographs © Oleksandr Kavun/Shutterstock (woman); © Ververidis Vasilis/Shutterstock (steps)

Avon Impulse and the Avon Impulse logo are registered trademarks of HarperCollins Publishers in the United States of America.

Avon and HarperCollins are registered trademarks of HarperCollins Publishers in the United States of America and other countries.

FIRST EDITION

19 20 21 22 23   HDC   10 9 8 7 6 5 4 3 2 1

For Elise.
Beloved daughter, cherished friend.

Waiting for a Rogue

CHAPTER ONE

Mildred's Millinery
Hampshire, England
March 1847

Caroline hid her disbelief with a ladylike cough and eyed the familiar aged shopkeeper. With an attempt at patience, she smiled and tried again.

"I beg your pardon," she said, a hint of confusion creeping into her voice, "but I don't believe I heard you correctly, Mildred. My aunt asked me to pick up a bonnet . . . *one* bonnet."

A bout of amused laughter caused the woman's shoulders to shake with mirth. "Oh no, my lady, you heard me a'right. Lady Frances ordered four, only she's never been by to pick them up." She shook her head. "They're such elaborate things too . . ."

To prove her point, Mildred reached over to raise the lids of the hatboxes that were stacked on the counter before them. The straw creations were more fancifully decorated with ribbons and flowers than current fashion dictated. In fact, the flashy style was more appropriate to the previous decade. Caroline knew the milliner was typically quite up on all the trends from London, so this came as a surprise.

"Did Lady Frances order these hats be designed in such a specific way?" she inquired innocently, her eyes widening at the copious layers of satin trim and multicolored feathers the final hat revealed.

"Oh yes, she was very particular." Mildred sounded almost apologetic, then smiled brightly from between the gray curls that framed her face.

Caroline's smile faltered and she felt the blood drain from her face. Her aunt knew Caroline did not wish to return to London in the spring, regardless of her parents and their feelings on the matter. Was this Frances's way of forcing the issue? It was possible, but unlikely. She didn't want to think on what the likeliest scenario actually was, but found herself considering it anyway—that these hats were not intended as part of a larger scheme to pressure Caroline into another useless season, but were simply a product of one of her Aunt Frances's most recent fantasies. One that would cost a pretty penny, although that concern was not of paramount importance to her at the moment.

It was how she was going to get the blasted things home.

If she'd taken the carriage, this little setback would hardly be any trouble at all. But of course she'd chosen to walk today given the mildness of the weather. Tapping her fingers against her lips, she scanned the cluttered storeroom behind the front counter.

"I don't suppose you've any extra staff on hand to make a delivery?"

"Wishing I did, my lady," replied the milliner as she replaced the lids upon the boxes, regarding the clock with stern disappointment. "If my nephew Simon were here on time as he should be, he could do it for ye. Or I could help with loading it into your carriage."

Caroline shook her head and directed her gaze out the window, the weak winter sunlight that had shone a moment before now darkening with the passage of a cloud. "I walked here today. However, Lady Frances was most anxious to receive her bonnet, er, *bonnets*, so I will take them home myself."

The shopkeeper stared. "On foot?"

"Both feet, even," said Caroline lightly, her tone sounding more self-assured than she felt, the four boxes mocking her from their place upon the counter. She smiled, cinching her green woolen cloak more tightly around her neck and raising the hood. "Would you mind assisting me to the door?"

A few minutes later and with a doubtful wave from Mildred, she was on her way, albeit awkwardly. The milliner had managed to secure the boxes in pairs with string for easier carrying, and Caroline teetered as gracefully as she could, balancing one set on either side of her as she dodged the mud along the edge of the road. Glancing up, it appeared that the worst of the clouds had passed for now, allowing a slice of sunshine to break through, hopefully giving her enough time to

arrive home without getting soaked. The journey to Willowford House was not long—under an hour by walking—but
she knew that after only a few minutes her arms would grow
weary from carrying these boxes.

Nothing to be done about it except to walk and keep her
head down. It would help her to concentrate on the sound
of the horses trotting by and try not to think on how their
riders were probably staring down at her with confusion, disdain, or both. Although even she could admit that the sight
of her trudging by herself into the country, beset by hatboxes, would appear quite strange, even to those who were
not aware that she was the Duke of Pemberton's daughter.

Not that she cared about anyone's opinion, especially
that of the Duke and Duchess of Pemberton, she thought
with a bitter pang. After all, it was their conspicuous absence
from her life that had served to mark her as somehow defec-
tive. And what was the *ton*, or anyone else to think, when
they'd simply elected to hide her away in the country with
her maiden aunt?

What was *she* even to think?

A fresh tide of heartache washed through her and she
steeled herself against it. Not for her parents. She'd long
given up on them. But it was Eliza's departure, and the circumstances that had surrounded it, that still shook Caroline
long after her friend had been forced to leave the neighboring
estate for good. And there was only one person responsible
for it all . . .

The American.

She scowled. Hadn't Eliza gone through enough after

being widowed with a young child—her father and brother killed in the same accident that took her husband? Life wasn't fair and Caroline knew it very well, but her friend had suffered far more than her share. It wasn't right that she then be evicted from the only home her daughter had ever known, just because the next male in line stepped forwards for his share.

It's the way of the world, people had told her. *Entailment is the law,* they had said.

Well the law was stupid, she thought, kicking a rock vengefully out of her way. And strangely enough, the law seemed designed to put females at a disadvantage. It was one of the reasons she did not wish to marry . . . aside from the fact that men had only proven to her, time and again, that they were undeserving of such commitment. She refused to be a either a brood mare or a decorative accessory for some foppish lord, and there was *no* way she would ever let herself be managed by such a man. Or any man, for that matter.

"I trust you won't make it easy for him," Eliza had said as she had pulled her close on her final day in Hampshire, struggling to smile through her tears.

Caroline's throat had constricted in sorrow. "Never."

Despite it all, Eliza had found a happy ending with her new husband, the incredibly mischievous Viscount Evanston. Caroline had even surprised herself by approving of the match. But there was no such change of heart for the Cartwick heir.

She glared down the road in the general direction of his newly acquired estate. Regardless of *the law,* he had still robbed her of one of the only people who loved her and caused an undue amount of pain in the process. He was simply another man trying to rule his little piece of the world without care for others, and she was only too happy to make it as difficult for him as possible. In fact, Caroline had already started by hampering his efforts to alter the boundary lines between their estates. It was a mystery how the lines had gone wrong to begin with, and she knew her recourse was limited, but he'd taken quite enough already, in her opinion. She would not sit idly by.

At some point, the hardened dirt street of town had given way to the hedgerows that lined the road leading towards home. Exhaling a sigh of relief, she set her boxes down upon the grassy ground underfoot. Caroline rolled her head around to loosen her shoulders, now aching with the persistent weight of the boxes, and flexed fingers that had grown numb from the brisk coolness of the air. Her hood had slipped off but she didn't mind so much now, when she was away from the curious stares of the townsfolk. Her hair was a thorough mess, however, with locks flying every conceivable way from their pins.

Depending on her current mood, Aunt Frances would either laugh in delight at her disheveled state, or deliver a sharp rebuke for looking like a heathen out of doors. Caroline could no longer be sure what kind of reception she would receive; she only feared for the day when her aunt might forget her entirely.

Her vision blurred as she bent down to retrieve her burden once more, but the sounds of an approaching horse stayed her hands and she squinted up ahead. It was a lone rider. Muttering under her breath, she hooked her fingers through the string handles and moved quickly off the road. To her consternation, the rider's pace slowed as he neared. In an attempt to avoid engaging him, she fixed her gaze to some distant point and tipped him a nod of barest acknowledgment. It was an indifferent gesture that she was certain would not encourage further conversation.

He started one anyway.

"Pardon me, but are you in need of assistance?" called the man.

The rich depth of his voice took her by surprise and she almost risked a glance upwards at his face. Caroline resisted the urge as it would only promote more interaction. Staring at the gleaming black leather of the boot that rested in the stirrup, she was likewise perturbed by the muscled leg that rose just above it, and by the long masculine fingers that held the reins in their commanding grip. She twitched her head anxiously in negation.

"No, sir, I am not, but thank you for your concern. Good day."

Caroline resumed walking, and for one fleeting moment she almost believed she'd successfully deterred the stranger until the horse's hooves could again be heard ambling closer.

"It seems you are rather fond of headgear, although I see you wear none yourself," he observed.

There was a hint of amusement in his tone, and she might have laughed if she hadn't been so taken by that voice again. He had an intriguing accent that was refined, yet had an edge to it she could not quite place. Caroline wasn't entirely comfortable with how it was affecting her, nor did she care to find herself feeling vulnerable in the company of an unknown man on an empty road. She felt the strongest need to get rid of him. And tug him closer. It was all very confusing.

"They're not mine," she replied hastily over her shoulder. "And while I appreciate your concern for my headgear, I really must be on my way."

Her heart sank when she heard him swing off his saddle to land solidly on the ground behind her. She knew there would be no ignoring him now, but perhaps she would find him as unattractive as his voice was enthralling. Spinning around to face him, she felt her breath seize inside her chest.

No such luck.

He was tall but not imposing, his body an enticing combination of lean angles and muscles with a powerful set of shoulders easily discernible beneath the lines of his sapphire-blue frock coat. The hands she'd admired before slid slowly off his horse's polished leather saddle while he surveyed her with interest, and she noticed the unusually short cut of his brown hair, the strong set of his jaw, the alluring curve of his lips and a slight dimple in the center of his chin.

There was something that made her want to stroke him with her fingertips. Caress his cheeks, his nose, his mouth. He had a sensuality that called to her, until recently ignored, primal instincts. Even her brief interest in the undeserving Lord Braxton had never sparked feelings like this.

Her gaze rested with tremulous fascination upon his eyes. They were of the lightest brown . . . glowing and golden.

She didn't think she'd ever seen anything quite like them. What was worse, she didn't want to stop looking.

The hatboxes slipped from her fingers to land on the ground.

With a tiny exclamation, she crouched down to collect her aunt's bonnets, one of which had managed to free itself in the midst of the chaos. Before she could reclaim the wayward headpiece, the stranger had managed to scoop it up, silencing her objection with another outstretched hand meant to assist her.

"No, thank you," she forced out shakily, untangling herself from her skirts and coming to a stand on her own.

The man raised his eyebrows and shrugged, then directed his attention to the decorative bonnet still in his grasp. He turned it this way then that, finally glancing towards her with hesitant inquiry.

"You have . . . extravagant taste," he noted, neatly dodging the bright spray of feathers as he turned the bonnet another time.

Caroline leaned forwards to snatch it from his hand, realizing too late that she'd come close enough to detect the skin-warmed scent of his shaving soap. She jerked back with a glare.

"I told you before," she said while trying to stuff the offensive thing back in its box, "it's not mine. Please don't look at it," she added.

He uttered a low laugh. "You dropped it out onto the road. How was I not to look at it?"

She could think of no response to that but a small *hmph*, which elicited a smile of amusement from the handsome stranger. With the boxes sealed and secured at last, she lifted them again and gave him what she hoped was a final nod of farewell. She felt too ridiculous at the moment to even attempt a more formal good-bye. Turning on her heel, she strode quickly away.

"Wait—"

His request only made her walk faster, but the slide of his fingers upon her sleeve halted her progress. She faced him with something nearing exasperation.

"What do you want from me, sir?" she asked. Although if she were being honest about it, part of her hoped there was an answer to that question.

The man pulled his hand away and patted the sleek black nose of his horse, still being towed dutifully behind him. "I think we started off on the wrong foot." He inclined into a shallow bow. "My name is Jonathan—"

His next words were ripped from the air by a crack of lightning that sent the rooks in the trees scattering noisily. They held each other's gaze in mutual alarm. He shook his head, switching topics altogether.

"How much farther do you have to walk?" he asked with a wary glance at the burgeoning sky, placing his hand gently behind her to usher her along.

"I, um—" It took a moment to gather her thoughts between the dazzle of the lightning and the heat of his hand pressing against her back. "Not much farther . . . just past the hill to Willowford House."

He stopped abruptly. "Did you say Willowford House?"

"Yes. Why?"

After a pause, he cleared his throat. "No reason."

The pressure of his hand was upon her back again. They resumed their walk in awkward silence, with Caroline casting furtive glances to ascertain the reason for the suddenness of his shift in mood. Finally, he said, "So what is your impression of the American?"

She turned to stare at him, but a simultaneous rumble of thunder prompted her feet to keep moving beneath her skirts. "The American?" she asked in confusion.

"The one who has moved into the Cartwick estate. I can only assume you've heard of him since he would be your closest neighbor."

Caroline scoffed. "Indeed, I have heard of him."

"And?"

"I'm not impressed so far."

His eyes were alight with interest. "Why not?"

She shifted the weight of the boxes to alleviate the strain on her fingers, and without breaking his stride, he reached down to take one set of hatboxes. At her murmur of thanks, he only tipped his head for her to continue.

"Well for one, the vile man is apparently unwilling to converse unless it is through his land agent."

He raised his brows. "So you have spoken to the land agent?"

"Through letters."

"And there is a dispute?"

She gave him a wry glance.

His mouth twisted. "I see. And what makes this American so vile? Or is it simply that you disagree with his views on this . . . land dispute?"

Their harried pace up the hill was making it difficult for her to catch her breath, but she was still able to shoot him an offended look. "Has anyone ever told you that you give your opinion quite freely?" she managed.

"I think you did, just now."

A lock of auburn hair worked free from its arrangement to slide down across her cheek and she brushed it away in annoyance. "Well yes, certainly I disagree with him," she said, eyeing the appearance of her driveway with some relief. The first cold sprinkling of rain had begun to fall amidst under another deep rumble from the sky. "But he has shown his true colors through his dismissive replies, the inflexibility of his agent and his inability to compromise over the slightest of errors. Not to mention he displaced a woman who is my friend—a widow with a child, no less. He is obviously a boorish man whose lack of concern for others show him to be *decidedly* American."

They approached the front of the house, and a footman dashed outside. The man relinquished his reins and accompanied Caroline up the stone steps. Once they reached the top, he grimly held out the pair of hatboxes he'd been carrying, the muscle in his jaw flexing.

"I wouldn't call a discrepancy of nearly five acres 'the slightest of errors,'" he said acidly.

Her mouth dropped open at his unexpected censure of her. "How can you know how many acres—"

"And," he interrupted, "I can't see how the entailment of the estate could possibly concern your friend any longer, as she has just been married to a viscount. But I am still more fascinated by how you are able to ascertain the blackness of a man's character . . . all without ever having met him. I'd say that's a better reflection of your own nature."

Before she could make sense of what he was saying, the front door flew open and they were greeted by Lady Frances, clearly overjoyed by the arrival of her festooned bonnets and in the midst of one of her better moods. "Oh Caroline, darling, thank you for fetching these for me," she sang, plucking the hatboxes from her nerveless grasp.

She paused upon noticing her niece's male companion, and a servant ferried off the boxes so she could extend her hand daintily in his direction, glancing at Caroline for an introduction. Grudgingly, and still confused, she complied.

"Sir, this is Lady Frances Rowe, my aunt . . ." She searched her memory, struggling to recall, her voice trailing off with the realization that she would not be able to complete the introduction. That she didn't even know this man's name.

"Lady Frances," he said drily, when it was clear that Caroline could not finish.

Without missing a beat, he took her aunt's hand in his own and placed a kiss neatly upon her knuckles. When he straightened, his eyes focused only on Caroline.

"It is a pleasure to meet you. My name is Jonathan Cartwick. The American."

CHAPTER TWO

Jonathan's eyes scanned the ridge while he waited for his meddlesome neighbor.

Now that he was viewing it in person, he supposed he could understand why Lady Caroline was putting up a fight about the loss of such a peaceful bit of land, but he still had no intention of backing down. The majestic hillside, dappled with silvery birch groves and tapering down into gently rolling meadows was stunning despite its current lack of spring flora. A lingering mist clung insistently to the early afternoon air, seeming to challenge the sun that glimmered faintly from above.

"They call it Windham Hill. And aye, it's a capital spot," muttered his land agent with a nod, as if reading his mind.

He cocked an eyebrow in his direction, determined to seem unimpressed. "What makes you say that, Mr. Conrad?"

The man scoffed lightly. "Well it's got to be the prettiest

place on the estate, in my opinion. The elevation provides such wondrous vistas of the lands below, and the trees give enough privacy to feel as if you're in your own little world. And just look at it." He waved a hand over the landscape. "Imagine this little copse come summertime."

Jonathan couldn't deny that it would be beautiful. In a few more months, this place would be awash in wildflowers, and almost against his will, Jonathan could imagine many a leisurely afternoon spent here—could feel the sunlight's warmth upon his closed eyelids as he reclined on a blanket among the tall grass. Could almost hear the linnets trilling insistently to each other from the trees. Could imagine the freshness of the air, so different and so very still compared to the sooty noise of New York.

"Fine. It is lovely," he admitted.

Not that he'd missed this part of the world. Not that he even remembered it other than bits and fragments of a happy and heedless childhood. His chest ached when he thought of what his parents had actually endured at the hands of the *ton*—the ostracism, the dirty looks, the sniping gossip—all while taking great steps to shield their children from the ugly fact that while they shared an esteemed family name, they were decidedly the wrong sort of Cartwicks. Their only crime, it seemed, was not being born into land holdings and money. They were merchants who earned their living through hard work, and they were proud of it. But every man had his limits.

So his father had done what most men wouldn't have had the courage to even attempt. He'd packed up his family and moved overseas to try his fortune there, and it was a gamble that had certainly paid off. Robert Cartwick's shipbuilding business had not only grown to become a shining example of entrepreneurial spirit along the New England coast, he hadn't required one wealthy snob to make it happen.

Jonathan tapped his fingers restlessly on the reins, his irritation rising. He had never met his father's cousin, Nicholas Cartwick, nor Reginald, the son who had recently perished. He didn't know what kind of people they were, and he didn't care. All he knew was that his father had not lived long enough to truly enjoy his success. Jonathan had barely been of age to take over the company affairs when he had died. Much too soon, his father was gone, and it led one to wonder: Had Robert been born to a privileged family, would he have lived longer? Did the derision of fashionable society contribute in any way to his early demise? After all, it had been no easy task to start over in a new land.

He also had to wonder if he had made the right choice coming here. It was impossible to tell just yet. All he knew was that it had felt *necessary* to claim the birthright his beloved father had been unable to enjoy, and now it was only the purest irony that the same circle of society snobs that had looked down their nose at his merchant father were now falling over themselves to welcome his son into their fold. Their duplicity was anything but surprising.

A hare bolted out from a cluster of bushes behind them, and the agent clutched at his chest, exhaling shakily, his face nearly as white as the whiskers that blanketed the sides of his face. Jonathan withdrew his pocket watch and checked the time.

"They're late," he muttered.

Conrad chortled obsequiously but could apparently think of nothing to add.

With a sigh, Jonathan walked his horse over to a particularly charming spot beneath a large ash at the top of the hill, the smooth branches sparsely ornamented with velvety black buds. He could hear the grass rustle and bend beneath the wind. There was certainly something comfortable about the place. Soothing.

He could appreciate this all now, but in a month . . . dear God, he could imagine the boredom. There were only so many turns about the garden one could take before completely and utterly losing your mind. It was partly why the vapid English existence repulsed him the way it did. Men and women of leisure and privilege who had never had to work an honest day in their lives. Idle rulers whose authority was based solely upon their social ranking and the good fortune of their births.

Women like *Lady* Caroline, for instance . . . her title acquired merely by being the offspring of a duke. He supposed her scorn was to be expected. Leave it to someone like her to find offense at the entailment of an estate, and to fight against the correction of a property line. From their brief interaction on the road, he could already see that she was no different than the aristocrats who had made his father's life a living hell.

Although . . . she was lovely. After all, there had been a
reason he'd delayed his ride into town the day they'd met.
Even upon discovering the truth of who she was, and after
hearing her scathing and uncensored assessment of his integ-
rity, he'd still found himself intrigued. By the thick dark hair
that gleamed with fiery abandon in the light. By the eyes that
shone with the fierceness of polished granite. And by the red
lips that had pursed at him in displeasure, yet still managed
to look so very soft . . .

He shifted in his saddle, earning a quiet whicker from
his horse. If she was anything like other aristocrats, Lady
Caroline likely had no real accomplishments of her own to
speak of, other than perhaps playing the piano or excelling
at needlework. Occupations that would not tax her feminine
mind excessively, as the English seemed determined to avoid
such a thing at all costs. The luxury afforded to a woman in
Lady Caroline's position would surely quell any of her more
intelligent objections, for a life of convenience for a beautiful
woman of rank was easily bought, as long as there was a man
present to pay for it. And loyalty was never guaranteed. He'd
found that out the hard way . . .

Stay on task, he thought with a jerk of his head.

Jonathan sighed. He might be forced to make nice with
the jackals who had driven his father to settle in America,
but he'd treat them about as well as they deserved. Lady
Caroline included.

The sudden sound of pounding hooves roused Jonathan
from the grim turn of his thoughts, and both he and Mr.
Conrad straightened. He squinted at the impending arrival

of the lady herself, this time free of hatboxes, accompanied by her family's own agent. The thin mist curled around the pair then retreated as they made haste to the meeting spot. He found his glance lingered over the curve of her hip, swathed in the dove-gray felted wool of her riding habit and graciously displayed by the way her leg curved around the pommel of her sidesaddle. The ladylike drape of skirts cascading down the horse's flank along with her regal posture completed the picture of airy refinement.

Jonathan straightened his back and gripped the brim of his top hat to raise it in wary greeting as they came to stop before them. Her agent spoke first.

"Greetings, Mr. Cartwick." A pair of serious blue eyes greeted him from beneath a brow topped with curly dark hair. "I am Reuben Wakefield, land agent to the Duke of Pemberton. Allow me to present—"

"Lady Caroline," Jonathan interrupted, his gaze shifting immediately to the woman in question. He had no patience for unnecessary introductions. "We meet again. I wonder why you are so insistent upon speaking to me when both these men could converse together and save us the trouble. This is a situation easily remedied."

She rolled her eyes heavenward. "I'm sure you would be happy to leave this to our agents, Mr. Cartwick. But the nature of this dispute would preclude that, I'm afraid."

"I can only assume you mean the nature of *your* dispute, because I see no cause for issue. It appears that the boundary between our estates is quite clear." He hitched his shoulders in a shrug. "I only seek to correct an error."

"An error of such little consequence that the previous owner saw fit to disregard it entirely," she said with a sniff, the tip of her nose turning a delicate shade of pink in the cold.

He accepted her point with a congenial nod, but his gaze was sharp. Both agents remained silently nearby, allowing the master and mistress to speak, clearly terrified of the explosive argument that could erupt at any moment.

"Yes, they did, although their indifference to the discrepancy was merely a willful acceptance of the mistake," he replied succinctly. "That is not how I do business."

Her gray eyes flashed with anger, like fathomless dark stars priming to explode. Intrigued, he felt an answering pulse of excitement course through him. A curious reaction.

"Yes, thank you for the reminder that this is simply business to you," she answered with a baleful stare. "And I'm sure you won't trouble us with your presence for longer than is absolutely necessary before you choose to lease Greystone Hall. But some of us must *live* here—"

Her words had taken on a biting tone that he did not like, and Jonathan interjected with an abrupt raise of his hand. The astonished way her mouth snapped shut told him she was not used to being silenced. Mr. Conrad fidgeted nervously beside him.

"Do you, in fact, own Willowford House and the surrounding lands?" he inquired almost pleasantly. He fought to suppress a smile at the venomous way her eyes narrowed at him.

"You must know already that I do not own this property," she answered in irritation.

He allowed his horse to amble a bit closer to her position while he surveyed her thoughtfully. There was some satisfaction in seeing the way her cheeks flushed beneath the mockery of his gaze.

"And you live here with your aunt who, I also assume, is not the owner of the estate?"

At his belaboring of the point, her agent attempted to insert himself. "Now see here, Mr. Cartwick," he said, gallantly intent on defending the lady's honor and jabbing his plump finger in Jonathan's direction. "I will not stand for this effrontery—"

"It was not my intention to insult," he clarified. "But unless you are the owner of this property, I cannot see the point in conversing with you at all."

"I am simply here to . . ." She paused, dipping her chin down in thought, then began again. "My only wish is to . . ."

"Waste my time?" he supplied helpfully, with a sardonic lift of his brows.

She pressed her lips together and looked away, probably in humiliation. Had she been a different sort of person it might have made him feel bad. Thankfully, she wasn't and he didn't. A violent clearing of throat from his left interrupted the acrimonious exchange before it could continue afresh, and Jonathan turned to regard Mr. Conrad who looked as if he were ready to faint off his steed.

"*Forgive him,* my lady," he begged with an excess of deference, his eyes bulging beneath his brow, now damp with perspiration. "What Mr. Cartwick means to say is that we welcome your opinions during this process, although any final input will have to be made by the Duke of Pemberton, of course."

The lady's head swiveled back to the conversation at hand. "That might prove difficult, as the duke is so often away on travel," she replied tightly. "Perhaps you are aware that he does not make his home here?"

Jonathan supposed he found that bit of information surprising, but he refused to get into the particulars of the man's familial relationships. "I will reach him wherever he may be located, rest assured." He bristled and jerked on the reins, his horse spinning around to face Mr. Wakefield. "Send me his most recent address. I'll be drafting a letter immediately upon my return to the house." He focused on his own agent. "Can any progress be made prior to receiving the approval of the duke?"

Mr. Conrad looked astounded that he would even ask such a thing. "No, sir." He looked uneasily at Lady Caroline. "Although we may be able to adopt a new understanding of the boundaries, even before the fence line can be adjusted?"

"Absolutely not," she declared with thinly veiled irritation. "Nothing changes until my father has his say on the matter."

Which would be a while, if her earlier talk of the duke's travel could be believed.

Oh, she was maddening. The feeling was mutual, he knew, so there was at least a little satisfaction in that. With an exasperated sigh, he turned around to approach her once more. Her long lashes swept down as she avoided his gaze, and Jonathan noticed her audible intake of breath as he drew near. She had been plenty outspoken up until now, so he wasn't sure why she would choose this moment to act demurely.

No matter. It was about time the little princess received some sort of reckoning.

"Well I'd been hoping to deal with matters of the estate quickly and efficiently, but you've just guaranteed that this will be a long, drawn-out process instead." He touched the edge of his hat and leaned forwards in a grandly exaggerated show of respect. "I look forward to becoming much better acquainted over this godforsaken scrap of land."

Her eyes met his then, luminous and surprising, but with that unflinching hardness she seemed to work very hard to preserve. In an odd moment of weakness, he found himself wondering what it would be like to see that stony gaze softened into warm pools of surrender. Then he wondered what on earth it would take.

Perhaps the brush of his lips against hers would render her too shocked to argue over some meaningless hillside . . .

His head twitched of its own volition—an unconscious attempt to banish the thought. He saw her expression change upon his momentary lapse, a subtle look of confusion dawning in those lovely eyes, and part of him wondered if she had guessed the sensual shift of his thoughts. Impossible, of course, but he almost wished she had. Part of him ached for an excuse to somehow feel her in his arms.

Lady Caroline looked to her agent and Mr. Wakefield obediently came to her side.

"I'll do my best to keep the interactions to a minimum,

Mr. Cartwick," she replied haughtily. "I can see now that there is no use in appealing to the better nature of a man who doesn't have one."

And with that last parting shot, she urged her horse on, leaving him to stare after her in silence.

Caroline swore she could feel Cartwick's unsettling golden gaze searing into her back, and felt her temperature rise accordingly. Leaning forwards, she prodded the temperate gray horse into a less sensible pace, the need to place as much distance as possible between her and the American growing greater by the second.

There had been a moment . . . she was sure of it . . . where his eyes had betrayed an awareness of her that was not limited to their rancorous discussion of fence lines . . .

No. She must have imagined it. And even if she hadn't, entertaining the idea of that man as anything other than an adversary wasn't acceptable. Not for her, and certainly not for the beloved friends who had been booted from their home because of him. Yes, Eliza had managed to settle safely with Viscount Evanston, but that was hardly the point. Entailment was such a dirty game to begin with; a game that women were not designed to win. Watching her friend lose it all before her very eyes had not just traumatized Eliza and her daughter, Rosa, but Caroline herself. She still agonized over the loss of her cherished neighbor, especially now that Lady Frances had taken a turn for the worse.

"My lady!"

Mr. Wakefield sounded out of breath as he attempted to catch up with her, and she pulled reluctantly on the reins to slow her horse, who whinnied softly in response. A subversive glance over her shoulder reassured her that Cartwick was not only out of earshot, but no longer visible. She turned to face the agent who approached with a loud sigh.

"Lady Caroline, I feel I must remind you—"

"There's no need," she said, cutting him off.

The man blinked, his dark head tilting to evaluate her. "So you know there is likely no winning this battle?"

She looked past him, back at the shape of the grassy knoll that had become her refuge over the years. At the little grove of trees that had stood patiently nearby while she had cried out her heartache for only them to hear, their leafy canopies sheltering her from wind and sky and the cruelty of the world beyond. The loss of this place was like another well-timed stab to her heart after what felt like a lifetime of such wounds.

The correction of the boundary between their estates might be inevitable, but she would not give up quietly, and especially not to a man like Cartwick. She would revel in causing him even a moment's frustration, although truth be told, she hoped to vex him substantially more than that.

"There may be no winning the battle," she agreed, tugging her kid gloves more snugly over her hands, "but I can still fight the war. Rather appropriate given his lineage, I think."

Wakefield glanced at her, perplexed. "The man is not American-born, my lady. His parents moved the children when they were still young."

She froze. "How young, exactly?"

"Mr. Cartwick was ten years old, I think."

His peculiar accent suddenly made a bit more sense. It held the subtle remainder of a British lilt with the underlying edge of something else that was not local. It was why she hadn't been able to place it when they had met on the road, although she'd been so distracted by the velvety richness of his actual voice that deciphering his accent had been the farthest thing from her mind. Somewhat closer to her mind, along with the way his nearness affected her, had been his topaz-colored eyes and the teasing light that had filled them . . . right up until her thoughtless slander of him. A remembrance of the embarrassing circumstances caused her stomach to lurch in mortification, and she turned to resume her course to the house.

"An interesting fact," she replied over her shoulder. "Not that it makes a difference. I'm sure it will have no effect on his decision to find a tenant for Greystone Hall and return to . . . to . . . wherever he is from in America."

"New England," Wakefield supplied, urging his horse to catch up with her once again. "And I'm not certain he can return. Not after the entailment."

"Well, I wish him luck in his pursuit of my parents. Where were they located last anyway?"

The question was asked nonchalantly, but an astute observer might have been able to guess at the subtle undercurrent of pain lying just barely beneath the words. And anyone with the slightest knowledge of her family history wouldn't have to guess at all.

"Spain, my lady," he replied, "but I believe they plan on returning to England soon."

Caroline lapsed into moody silence, a heavy bitterness rising in her throat. She choked it down, as she always did. What wonders the world must hold for them. Wondrous enough to desert their only child in the Hampshire countryside to either marry or rot. They'd made it clear their preference was marriage and she supposed she ought to be grateful for that, although she knew what drove their motivations. One spinster in the family was quite enough of a drain on the Pemberton purse already; *two* spinsters just simply wouldn't do.

Before long, their horses' hooves were clattering into the side courtyard and the stableboy dashed out immediately to assist her. After requesting her agent keep her apprised of any new information concerning correspondence between Cartwick and her parents, he took his leave and she rushed into the house to find her aunt scratching away at a letter in the library. A cup of steaming tea was positioned on the desk within easy reach. The scene was so normal, Caroline found herself smiling despite her low mood.

"Hello, Auntie," she said, thrilled to see her engaged in correspondence after a long stretch of having lost interest. Caroline came closer, being careful to adjust the uneven hem of her riding skirt so as not to trip over herself. "And who, may I ask, is to receive the pleasure of this particular letter?"

Lady Frances kept her head down, gray hair pulled back into a severe bun with only a few tendrils escaping down alongside her ears. She remained in that position until she had finished the sentence she'd been writing, then set the pen aside and turned in her floral chintz armchair to regard Caroline with a smile. She was relieved by the lightness of her aunt's expression. It was a welcome change from the worry and forgetfulness that had plagued Frances these past months, and it was good to see her aunt feeling more like her usual self.

"I'm so glad to see you, dear," she said, hooking a finger around the china handle of her cup and taking a small sip of her tea. "Before I answer your question, please tell me . . . did you and Mr. Cartwick come to some amicable understanding?"

Caroline's brow lowered in reflexive response to the mere mention of him. "No, and what's more, I don't believe we ever will. He's writing to Father as we speak."

Her aunt's faded eyes squinted up at her in steady evaluation. "I still think you should try," she said. "He may be set upon righting the boundaries, but if you two could at least be friends he might give you permission to—"

"I don't want his permission!" she exclaimed, surprising them both. Caroline inhaled deeply through her nose, then smoothed her hands over the ash-colored skirts of her riding habit. She cleared her throat. "Forgive me, Auntie. I just can't abide the thought of requiring his approval to do anything when his very presence is an irritant. I look at him and I see . . . I see . . ."

Frances reached over to clasp her trembling hand. "You see the man who wronged your friend."

"*Yes*," she breathed with relief. Thank goodness someone understood at last.

Her aunt nodded. "Do you know what I see when I look at him?"

Caroline tensed, her body turning rigid. After years of attending the season with Frances, she knew exactly what was coming.

"No, don't say it—"

"I see a wealthy and attractive man," Frances continued, confirming her fears. "And I'm not the lady in need of a husband."

"Who said I needed a husband?" Caroline said, then immediately regretted the outburst when her aunt's gaze sharpened in response. Pressing her lips tightly together, she glanced down at her hands as Frances rose from her seat to face her.

"I know you value your independence, Caroline," she said quietly, firmly. "And I know you had such high hopes for Lord Braxton during your last season."

"I had no such thing for Lord Braxton—"

"Yes, my dear. You did. And I'll never forgive myself for the part I played in your losing him—"

Caroline shook her head vehemently. "I won't stand to have you blame yourself for that man's behavior. If he had truly cared for me, he wouldn't have married the first lady to look at him once we left London."

"Yes," Frances agreed. "He was fickle. But there comes a time when you must face the reality of your situation, and one disappointment does not turn you into a spinster, no matter what the *ton* says. Sometimes I think you resist simply for the sake of resisting, and that will not do." She squeezed her hands tightly. "You cannot ignore your duty to this family. You must get married, and soon."

"Duty?" Caroline jerked her hands away in a sudden flare of temper. "What a notion! Was there no obligation owed to me by my parents these past many years?"

Of course, she didn't expect Frances to respond. How could her aunt truly take her side when the very people who had abandoned their own daughter had also provided her spinster aunt with a home and provisions?

Frances turned her back and seated herself at the desk once more. Retrieving the pen, she signed her name with a flourish while Caroline watched sullenly from behind, then set the missive aside to dry.

"I understand how you must feel, but marriage is better if you can manage it, my dear," she said, glancing over her shoulder with a melancholy smile. "I hope you would trust my opinion on the matter, given the course of my own life. And if familial obligation cannot motivate you, then perhaps you should consider what not marrying would mean for you and your future."

Caroline grumbled under her breath and picked fitfully at the lace on her sleeve. She would gladly earn her parents' bad opinion forever than consider marrying the usurping American.

"I think I would rather grow old alone than settle on a man with no regard for his effect on the lives of people around him. He is not nice, Auntie, I don't care how attractive he is."

Her aunt's eyes grew alert. "So, you do think him attractive?"

"I, er . . . well—" Caroline flushed up to her hairline, a flood of heat marking the precise path of her mortification. "Fine. I suppose I can't deny that he possesses some pleasing features. But every time he opens his mouth—"

Lady Frances abruptly rotated back in her chair and began folding her letter. "What about you, darling? I know I've taught you how to behave in civilized company, and yet for some reason I feel you disregard it all with this man, in correspondence and in person." The parchment crinkled beneath her hands. "I'd say you set the tone before he even arrived at Greystone Hall."

Caroline could bear it no longer. First her parents, and now her aunt? Scalding tears threatened to spill past her lashes and she swallowed against the sudden lump in her throat. She stared as Frances sealed the letter with red wax.

"Aunt Frances," she said hoarsely, "my feelings for him are a direct result of his actions and his words. And marriage to him . . . or anyone . . . is out of the question. But especially him."

Her aunt stared at her, then stood and tugged on the bellpull. "Can you tell me why?"

Because he hurt my friends . . .

Because men are unworthy creatures . . .

Because I've grown weary of disappointment . . .

She only shook her head, wishing she could be honest but knowing that the truth might only serve to break her aunt's heart. She'd already said too much, as it was. The appearance of a footman at the door saved her from the need to provide an immediate response, and her aunt handed him the letter she'd been working on. He inclined into a polite bow and then left, closing the door quietly behind him, and Frances touched her upswept hair before aiming a long-suffering look in Caroline's direction.

"Well, whatever the reasons for your dislike, I hope you work through them quickly."

Dread turned her icy cold from head to toe. "Why? What do you mean?" she asked slowly, the words laced with caution.

Her aunt came forwards and placed her hands upon Caroline's shoulders.

"Because that letter was our acceptance of an invitation to dine with Mr. Cartwick and his mother tomorrow evening."

CHAPTER THREE

Y ou did *what?*"

Startled, Dorothea Cartwick glanced up from her seat near the fireplace, temporarily forgetting the menu she'd been reviewing with the housekeeper. Jonathan was incensed to detect a smile lurking behind his mother's warm brown eyes, but there so often was one. It was simply her way.

With a nod, she dismissed the housekeeper, waiting until the woman had fully exited the drawing room before turning back to regard him with amusement.

"Come now, my dear. Surely you didn't expect me to shun our new neighbors?"

He scoffed. "Not any more than they would like to shun us."

"I don't know what you mean, Jonathan," she said, folding her hands together primly. "Lady Frances was quite amicable when I called on her today."

A moment of silence ensued. "You called on her?"

"Yes, I did. While you were off trying to make enemies with her niece, I was visiting the aunt and inviting the two of them to dinner."

Sighing, he ran a hand through his hair. His mother had always possessed a spirited nature, one that had served him and his family well as they had carved out a new existence for themselves across the ocean. While he admired her initiative, he held no real hope of her forging a truce with Pemberton's daughter . . . not as long as the girl insisted on being an unmanageable brat.

"You're wasting your time. Even if Lady Frances were a saint, her niece cannot be tolerated." He felt himself scowling in recollection of her haughtiness. "I've never met such an entitled woman in all my life. To think she thought she could insert herself into a situation where she doesn't belong." His eyes raised to the ceiling.

His mother appeared to consider his words thoughtfully, plucking softly at the polished jet necklace that hung around her neck. Despite his father's death some five years before, and the fact that she no longer adhered to the requirements the traditional mourning period called for, there was always a hint of it in her daily attire; a dangle of jet or onyx; a flounce of black lace on an otherwise colorful dress. He knew his father was never far from her thoughts although she did not like to speak of his loss. Her natural fortitude and happy disposition demanded she carry on without him, however much he was missed, and she threw herself wholeheartedly into supporting her sons instead.

"Hmm, I wonder," she said at last. "Does she not have a right to be concerned about a situation involving her home?"

Jonathan crossed over to stand behind a wine-colored armchair, his hands sliding restlessly over the top of it. He was trying to appear casual but could feel his fingertips digging into the rich velvet upholstery.

"She absolutely has the right. But the matter still doesn't involve her."

Her eyes were no longer smiling. "I happen to disagree. And I don't think you believe it either."

"And why do you say that?" he asked, tamping down his irritation. If there was any woman less deserving of his mother's sympathy than Lady Caroline, he would be hard-pressed to name her.

"Well, for one, I am here with you." She tipped her head over the various menus in her hands, the silver threads in her otherwise dark hair catching the light that filtered in through the windows. "I have no real authority over this estate, and yet I know you value my input. I wouldn't be here if you did not. You obviously, however, do not value hers. Why?"

He stared at her, in growing disbelief over the line of her questioning. "Your input is valuable because I know you to be an intelligent person, while I have seen nothing of her intelligence so far. She appears to operate at the mercy of her emotions," he said with a dismissive wave of his hand. "I don't have time to deal with such ridiculousness."

"On the contrary, you may have more time than you think if the Duke of Pemberton is so difficult to pin down," she countered with a sober laugh. "Don't you think you might be overreacting a bit? This seems like a bitterness our new neighbor doesn't quite deserve. At least not yet."

"Are you implying something?" he asked with a sigh, knowing full well what she was implying.

"I just worry about you, dear. I worry that the way things ended with Letitia might keep you from treating other women . . . fairly."

"This has *nothing* to do with Letitia."

His mother only nodded, surely detecting the annoyance in his voice.

"Besides," he added, finally coming around the armchair to drop down into the cushioned seat, "her position is indefensible. The fence line is wrong. And not just a few feet over to one side; it is significantly wrong. I'm rather surprised that Reginald Cartwick did not bother to fix it while he was alive."

She set a menu off to the side, having narrowed down her selections for what was sure to be one hell of a dinner. Literally.

"It is curious, for certain," she agreed. "Surely, he knew? He and the duke both must have known—"

"But that's another thing. She mentioned that her father doesn't live at Willowford House. It could be he didn't know, as I imagine he's got estates all over the country and agents with which to manage them, albeit poorly. But doesn't it strike you as a little strange that the duke's daughter lives alone with her aunt?"

A tiny crease had appeared between the dark wings of

his mother's brow. "Yes, it does seem strange. And maybe a little sad."

He leaned forwards to rest his elbows on top of his knees and shook his head. "I think you are being too generous a judge of her character. Trust me, she will not hold back when the time comes to judge you."

"I understand you two have had your differences already," she replied evenly. "I also understand the resentment you hold towards the aristocracy. I share some of those same reservations. But it is still no reason to be unpleasant to a woman you hardly know, and a neighbor, no less."

He viewed his mother in sardonic contemplation. "Lady Caroline is being difficult simply because she can. And on the first day we met, she told me precisely what she thought of me, even though we'd never met before."

Mrs. Cartwick perked up. "She did? You didn't mention that. Only that you'd seen her on the road and escorted her to her house."

"Yes, for all the good being a gentleman does around her," he muttered darkly.

Her eyes held the barest hint of suspicion. "Why would she speak so freely to a new acquaintance? Especially one she was eager to criticize?"

"It's difficult to explain. I never had the chance to make myself known. And as for why she would speak freely, I think you'll need to meet her to fully understand." He paused. "Also, I suppose I asked her opinion."

She stared blankly. "You asked her about—"

"Her thoughts on the new owner of the Cartwick estate."

There was silence first, then the sound of his mother's laughter. He glowered at her until her amusement had subsided into soft chuckles of mirth, and she wiped at her eyes while attempting to compose herself. Rising to make her way to the door, she placed an affectionate hand on his arm as she passed. Another giggle managed to escape on her way. Curling his fists at his side, he asked, although he was almost afraid to.

"What is it that you find so very funny?"

She turned to face him, her face flushed with the effort to suppress her laughter.

"It's you, my darling," she said as seriously as she could and pausing for a moment to catch her breath. "It's you trying to act so very uninterested in her."

Caroline peered out the carriage window at the night sky. Through the jostling darkness, there wasn't much to see except the trees that stood like shadowy sentinels along the road leading to Greystone Hall. She regarded them moodily before sinking back against the seat cushions in a sulk, her gloved fingers twisting around each other in apprehension. Soon she and Frances would arrive at Eliza's old home, and she wasn't sure she could pretend to behave as if none of it bothered her. As if the man who had taken her friend's place didn't bother her.

"Cheer up, for heaven's sake," came her aunt's voice from beside her. "This isn't a funeral."

She glanced over with a flutter of her eyelids to meet Lady

Frances's cool gaze. "It might as well be a funeral; a farewell to my illusion of free will. Forced to share company with a man whom I despise—"

"Now you're being dramatic, my dear," Frances replied with a small smile. She reached over to unwind Caroline's fingers, then gripped one of her chilled hands inside her own and squeezed it tightly. "It's only dinner. A chance to get to know these people a little better." At Caroline's unmoving expression, she added, "I don't expect you to be cheerful, but I do expect you to smile."

She had to laugh at her aunt's demand. "You may very well discover how unfriendly a smile can be."

"While I cannot stop you from being uncivil outside my presence, I do expect a little more of you when I am here at your side," she stated, frowning. "And if you can't manage to be polite at a private country dinner with four people in attendance, then perhaps it's time for you to head back to London for another season."

"No!" she exclaimed with wide eyes, seeing that Frances indeed meant business. "I'll be good. I promise."

Frances patted Caroline's hand in approval and stared at her meaningfully. "That's more like it."

The carriage springs creaked noisily as the vehicle came to a halt in front of Eliza's former home. The footman opened the door and an unwelcome wave of guilt washed over her as she gazed up, eyes wandering across the familiar gray stone facade of the house. What would her friend think of her now—arriving to dine with the new master of the Cartwick estate after she and Rosa had been turned out so unfeelingly? If only her aunt hadn't taken steps behind her back to smooth things over, she could be back at Willowford House right now, safe in the knowledge that she'd not blurred the lines between her and the invasive new resident.

Caroline tipped her chin up a bit higher, reminding herself that she was in complete control. There would be no blurring of lines; not tonight or any other night. In fact, she'd do her best not to even look at him.

After waiting for her aunt to disembark, she took the footman's hand and brushed her skirts aside to join her on the drive. A thick garnet cloak concealed her aunt's high-necked velvet dress in a shade of rich, dark chocolate brown, trimmed in ivory lace. Caroline couldn't ignore the relief she felt at seeing Frances looking so dignified and poised. Privately, she was still anxious about whether or not her aunt would be able to make it through the night without suffering some kind of setback, but she wasn't nearly as worried in tonight's company as she had been in London. It wasn't as if she and Frances would have to flee in the middle of the night to avoid scandal, as they had before. They would merely ride back to Willowford House, and it would be just the excuse she needed to never speak to Mr. Cartwick again.

Standing there to greet them was the man himself dressed immaculately in black-and-white formal dinner attire. The sight of him jarred her carefully structured defenses, and she found herself admiring how well he looked, the cut of his jacket highlighting the lines of his naturally pleasing male form. Upon realizing her mistake, she forced her eyes upwards to glance at him in awkwardly held silence.

He held her gaze, daring her to misbehave, but she resisted the urge to level him with a glare and simply lowered into a curtsy instead. Her aunt did likewise, smiling like a young girl when he approached to clasp her hand in his own. She was regretting the fact that Frances was never able to resist a good-looking man. Caroline sighed inwardly and prayed for the fortitude she would require to endure this.

"Lady Frances, such a pleasure to see you again," he murmured over her gloved fingers with a bow.

Caroline observed his lips as they grazed the back of her aunt's knuckles, and she glanced quickly away. Pleasantries were exchanged while she stood off to the side, staring down at the silvery blue satin skirts that showed between the folds of her forest green cloak. Moments later, as she had predicted, he merely bowed in her direction, abstaining from the effusive courtesy he had shown to Frances.

"Lady Caroline."

Having already curtsied and feeling annoyed at the obvious slight and her own irrational disappointment, she tipped her head in mute reply then gazed past to the woman standing behind him on the drive. Thankfully, he caught the hint and stepped aside with an outstretched arm.

"Allow me to introduce my mother, Mrs. Dorothea Cartwick."

Mrs. Cartwick smiled warmly and came forwards as if it had taken every ounce of restraint to wait, her large brown eyes shining in anticipation. She was a handsome woman, and the violet shade of her dress complimented her thick sable hair nicely. The black accents of silk and lace did not escape Caroline's attention, though, and she wondered if the woman still mourned for her husband.

In an artless but charming expression of her excitement, Mrs. Cartwick reached out to squeeze both women's hands at one time. "It is good to meet you, my ladies," she said with a bright smile. "I've heard so much about you from my son."

An almost imperceptible snort of laughter escaped Caroline before she could prevent it. She could imagine what things Jonathan Cartwick might have said about her, and they would not be flattering in the least. Clearing her throat, Caroline glanced at her hostess and was surprised by the tiny wink that greeted her. She found herself liking the woman despite her efforts against it. The woman's unfashionable candor was surprisingly refreshing.

Lady Frances attempted to shake the woman's hand in awkward fashion, then gave up and withdrew her hand with a polished smile. "Thank you for the invitation to dinner."

"It is my pleasure, of course." She aimed a look in her son's direction. "Let us go inside and escape this frigid air."

To Caroline's horror, Jonathan Cartwick extended an elbow in her direction, his reluctant gaze partially illuminated by the nearby torches. The older women had already started their way up the stairs together, Aunt Frances already at ease and chatting with their amicable hostess. She supposed she could just ignore him and proceed into the house on her own, but even her brazenness had its limits.

Her hand stretched out towards the gleaming black broadcloth of his sleeve that hovered, waiting for her. The grim silence she received told her that the gesture was borne out of simple formality, but she supposed a tiny part of her was grateful that he was offering his arm at all. She hesitated, then came closer to slide her palm over the warm strength of his arm.

Butterflies flew fickle patterns in her stomach as that familiar scent of shaving soap, the same intoxicating smell she'd detected upon the day they'd met, radiated off of him with the heat of his body. There were also hints of his fresh linen shirt, crisp starch and some other nameless, dizzying element that seemed to be uniquely his own. Swaying briefly, she righted herself and noticed the way his gaze flicked over to the side just a fraction.

"Are you well?"

The quiet inquiry sounded uninterested, almost annoyed, but Caroline saw that a tiny notch had formed between his brows. It was most likely exasperation that had prompted its appearance. She couldn't imagine it was concern.

"Yes," she forced out in a voice resembling a croak. His nearness was affecting her strangely. Swallowing hard, she continued in as bored a manner as she could muster, "Let us follow."

Without further delay, he strode towards the steps and took her along with him. Caroline hurriedly clutched at her skirts with her free hand to keep from stepping on the fine material as his legs were long and his pace a touch faster than she would have liked. She was certain he only wished to be rid of her as expeditiously as possible, but she refused to give him any reason for thinking he could upset her in the slightest. She needed to present her most immovable and unshakeable self to him tonight, and goodness knew she had plenty of experience in pretending to be all right when she was not.

Before Caroline could truly process what was happening, she was in the foyer and Cartwick had released her, striding into the drawing room without another look. The butler came forwards to divest her of her cloak, and she continued her harried pace to join the group, in a rush to not be left behind.

Then she found herself staring in speechless surprise at the interior of Eliza's old drawing room. The settee Eliza used to prefer for needlepoint work . . . the lovely old grandfather clock her friend had hated with a passion . . . the fireplace by which they'd shared many cups of tea and conversations. Caroline had spent long comfortable afternoons in this place with her friend, and now she felt like the worst kind of traitor, sharing the same space with the American.

She could see the wallpaper had been changed from its former print of gold-and-peach tones, to a pattern scattered across a light bluish-green background, and found the change pleasing, which she immediately felt guilt about. The contrast of newness and familiarity was to be expected, yet it still came as a shock. Caroline worked to leash her emotions before she made a fool of herself. It would not do to lose control in front of these people, especially when she had already worked so hard to craft an attitude of surly indifference.

Meanwhile, Cartwick stood nearby, his dazzling amber eyes watching her like a hawk marking the movement of its prey. He was probably loving every second of her struggle. A fresh wave of loathing for the man poured through her like a tide of poison, although she knew she was upset with herself too. Hadn't she allowed herself to enjoy the feeling of his arm beneath her hand? How good the rest of him might feel had been the next natural thought to occur and was yet another reason why their closeness should be avoided. Little wonder, then, that her pride now assailed her with stinging barbs of embarrassment. Mrs. Cartwick's voice roused Caroline from her reflections.

"Lady Caroline, is the house much as you remember it?"

The question was bold given Caroline's history of bitterness on the subject, and she found Mrs. Cartwick gazing at her in pleasant expectation, her dark eyes wide with curiosity. Beside her, Frances appeared similarly interested in Caroline's response, while Jonathan Cartwick crossed to the tall windows across the room.

"I—" Her voice awkwardly faltered as her eyes moved about the beloved surroundings, Eliza's presence nearly palpable to her even under these strange circumstances. She crossed her arms around her torso and attempted a fraction of a smile for the sake of her hostess. "There are changes here and there, of course, but I can still see my friend's influence in these rooms."

The woman beamed. "I believe Lady Eliza made many charming additions."

"Yes, she did," Caroline replied. Then she added, "Nicholas Cartwick and his wife also contributed quite a lot to the beauty of the estate."

Her aunt threw a dark look in her direction. It was a reminder to maintain the peace, but there was no need. Caroline found it difficult to be angry with Mrs. Cartwick, who clearly had no intention of offending—unlike her son who seemed to take advantage of every opportunity.

Dorothea nodded warmly. "I have heard that, as well."

The women resumed their soft conversing and Caroline elected to seat herself on the settee, glancing over to where Mr. Cartwick stood by the windows. He stared out at the nearly lightless drive below. Since the torches outside provided very little in the way of illumination, he couldn't be seeing much. And while they did not care for each other's company, she couldn't help but feel dejected at his insistent ignoring of her, particularly since she had been invited here as a guest.

But Lord Braxton had taught her much throughout the course of her last season, with perhaps the most important lessons being not to lower your defenses to any man, and don't expect too much of them if you do. Physical attraction was the surest path to a difficult situation, but it was also the thing most out of her control. Even though she held Jonathan Cartwick in the highest contempt, she could still sense the danger in being around him.

A small *ahem* succeeded in catching his attention, but she was quick to cast her eyes elsewhere when he turned, his gaze landing squarely upon her. He remained where he was for a moment, then approached warily as if he didn't trust her not to cause a scene. Part of her wanted to, of course, while the other part—the one that was incredibly curious to know if he found her at all appealing—hoped to surprise him by being docile and compliant.

Cartwick stopped to eye her critically. "Are you in need of a drink, my lady?" he asked. "It seems your throat has been troubling you this evening."

Any thoughts of compliance were dashed by his sarcasm. "Why yes, I foresee the need for multiple drinks if I am to somehow survive this night," she said sweetly. Her eyes flicked quickly to the women on the other side of the room to ensure they had not been overheard, but his quiet scoff regained her attention.

"Is that any way for a lady to speak?"

She straightened her posture and ran a gloved hand along the pearl and diamond necklace that circled her throat. "Am I to believe that you think me a lady?" she asked wryly. Noticing the way he followed the course of her fingertips, she swiftly returned her hands back to the decadent swaths of satin that covered her lap.

"No more than I am to believe you think me a gentleman," he replied evenly, seating himself in a cushioned armchair across from her.

The casual way he draped an elbow over the back of the chair caused her already rapid pulse to stutter out of control. Caroline clung to her animosity in an effort to subdue her more inappropriate responses to this man, but that same urge she'd felt before soared inside of her again.

"Is it not customary to make polite conversation with ladies where you come from?" she asked, hoping he would not notice the nervous tremor in her voice. "You're rather bad at it, if it is."

The lopsided grin that flickered briefly across his face was a revelation. So was the dimple she had not known he'd possessed. Thankfully, it disappeared almost as quickly as it had arrived, and she waited in something like anticipation of his next targeted jab.

"When I meet one, I'll be sure to practice sufficiently," he answered, nonchalantly examining the edge of his coat sleeve.

Her reaction could have been quantified as a gasp, except her lungs lacked the oxygen to produce a sound. In fact, she noticed the room had gone strangely quiet, and both she and Cartwick glanced over to where Mrs. Cartwick and her aunt were standing, observing them with serious, and possibly displeased, expressions. It seemed that part of their brief conversation may have been overheard after all.

"I certainly hope you two are being polite," Frances said lightly, her forehead creased in concern.

Feeling sheepish, Caroline stood to prevent things from continuing as they had, and Mr. Cartwick rose to cross back over to the windows.

"Well, I—"

The sudden entrance of the butler to announce dinner saved her from the necessity of finishing her thought, but could not rescue her from the look of censure she received from Lady Frances. Their hostess also seemed perturbed, but only gestured to her son with an outstretched hand.

"After you."

Caroline could see the visible rise and fall of his shoulders as he sighed in annoyance. Of course it was expected that, as a gentleman, he would escort her into the dining room. She nearly laughed at his reaction, but instead raised her eyebrows expectantly when he extended his arm to her once again.

"I should have known tonight would be miserable," he muttered under his breath.

Her breath quickened when she slid her hand around his arm and stepped close. "You should know something else too, Mr. Cartwick," she said.

He glanced down at her. "And what is that?"

She rose up on her toes to deliver a vengeful whisper as they began walking out of the drawing room.

"Your new wallpaper is atrocious."

Chapter Four

Jonathan twirled the stem of his crystal wineglass between his fingers, contemplating Lady Caroline from his seat at the head of the table. In a flash of intuition—most likely resulting from their earlier contention—his mother had changed the seating arrangement so Lady Frances, instead of her niece, was closest to him. Instead of being offended as one might normally be, Caroline seemed almost relieved. When not engaged in conversation with the other women, she ate her meal in silence with what seemed like an unnatural dedication to the task. He did not mind the seating switch either as it provided him the freedom with which to surreptitiously view her from afar.

His gaze traveled furtively over her countenance as she took a small sip of her carrot soup, entranced by the lushness of her lips and the way they pursed forwards around the edge of her spoon. There could be no doubt regarding her beauty.

He might have wondered at her inability to find a husband during the course of her past seasons, except for the obvious issue of her abrasiveness. Aristocrats did not find that behavior at all charming, not even from the daughter of a duke. It held no appeal for him either, but he couldn't deny that he still found her interesting. And her fiercely delivered comment about his wallpaper had only managed to entertain him rather than affront, as he was certain was her purpose.

Most interesting to him at the moment, however, was her abundance of seemingly effortless sensuality. It was impossible not to notice, and even easier to see in those moments when she was being quiet. The way the candlelight reflected softly against the fiery glow of her hair. The graceful slope of her nose and the light scattering of tiny freckles across it. The dark lashes that lowered to conceal eyes that glowed brightly, like polished agates and moonstone . . .

"—is that so, Mr. Cartwick?"

His gaze snapped over to Lady Frances, who was obviously awaiting the answer to a question he had not heard. Dorothea's eyes were overly bright as she took a sip of wine, and Jonathan straightened in his chair with a frown.

"My apologies . . . what was the question?"

Frances dabbed the corner of her mouth with her napkin. "I was inquiring about the nature of your business in America," she said. "Is it true, as I have heard, that you have found great success?"

Jonathan regarded the elder woman's curious expression and found no malice lingering there. She could quite possibly be the only member of the *ton* who would ask such a question

without a show of disdain. Lady Caroline raised the spoon
to her lips once more, but her gaze did raise ever so slightly,
displaying the barest show of interest.

"I suppose you could call it that. We build ships. Excellent ones. And the demand in the industry has increased over
the past two decades to the point that we build a steady and
ever-increasing supply of vessels for fishing companies."

Lady Frances regarded him in confusion. "But your father
had no maritime or shipbuilding experience while living in
England, correct?"

"He did not possess those particular skills as an English
merchant, but he owned a wealth of intelligence and was
highly motivated as an American entrepreneur. His charisma earned him the respect of men who could teach him
the necessary skills. When they grew old, those same men
sold their share of the business to my father, who left it to me
upon his death."

"And your younger brother has now assumed the mantle of
responsibility?" asked Frances, leaning back in her chair as her
soup bowl was removed. "Is he the sole remaining Cartwick in
America?"

"He is."

"You don't sound happy about that," Caroline said sharply.
"Perhaps you should have stayed where you were."

Lady Frances pivoted in her chair to lance her niece with
a dark look, and Caroline had the good sense to look away
in shame. It was almost as if the words had escaped her lips
before she'd been able to really consider them, which was just
more confirmation that they reflected her true feelings. He

could only imagine her disdain if he were to tell her the truth of things. That he wasn't happy here. That he wasn't certain why he'd left everything he loved in America to return to England. That he didn't feel like saying *no* was an option.

Jonathan raised his napkin to touch the corner of his mouth and regarded Lady Caroline with a neutral expression. "Perhaps you're right. Leaving my father's business . . . and my home . . . for such a reception here was a difficult decision to make. But my brother is just as capable as I ever was, and I rest easy knowing the company is in good hands."

"Robert Cartwick was the kindest, most amiable man. Hardworking too," his mother said with a small smile and a wistful look, as if momentarily lost in a recollection of her treasured husband. Remembering herself, she hastily reached down to straighten her silverware upon the linen tablecloth. "My sons remind me of him very much."

Jonathan smiled warmly at her for just a moment before refolding the napkin on his lap. "I'd venture to say you had something to do with that, Mother, although I don't believe everyone shares your good opinion of me."

Naturally his eyes sought Caroline, who blushed but kept silent for once despite his goading.

Dinner passed slowly, with Mrs. Cartwick and Lady Frances chatting animatedly with one another while he and Caroline contributed fragments of conversation when prompted. Their limited participation was for the best, really, and yet he couldn't dismiss the pervasive disappointment that kept him from enjoying himself.

For some incomprehensible reason, Jonathan was intrigued by the woman, and part of him was eager to know her better while the more sensible part told him to run away. Hadn't Letitia put him through enough? Had he not learned that being miserable by one's self was much preferable to being miserable because of another?

Still, he'd been stopping himself all evening from contemplating the feel of her small hand wrapped around his elbow, and the enticing pressure of her breast against his arm when she'd risen on her tiptoes to insult his drawing room décor.

Your wallpaper is atrocious.

Out of all the things she could have possibly said, he was incredibly amused she had chosen that. Though his amusement had immediately dissolved at the feel of her, and when the silky warmth of her whisper had caressed his cheek, the beginnings of lust had stirred briefly in its place.

No, he'd thought fiercely. *Not her.* Lady Caroline was nothing but trouble in a lovely little package. Her biting retorts were a reassuring sign of her intelligence, although she wielded it with the delicacy of a battle-ax. And even though she tended to rashness and often rushed to judgment, he was annoyed to find he could not dismiss her altogether as the prissy daughter of a duke.

When the meal was finished and the party had moved into the parlor, he poured himself a brandy at the sideboard while the women took tea. His mother had made efforts to include Caroline this evening, but still she removed herself to stand alone by the piano while the older women were seated cozily on the couch.

He heaved a sigh. Considering everything, he supposed his mother was right. Caroline might like to overstep traditional boundaries, both figuratively and literally, but perhaps since she was their guest, he could at least *try* to be amiable. Looking at her out of the corner of his eye, he tossed back his drink and returned the glass to the sideboard, his stomach tensing in anticipation. There was no way of knowing whether she would greet him with a smile or a hiss.

The lady stood immobile, running her fingers absently along the gleaming rosewood piano case, her rich auburn coiffure studded with pearls displaying her slender neck to perfection. The glimmering light from the candelabras fell softly upon gently rounded, bare shoulders, and he took a step closer to gain her attention. Caroline jerked in surprise at his appearance, and while she did not cheerfully welcome him, she also did not scowl.

"You seem bored, my lady," he said in a low voice.

Her back stiffened and she regarded him with flared nostrils. "You smell like brandy."

A smile tugged at the corner of his mouth. "It wasn't an insult, simply an observation," he replied. Then trying again, "Are you bored?"

Her eyes widened, then she looked away and shook her head. "No."

"What are you, then?"

"I'd rather not talk about it."

Jonathan viewed her in silence, wanting to press the question although he knew it would be ungentlemanly of him to do so. Instead, he noticed the way she held her hand on top of the piano. It reminded him of an affectionate gesture. Protective. He supposed that made sense given her familiarity with this house and the things in it.

"Do you play?" he finally asked.

"Yes, of course," she replied, her head still lowered.

"Will you play something for me?"

Caroline's eyes lifted. Instantly, his heart doubled its pace.

"For you? No. Although—" she trailed off with a sigh. "I do owe you an apology for what I said at dinner."

A rise of conflicting emotions caused Jonathan to pause; the obvious discontent at her rejection, and the ensuing astonishment at her apology. He tried to gather his thoughts although at the moment, standing near enough to discern the faint drift of her rosewater perfume, he could not quite remember to which comment she was referring.

"Remind me, if you will," he managed.

"It's surprising you've forgotten. I—I made an unkind remark."

"Ah, yes," he said, nodding and folding his hands behind his back. "Perhaps I should have stayed where I was."

She blushed and briefly caught her bottom lip between her teeth—her full, luscious bottom lip that was the color of ripened summer strawberries. How he wished she wouldn't do that. When it was finally released he felt his body relax considerably, although with her still so very close to him he would never be entirely at ease.

"Yes. Well, I shouldn't have said it," she said.

"Has that ever stopped you before?" he asked, needing to steer his mind away from thoughts of ravishing her velvety lips with his own eager mouth. His willingness to make peace was disappearing. An argument seemed preferable to this . . . this damned *pull* that seemed to intensify each time the two of them met. "You seem to speak your mind most freely whenever you like."

Her eyebrows lowered. "You are not particularly gracious when accepting apologies."

"Well perhaps you should have just played the piano, like I asked, and saved us the inconvenience of conversation—"

He broke off at the sound of a commotion behind him, and Caroline's face grew taut with alarm. Turning, he saw Lady Frances abruptly swat at the empty space on the couch beside her.

"*No!*"

Mrs. Cartwick sat motionless, frozen on the other side of the couch, her eyes wide. Jonathan frowned, unsure of what the trouble was yet, and stepped forwards to assist.

"Is there something I can—"

Lady Caroline beat him to it, though, shouldering hurriedly past to assist her aunt.

"Auntie, you look tired," she said hurriedly. "Here, let me help you. We can return home if you like."

Frances still stared at the empty space on the couch, jabbing a finger at it for emphasis.

"Naughty!" she cried.

Caroline gently grasped the lady's arm and helped her rise to a stand, her worried expression plain to see. The moment made an impression on him, as he would not have thought her capable of such tenderness or concern. Anytime he was with her, she was pricklier than an angry hedgehog, but it was clear this was no ordinary situation.

Frances stared at her niece in confusion and Caroline leaned in, her head tilting close to whisper softly to her aunt. One hand was placed firmly on Frances's shoulder while her other hand rubbed her back in soothing circles, and the whispering continued until finally Frances relented with a beleaguered nod.

He strode forwards and touched Caroline's elbow. "What can I do?" he asked.

"Yes," his mother added, nodding. "We'd like to help."

Caroline refused to acknowledge his offer, pulling away to slide an arm around her aunt and glancing at his mother instead.

"I fear my aunt has overexerted herself," she said. "Would you be so kind as to call our carriage around?"

Mrs. Cartwick rushed over to tug on the bellpull then opened the door of the parlor. "Of course, my dear," she said, her fingers clasped together in a worried tangle.

"Is there anything else you need?" he asked, trying again. This time he did not make the mistake of touching her.

Her answer was short and to the point. "No, thank you."

Then she was ushering her aunt out before anything else could be said, giving barely enough time for the butler to fetch their cloaks. Jonathan and his mother followed them in dismay as the ladies flew down the front steps to board their carriage, hands extended in farewell with no real hopes of reciprocation. The vehicle lurched down the drive, turned the corner and disappeared, a lingering remnant of Caroline's perfume still drifting lightly upon the wind. The delicate scent of roses was as alluring as the lady herself.

After such a sudden departure, it was the only indication she'd been there at all.

"Thank you, Meggie. I'll be in my room if you need me."

Caroline turned the knob and slipped into the hallway. She closed the door quietly behind her and sank against the oak panel with a pained sigh. Glancing down at her dress, she gripped the bodice and tugged it straight. It had twisted uncomfortably when she'd been lying next to Frances in bed, arm wrapped around her aunt's waist, praying for sleep to claim the woman at last. It had been half past three o'clock when the mercy had finally happened. She squeezed her eyes shut.

What do I do? Oh, what do I do . . .

Caroline willed herself not to cry. She had learned long ago that crying never did any good, but still the annoying urge came over her from time to time. The muscles in her jaw tensed as she staved off the wave of emotion, and when she was satisfied the moment had passed, she pushed off the door and started walking to her room.

She had hoped—she had truly thought—that her aunt had been improving. In hindsight, her supposition had not just been wishful, it had been foolish. These things did not typically get better with age. They got worse. She knew the signs of what they called *senile dementia.* Her aunt's hallucinations of pet rabbits she'd owned as a child was most likely an indication of the severity of her case, but calling for the physician was not an option. Caroline would never allow Frances, the only true mother she'd ever had, to be taken away to a lunatic asylum so she could live out the rest of her days in a windowless room. A horrid place where she would sleep upon a straw bed while the screams of the other residents echoed loudly throughout the halls.

It was also why her parents could not discover the truth. Such selfish creatures would only seek to make their own existence less distressing, and an elderly woman with diminished mental capacity would be highly inconvenient for them. It would be off to the asylum for poor Lady Frances, regardless of her distinguished pedigree or upbringing, and irrespective of the fact she was the duke's very own sister.

Her biggest regret was that this recent lapse had happened in front of others. And not just *any* others . . . the American scoundrel and his mother. She did not know Mrs. Cartwick well enough to assess whether or not she was a gossipy sort of woman, but Jonathan Cartwick already thought badly of her—a fact that troubled her more now than it had upon his arrival in England when he was nothing but a faceless enemy.

With a tiny groan of impatience, she cast all thoughts of him out of her mind, her pace hastening. Once reaching her room, she ducked silently inside. The welcome *click* of the door latch caused relief to flood through her from head to toe.

She started towards her vanity table then stopped, electing to sink down against the edge of the bed instead.

Her mass of silvery blue skirts spilled out to the sides around her. She hadn't had the chance to change out of her finery yet. Caring for Lady Frances had been the task of utmost importance on her mind tonight, and that brief hint of her aunt's troubles at Greystone Hall had continued in a prolonged event that had stretched throughout the rest of the evening back at home. Now her aunt lay resting in bed, comfortable in her nightgown, sleeping peacefully the last time she saw her. That could change quickly, Caroline knew.

Leaning forwards, she propped her elbows on her knees and cradled her head in her hands to massage her aching temples. She would need to hire more staff. It made no sense to continue on in this way . . . she needed to make adjustments now before things took an even more conspicuous turn for the worse. It was best for Frances's comfort and safety, after all. And much as the thought killed her, perhaps it was best to limit her aunt's exposure to outside society, even here in the country. Frances would be mortified if she were to be seen acting out. Tonight, the damage had been minimal, she hoped. But next time she couldn't be sure. There simply couldn't be a next time.

With a quiet grumble, she mentally kicked herself. Hadn't she learned her lesson after Lord Evanston had helped them leave London during the season? It had cost her everything to avoid the scandal that would have ensued if Frances acted out in society. Her courtship with Lord Braxton had been one casualty. Her reputation was another, and the local peers had not turned a blind eye to her predawn flight with a notorious rake. Just thinking about their constant slander of her was enough to make her stomach churn.

Rising from the bed, she crossed over to seat herself at the vanity, unfastening the pearl and diamond necklace around her neck. She found herself staring off into space, lost to her own melancholy thoughts. The thought of most concern was whether or not the American could be trusted to keep his mouth shut.

She would worry about that later. For now, she needed to get some necessary rest. After an acute episode of agitation, her aunt often required a day of close watching and assistance. If Caroline was lucky, that would be all she needed for a while. If not, she would need to be close at hand for days.

Caroline knew she could ring the bell and wake her lady's maid to help her out of her gown, but she was so tired and it was so very late. Her eyelids drooped heavily as she raised her arms to pluck the bejeweled pins from her hair. One by one, she slid them out and laid them upon the table, the auburn locks gradually uncoiling to fall in russet waves down her back, then she took the silver brush and briefly ran it through her hair. She only wanted to get the worst of the tangles worked through—there was just no energy for the rest.

A tear landed with a soft *plunk* on her skirt. She glanced down in surprise at the dark spot that widened across the expensive satin.

Crying has never done a bit of good.

No, it hadn't. And she would not start crying now.

With a weary sigh, she brushed the back of her hand

across the wet tracks upon her face. Then Caroline pushed herself upwards to a stand and stumbled across the room to flop facedown upon her bed.

Jonathan dug his heels into the sides of his bay, and the horse immediately responded to the demand by lowering its head and increasing his pace upon the worn country road.

Against common sense—but in line with the dictates of courtesy—he had decided to ride to Willowford House to check on the status of Lady Frances. His mother had not found the past two days of silence reassuring in the least, and even he had to admit that he would like confirmation that all was well with the women after what had occurred during the dinner party.

Woman, he corrected himself. *You are inquiring about Lady Frances.*

But part of him knew that wasn't true. He couldn't help his thoughts from wandering to the beauty with dark hair that glittered with the intensity of a thousand rubies.

He snapped the reins in irritation. He needed to stop being a fool. Lady Caroline was the daughter of a duke and entirely uninterested. One could even say she was repelled by him. He'd never be able to kiss her anyway because that tempting mouth would never cease spitting venom in his direction.

She was pleasing to look at but that was as close as he'd ever be, and what was more, he was glad of it. The woman was entitled and arrogant, just like all the others of her ilk. She could go make some other man miserable; Lord knew she'd already succeeded with him in their short time of knowing one another.

With a deep breath, he turned in and proceeded up the drive to stop before the stately ducal residence. After relinquishing his horse, he vaulted the stone steps two at a time. The heavy front door swung open to reveal a formidable butler who was tall with a slightly rounded belly, a full head of silvery gray hair, and a hawkish nose. He looked down that nose with a hooded gaze to assess the man standing before him now.

"Mmm . . . yes," he said. The man's dignified affectation made it sound like one word. "May I help you?"

"I am Jonathan Cartwick from Greystone Hall," he said, gesturing in the general direction of his estate. "Is the lady of the house at home?"

"Mmm. Lady Frances is not inclined to receive visitors at the moment." He started to back away.

"One moment, if you please," Jonathan said with a staying hand on the door. "What of Lady Caroline? Is she available? I must speak to one of them," he added. "It is a matter of some importance."

The butler's steely gaze was sharp while he considered his request. Finally, it eased just a fraction.

"You will find Lady Caroline out back."

Jonathan blinked. "Outside?"

"Indeed."

The door slowly closed in his face.

He uttered a small, disbelieving laugh, then turned on his

heel to retrace his path down the steps. Ornamental gardens surrounded the grand house. Hedges had been trimmed and shaped into unyielding submission. The bare fingers of leafless willow trees drooped and swayed in the considerable breeze, and multiple terraces with balustrades surrounded the sides and rear of the house. Jonathan knew the duke owned many other properties throughout the country, and the fact that this was probably one of his less ornate holdings set his teeth on edge.

Walking along the gravel lined path, he continued until he was greeted by the quiet *shoop* of an arrow piercing a target at high velocity. And there she was—like some aristocratic version of Artemis—practicing archery on the back lawn with a cup of tea perched upon a small table beside her.

For a moment, she did not see him and was wholly consumed by her focus upon the target and her draw on the longbow. This allowed him a few seconds in which to observe her unnoticed. A lock of dark auburn hair had been teased out by the wind and it swayed and bounced along the nape of her neck. Her informal day dress of champagne-colored muslin was trimmed with lace and enveloped her body in a most . . . flattering way. Jonathan was surprised to see she was not wearing a cloak or something warmer. In fact, it almost appeared as if she'd been reading in the library when the desire to practice archery suddenly took her.

The high round neckline concealed her skin, but the fit of her bodice only illustrated the petite curves beneath. Suddenly he had the most infuriating desire simply stride right over and pull her into his arms. To feel that softness molded against him. To shock her with his touch, then tease her with his kiss—

God, no.

He cleared his throat loudly and she loosed an arrow in surprise, the projectile skittering off awkwardly into the rosebushes. His answering smile was instantly countered by her frown, and she lowered her bow.

"Mr. Cartwick. What are you doing here?"

Her discomfort was gratifying, and he wondered at its exact cause. Was it merely that he had startled her? Or could it be something else . . .

Banishing the thought, he came closer to where she stood. "Forgive me, Lady Caroline. I'd hoped for conversation but I see I've interrupted your archery practice instead."

Lady Caroline's frown deepened and she cast a sheepish look at the target. "I was doing fine until you showed up here, uninvited."

Jonathan smiled at her, a bit too politely. "I believe you."

Every inch of her exposed skin turned pink, from her chest right up to the delicate tips of her ears. Her eyes somehow grew darker yet brighter, and that same thrill he'd felt before in her presence expanded again within his chest.

"Why are you here?" she demanded.

He gazed at her in fascination. *Answer her, you fool.*

Jonathan smoothed a hand over his cravat. He wasn't going to be able to resist teasing her. It was just too tempting. "I came to ask after the welfare of your aunt," he finally said. "But I have time to join you, if you like. Perhaps offer a few pointers."

The surprise on her face made his visit entirely worthwhile, even if she were to turn him away this instant. She placed a haughty hand on her hip.

"The Duke of Pemberton, himself, taught me how to use a bow."

He felt his mouth quirk upwards. "I see."

"Besides, what do you know of archery?"

It was impossible to not want to provoke the little minx when she was so provocative herself. He closed the remaining distance between them and took the bow out of her hands.

"You are about to find out, my lady."

She rolled her eyes while he examined the longbow; flexible and fine and constructed of yew. He would have used a larger, heavier bow under normal circumstances, but adjustments in calculations could be made . . .

Pivoting around, he assumed the proper stance, planting his feet shoulder width apart. Jonathan performed a test draw on the bowstring, pulling back to his ear, then keeping hold of the string, he released it before turning around to slide an arrow slowly out of the quiver at Caroline's hip. This earned him an offended glare that he relished. He turned away, nocked the arrow and took his aim.

"Oh, please," sighed Caroline from behind him. "What a pointless display—"

He breathed out in a prolonged exhale and released the arrow, the shot making the same *shoop* noise as hers had before.

Only this time, it drove directly into the heart of the bull's-eye.

He stood there for a moment in satisfied silence, then turned back to revel in the shocked expression on her face. Reaching down with his free hand to grasp the delicate china cup, he took a sip of her tea before setting it back on its saucer with a tiny, satisfying *clink.*

"Would you like that lesson now?" he asked with a grin.

CHAPTER FIVE

Caroline stared at Mr. Cartwick, the unexpected excitement at finding him so near having quickly transformed into annoyance. There was no way to convince him that normally she was an excellent shot. That after days of worrying and caring for her Aunt Frances, she was just having a bad afternoon. And the longer he looked at her with those incredible eyes of his, the more she knew she would keep losing her aim. It was useless.

"No, thank you, sir. I practice only for my own pleasure, which you have seen fit to ruin today. I believe I am done for now."

She stepped away, intent on retrieving her arrows, but the gentle pressure of his hand upon her own halted her progress. Surprised, she glanced up at him to find a contrite expression on his face.

"Apologies, my lady," he said in a voice that was rich with

his singular accent that was a fascinating blend of two different worlds. "I would never wish to interrupt anything that
brings you pleasure." He paused, the heat from that incredible gaze causing her to look away.

Surely he hadn't meant for his words to sound so . . .
seductive.

"F-fine, then," she stammered. "In that case, you are free
to leave."

"But would it not please you even more to strike the target
precisely where you are aiming?"

Silly her. She thought he was going to be polite. "Mr.
Cartwick," she seethed, "if you are not careful, I will be
aiming at you next time."

"Fair enough," he said, clearly struggling to keep his composure. "And if you move your aim to the left, you may very
well hit me."

Caroline's eyes widened in disbelief. Ooh, he was impossible. Turning on her heel, she stormed across the lawn and
began yanking arrows out of the target. One . . . two . . . Yes,
she was tending to err on the right side today.

"Do you see?" he asked, ambling closer to where she stood.

Upon being caught, she resumed removing her arrows
with sharp tugs. "I'm not sure what you mean, but—"

"Come now. Don't be stubborn," he admonished softly,
stopping before her and causing her heart to hammer insistently beneath her ribs. "A minor form correction is likely all
that's required."

"My form is fine," she argued.

His glance dropped to graze across the fit of her bodice,

the filmy drape of her skirts, as if to ascertain the truth of her statement. He took his time, and only when he was done did his eyes meet hers again. Caroline could feel herself growing hot in embarrassment, indignation and . . . something else.

Had Lord Braxton ever looked at her that way? Even if he had, she doubted it would have stirred the same restless craving deep inside of her.

Clearing his throat, Cartwick came forwards and began pulling arrows out of the target for her. She watched him in carefully subdued amazement.

"Your form is admirable," he agreed boldly, sending a flare of heat up into her cheeks. "But as I'm sure you are aware, if your aim is off then something is not right. Would you like me to help you figure it out?"

Caroline wanted to give him a proper setdown of some sort, but found herself unwilling to send him away. Pursing her lips in what she hoped appeared to be reluctance, she gathered the arrows and slid them back in her quiver, being careful not to meet his eyes.

"I suppose."

She marched back to the table and took a sip of her now lukewarm tea, remembering too late that he had taken a drink from it before when he'd been showing off. The knowledge didn't bother her . . . but it did seem rather too intimate . . . almost like sharing a kiss.

Nervously, she glanced up at his face and saw his color had heightened. Perhaps he felt the same way.

Cartwick approached, then offered the longbow back to her. "Assume your usual stance when you are ready," he said.

Turning her back to him, she widened her feet to roughly shoulder width apart and angled them slightly outwards with the bow lowered to her side. He circled around her, examining her stance carefully, and a corresponding sheen of perspiration broke out upon her forehead despite the chilliness of the air . . . and despite the fact that she didn't like this man. Did *not* like him. A fact that didn't affect his inconvenient appeal at all.

"That's good," he said. "Try straightening your back just a little."

Caroline knew what proper form was. But for some odd reason, she hoped to prolong this little interlude. She brought her shoulder blades back slightly instead.

"No, no. Your lower back. May I?" he inquired with a questioning glance, his hands raised.

Oh—

He was asking permission to touch her. She knew she shouldn't let him, and yet before she could refuse, found she had already tipped him a tiny nod of assent.

Cartwick moved closer and her lungs began to struggle. The pressure of his hand, confident and warm, slid across the small of her back and caused her to jump. He glanced at her.

"Is this all right?"

"Y-yes, I—" She paused to compose herself. "It's fine."

"Good. Now curl your back against my palm, as if you are trying to push it away. There—stop." He smoothed his hand over the line her spine had created, a wave of sparks chasing after the pathway of his fingertips. "This likely feels curved, but you had too much arch before. You have now corrected it."

It did feel strange, but not nearly as strange as it felt to have a man's hands on her. It made the close hold of a waltz feel tame and harmless in comparison. He stepped away and Caroline exhaled in relief.

"Now draw and hold."

Raising her bow, she nocked an arrow and hooked her fingers around the bowstring. Pulling back toward her right ear, focusing on her target, she tried to ignore the fact that he was standing so near.

"This elbow is rotated too far." His fingers touched the arm that was holding the bow.

Oh, she knew. But some devilish part of her wondered if she could get him to touch her again. Releasing her draw on the bowstring, she stared at him. "It is not—"

Cartwick again reached out, taking her arm in his hands and gently guiding her back into position.

"If your concern is simply hitting anywhere on the target, then you're right," he replied. "If, however, you are interested in bull's-eyes . . ." He gripped her elbow and rotated it downwards. ". . . then you will need to perfect your alignment."

Caroline accepted the correction with a sigh, even as a shudder of awareness traveled through her. He was so very, *very* close. Cartwick released her arm to step back, and her eyes darted across his black frock coat, the gray fitted waistcoat beneath that clung to his broad chest like a second skin. He was so near that she could see the pulse in his neck, feel the heat from his body. The shameless urge to press herself against him, to sink into his arms and taste the warm skin that was visible above his collar, was nearly overwhelming. It was something she'd never felt before. Noting her difficulty, his brow creased in concern.

"Perhaps you are tired."

"I, no—I feel fine," she replied, shaking her head. "Please continue."

He eyed her distrustfully before resuming. "As you wish. I believe your shoulders also need to be more open. This is the primary reason why your arrows consistently strike to the right of your target."

She opened her shoulders a tiny bit, but not enough to make much of a difference. Meanwhile, her nerves sang in anticipatory delight.

Perhaps the ton *is right,* she thought shamefully. *I am a wicked girl.*

Cartwick did nothing for a moment, perhaps considering how to make the adjustment without being too inappropriate, and Caroline kept her eyes focused down the lawn the whole time while she awaited his instruction. She couldn't look at him again. Not when he was so near. Not when he was about to touch her again.

He circled around, coming to a stop behind her. Places Caroline had hardly ever thought about became unwittingly alive with him standing there. Cartwick was so near she could feel his breath caressing the side of her neck. Her arms trembled as she held her position, and she jumped a little when his hands slid over the tops of her shoulders, the thin muslin doing very little to disguise the incendiary potency of his touch.

"Like this, my lady," he said softly.

He gently exerted force on Caroline's shoulders, pulling them back into proper position. Her posture improved instantly and her arms fell into place, creating one seamless pathway to the target. His hands fell away, but before she could breathe a sigh of relief, he had slid them lower into a possessive clasp around her waist. She gasped.

"Mr. Cartwick, I don't—"

Her objection was silenced when she felt his hands increase their pressure, rotating her hips just a fraction so they were facing straight ahead. His right hand traveled upwards to lightly tuck a stray lock of hair around the side of her neck, then returned immediately to its place around her waist.

"One clean line. Everything in alignment," he murmured near her ear.

What was it that made her ache for him with all of her being? Her wayward imagination wondered what it would be like if he simply tugged her back against him. She envisioned one hand snaking its way down below her belly while the other rose higher to seek her breasts, the heated brush of his lips upon her neck. She couldn't help it . . . she felt so deliciously vulnerable with him standing behind her.

Then she experienced a moment of clarity. Here she was, imagining this man ravishing her outside on her own back lawn. *And this was not just any man.* He was the American. The one who was now living in the house that Eliza had been forced to vacate. Eliza . . . who'd been like a sister to her, and whose parting words still rang in Caroline's head.

I trust you won't make it easy for him.

She struggled to be loyal for the sake of her friend, but his strong hands were still on her waist.

"Please unhand me, sir," she forced out, "so I can make this shot."

His hands jerked away, allowing for some much-needed concentration. Inhaling deeply, she focused on her target down the lawn, released her breath and took the shot.

Shoop.

She had overcorrected. The arrow hit just to the left of center, but it was still a good shot. Turning, she saw Cartwick nodding in approval.

"Well done."

It was probably the best she'd be able to do with him anywhere nearby, and that thought immediately led to another one.

Do I affect him the same way?

She wanted to find out. Releasing her draw, she extended the bow in his direction.

"Can you do better, Mr. Cartwick?"

He tipped her a smile. "I've already shown that I can."

"Then there should be no problem duplicating your success," she said with a shrug.

Cartwick stared at the bow in amused silence, then slid it from her hands. She offered him an arrow from her quiver then moved back, wrapping her arms around her midsection, being certain to stay in his periphery.

He found his footing, nocked the arrow and pulled back on the bowstring. It appeared his focus was entirely on the target and on the arrow that would pierce it. His gaze was steady, brow lowered, jaw tight—and all at once she saw the face of the man who had run a prosperous shipbuilding company. Serious and determined, she couldn't imagine anyone standing in his way. Failure was simply not an option.

So Caroline raised a hand and slowly, as if lost in thought, traced her fingertips across her lips.

With a blink, his grip slipped and he released the bowstring too soon, sending the projectile high to miss the circular area entirely. He stared down the lawn, glowering as if his arrow had betrayed him, and an unmistakable sense of satisfaction raced through her. She shook her head in mournful contemplation.

"Oh, dear. Perhaps you would appreciate some guidance?" she asked innocently.

Cartwick's gaze snapped over to her. He opened his mouth to reply, seemed to think better of it and shook his head instead.

"Fine, then. I suppose I win." Setting her bow against the table, she lifted her tea and began walking to the house, leaving him to follow or not as he wished.

"Why am I not surprised," he muttered behind her.

She spun around. "Remind me, Mr. Cartwick. Why did you come here today?"

"I came here today to ask after your aunt, as I said earlier," he replied.

Drat. She didn't want to talk about her aunt. Not to anyone, but especially not to him. She started walking again.

"Lady Frances is doing well," she casually mentioned over

her shoulder. "Your inquiry is appreciated but entirely unnecessary. It had grown late and she was tired."

The masculine waft of starch and soap meant he was still following her closely. She felt inordinately irritated at the foolish flutters in her stomach.

"Was it as simple as being tired?" he asked, his voice deep and velvety. "It almost seemed as if it could have been something else."

This was not good, Caroline knew. She felt the blood drain from her face and stopped once more to turn around.

"What do you mean, exactly?" she demanded. "Are you implying something?"

An English gentleman would know better than to ask such questions of a lady, and she would be happy to shame him into compliance, if need be. As it turned out, Cartwick was properly chastened, his golden gaze dipping down to the grass in realization.

"My apologies for causing offense. I ask only out of concern for your aunt."

"My aunt is well," she repeated tersely. "Thank you."

Pivoting on her heel, she resumed her course. Again, his pace matched hers . . . it would seem he was intent on following her into the house. If she were being polite, she would have invited him in herself, but she was unsure of Frances's whereabouts and state of dress. Meggie tried to keep an eye on her aunt, but had other duties to tend to on occasion. Caroline would rather not encourage more scandal at this point. Still, it would cause just as much suspicion, perhaps, to be rude to a visitor.

Her head was still a muddle when he asked her one more thing.

"Will you be attending Lord and Lady Hedridge's ball?"

An icy chill chased over her skin. Baron Hedridge's wife was one of the biggest gossips in Hampshire. She was also the lady who'd showed Caroline the least mercy after the events of the last season. As the Duke of Pemberton's daughter, Caroline was always invited to their balls and soirées, but she often declined in an attempt to avoid the whispered sniping. And there was always sniping about Caroline's reputation, whispered and otherwise. They'd never let her forget that *they knew* she'd left London with Lord Evanston. What they would never know, if she could help it, was why.

The china teacup she was holding rattled noisily on its saucer as she stared at him, trying to remember to breathe.

"Why do you ask?"

He blinked. "Well I suppose I was curious, since my mother convinced me to accept their invitation."

"No doubt they will be eager to satisfy any curiosity you or your mother may have, Mr. Cartwick. Now if you will excuse me, I have matters I must attend to—"

She turned to leave but he reached out to curl his fingertips around her elbow. A now familiar thrill seared a burning pathway up her arm, and she leveled a glare at him. This would all be so much easier if she weren't fighting against this blasted attraction.

"How could my question have possibly caused you offense?" he asked with a confused frown.

Because soon you will be sniping with them. Joining in their gossip. Laughing at me while you occupy my friend's home, and laughing harder, still, when you and your land agent take away my hillside.

Tears pricked at her eyes and she tugged her arm away.

"Mr. Cartwick, please. I need you to leave."

He recoiled at her words, and his eyes went from a congenial amber to black within the span of a heartbeat. Cartwick viewed her with a sardonic tip of his hat.

"Understood. I wish your aunt well."

Caroline watched him leave the way he'd come, his stride long and powerful, the gravel crunching loudly beneath his boots. And although she had achieved her intended goal of driving him away, she couldn't quite explain why it didn't make her feel any better, or why she felt a sharp slice of regret at his parting.

Jonathan glanced over at his host for the evening, Baron Hedridge, who was crossing the floor in a quadrille with his wife and three other couples. The man was competent enough as a dancer, although it was easily deduced that the baroness was at least thirty years his junior. The baroness, by comparison, was quick and light, chatting sociably with the other guests throughout.

Dear God, he wasn't certain if he'd be able to make it through tonight, prancing about like an aristocrat and laughing at terrible jokes. He was an imposter. One who had no interest in imitating the very sort of people who had made his father miserable before, and it all felt like some exercise in play-acting compared to his gritty upbringing in America. He and his brother running through the shipyards, covered in mud and playing with swords made from wood they had taken from the lumber piles, seemed to him more real than any farcical pretense of civility in this ballroom tonight. His brow lowered into a surly frown.

Oh, to place such enormous importance on things like balls and dinners.

A vision of Lady Caroline, practicing archery with a cup of tea, entered his mind before he could prevent it. Had she been here tonight, he would have expected her to ignore him for the duration. Still the evening would have been more interesting. Her earlier dismissal of him had stung, but he could admit that there was something appealing in her unconventional ways . . . in her guileless banter . . . in the way she had caressed her lips while he'd been lining up his target . . .

Clenching his teeth, he dragged his thoughts away from anything to do with her mouth. Clearly she despised these people. And against his better judgment, he wanted to find out why. Needed to learn more about his beautiful, but vexing, neighbor.

No doubt they will be eager to satisfy any curiosity you may have, Mr. Cartwick.

They meaning Lord and Lady Hedridge.

What could she have meant?

"The punch is tolerable, Jonathan. You should have some."

With a blink, he glanced down at his mother, who was

staring straight ahead, drink in hand. He leaned down to whisper in her ear.

"When can we leave?"

She turned to eye him accusingly, setting her dangling onyx earrings swaying. "My goodness, you can do better than that. You've only danced with two ladies tonight and stubbornly refused to ask for any more, even though it appears you've already made quite an impression . . ."

He followed her glance to the young women he'd danced with earlier, suddenly feeling outnumbered. They were perhaps sixteen years old, and they gazed at him with a ferocity that was startling. The girls affected to be demure, he could tell, although the hungry gleam in their eyes was difficult to ignore. Was this what passed for flirtation here in the English countryside? His eyes widened and he turned his head to stare unseeingly at a potted plant.

"Perhaps they should learn to control their expressions a bit better."

Mrs. Cartwick raised a hand to conceal her sudden laugh. "It is terrifying," she admitted, then scanned the ballroom. "But surely there must be someone here tonight who could interest you in another dance?"

"I don't think so," he said. "I'd rather drink the entire bowl of that vile punch than dance with another girl who's just come out . . . especially if *that* is the result." Jonathan twitched his head in the direction of the maidens who still stared eagerly in his direction. "Besides, why they would have such an interest in an American is beyond me. Not while there are all these lazy lords to choose from."

His mother snapped out her fan, fluttering it before her in an attempt to cool down in the stifling heat of the room. "You are more than wealthy in your own right, although I'm surely not the best person to ask about your other charms." Her eyes rotated slyly up to his face. "Perhaps Lady Caroline might be better able to enlighten you?"

He jerked his head in surprise. "What—"

"*Mr. Cartwick,*" came the effusive greeting of his hostess, just approaching to his left. Baroness Hedridge curtsied before him in all her golden blonde, topaz satin-swathed glamour. She was the outer picture of welcoming warmth, although he did not fail to notice the cold azure gaze that was riveted solely on him. Finally, it shifted to his mother. "And Mrs. Cartwick. So good to have you join us this evening for our little party," she said, gesturing to the large crowd of glittering attendees with a musical laugh that he supposed was meant to convey modesty.

His jaw clenched down on his smile, preventing it from fully showing. He forced himself into a perfunctory bow, while the beginning strains of the orchestra's next piece provide a musical backdrop for their unpleasant conversation.

"My lady. Thank you for inviting us here tonight," he managed.

"Oh, no thanks are necessary, sir. I would hardly be doing my duty to country society if I didn't invite the most handsome bachelor in recent memory to grace our little part of England. And his mother, of course," she added with a tiny smile.

Mrs. Cartwick added a small smile of her own, deftly ignoring the subtle slight. "We've met some lovely neighbors already, but this is our first ball back in England."

"It's our first ball in England, ever," Jonathan corrected under his breath.

His mother swiftly closed her fan and just happened to smack his arm in what was definitely not a coincidence. The baroness's eyes sparkled in delight.

"Do tell. Have you met the inhabitants of Willowford House?"

Jonathan could feel his distaste growing at the predatory excitement with which the baroness had asked her question.

"Yes," answered his mother before he could reply. "We had both Lady Frances and Lady Caroline over for dinner. It was a splendid time."

"Was it?" Baroness Hedridge raised her eyebrows. "Well, any time spent in their company is sure to prove interesting." She turned to her husband who had just joined the group. "Wouldn't you agree, my dear?"

The baron gripped the gleaming lapels of his formal black jacket and viewed his young wife with a smile. "You know I agree with you on most everything, darling. Who are we discussing that is so very intriguing?"

"Why, Lady Caroline, of course," she said, curling a perfectly manicured hand over his forearm. Jonathan had the sense that these two together made quite a formidable—and bloodthirsty—team. "And Lady Frances. I was just telling these good people how very *interesting* they can be."

Hedridge's bushy gray eyebrows lifted high onto his forehead and he chuckled scandalously. "Yes. Interesting is one way to describe them, especially after last year's season."

He felt his body tense in anticipation of whatever rubbish was forthcoming, although he could not deny his curiosity where Caroline was concerned.

"Why do you say that?" he nearly growled.

Lady Hedridge's icy eyes widened to near comical proportions. "Well, haven't you heard? Surely you must have, by now." At their blank looks, she uttered a shrill laugh and waved a dismissive hand in the air. "Lady Caroline was heartlessly jilted during last year's season. It was done quite out in the open for the public to see too. Poor creature." She tutted in false sympathy, her pleasure in sharing the dire news oozing out from her like some disgusting contagion.

"No!" his mother said, aghast. "Oh, how hard that must have been on her."

She was appropriately horrified, while Jonathan thought the information may have actually explained a few things. Although his heart clenched upon hearing it in such a way, so callously delivered. He, too, had once been the victim of a fickle love and would not wish that pain on anyone—not even the temperamental Lady Caroline.

"Oh, it was." Lady Hedridge nodded. "We'd all believed Lord Braxton's request for *her* hand to be a foregone conclusion at that point, but then he surprised everyone by offering for another." She tipped her head in thought. "Perhaps it made sense, though, given that she left London in the dead of night with one of the *ton*'s most notorious rakes."

Her last sentence hung in the air leaving silence in its wake. He was stunned at such an accusation, brandished in the presence of others. Given what little he knew of Caroline already, something didn't seem to fit. What did seem to fit, however, was why she'd suddenly gotten upset when he'd made mention of attending this ball.

And here . . . now . . . in this ballroom? He needed to check his emotions, and quickly.

Neither he or his mother uttered a word of reply, and at their unsmiling silence, the lady finally submitted with a coquettish laugh, intent on driving her point home.

"Rumor has it she departed with Lord Evanston, of course, not that anyone could blame her," she said, a blush brightening her complexion. Lord Hedridge wagged a finger at her in amused censure.

Jonathan inhaled sharply through his nose. "You speak rather plainly," he said at last, his cheeks burning in annoyance.

His mother cleared her throat and took a mortified sip of her punch.

Entertained by his offense, the baroness tittered once more. "But my dear Mr. Cartwick, why mince words? The man is intolerably handsome, at least that's what I've heard," she added quickly with a wink to her increasingly disgruntled husband.

Lord Evanston . . . why have I heard that name before?

He struggled, searching for a fragment of thought that was eluding him. There was a piece to this puzzle that he was simply not seeing . . .

"Is that not the man now married to Reginald Cartwick's widow?" asked his mother softly, deep in thought, glancing at Jonathan for confirmation.

Realization struck him like a frigid wave from the Atlantic.

Yes. It was the very same man. And Lady Caroline had just become that much more of a mystery.

CHAPTER SIX

With Eliza's note tucked safely away in her pocket, Caroline decided to take advantage of the first truly sunny day she'd seen in months by heading out to Windham Hill. It was a long walk across the estate and over the fields to get there. Normally she would have ridden her horse, but today she felt the need to make the journey on foot, and her skirts dragged over the uneven terrain as she made her way.

It had been nearly two weeks since the Hedridges' ball, and her usual tactic of ignoring the *ton* wasn't proving as effective this time, and she had an idea why.

The American.

As much as she didn't like to admit it, the idea of Mr. Cartwick believing any of the gossip about her was troublesome. It shouldn't have mattered. But she knew what stories the baroness could conjure up. And Eliza's most recent letter had given her plenty of cause for concern.

Removing it now from within the folds of her skirt, she unfolded the parchment to squint at it in the bright glow of the afternoon sun, her gaze lingering on one passage in particular:

I thought you should be aware that word has been circulating about your hasty departure with Thomas from last year's season. I'd hoped enough time had passed and the ton had lost interest, but this does not seem to be the case. Do not worry yourself over us; Thomas couldn't care less and would even enjoy the attention were it not for how the talk might affect you and me. It does not affect me . . . my only concern at this point is how it might possibly affect you.

She sighed and hung her head, folding the note and tucking it back into her pocket. Her eyes burned and she squeezed them shut, her walking boots still somehow able to navigate the uneven terrain with which she had grown so familiar over the years. Thomas was worried for her, Eliza was worried for her, and the only thing filling Caroline with an unsteady terror was the possible reveal of Lady Frances's deterioration. It was sure to come out if these jackals kept prying into her affairs.

Of course, there were her marriage prospects to consider. But that would only matter if she were actually considering marriage. Still, the idea of Jonathan Cartwick laughing alongside Lady Hedridge, those captivating eyes alight, caused her stomach to roil unpleasantly. If it bothered her this much when she couldn't stand the man, she could only imagine the pain if she did somehow like him. Truth be told, it bothered her more than it should.

I trust you won't make it easy for him.

Her breathing grew shallow, the cage of her ribs seeming to crush down against her lungs. Caroline had felt this way many times throughout her life, and often. It usually happened when the frustration and helplessness of her situation made all her efforts seem futile, the pent-up energy rising high enough to choke her.

Briefly considering whether she should turn around, Caroline pushed herself further, her marching stride through the tall grass consistent and unrelenting. Soon her lungs released their hold and loosened, allowing her to take grateful gulps of air by the time the hill came into view up ahead. A carpet of blue, woven gracefully between the trees, greeted her and she laughed out loud, running the rest of the way. She felt like a child again as she fell to her knees in the partial shade of the still budding trees. Caroline plucked a fistful of the early blooming bluebells and raised the succulent flowers up to her nose.

Inhaling their fragrance, she let out a happy sigh, contented for a moment, and her hands dropped into her lap. How she enjoyed these flowers and the folklore that surrounded them in shadowy intrigue. Some of the stories bordered on sinister, while others were lively and fun. But her favorite had to be—

The jingle of a harness startled Caroline from her daydream and she sat up straight, turning her head apprehensively to spot a white horse standing on the other side of the grove, its head lowered to graze on the flowers at its feet.

Mr. Cartwick didn't ride that horse . . . or did he?

Unable to recall his steed from the day they'd met on the road, she rose on wobbly legs to venture closer. Her hand trailed across the rough surface of the tree trunks and she peered around as she went, afraid of who she might find. Would it be worse to discover an unknown man or the American? Who she saw certainly surprised her. Cartwick's gray-haired land agent, Mr. Conrad, was seated with his eyes closed, leaning against the trunk of a tree. Caroline took a deep breath.

"What are you doing here?"

The man jerked in surprise and his top hat fell off his head. "I, er—" He raised a finger in pause and leaned over to retrieve his wayward hat, then scrambled to his feet and straightened, his eyes round in apprehension. "Mr. Cartwick is set to meet me here in five minutes—"

Her eyes narrowed. "Oh, is he?"

"Indeed, my lady. Knowing his fondness for punctuality, I decided to arrive early and, ah! There he is," he said, pointing behind her and removing a kerchief from his pocket to mop his brow in relief.

Caroline whirled around. There was his majestic bay—she remembered it now—the horse walking idly in her direction through the scattered fence of silvery trees. Cartwick had been all but silent or else she would have spotted him sooner, and the shock of finding him there caused her to fall quiet too. His eyes caught hers as he approached, and he brought his horse to a stop with a brief tug on the reins. Cartwick looked down at his hands with a sigh.

"Mr. Conrad, perhaps now is not the best time for this."

"I quite agree, sir," answered the land agent who was already hurrying over to fetch his horse. "I'll await word of our rescheduled meeting." He paused for a moment, shooting a slightly terrified glance in Caroline's direction. "Good day to you, my lady."

She pressed her lips together and nodded to the man. He was attempting politeness, after all, and he was leaving, which was even more important. Conrad mounted his horse and with a lift of his hat to both of them, spurred the animal into a gallop for a hasty retreat. The agent disappeared down the hillside, and in the space of a breath, Caroline realized she was now alone with Cartwick. Again. And with him staring down at her from his position on his horse, she could see the muscular clamp of his thighs around the saddle, the calloused surface of his palms as he relaxed them around the reins and the breadth of his chest beneath his brocade waistcoat. Not unpleasantly, it reminded her of the day they had met.

Caroline glanced away, striving for nonchalance. "If you aren't coming down off your horse, feel free to follow your land agent," she said with a sniff. "I don't even want to know your purpose in coming out here today."

Cartwick's eyebrows raised, and he swung nimbly off his horse to land on the ground.

"Is that better?" he asked.

Had she just goaded him into staying? Frowning, she said nothing and walked away while he looped his reins around a tree. Her heart was pounding frantically in her chest and she had a few guesses as to why. She couldn't help but notice that his masculine form, clad in a striking black frock coat, seemed larger in the screened privacy of the grove. They were alone here, in relative seclusion, and the knowledge caused Caroline's body to tremble excitedly. And the knowledge that she had so little control over herself in his presence was disheartening to say the least.

No longer feeling cheerful, she tossed the cluster of bluebells she'd been holding tightly in her fist, sending them tumbling to the ground.

"No," she heard him say, his footsteps approaching. "Don't do that."

She watched in surprise as Cartwick dropped to his knees to retrieve the flowers. Rising to a stand, he paused, then extended them back out in Caroline's direction. She stared at them.

"What does it matter to you?"

His broad shoulders raised in a shrug. "You just seemed so very peaceful earlier, when you picked them." He hesitated, his eyes scanning over his offering, seeing the way the green stems had been mashed together.

Caroline snatched them from his grasp, her cheeks burning. "You were watching me?"

"It was incidental, I assure you."

"Well I'm not sure why you stayed, Mr. Cartwick. I've nothing to say to you," she said, squaring her shoulders.

"Oh? Now that would be a first."

Caroline met his gaze and took in that enthralling mix of soft brown and warm amber. Her strongest inclination was to pull him into the sunlight so she could see every detail of those extraordinary eyes for herself. Instead she clenched her fists, feeling her body stiffen in challenge.

"I find it funny that you would say such a thing when just over a fortnight ago you willingly entered the vipers' den of gossips." Her voice sounded more offended than she'd been hoping to let on.

A shadow passed across his face. "Truly," he conceded. "Lord and Lady Hedridge are the worst sort of rumormongers."

Caroline flinched. What had they told him? If Eliza's letter was any sort of clue, she had a feeling she knew exactly. She needed an escape. The possibility of being cornered with an awkward question was best avoided.

"Yes, I believe I knew that. Good-bye, Mr. Cartwick. I'm going to walk back—"

"Is it true that your last season was exceptionally difficult?"

Frozen in place, her mouth fell open in silence before she could formulate her words. Caroline hadn't actually expected him to voice such a personal question to her, but with him all bets were surely off. She was unsure whether he was implying something less than ideal about her character, but the discovery of her aunt's illness was a chance she was unwilling to take. She would have to avoid that topic, and focus on the other. Girding herself against his judgments, she met his gaze.

"If you are vaguely referring to my being jilted by Lord Braxton, you should know it is a most impolite thing to do."

Cartwick looked away. "I did not intend to speak lightly of such a thing," he muttered. "But I struggle to understand you sometimes."

"Do you need to?" she asked, gesturing beyond them to the hillside that was dappled in golden sun. "It seems your priorities have been very clear since your arrival. What difference does one neighbor make, and what can possibly be gained from learning about her failed season?"

Cartwick shoved his hands into his pockets, considering her question.

"I admit, there is nothing to be gained," he said at last. "Perhaps only an answer."

"An answer regarding *what?*" she asked incredulously.

He took a step closer and she tensed in response, staring helplessly as his eyes dropped to the bluebell-carpeted ground beneath their feet. "An answer to the question of why you seem to harbor such disgust for me, when you must be capable of civility, and even softness." The muscle in his jaw clenched. "Were you not kind to Lord Braxton?"

Caroline uttered a quiet laugh that was entirely without humor. "Oh yes, I was kind to him, and he repaid me with humiliation. But since when are we comparing you to a man who once courted me?"

A quick twitch of his head. "We're not. I mean—that was not my aim."

"Then what, exactly, is your aim?"

Cartwick's lips twisted, and she had the inconceivable urge to tug on the lapels of his coat . . . to taste that tempting mouth until his resistance slipped . . . until he was gripping her tightly, hands on her waist as they'd been once before . . . ravishing her with slick openmouthed kisses of his own . . .

Caroline fidgeted with her flowers nervously. She'd never even been kissed and had precious little idea what she was thinking about, although her body did seem to have ideas of its own. His vocalized ponderings about her former suitor had certainly managed to rouse all sorts of . . . feminine feelings. Impulses that were better left unexplored, especially with him.

He finally made a sound of annoyance. "Nothing . . . there is no aim other than to correct this blasted boundary as quickly as possible."

Her posture straightened. "Fine."

"Fine," he bit back, reaching upwards to snap off a thin branch from an overhanging tree.

"I can't promise I won't try to make things difficult for you." She owed Eliza, after all.

Cartwick rolled his eyes. "Would it please you to know that you already have?" He whipped the branch at a patch of bluebells near his feet.

"Yes. And you really shouldn't do that," she said.

He paused. "Why not?"

Caroline lifted her flowers and twirled them around. "Legend has it that a field of bluebells is intricately woven with fairy enchantments."

"Ah," he said, casting his eyes cautiously about the blue carpet at their feet. "And why would that worry me?"

"Because," she replied, "the fairies are not known for being nice to humans. Especially uninvited Americans who think they know everything."

He stared for a moment, then threw his head back in laughter. It both unnerved and delighted her to think she had been the cause. She frowned as her gaze lingered upon the dimple that had shown itself again . . . across the sharp line of his jaw that glinted with just a hint of stubble . . .

"Tell me, Lady Caroline," he said through his mirth, wresting her attention back from her more inappropriate musings. "What else does legend say?"

She removed a single flower from the cluster in her hands and pinched it between her fingers, holding the trembling bloom that was precariously attached to its stalk. "Well, according to folklore, if one hears a bluebell ring out loud, they'll soon be dead."

His smile vanished. "I don't care for that particular historical tidbit."

"I didn't say it was all sunshine and romance," she replied, tossing the flower to the ground.

"Romance," he said evaluatively, coming closer, tapping the branch in a staccato rhythm against his thigh. She swallowed hard, struggling to hear him against the heartbeat thundering loudly in her ears. "I'm not surprised you would spurn such a notion."

"You don't know anything about me," she replied in a low voice, suddenly worried.

He shook his head slowly, his amber eyes never leaving her face. "That's not entirely true."

Oh, God. What did they tell him?

Caroline stumbled backwards. She couldn't bear the

thought of receiving any censure from this man based on the lies he may have heard. If she had behaved scandalously in London, it had been solely out of love and the necessity of protecting her aunt. She extended a finger in his direction.

"Say nothing else . . . I don't want to hear it. To be honest, I'm not surprised that you would blindly accept the word of people like the baron and his wife."

The branch ceased its incessant tapping upon his leg, and his gaze grew bright. "Likewise, I am unsurprised at your judgment of me. It seems to be the one trait of yours I can rely on with any certainty." His mouth clenched shut and he turned his head to the side. "If you wish to avoid others drawing their own conclusions about you, perhaps you shouldn't pride yourself on being such an enigma."

"So, if I don't wish for my private affairs to be constantly picked apart by the hungry vultures of the *ton*, I must be at fault in some way?" Caroline laughed harshly. "Oh, Mr. Cartwick . . . welcome to England. You'll fit right in."

Throwing the rest of her flowers aside, she stomped past him out of the grove and through the long grass that led back to Willowford House. Her rapid breathing and the rustling of her tangled skirts were the only noises she could discern at first in her rush to escape him, until his boots could be heard hurrying through the grass behind her.

"Caroline—"

She spun around in fury at his presumptuous familiarity.

Cartwick halted and placed one hand above his eyes as if his head had suddenly started to pound. "*Lady* Caroline—"

His hand fell away, and when he glanced up, whatever

words were next suddenly died on his lips. She saw that his gaze was focused on something beyond her, and when she turned and spotted what had caught his eye, a cold bloom of dread took root in her chest.

It was a figure dressed in white, zigzagging haphazardly across the field below.

No, she thought weakly. *It couldn't be—*

Before she had a chance to think about all the ways this could be disastrous for her, she picked up her skirts and bolted down the hillside. She did not hear Cartwick following but knew it would happen eventually given the urgency of her reaction.

Gravity tugged her to her destination, and before long it took more effort to keep her from toppling over headfirst than it did to keep a fast pace. Still, the white shape in the distance remained an ever-elusive speck, and she realized in the midst of her panting exertion that it was much farther away than she'd initially believed—or maybe it was only her panic making it seem that way. She'd made the journey from Willowford House to Windham Hill hundreds of times, but never truly appreciated the steepness of the incline or the distance from home, especially since she usually rode her horse.

The pounding of hoofbeats caught her attention and she turned to glance behind her, tripping slightly as she did. Cartwick pulled hard on the reins to stop his bay just short of her position, the grave look on his face holding a hint of confusion. He still wasn't aware of exactly what was happening, but he would know very soon.

He pulled his foot out of the stirrup and reached toward her.

"Get on."

There was no more time for anger or hurt feelings; Caroline simply placed her foot in the stirrup and let him take her hand, warm and strong around hers. She gathered her skirts tightly then pushed off. In one swift motion he swung her around so she came to rest just behind the saddle, inching as close to him as she could to avoid flying off the back of the horse. Cartwick gripped her wrists and tugged them roughly around his waist. Lowering her head, she gasped quietly against the hard plane of his back, locking her hands together before he took the reins again and jabbed his heels into the horse's flanks with a sharp yell. The bay took off and she tightened her hold, some disbelieving part of her unable to ignore the way she was pressed against him.

But this was not the time for such thoughts. His horse flew down the hill and she jostled wildly upon its back, clinging tightly to Cartwick. It was as thrilling as it was terrifying, and after what seemed like forever—but had likely only been half a minute—the ground evened out into gently rolling meadows. The ride became less bumpy as the figure in white came startlingly and painfully into view.

It was indeed Lady Frances, and although her appearance was in disarray with gray hair unbound and eyes darting wildly, she was at least covered by her ivory morning wrapper. It was not entirely appropriate for out of doors, but it was a far sight better than the chemise Caroline feared it had been from her distant viewpoint on the hillside. They'd only just pulled up beside her when Caroline slid off the horse that had not quite stopped yet, narrowly avoiding its stomping hooves. She heard Cartwick call out. In anger? Concern? It was hard to tell.

"Caroline!"

Ignoring him, she lurched forwards and gripped Frances's shoulders in both of her shaking hands.

"*Auntie,*" she cried, her gaze scanning hurriedly for any signs of injury. "What are you doing here? Why are you not inside?"

Cartwick had dismounted to approach the group from behind, and she felt his hand slide protectively under her upper arm. Her eyes flicked up to his briefly, and Zeus himself could not have been more intimidating with the expression of thunderous disapproval that greeted her. No matter. She turned back to Frances.

Her aunt's filmy hair floated upon an errant breeze and her confused expression sharpened into focus, one motivated by determination. She leaned forwards as if imparting a great secret.

"I need to find Crumpet."

Caroline's heart sank.

Cartwick's hold on her arm suddenly loosened. He didn't say anything, thank goodness, but she could tell he was trying to piece together what was happening.

"Auntie, Crumpet made his way back to the house. In fact," she added confidently, "he's with Meggie right now." She tugged the wrapper more firmly around her aunt's delicate frame.

Speaking of Meggie, the maid would have some explaining to do. Caroline assumed Frances had been assisted in dressing this morning, so how Frances was able to slip out of the house undetected was still yet to be heard. But Caroline needed more staff and she knew it. She'd been advertising in the village but had yet to find any capable candidates who were trustworthy enough to both care for her aunt and keep her condition a secret.

"Oh," Frances said in a quiet voice, her eyes roving across the meadow. "I'm sure I saw him dash through the grass—"

To Caroline's surprise, Cartwick stepped closer and bowed deeply to Lady Frances, as if there was nothing odd about the fact he was greeting her in a field when she was wearing little more than her nightclothes.

"My lady, would you care for a ride back to Willowford House?"

It was unclear at the moment if her aunt recognized her American neighbor, but one thing was for sure if her blushing smile was any indication. Caroline had to grin. She wasn't sure how such an adorable flirt had not managed to land herself a husband in her earlier years. Frances did not like to speak of it.

"How kind of you to ask," she said with a tinkling laugh, "although I don't think I can lift myself up onto your saddle."

He extended his hand with a flourish. "I am at your service."

Watching Cartwick treat her aunt with such gentlemanly respect did something strange to Caroline's insides. She'd never believed this man, or any man, could be capable of that level of kindness. A sensation like warm honey flowed through her chest, warming her frozen limbs, breathing life into her body, little by little. It was a small change . . . barely noticeable . . . but she could almost feel a tiny crack forming in the ice that had long encased her heart.

And that same heart sank at the knowledge of who had caused it.

CHAPTER SEVEN

The sun had begun to lower in the sky, bathing the tree-lined landscape in luminous pink and lavender hues, and Caroline watched it go down from her aunt's bedchamber window. She exhaled a prolonged sigh that fogged the glass and obscured her vision of the beautiful sunset. After a trying but not unexpected struggle during her bath, Frances was settled at last and dressed in a fresh nightgown, nestled cozily among the blankets on her bed. Caroline glanced down at her skirts, made heavier and darkened by the water that had soaked them earlier, and shook them out with another sigh.

"Can you tell me what's wrong, dear?"

She glanced at her aunt, who had set aside her book to regard her in worry. Her earlier confusion had already seemed to pass, but Caroline was reluctant to leave her alone for fear that it would return. It often did when the sun went down; a phenomenon that she could not explain but tried to guard against, nonetheless. Meggie had gone belowstairs for a bit of dinner but would be back shortly to relieve Caroline, who would return later to sleep beside her aunt.

"Oh Auntie, I wouldn't want to trouble you," she replied, crossing the room to lean against a mahogany poster at the corner of the bed.

Meggie had been reprimanded for her lapse today, but Caroline's remonstration of the beleaguered housemaid didn't really have much teeth behind it. Not when the woman was already performing a job that was above and beyond what would normally be expected of a servant in her position. At this point, the housework could go hang for all she cared.

And of course, she could *never* tell her aunt about the other thing that was troubling her. Namely their American neighbor, who had behaved with chivalry today, even after their earlier argument.

Frances was often out of sorts but still a highly perceptive woman. She placed a bookmark between the pages then closed her book and set it aside. Smiling gently, she patted the spot next to her on the coverlet.

"It's no trouble, my goodness. Now come here. Is it still to do with Lord Braxton?"

Caroline uttered a weary laugh and sank down beside her aunt. "I only wish it were. Such a simple man posed such simple problems."

"When has heartbreak ever been simple?"

"I wouldn't go so far as to call it heartbreak, Auntie," she replied. Not any longer, when her most conflicting feelings so far originated with the one man she was determined to loathe. "And heartbreak is surprisingly simple. I think it is love that poses the biggest challenge."

Frances held her gaze solemnly. "You are wiser than your years, little Caro."

She flinched at the endearment. It was a sobriquet that her aunt almost exclusively used when in the midst of an episode. Searching Frances's gaze for signs of confusion, Caroline only found sincerity within her clouded eyes. Although her aunt meant well, she would probably not remember this conversation tomorrow.

Caroline took her hand inside her own and gave it a tight squeeze. "I can think of many people who would happily disagree with you on that."

"Like who?" Frances asked, mildly offended at the notion.

"Like the American, for starters."

"*Pfft*, the American. What does he know? Wait," her aunt added with a thoughtful pause. "The handsome American?"

She shifted uneasily. "Well, if you think him handsome, I won't argue with you—just how many Americans do you know?"

"The same handsome American who gave me a ride on his horse?" Frances asked, ignoring her question.

Caroline stared. "You remember?"

"Remember? I'm not likely to forget that anytime soon." Frances's eyes gleamed with mischief. "If I were you, I'd quit wasting my sorrows on the likes of Lord Braxton and set my cap at him."

"I don't *care* about Lord Braxton, and I've no intention

of setting my cap at Cartwick or any other man, Auntie. I've told you that before," she bristled.

Frances shook her head and clucked her tongue. "That's too bad."

Caroline didn't like the ominous sound of that.

"Why?" she asked, preparing herself for the worst.

Her aunt reached down to retrieve her bookmark, sliding it out from the pages of her book to hold it aloft so Caroline could see. The bookmark was actually a letter; a rectangle of neatly folded parchment with loopy penmanship on the front. It was handwriting she recognized, although the letters were so rarely addressed to her.

"Because your parents are on their way home," said Frances. "And they are quite set upon finding you a husband themselves."

Jonathan paced down the length of Caroline's drawing room for what seemed like the thousandth time, the carpet upon the hardwood floor deadening the sound from his boots.

He broke off from his anxious pattern to cross over to the window, swatting the gauzy curtain aside before leaning against the edge of the casement. After today's events, it had become increasingly clear that Lady Frances was suffering from some type of malady, and that Caroline was already aware of it. Not clear was how long it had been going on, but he had seen signs of it at the dinner party a few weeks earlier.

As Caroline had rushed Frances upstairs for a bath and change of dress, she had shooed him away in an attempt to dismiss him, probably regretting the fact that he'd been there to witness it at all. But the lady had yet to find out that he was not so easily dismissed, especially when it was clear the two women needed some kind of help. And while he would never outwardly admit to caring for Caroline's good opinion, he couldn't help but be bothered that she viewed him with such abhorrence.

You must be capable of civility, and even softness . . .

He quietly swore at his remembrance of the uttered statement, and heat spread up his neck to flood his face. It was something he'd had no business saying to her, especially when the only possible outcomes were stoking her anger or heightening his awareness of her as a woman.

Then there was the question of what had taken place in London. Something must have occurred to cause her to flee in the middle of the night.

And then there was the obvious question being alluded to by the *ton*. Had she invited Eliza's future husband into her bed . . . even briefly?

He pushed away from the casement and resumed his pacing across the floor. No. That notion still didn't make sense to him. She was a mystery, it was true, but she also seemed fiercely loyal to her friend. Evanston must have been courting Eliza at that point—Jonathan just couldn't conceive of a time when Caroline would betray her in such a way. And wouldn't it be awful to have the gossips spread such a lie . . . especially if it wasn't even true?

Jonathan shook his head with a troubled sigh. This was taking too long. He needed to either find out what was happening or leave. Lady Frances was surely finished with her bath and resting in her bedchamber by now. No doubt Caroline would be furious at finding him still at Willowford House, but it would be worth a few angry words from her if he could just know they were fine, at least for the time being.

His eyes darted to the bellpull, but he decided against it. Loyal servants would have no problem lying to his face for their mistress. Instead, he strode from the drawing room and into the foyer, listening for signs of action or movement. He approached the foot of the stairs and then stopped, discerning the quiet sound of weeping coming from upstairs, drifting down the sloping curve of the staircase. It could be a maid, or Lady Frances. Or it could be Caroline . . .

Knowing he was about to break a thousand rules of buttoned-up English propriety, he ventured slowly to the noise, his boots claiming one stair at a time, until he rounded the corner of the upper hallway. And there he found her— face buried in her hands, forehead pressed against the wall, auburn hair mussed and slipping loose from its pins. Crying.

A peculiar tension built within his chest at the sight of her pose. It was almost unbearable to watch and do nothing while her shoulders hitched with each softly muffled sob. Here was the softness she was not willing to show him. The suffering that lurked behind her blustery demeanor. He'd wanted to know this more vulnerable side of her, but part of him regretted actually seeing it. This was much too personal, and he felt it with an intensity that he did not care to think about.

But he was damned if he was leaving her like this now. In full anticipation of her rage, he hesitantly approached, and with each quiet step his heartbeat seemed to triple its pace. Finally, he stopped beside her, his eyes traveling over the rounded curve of her back before sliding a gentle hand over her shoulder.

"Lady Caroline," he whispered.

With a gasp, her head jerked upwards and his jaw dropped at the sight of her. Normally vibrant gray eyes, now dull, red-lined and weary, stared at him. The porcelain luster of her cheeks had vanished, replaced with a distressed flush and the glistening sheen of her tears. Her dress was crumpled and appeared to have been splashed with what he guessed was bathwater. The total picture of disarray was a jarring contrast to the polished and perfect image she always tried to present.

She viewed him for a moment in paralyzed shock.

"What are you doing here?"

Any verbal explanation from him would not serve as a sufficient answer. Jonathan had stayed after her offhanded dismissal because something inside him would not allow him to leave. If pressed, he wasn't even sure that he could properly explain the reason. So choosing to remain silent, he did the absolute opposite of what she would expect.

He stepped closer and tugged her into his arms.

Caroline's body turned rigid. She brought her fists up against his chest and pushed.

"Don't—"

His hold loosened but his hands remained on her back, crisscrossing soothing patterns over the tense muscles, willing her to relax. Set on resisting, she continued to shake her head while her breath hitched audibly.

"I don't know what you think of me, Mr. Cartwick, but—"

"And I don't know what you think of me, my lady," he murmured, pulling back to hold her uneasy gaze, bringing one hand forwards to trace his knuckles across the curve of her damp cheek. "But I would comfort you if you will let me."

Caroline froze in his arms, staring up at him in dismay. "I-I'm not sure what you . . . I don't n-need any . . ."

Her face crumpled and he felt that same disconcerting pressure in his chest as she collapsed to bury her face against it, her cries partially absorbed by his linen shirtfront. The hands she'd used only moments before to push him away were now curled around the fabric, gripping tightly to pull him closer. Not knowing what else to do, he let his arms enfold her shivering form. He lowered his chin against her head and whispered quietly against the disheveled arrangement of her hair.

"Shhh," he said, taking a moment to greedily inhale the faint scent of rosewater he'd begun to associate exclusively with her. "It will be all right . . ."

She pulled back and shook her head once more, sending an errant teardrop flying off the end of her nose. "You can't say that," she muttered, staring straight ahead at the lawn of his shirt.

"I can say it," he corrected with some irritation, "but of course, it doesn't mean it's true. Let me try to comfort you, for God's sake."

Caroline relented, tipping a watery glance upwards to

meet his gaze. She seemed to finally understand that, at least in this moment, he posed no threat to her. To his considerable surprise, her hands spread out upon his chest. She regarded them thoughtfully, her stormy eyes dark and unreadable, the delicate pressure of her fingertips leaving burning pathways through the fabric.

"You can't comfort me," she replied hoarsely. "You shouldn't try."

Sweet Jesus, *yes* he wanted to comfort her, even though she'd brought him nothing but annoyance so far, and he knew precisely how he would go about it.

But she had her own ideas too, it seemed.

Her fingers moved as if they had a will of their own, and with each brush against the taut muscles of his chest, Jonathan's breathing became shallower and more labored. His hands, too, coursed over her back, down her sides, slowly but eagerly, until lowering to wrap possessively around the slim indent of her waist.

The shared intimacy was shocking . . . the feel of her tucked safely within his arms . . . her hands on him in an appreciative exploration he'd had no reason to anticipate. He yearned to explore her as well, and longed for her to allow it. It would be the greatest gift, to make her mindless with pleasure, to hear her breathing grow faster, have her call out his name—

He released her and Caroline wobbled unsteadily on her feet then started setting herself to rights. She diligently re-pinned her hair, tidied her bodice and swiped at the tears on her cheeks with the heels of her hands.

Surely she had been taken aback by his abruptness, but the shamed blush that crept up her cheeks told him she already knew a line had been crossed between them. Shoving her away had been the only reaction that made sense, and preferable to where his mind had been headed.

Jonathan retrieved a handkerchief from his pocket and held it out. She hesitated then accepted his offer, being careful to not allow their fingertips to touch when she slid it out of his hand. Caroline sniffed and dabbed gently at her eyes, and something shifted within him at the sight of his monogrammed kerchief brushing away her tears. Clenching his teeth, he waited and silently wished he'd never come upstairs.

What he needed right now was for her to toss out one of her barbed comments. *Anything* to get his mind off how good it had felt to hold the infuriating vixen in his arms. His eyes scanned around the hallway . . . at the light fixtures . . . the wallpaper . . . trying to avoid the only thing he wanted to look at with a fiery intensity. He ended up looking at her anyway, once again noticing that her dress was half-soaked.

"May I ask what happened to your dress?"

She gave him a long-suffering look, then sighed and glanced away. "Lady Frances did not desire a bath."

His inclination was to smile at the image of Caroline trying to bathe the feisty older woman and getting splashed mightily for her trouble, but her state of disarray and emotional upheaval suppressed any amusement.

"Did you have assistance?" he asked.

Caroline smoothed down the front of her skirts and straightened her spine. It appeared she was about to reclaim her sense of empowerment and probably at his expense. For once, he welcomed it.

"None of this is your business, Mr. Cartwick," she replied primly.

"Normally, I might agree with you. But after I give barely clothed ladies a ride on my horse, I tend to make it my business." Jonathan widened his stance and folded his arms across his chest.

"Does that happen to you often?" she asked, her eyes widening in shock.

"Do you really care to know?"

Caroline leaned back against the wall. She folded her own arms in a mirror image of his defensive posture, but it had a rather different effect than what she was probably trying to achieve. Cursing his own weaknesses, he tore his eyes away from the delectable way she'd pushed her breasts upwards and forced himself to meet her gaze, praying for the patience of a saint.

"This house is full of servants, and Meggie was with me. Of course I had assistance."

"And yet," he replied, "she still managed to find her way out of doors, despite your abundant staffing."

He knew she was bluffing anyways; had not missed the layer of dust upon the mantel downstairs, nor how the carpets were clearly overdue for a cleaning. Jonathan craned his neck to view the empty hallway with a healthy dose of skepticism.

The confidence fled from her eyes. "Yes, she did. And I need you to assure me of your silence on this subject, especially given your choice of company in recent weeks."

His expression turned serious. "You and I may have our disagreements, but I would never allow that to affect an innocent person. I would certainly not gossip about your aunt's . . . affliction. And yes," he added, "I do take offense that you believe I would stoop so low."

She squared her shoulders. "And here I thought you only cared about yourself."

Jonathan couldn't tell if she was being serious or not, and felt his temper rising. "I care about a *hell* of a lot more than just myself," he snapped. Anger, hot and heavy, started in his chest and flowed outwards in palpable thick waves. "I can tell you I even cared when you leaped off my horse like an idiot."

Caroline's mouth fell open in outrage. "Spoken like a gentleman!"

"I never claimed to be a gentleman."

"Well I thank you, but please spare me the honor of your concern next time. I'm sure there must be another property line somewhere that requires your attention more."

"The property line near Windham Hill required my attention today," he pointed out, his irritation increasing rapidly. "But I was forced to delay my meeting after finding a trespasser on my land. Although if that trespasser doesn't care enough to not throw herself under the hooves of my horse, then I suppose she won't be troubling me much longer."

She glared at him, her eyes shooting sparks. "And you'd like that, wouldn't you?"

"Does it seem like I'd like it?"

Caroline pushed away from the wall but he had already

stepped forwards. She bumped into his chest and froze, stiffening in surprise.

"What are you—"

Transfixed by the luscious ripe redness of her lips, he realized too late that it had been desire, possibly just as much as his concern, that had led him straight up the stairs and into this reckless argument.

Without uttering a word of explanation, Jonathan lowered his head and kissed the Duke of Pemberton's daughter in what was sure to be a colossal mistake.

If Caroline was surprised when he'd pressed against her, she was utterly overwhelmed when his lips came crashing down over hers. But it didn't take long to adjust. Her body had been primed from weeks of longing for him—the desperate struggle to hate him while aching to be closer.

His mouth was slick and hot, dragging across her lips in every fulfillment of her inexperienced girlish fantasies. And just like in those daydreams, she did not play the part of the passive submitting damsel. Tipping her head up to meet him, she matched his every move . . . every vertigo-inducing tangle of their lips, each tantalizing dart of his tongue. Her hands sought the sides of his face, needing to preserve the closeness, savoring the rough scrape of his jaw beneath her sensitized palms.

Caroline had no clue if she was kissing him properly—or if there was such a thing as a proper kiss—but Cartwick groaned quietly as he lunged down to plunder her mouth again, a hopeful indicator that she was doing well. She had the good sense to be scared for just a fraction of a second before he pulled away to gaze at her, his chest heaving as he struggled to regain his breath.

"Christ, Caroline . . . you drive me mad."

The roughly whispered admission caused her body to come alive in unsettling ways, and in unsettling places. Disturbing, but oh, it was pleasing too. Relinquishing control over herself was the last thing on earth she should be doing, yet she could only stare up at him . . . at his mouth . . . wishing he would kiss her again.

She didn't have to wait long. Cartwick dived down once more, softening the play of his lips for just a moment before flicking the velvety wetness of his tongue inside her parted mouth. Caroline jerked at the contact, then passion robbed her of thought and her hands involuntarily curled around the back of his head, her fingers weaving through his hair to pull him closer, kiss him harder. She was rewarded with another groan from him, this one louder than the first, and he moved his hands from her arms to the wall on either side of her, framing Caroline between them.

He was obviously mindful that her aunt was resting just down the hallway and there might be servants nearby, but his caution did not carry over to the way his teeth closed sharply over her bottom lip, nor how he was flattening her against the wall with the hard press of his body. She whimpered, the unbearable pleasure forcing the cry to rise helplessly from her throat, and he released her lip to caress the swollen place with the tip of his tongue.

The mere curiosity that had interested her before had exploded into a full-blown need that burned straight down through to her core. She wanted to feel his hands on her, all over, touching everywhere, but he insisted on maintaining some distance by keeping them firmly planted on the wall. Trapping her, but never touching.

Crying out in frustration, she wrapped her arms greedily around his neck to kiss him again, returning the bite he'd paid to her with a nip of her own. His body froze and went rigid, hovering just inches away from hers, and she could sense he was possibly on the verge of losing control.

It snapped her out of her trance and she shoved him away with all her might.

Then she slapped him for good measure.

His head rocked to the side and he stood frozen, in shocked silence, staring incredulously at the wall. Caroline's mouth moved silently, struggling to find her words even as she was sickened by her own remorse. She hadn't meant to strike him and could not justify it in the least. After all, she had eagerly reciprocated his advances, even if they had initially surprised her.

"I apologize," she said softly in a voice that didn't quite sound like her own. "I-I don't know what came over me."

Cartwick rubbed a hand over his cheek, then he straightened and tugged sharply down on his coat.

"I shouldn't have kissed you," he replied succinctly.

While she couldn't disagree, she wasn't sorry that he had. Her body was still trembling with exhilaration; a feeling she already wanted more of. Much more. Her conscience screamed at her from the depths of her psyche.

"You're right," Caroline said sternly, remembering herself. She planted her hands on her hips, trying to appear stronger than she felt. "You should leave."

An immediate coolness registered behind the previously warm amber gaze, and he viewed her for a moment longer before giving her a curt nod and turning on his heel. She felt another shock wave of regret as she stood there, watching him go, finding it more confounding than her guilt about the slap had been.

And now she had to wonder how she would ever be able to face him again.

CHAPTER EIGHT

Tossing his reins to an awaiting stableboy, Jonathan exited the musty interior of the stables, crossed the yard and bounded up the front steps of Greystone Hall. One long day had passed since his ill-considered kiss with Lady Caroline, and his muscles were still tightly coiled in tension, the length of his body fraught with anxiety and frustration.

It had been the worst idea imaginable—the most foolish thing by far—for him to sacrifice common sense in favor of that stolen moment with her, and he was considerably worried by his lack of discipline. Could he ever really trust himself around her again?

And though he had tried, he could not forget how she had kissed him too. So unlike a shrinking debutante and so very like the enchantress he knew she would be once she had surrendered to her passion at last.

But then, of course, she had slapped him.

Jonathan was frowning as he entered the foyer, and the butler was immediately at his side to divest him of his riding jacket. But before he could proceed upstairs, he heard his mother's approaching footsteps echoing loudly upon the checked tile floors. Her sudden appearance indicated she'd been waiting for his arrival, which she probably had since he'd taken great pains to avoid her yesterday. After his accidental meeting with Caroline, he'd been in no mood to pretend all was well.

"There you are!" she said. "You've been busy these past two days, and just look at how much you've missed. We've received a letter from your brother this morning."

Jonathan's cares were forgotten in an instant. "Did we?" he asked brightly. "And how is James faring at the shipyard?"

"Not so fast," she said with a wry smile, her gaze turning hooded. "I want to know why you've been avoiding me, first."

He grumbled in irritation then tipped a nod to the butler. After the man had left, he guided his mother into the drawing room with a sigh.

"My meeting with Mr. Conrad did not go as planned yesterday."

"Oh?" She tipped her head, the gray filaments in her hair catching the late morning light streaming in from the windows. "What was the problem?"

He shot her a pointed look. "Lady Caroline was the problem."

Mrs. Cartwick's eyes grew round with surprise, then

she burst out laughing. "But how could she possibly have known of your meeting?" she asked, trying to stifle her amusement.

"I don't believe she did." He crossed over to the sideboard and poured himself a drink. "It seems she really does enjoy that particular spot of land and was simply taking advantage of the fine weather."

His mother eyed him in concern. "A bit early for brandy, isn't it?"

"Yes," he replied, tipping his glass upwards for a drink. He hissed at the sweet burn of the alcohol and squeezed his eyes shut. "Yes, it is."

"Oh goodness. It was that bad, then?"

Jonathan frowned and polished off the rest of his drink before setting the glass down to face her. "It wasn't meeting her there that was the worst of it, surprisingly enough. She was as argumentative as ever, but . . . it was what followed after that gave me the most cause for concern."

Mrs. Cartwick crossed over to the settee and lowered herself down as if in preparation for what he was about to say. "And what was it that followed?" she asked quietly.

Guilt flashed through him. He could not divulge what had taken place between them yesterday. And although he knew his mother could be trusted, Jonathan's lack of manners and self-control around a highborn aristocrat's daughter would absolutely be cause for condemnation. It was all better left unsaid. Besides, the seriousness of the situation with Frances took precedence over any of his more . . . romantic . . . dealings with the woman's niece.

Seating himself in an armchair opposite her, he ran his fingers distractedly through his hair before leaning forwards to plant his elbows on his knees. "Well, Lady Frances made an unexpected appearance too, in little more than her night-gown."

His mother's shocked reaction might have been comical given alternative circumstances, but in this case, it was perfectly fitting.

"I—" Snapping her mouth shut to collect herself, she tried again. "I see."

"Yes," he agreed, scrubbing his face between his hands. "Now you see. Her aunt had somehow ventured outside without being detected by the household staff, and I escorted both of them back to Willowford House. Obviously, Lady Caroline regretted me being there to witness the event."

"I would say she did, the poor dear. The decline of a loved one is such a private matter," her mother added sadly. "Do you think there is anything we can do to help?"

Her response was unsurprising, as she had firsthand experience with the agony of watching a loved one fade before your very eyes. After years of ostracism and poverty in England, followed by the massive undertaking of doing business in America, the stresses of life had caught up to his father. Robert Cartwick's heart had soldiered on, stubborn but failing, for the better part of a year before the release of death finally took him.

"Perhaps," he answered. "I've been giving it much thought—it seems that more staff might be helpful. We could spare one or two servants for a period of time?"

"She will likely resist, not wanting to place herself in a position of owing you in any way."

"Yes," he said with a sigh. "I'm sure she will."

"Do you think she would take offense at our offer?"

"I've yet to find a subject on which she doesn't take offense," Jonathan said, "but she needs the help. That much is certain. Perhaps she would find it less offensive if you made the offer and not I."

Mrs. Cartwick nodded. "We will call on her tomorrow, but I still think you should be the one to speak with her. You two may enjoy your arguments, but regardless of what you think, I feel she holds you in some esteem."

Although the shock had lessened over the past day, the sting from her slap still resonated throughout his being, leaving him feeling hollow and foolish. Jonathan shook his head.

"I think you're wrong. And I do not enjoy arguing with her," he added.

She gave him a hint of a smile. "If you say so. In any case, I'll speak to the staff later today and come up with a plan." Leaning back against the burgundy cushions, she evaluated him curiously, folding her hands over her lap. "I must admit I am surprised by your ready willingness to help, knowing how you feel about the peerage, and after hearing those terrible rumors from Lady Hedridge."

His gaze lifted to meet hers, not missing the unmistakable twinkle lurking there. She was fishing for information that he was unwilling to provide. He shrugged in practiced indifference.

"I would expect you to be more surprised if I had taken the baroness at her word."

Her eyes were steady. "Perhaps you're right," she said. He could tell she wasn't entirely convinced by his casual treatment of the subject, but he didn't need to convince her. He just needed her to stop asking questions.

In an effort to curtail her asking any more of them, Jonathan stood and approached his mother, hand outstretched, a smile playing about his lips.

"Now I'd like to see that letter from James, if you please."

"**O**uch!"

Caroline's breath hissed between her teeth and she sucked on her finger. Tasting the coppery tang of her own blood, she withdrew her hand to stare forlornly at her tiny wound. Frances's dry admonishment came from her place on the couch beside her.

"If you're not more careful with your needle, my dear, you'll be embroidering a field of poppies instead of that rose you'd been planning."

"I should have thought by now that your expectations regarding my needlework would be set appropriately low, Auntie," she countered. "It has never been my forte."

Caroline glanced over at Frances who was pushing her needle with ease through her circular embroidery hoop, creating lovely stitches of colored thread without seemingly any effort. The beginnings of an intricate pattern were starting to emerge—a bouquet of pink peonies and purple lilacs had taken shape already, lovely and distinct. It was the work of an experienced and delicate hand. Her work, on the other hand, was not nearly as refined nor as swiftly performed.

She stared down at the sad beginnings of the thorny stem she'd been stitching, then sighed and set her hoop aside to gaze longingly out the windows. It was another fine spring day. A bit chilly, perhaps raining a little, but what she wouldn't give to go outside and walk into town. The reality was that Frances needed more supervision nowadays, and Meggie was overworked. Caroline had always enjoyed her aunt's company, not just for the fact that she was quite possibly the only relative who cared about Caroline, although that did place her well above all others. Even her judgments on her embroidery and lack of suitors brought Caroline amusement. Usually.

Her parents' decision to return home had been anything but amusing, of course, but the news was no surprise. Caroline had always known that her surly attitude towards the marriage mart and its unsatisfactory offerings would wear thin with the duke and duchess. Many times, she'd imagined the day they would drag themselves back home to be reunited with their disappointment of a daughter. In her younger years, there had been anticipation, even excitement. Now there was only dread . . . and contempt.

"Is something wrong?" asked her aunt, head still lowered over her work.

She smiled. "No, Auntie."

But yes, of course there was. Her parents would be arriving in a few weeks, which meant they would soon be seeing

Frances's condition for themselves. The first thing they would do would be to have the family physician whisk her aunt away to an asylum. The second thing they would do would be to marry Caroline off to a man who was not terribly choosy . . . a man who would find any of her more objectionable qualities or rumored ruination slightly less important than the fact that she was still the Duke of Pemberton's daughter. She had a feeling they already had a list of local candidates in mind. A list that she already knew would never include the tempting Mr. Cartwick, thank goodness . . . even if the memory of their moments together had been keeping her awake well into the night.

Her throat constricted. In a way, those illicit events had made her question her own sense of identity. She felt unmoored, adrift. Who was she if not a loyal friend to Eliza? Who was the woman in the hallway that had returned the hungry kisses of the hated Cartwick heir, then callously slapped him upon realizing her mistake?

Squaring her jaw, she retrieved her embroidery hoop and set to stitching again, her needle piercing the fine cloth with more vigor than was required. The sound of a carriage pulling up on the drive caught her attention. Caroline looked over at Frances in surprise, only to stab her finger yet again.

"Ow!" she exclaimed angrily, hurling the hoop down onto the couch.

She could have sworn she heard her aunt snicker before standing and crossing over to peer out the windows, then Frances's wrinkled fingers rose to her lips.

"Oh—"

Immediately, her aunt began tidying her hair and smoothing over her skirts, giving Caroline a potential clue about the identity of their caller. Her heart sank down into her shoes.

"Is it the American?" she asked.

Frances turned to give her a disapproving look. "You know, you really should stop calling him that."

"So it is him, then," Caroline said. She sighed and set her needlework on the side table.

"And his delightful mother."

She paused. "Both of them?"

Oh no. What if Mrs. Cartwick had somehow learned about their kiss yesterday, and was now showing up to demand their marriage?

The drawing room revolved slowly around her, and she reached out to steady herself on the arm of a chair. Jumping to conclusions would do no good at all. Besides, he would no sooner confess the truth of their kiss than relent on the property line dispute near Windham Hill. She needed to breathe and act normally. They were just here for a social call; she was sure of it.

A sharp rap upon the door preceded the butler's entrance, and he greeted them with a bow. Before he could announce the arrival, Caroline interrupted.

"We know the Cartwicks are here, Taylor. Please send them in. And some tea as well."

He lowered into another bow. "As you wish, my lady."

She'd hardly had time to still her trembling hands before

Jonathan Cartwick and his mother entered the drawing room, bowing and curtsying their respective greetings.

"It is so lovely to see you both again," effused Mrs. Cartwick. "I hope you don't mind our stopping by." The woman hesitated, her eyes growing large. "Do you mind?"

In her typical fashion, she behaved with a frankness that the British would typically find uncouth. It was a lightness of manner that made Caroline relax the tiniest bit, putting her at ease even as Jonathan's presence caused its expected turmoil.

"Not at all," replied Frances. "Please be seated," she said, gesturing to the settee.

Caroline stole a glimpse of Cartwick, and noticed his gaze was studiously affixed to her aunt. He was making a very deliberate effort to avoid looking at her in any way.

While Frances and Mrs. Cartwick launched into the niceties, Jonathan continued to ignore her, which suited her just fine. Not just because she didn't feel like arguing at the moment, but because it gave her the rare opportunity to admire him, unobserved.

Caroline remembered threading that light brown hair between her fingers; thick wavy hair that had brushed against her palms as she pulled him down to kiss her even deeper. She remembered the press of those wicked lips against her own, and the sly darting of his tongue. She could recall the deep, reverberating groans that had issued from his throat, as if it had taken every bit of restraint he possessed to keep his hands pressed firmly on the wall behind her . . .

His eyes shifted over to meet hers. And in that moment, she knew that he was remembering it too.

A heated flush crept over her face.

Luckily, Taylor made his timely entrance with the tea cart, and everyone's focus shifted. Frances glanced over at her.

"Be a dear and pour Mr. Cartwick a cup of tea. He looks like he could use it."

His dark brow raised in amusement. "Do I now?"

Her aunt surveyed him with a wry smile. "Well, you look like you could use something."

Caroline decided to spare him any further teasing and rose to retrieve his tea. The ladies mercifully resumed their chatting—something about artwork from what she could hear—and she approached him hesitantly with his cup and saucer. Cartwick accepted her offering without so much as an upwards glance.

"Thank you," he said gruffly.

She nodded in reply, then returned to pour for her aunt and Mrs. Cartwick. When that was finished, she seated herself once more and laced her fingers together nervously upon the yellow muslin of her skirts.

"Are you not having tea?" he murmured .

Caroline glanced up to find his amber eyes locked on to hers, sending tiny shivers of awareness chasing across her skin.

"I'm not in the mood for tea," she said. Although truthfully, she was more afraid of spilling it on herself given the current state of her nerves.

He considered her answer. "What are you in the mood

for?" he asked, setting his cup aside. His gaze dipped slightly to her left, landing on the side table next to her. "Needlework?"

Caroline almost groaned out loud. She should have hidden the blasted thing away, but it wasn't like she'd had a lot of time to tidy for visitors.

"No, as a matter of fact, I am not fond of needlework," she said, hoping to discourage any further talk on the subject.

His eyebrows raised. "May I see?"

She shrugged but could feel herself flare crimson in mortification. "If you must," she said, reaching across to hand him her hoop.

Cartwick held it in his hands, squinted, then turned it upside down to squint at it some more.

"Is it a walking stick?" he asked.

Caroline scowled. "It's not finished, for heaven's sake. Obviously, it's a stem."

"Obviously . . ." he said slowly, rotating the hoop to the side to find a better angle. "And what are these bumps along the, er, stem?"

Her eyes narrowed further. "They are thorns."

"Ah," he said, lifting his gaze to catch hers. "Well, that makes sense at least."

"Why?" she asked in irritation. "Let me guess . . . because you think I have a prickly disposition?"

Cartwick leaned forwards to lower his voice. "After the other day, do you really need to ask me that?"

She was certain her entire body blushed pink at his words. With a cautious glance at her aunt on the far end of the couch, she whispered a reply. "I said I was sorry."

He handed her back the embroidery hoop. "And I said I shouldn't have done it. Lesson learned."

"Oh, did you truly require that particular lesson? The one that instructs all gentlemen *not* to ravish innocent women?"

Cartwick shook his head. "Of all the words one could use to describe you, Lady Caroline, *innocent* is probably not the first one I would—"

Closing his teeth shut over his next words, he glanced over to their companions who were still chatting with one another. With a swipe of his hand over his face, he sighed then nodded at the needlework in her hands.

"I'm surprised it's not a bluebell."

She blinked at him, then stared down at her pathetic representation of a stem. She was a little surprised by the thoughtfulness of his comment, especially when he'd been in the middle of delivering a withering assessment of her character. Either way, she was glad to steer the conversation away from anything having to do with their kiss. She could not pass that place in the hallway without every nerve ending spontaneously igniting in fiery remembrance of the event.

"I—well I suppose it could have been," she stammered. "But Lady Frances requested a rose."

"Ah," he said, the reserve behind his eyes softening just a bit. "Well then I have no doubt she will like it very much."

It shouldn't have pleased her to hear him say such things, and yet she couldn't help but feel a corresponding warmth expanding inside her chest. It also should have been easier to glance away, but again she found herself snared by the man's hypnotic gaze, which had just lowered to her lips in a way that was highly disconcerting.

The *clink* of teacups upon their saucers interrupted the spell, and Caroline jumped a little in her seat then set her needlework aside. Both Mrs. Cartwick and Frances abruptly rose to a stand.

"Mrs. Cartwick has requested to see the gallery," said Frances. "Would you care to join us?"

She and Cartwick stood as well, but before they could respond to the question, Caroline saw the subtle but pointed look Mrs. Cartwick gave to her son before answering her aunt herself.

"Ah, but then I wouldn't have your company all to myself, Lady Frances," she said warmly.

And suddenly, Caroline felt as if this friendly visit might have been part of a larger scheme. Perhaps Mrs. Cartwick *had* heard of their kiss and was intent on giving him a moment of privacy to make a proper offer for her hand. Cold sweat broke out beneath the squeezing confines of her corset.

He doesn't even like you, and he certainly isn't the type of man to be pressured into an arrangement by his mother.

Frances smiled at Mrs. Cartwick. "Very well." Now it was her turn to lance Caroline with a meaningful look. "I trust you will treat our guest with the civility he deserves."

Caroline viewed him sardonically and held her tongue, simply nodding instead. She waited until the ladies had left the room completely before leveling him with an accusatory look.

"What is this all about?"

He paused, then shoved his hands down into his pockets and tipped his head quizzically. "What do you think?"

"You really want to know?"

He smiled in thought. "I really do."

"Fine. I believe you intend to entrap me into marriage after our kiss the other day."

She didn't think it was possible for a man to look more shocked than Jonathan Cartwick appeared at that very moment, wide-eyed, his jaw slack. In fact, the magnitude of his surprise was anything but complimentary, and suddenly she very much wished she had kept her mouth shut about that particular suspicion.

"I—" His voice was a ragged scrape from his throat. "I can assure you that nothing is farther from the truth."

Caroline's heart squeezed painfully tight. The blunt words were just another reminder that nobody wanted her in their lives. Not her parents, not Lord Braxton and not even the dishonorable Mr. Cartwick.

Her expression must have betrayed some of what she was feeling, for his demeanor changed at once and he stepped forwards to take her hands in his.

"I don't wish for you to misunderstand me," he murmured, the brush of the callouses on his palms a strangely sensual feeling against her own bare hands. She was suddenly aware of how close they were again. "Kissing you was quite . . . pleasing. But that alone is not the basis for any marriage that I would wish to be a part of."

Willing away the rise of her embarrassment, she tore her

hands out of his grasp. "Fine, it was a silly notion," she said. "I understand."

"No, I don't think you do," he replied slowly. "And I must say I'm a little confused at your reaction since we both know I represent everything you seem to despise."

So he had seen her hurt. The knowledge made her feel strange and vulnerable, something that had started to happen more and more in his presence. Taking a second to recover, her eyes lingered over the golden-brown waves of his hair and the singular eyes that matched. The sharp angles of his cheekbones, strong line of his nose, appealing jut of his chin with the tiny indent in the middle . . . the man was all masculinity. Lean muscle and hard surfaces. Even his hands were roughened with work, which was highly unfashionable but somehow so incredibly attractive. It would be easy to imagine the feel of those hands as they slid across the more sensitive areas of her body . . .

Caroline clasped her fingers together in front of her skirts and gazed at him with as much neutrality as she could muster.

"There's no reaction," she said calmly.

"Are you sure?"

She crossed the room to finally pour herself some tea. "Don't flatter yourself, Mr. Cartwick," she said, adding a touch of cream then blowing lightly on the steaming drink. "I'm only wondering why you won't get to the point and tell me why you are here."

A nervous shadow passed over his countenance, and

Caroline felt her own sense of unease increasing. When he gestured to the couch, she found herself sinking down without objection, and Cartwick lowered down beside her, turning slightly to view her more easily from where he was seated. His hand passed down over the length of his midnight blue cravat.

"I would like to offer my assistance, should you permit me," he said quietly. "I am here to help both you and Lady Frances."

CHAPTER NINE

The confusion that spread across Caroline's lovely face rapidly transformed into something more like horror.

"Help us?" she asked with an almost imperceptible twitch of her head. "What do you mean?"

Jonathan shifted uncomfortably. Her hackles were already up, meaning this was going to be tougher than he'd originally thought—although he'd never been foolish enough to think it would be easy. His next words needed to be chosen with care.

"Well, first," he said earnestly, "I would like to emphasize that your acceptance of my assistance would not oblige you to me in any way."

She eyed him with skepticism. "You and I both know that any bargain made between a man and a woman has the potential for unforeseen complications, including obligation."

"I knew that you would think that, and again I would like to assure you of my honor in this regard."

"You will forgive me if I reserve my judgment for the time being."

"Of course," he replied. "But if the notion of my honor gives you pause, then perhaps you will accept the word of Mrs. Cartwick instead."

Her gaze snapped back over to his, the gray pools of her eyes blowing wide in panic. "What kind of offer is this?" She shot to her feet. "What have you told her?"

Jonathan stood and came close to grip her upper arms. He could feel her trembling beneath his hands.

"My lady," he murmured, "I told her only as much as she needed to know, and she wishes to be of help. We have two members of our household staff that we can offer to assist with your aunt, at least until you are able to secure staff of your own. Or for longer, if you like."

With one agile twist of her body, she slipped out of his grasp and marched over to the door, flinging it open then rounding on him with a hostile stare. "Get out."

Even he wasn't prepared for that reaction, and he thought he'd been ready for anything.

"*Why?*"

"I knew you would start telling others about Lady Frances," she said, turning to pace fretfully. "I knew I would come to regret you being there to witness . . . to see her . . ."

His brow lowered and he strode toward her, angry now, trying to keep himself from throttling the girl. "I have done nothing of the kind," he growled, shocking her into silence. "You take every word out of my mouth as a personal affront, even if it is meant as a kindness, and I'll be damned if I will continue to listen to your insults."

Caroline's face paled, casting the scattering of her tiny golden freckles into stark relief. Her dazed eyes drifted away from his own, down to his chest and finally to the carpeted floor. Then with the briefest of nods she spun around and dashed from the room. Jonathan stood there for a moment, staring solemnly after the frothy feminine mass of yellow skirts that hurried away from him across the foyer.

Christ, he thought, running a hand through his hair. *Now I've done it.*

Jonathan charged out to follow Caroline down the hall and into the music room. A gleaming piano was stationed proudly at the far end of the room, and Caroline had dropped into an armchair nearby, leaning over to cradle her head in her hands. The sight of her like that, defeated and over-whelmed, reminded him of when he had discovered her in the hallway, and he felt that peculiar sensation in his chest once again. The one that squeezed his heart, making him feel as if her problems were somehow actually his.

How could you help a woman who made it so very difficult to even try? He approached slowly and she remained curled over in her seat, despondent, shaking her head. He took another step closer.

"Just accept the help," he said, placing one hand lightly on the back of her chair. "I know you could use it—I am surprised the duke is not more involved."

Caroline's head continued to move from side to side, a

silky auburn lock sliding free from her upswept hair with the repeated movement. "You don't understand," she said with a wretched glance. "I don't want him to know. Do you know where they put people with her condition? It's bad enough you had to see it, but now your mother, and soon my parents—"

He blinked. "Your parents?"

She stood and walked to the piano, spreading her hands across the polished rosewood surface. "Yes. My parents will be arriving soon to marry me off," she said matter-of-factly. "It's simply not fashionable to support a spinster daughter. Especially a stubborn one like me."

"I—" Jonathan stared after her, his lungs squeezing. Then crossing the room, he came to a stop beside her. "I see," he said at last, "although I would hesitate to call you a spinster just yet."

"Would you?" she asked with a laugh entirely devoid of humor. "I've told anyone who would listen that I have no intention of ever marrying. My parents demanded I attend the season again this year, and I only managed to avoid it because it was impossible for them to impose their will from hundreds of miles away. Now it seems they are coming home to force the issue."

"Will they take you to London?" he asked, shaking his head, his mind still reeling in disbelief.

Caroline turned to face him, her expression unreadable. "I doubt it. That's rather a lot of money to spend, and with my reputation in its current state, they will probably settle on some eligible peer here in the country. Perhaps one who owes them a favor."

Pain shot through his jaw and he realized he was clenching his teeth. Jonathan found he had a visceral reaction to seeing this bright and intelligent—albeit temperamental—woman being offered up to the first willing lord in a marriage she did not want. It made him hate the aristocracy all over again. And oddly enough, he realized he'd stopped including both her and Lady Frances in that group at some point.

He was also forced to admit that the thought of her marrying another bothered him.

"I am sorry to hear that," he said. And he honestly was.

"Don't be," she quipped. "In one fell swoop, you will rid yourself of an annoying neighbor and her troubled aunt, while gaining Windham Hill in the—"

He silenced her with a black look. "Stop."

She relented, lapsing into silence with a sigh. Stretching out an arm, she ran her graceful fingers along the artfully carved edge of the piano case.

"That piano looks to be nearly a duplicate of my own."

"It is identical," she confirmed, her voice dreamy and lost in thought. "It was a gift."

"Oh? From whom?" he asked, walking around the side to view it more closely.

Caroline reached over to softly plunk one of the ivory keys. "Nicholas Cartwick."

Jonathan stared at her. "Reginald Cartwick's father?"

"Yes."

Her eyes found his and registered the surprise she found there. Jonathan smoothed a hand over his cravat and tried again.

"Forgive me. Was he close to the duke?"

"No, not particularly," she said slowly, gradually relaxing. "And Reginald and I were not playmates due to our difference in age. But his parents grew very close to both Lady Frances and me." A ghost of a smile flickered across her face for a moment. "In fact, Isabelle taught me how to play on the piano at Greystone Hall."

It was an answer to just one of the many questions he had about her. She was sad near pianos because they reminded her of those who had cared for her . . . treasured friends who were no longer alive. Friends who, along with her aunt, had probably been more like parents to her than the Duke and Duchess of Pemberton had ever been.

And now she would once again be faced with their cold disregard. Parents who would rather get rid of her than get to know her. Her father, who she feared would commit Frances, his own sister, to an asylum.

In other words, the worst kind of people.

Jonathan had been wrong. This hadn't just answered one question—it had answered many. And God help him, but he wanted to kiss her again. Slowly. Thoroughly. Until her considerable worries had been soothed away and replaced with that same desire she had given him a glimpse of that day before.

Forcing down the urge with willpower he didn't even know he had, he cautiously came closer, ignoring the heavy tension of arousal that had settled in his limbs. "My piano in America was much like this one," he observed. "But it was made by a company in Boston. Hallet and Davis."

She glanced up, eyes alight with newfound interest. "I haven't heard of them."

"They only started producing pianos a few years ago, so that's not surprising."

Caroline's brow creased in confusion. "You bought a lovely new piano and then left it behind?"

"I did. But I imagine my brother, James, is taking very good care of it."

She eyed him curiously. "Do you play?"

"A little," he said with a modest shrug.

She softly smiled. "Given the rough feel of your hands, I would have guessed you were using them for building your own ships, not playing the piano." Her tone was teasing. It was a pleasant change.

"Well, I was an apprentice for years and did assist my builders when necessary. My hands are still coarse, I suppose, but they were also able to coax out a tune," he said, glancing down at his palms, stretching his long fingers out to survey the calloused surface. "I never stopped to think that they might offend a lady such as yourself."

A pretty wash of color infused her cheeks. "I never said I found them offensive."

Jonathan forced himself to maintain control. It was not easy when he found himself overwhelmed from the sudden heat her words had incited.

"Well, I—" His voice sounded rusty, unused, and he swallowed before making another attempt to speak. "I am glad of it."

He was almost relieved to hear footsteps and conversation

growing louder in the foyer. His mother and Lady Frances were returning from their viewing of the gallery, no doubt, and he glanced over to the open door. The ladies would be expecting to find them in the drawing room, so he and Caroline had but a moment before being discovered. Remembering his purpose, he swiftly skirted the edge of the piano to join her.

"Lady Frances will be here soon, my lady," he said in a hushed voice. "Tell me you'll accept the help."

Caroline stiffened and gazed up at him, her mouth moving wordlessly before she looked away at last.

"Mr. Cartwick, I-I can't," she said, pressing her lips together and staring down at her hands.

"For God's sake, why? This help is freely offered."

He could see her tears threatening under the weight of his reply, but she took a deep breath and shook her head again, much as she had earlier when he'd started this conversation. "And I thank you and your mother for the kind gesture—"

His eyebrows flew upwards in astonishment. "This is more than just a *gesture*—"

"Oh, there you two are!"

Jonathan straightened immediately. His mother stood at the entrance to the music room, looking worried, and only then did he realize how unfriendly things must have looked from her perspective. Lady Frances was at her side, smiling and seemingly unaware of the frantic exchange that had been occurring only a moment before. Caroline brushed past him and crossed the room to stand beside her aunt.

"I apologize, Mrs. Cartwick," she said, looping her arm through Frances's, her mouth pursed with regret, "but it turns out this wasn't exactly the best time for guests, after all."

A shock of disappointment caused him to flinch, and he took a step in her direction, hand outstretched.

"Lady Caroline, let us discuss things further—"

"I'll thank you to drop the subject if you please, Mr. Cartwick," she answered quickly, shooting him a warning glance and leaning over to tug on the bellpull. "Taylor will call your carriage around and escort you outside."

And with little more than a parting nod, Caroline ushered her aunt out of the room, leaving Jonathan and Mrs. Cartwick to stare at each other in speechless surprise.

S*hoop.*

The arrow tucked itself neatly underneath her last one, both projectiles still straying to the right of the bull's-eye in irritating fashion. With a quiet growl of annoyance, she slid another from her quiver and drew back the bowstring yet again.

What she ought to be doing was trying to nap, as her aunt was resting peacefully in her bedchamber and she had not slept much the night before. Come to think of it, she had not truly been able to sleep well since Jonathan Cartwick had moved into Greystone Hall. Frances's bouts of evening difficulties only made matters more trying. Caroline had noticed her aunt's episodes were no longer exclusively occurring at night, as that day in the field had shown, although her mental faculties were still relatively sharp otherwise.

It was easier to convince herself that the situation wasn't so bad when Frances was her usual self, but she knew denial would only take her so far. Part of her very much regretted spurning the Cartwicks' offer the day before because Jonathan was right . . . she needed help.

Frowning at the target ahead, she tried to recall his instructions to her that day he had happened upon her practicing. What was it he had said? Aim more to the left . . .

Straighten your back.

Ah yes, that was it. And now against her own will, she was remembering the slide of his palm over her lower back, the illicit shock of contact and the way her body had awakened to him with just the lightest touch.

Caroline banished the thoughts immediately and flattened her spine the way he had shown her. A sudden gust of wind rushed around her skirts and whipped her hair into her face. Twitching her head to clear her eyes, she felt the familiar frustration welling inside of her until her chest threatened to burst.

She had longed to accept his offer. But things had grown . . . complicated . . . between them lately, and putting herself in a position that depended upon both his charity and his secrecy was not the wisest move. Plus, it would amount to a partnership of sorts, and she couldn't imagine trying to explain that to Eliza.

Shoop.

Again, the arrow struck right of center. She scowled and retrieved another arrow from her quiver. Drawing again on the bowstring, she straightened her back once more while searching for another piece of advice he had given her on that blustery afternoon.

Rotate your elbow.

Caroline checked her elbow to find it was indeed turned too far upwards and corrected the rotation. She'd been exaggerating her ignorance on that day with Jonathan, but she'd definitely been having more trouble since the problems with Frances had become so much worse.

Shoop.

Shading her eyes with a hand, Caroline squinted down the lawn. Her aim had struck slightly more to the left that time, and she broke into a grin. As much as she'd wanted to discount his assistance at the time, she couldn't dismiss Cartwick's masterful and seemingly effortless shot into the bull's-eye, or the way arousal had flashed within her at the sight of him—calm, confident and at ease taking charge. Part of his appeal was his ability to challenge her.

In fact, Cartwick's magnetism seemed to increase every time he came near her, and she had grown to fear any future meeting with him. The likelihood of shamelessly throwing herself into his arms only seemed to increase with each passing second.

Christ, Caroline . . . you drive me mad.

She turned her head sharply as if to drive away the thought. She couldn't let herself think of how his words had driven *her* mad. Couldn't bear to think about the lean muscles acquired from his years of shipbuilding, or the way her fingertips had eagerly traversed the planes of his chest in her feverish attempt to get closer. Or the dizzying press of his mouth against hers and how good it had felt when he'd kissed her deeper. And the thrilling sounds of the groans he had been unable to suppress . . .

I care about a hell of a lot more than just myself.

Open your shoulders.

Inhaling sharply through her nose, Caroline grasped weakly at the memory of his words and pulled on the bowstring once again, straightening her back, correcting her elbow and adjusting her shoulders until she was in perfect alignment with her target. She released her breath in a long exhale.

Shoop.

Straight through the bull's-eye.

Caroline stared in astonishment then let out a whoop of celebration.

"Yes!" she cried.

Smiling like a fool, she pumped her bow high into the air and spun around in a dance of unparalleled joy, then stopped to simply admire the sight of her arrow buried in the middle of her target. Glancing at the house and seeing no one, she set her longbow down and reached into her skirt pocket, pulling out a handkerchief. She stared at it, a little ashamed of herself, running her fingertips across the soft linen square.

Cartwick had forgotten his handkerchief after their kiss in the upstairs hallway, but since he'd just been slapped it was unsurprising that he'd left in haste. It was only later that afternoon that she discovered the item safely tucked away in her pocket. The bit of fabric showed a tiny monogram on the corner, $\mathcal{JRC}$, and still held the enthralling scent of its owner. Her pulse galvanized at his singular masculine smell. Starch and a hint of cedar and sandalwood mingled together in erotic harmony with his own delicious aroma.

Caroline was more than a little worried that she might be infatuated with the man. Although, truth be told, she knew so little of these things it was difficult for her to tell. She'd fancied herself in love with Lord Braxton at one time too— had thought the feeling was reciprocated—only to discover how easily she could be replaced.

With a troubled sigh, Caroline hid the handkerchief inside her pocket once more. Eliza would view her as a traitor for even considering him. The two of them had already kissed, and that was bad enough. But if things were to progress even further? Even if he did want to marry her, which he did not, there was no way she could ever become the next mistress of Greystone Hall. It would be an inexcusable slap in the face to her friend, the prior mistress.

Suddenly archery didn't seem so exciting. Unfastening the quiver from around her waist, she set it down beside her bow and began her return to the house when she was interrupted by the appearance of Meggie outside on the back steps. The maid's forehead was creased in concern.

"Begging your pardon, my lady, but Lady Frances wishes to speak with you—"

Caroline's boots crunched in the gravel and she came to a stop, smiling quizzically. "Then, by all means, let her speak to me."

"I would, but she won't come outside," Meggie said, glancing uncomfortably back to the house.

Craning her neck, Caroline looked through the garden to the glass windows that lined the rear of the house. A pale face in the interior gloom peered back out at her, and she waved a hand at her aunt. With no indication she had seen her, Frances pivoted around and walked away from the window, concealing herself further in the shadows.

"Can she not see me, Meggie?"

The maid nodded and glanced back at the house in apprehension. "She can see you, my lady. It's not her sight that is the problem . . ."

"What is the problem, then?" she asked with a frown, swatting away a tendril of hair that had come loose in the wind.

"Well, it's, er—"

The maid was twisting her hands together, and the fine hairs on Caroline's forearms lifted in nervous anticipation. Taylor was the next person to exit onto the back terrace, and his eyes quickly found her. The normally distinguished butler was wide-eyed and upset; something unusual for him.

"Apologies, my lady—"

"For goodness' sake," she said, her frantic eyes darting between the two servants. "Please tell me what's wrong!"

Meggie's face turned pale. "I think that . . . it seems to be . . ."

The maid stammered then gave up, shooting a pleading look at Taylor who responded by bowing his head with a solemn sigh. Caroline stared at him, trying to quell the trembling of her limbs that had just begun, and he placed a comforting hand on her shoulder.

"My lady, it seems that—at least for this moment—Lady Frances doesn't who you are."

CHAPTER TEN

Jonathan scanned the contents of the letter once more, then sighed and set it aside. The Duke of Pemberton was truly on his way home.

The correspondence had made no mention of any upcoming efforts to marry off his daughter. He supposed it wouldn't have been relevant in these circumstances unless they'd been actively considering him as a candidate. But they would no more give their approval for Caroline to marry an American shipbuilder than they would promise her hand to a lowly fishmonger. Hopeless notion that it was, his exclusion from the running of eligible men did grate on him. It was typical of their ilk. Returning to England and expecting his family to be treated any differently than before was the ultimate naivete, and he reminded himself not to be foolish, especially where the duke's daughter was concerned.

The letter had merely stated that the property lines would

be addressed and resolved, and while the news should have brought him a considerable amount of relief, he found himself sitting here instead, contemplating, wondering if there was still something that had been missed. *Something* about the situation still didn't quite add up, and even though every document he had showed that he was in the right, he couldn't help but feel apprehensive about making any permanent adjustments to the boundaries. He also couldn't deny that his growing feelings for Caroline, vexing as she was, could constitute part of his reluctance.

Jonathan ran a hand along the back of his neck and sighed. His dealings here had become incredibly complicated. It had been much easier before to vilify the woman when she had been resolutely against any effort to make peace. Now they were at least civil to each other, but he knew that for her to diverge from the notion that he was a self-serving interloper would make her feel as if she had wronged her friend. No . . . it was pointless to think about Lady Caroline as anything but an intriguing neighbor. A surprising and intelligent woman who had suffered at the hands of the *ton*, of the inconstant Lord Braxton . . . even her own parents. And with her parents' renewed determination to see her married to a lord, she would certainly suffer more before this was all said and done.

His thoughts strayed dangerously again to the auburn-haired beauty, and he pushed back from the scarred oak surface of his desk, stood and crossed over to the window of his study. Bracing a hand against the casement, he cast his gaze across the gardens behind the estate, noting it was another lovely day, if a bit windy. He reflected on his home back in New England. For as much as he'd loved life in America and as often as he missed his brother, he knew his new life here was an attempt to fill some inexplicable need. He was still in the process of figuring out exactly what that was.

Recognition? Retribution? Jonathan couldn't quite put his finger on it, but what he did know was that dealing with his neighborly adversary had become one of the things he looked forward to the most.

With a restless growl, he returned to his desk and sank back down into his butter-soft leather chair to examine the parchment leaves of the letter again. He found it hard to believe that the duke and duchess were entirely ignorant of Lady Frances's condition. But if it was true, then that made Caroline's unwillingness to let him help her even more troubling. Would it not be more likely for the duke to whisk his sister away to an asylum if he were to come home to discover insufficient staffing and no plan in place? Even Caroline's concerns about privacy and misplaced gossip seemed small in comparison, although he understood her worry over that as well.

Leaning an elbow on the arm of his chair, Jonathan's mind wandered again, this time in recollection of her shining gray eyes. There was nothing quite like them; eyes like dark stars, simmering with contained energy. Despite his best efforts, his thoughts often lingered upon the interlude they had shared, and the tantalizing softness of her lips against his. He found the idea of such a vital spirit wed to a curmudgeonly old lord did not sit well with him. The notion of somehow being able to convince her to marry *him*, however, seemed just as preposterous.

A soft knock sounded upon his study door, and his head jerked up.

"Yes?"

The heavy wooden portal opened to reveal his butler, Shaw, who crossed the threshold and addressed him in a curiously hushed voice.

"Pardon the interruption, Mr. Cartwick, but Lady Caroline has arrived."

Jonathan's breathing stopped to hover anxiously inside his lungs. He was not expecting her, and after how she had dismissed him the last time they'd met, this visit was . . . surprising. His throat went dry, and he swallowed before attempting to speak again.

"Did she state the purpose of her call?"

The man shook his head. "No, sir. And Mrs. Cartwick is still in the village and not here to receive her."

It would have to be him, then. "I'll receive her here in the study," he said, shuffling his papers—including the duke's letter—into a tidy stack and depositing them in a desk drawer. "You may send her in."

Shaw departed with a nod and Jonathan took a cursory glance at the informal state of his own attire. Brown trousers, white linen shirt with no cravat and lack of waistcoat could hardly be considered appropriate clothing for greeting a lady in his own home. But his worries were dispelled when Caroline appeared at the door, bedecked in one of the large and conspicuously atrocious bonnets she'd been carrying on the first day they had met. She was beautiful as always, but the thrill of seeing her in his private study was nearly offset by his amusement at her choice of headgear, festooned as it was by iridescent feathers and multicolored folds of satin.

The butler closed the door behind her and Jonathan rose from his seat, gesturing for her to come closer with a stifled laugh that he masterfully transformed into a smile.

"Please be seated, my lady," he said pleasantly. "Perhaps you would like an extra seat for your considerable bonnet?"

Caroline froze in mid-step, her hands flying upwards to the creation, then she was swiftly tugging at the ribbon fastened beneath her chin. She ripped the decorative straw headpiece hastily off her head and tossed it into the chair as he'd suggested.

"I'd forgotten about it," she muttered. "My aunt insisted on my wearing it today."

Any opportunity to see the russet shimmer of her hair was a welcome one, and he admired her openly before realizing what she'd said was not in line with her usual snappy retorts. She was also here unannounced, and now that he was looking closer, he could see that the normally stalwart Lady Caroline was pale and shaken.

"You are unwell," he said in alarm, stepping clear of his chair with the intent of approaching her.

"Stop, please," she said, staying him with a raised hand. "I don't plan on staying long but I need to say something without my head getting . . . muddled. By you."

He stopped, and with a small bow in her direction, attempted to respond.

"I would not flatter myself into thinking my presence could affect you in such a way. But if—"

"You know it does," she said, interrupting. "So please stay on your side of the desk."

Her admission was gratifying. Briefly, he envisioned her reaction if he were to come nearer anyway, not hesitating until he had pressed her against the door behind her, mercilessly savoring the sweet taste of her mouth until the color had revived in her face. Given the seriousness of her countenance, he steered his thoughts in a more appropriate direction and obeyed, seating himself once more and nodding to the chair before her.

"Won't you sit, at least?" he asked.

She twitched her head and glanced away. "No, thank you. I only want to know if your generous offer of extra staffing is still available to me."

Jonathan stared. Something was definitely wrong. He leaned forwards on his elbows to regard her intently.

"Will you tell me what has happened?"

Her chin quivered slightly. "It was y-yesterday afternoon. Lady Frances, she . . ." Her voice trailed off and she fidgeted with her hands before raising her eyes to meet his. "My aunt is having more trouble with her memory. She forgot . . . who I was . . . and . . ."

Caroline trailed off, and he worked to grasp the magnitude of what she had just told him. Lady Frances had forgotten her own niece, the one person who loved her best in this world.

Jonathan cleared his throat as a suspicious emotion rose

to thicken his voice. It was something like sadness. Like his heart aching on this woman's behalf.

"Has her lapse persisted?" he forced out. "How is she today?"

She shook her head as if to somehow dismiss the severity of the situation and smiled bravely. "No, I was familiar to her this morning. The only sign of anything out of the ordinary was her demanding that I wear this bonnet."

He couldn't prevent his answering smile, and glanced over at the item in question. "Is this not a style she would normally find pleasing?"

"Perhaps as a little girl," she said, eyeing the headgear warily from where she stood. "Or maybe a decade ago. You must understand, Mr. Cartwick, my aunt has spent the past few summers in London. Normally, she would know which pieces were especially . . . out of fashion."

"I believe it. From what I know of her, she possesses a keen intellect."

"Yes. When she is herself, she is very sharp. It's just that soothing her agitation will be much more difficult from this point on if she cannot remember who I am, and I have come here today to see if your offer still stands," she said in a choked voice.

Jonathan was overwhelmed by both her confession and her request. The pain must have been unbearable for her to come to him like this. He couldn't really imagine it. Hidden away in the country with no Pemberton parent in sight, trotted out to London each year for the sole purpose of getting rid of you, then watching your only loved one fade into some nameless oblivion. No wonder she felt the need to constantly defend both herself and her aunt from every conceivable threat.

He wasn't certain when the change had taken place, when his irritating highborn neighbor had managed to breach his heart, but Jonathan found he would gladly remove himself from that list of worries. Would do all that he could to keep her from worrying about anything, were it possible.

Rising, he slowly rounded the desk. Her eyes widened but remained on his when he stopped before her, and he reached out to surround her chilled fingers with the warm strength of his own. She not only allowed it, she returned his grasp.

"Of course my offer still stands," Jonathan said, his voice sounding huskier than he'd intended. "You will have two members of my staff at your immediate disposal. Anything else you might require will be yours as well."

Her expression changed, relief spreading across her features like the rolling of a wave across the ocean, and she gripped his hand tighter.

"I would ask, although it may be too much, that you might defend my efforts to continue caring for Lady Frances at Willowford House as well. My parents will likely not heed my opinion on the matter, but I can't allow them to move her into an asylum. They may listen to you."

Jonathan nodded. "It would be most effective if we were to present a unified front. Although my opinion may mean very little to them, you may be assured of my support. Please know that I will do whatever I can," he said with a gentle squeeze of his fingers.

Gratitude transformed into reluctant skepticism behind her slate-colored eyes. "But why?" she asked with a sad shake of her head. "Why help me at all when I've only caused you trouble from the start?"

"Trouble?" He laughed. "No. Mischief . . . perhaps. But I would not trade you for a more placid neighbor. Trust me on this." His eyes danced lightly over the diminutive angle of her nose, across the delightful smattering of tiny freckles and down to the lips that had thankfully returned to their tempting strawberry hue. God, how he yearned to kiss her. "In fact, I think a less formidable woman would be rather boring."

Caroline blushed, the color in her cheeks rising to match her lips. "If you were to ask the *ton*, they would tell you that I am hardly formidable."

"Good thing I wasn't asking the *ton*." Lifting her hand, he brushed his lips across her knuckles, his eyes closing at the feel of her.

Her quiet intake of breath was easily heard in the silence of his study, and he wondered how she was looking at him in this moment. Normally, a kiss on the hand wouldn't be cause for any sort of notice, but he meant this one differently and felt like she knew it. It was a commitment—a promise made in her time of need—sealed now with his mouth upon her soft skin.

When he relinquished his hold, she took a quick step

backwards then retrieved her bonnet, affixing it to her head in outwards preparation for her departure. It was almost painful for him to see the lovely ruby sheen of her hair covered once more by that feathered abomination, but the sight of her leaving was profoundly more upsetting.

"I thank you, Mr. Cartwick. Most humbly," she said and crossed to the door, her fingers working on tying the fuchsia ribbon. "We can discuss the particulars at a later date—"

"Why not discuss them now?" he asked.

Gazing at the floor, her fingers remained unusually absorbed in their task. "I-I suppose we could, but I have other errands to attend to this afternoon."

"Don't," he said.

Caroline cinched the bow and glanced at him cautiously. "Don't what?"

"Don't leave like this. Not again." Jonathan strode to where she stood by the door and saw her stiffen. He stopped before reaching her but leaned in, dodging a feathery protrusion from her bonnet to speak into her ear. "I'm glad you came to me for help," he murmured.

Her eyes drifted closed at his nearness, then snapped back open. "And please know that I will send payment just as soon as I am able to acquire the necessary funds from my parents—"

He inhaled slowly through his nose. "I will accept no payment from you. You know that," he admonished, his chin scraping softly against her jaw.

"P-please," she stammered through trembling lips. "You don't have to kiss me."

He tilted his head to regard her in surprise. "If I kiss you again, it will be because I desire it."

The anxious rise and fall of her breath paused for a brief moment, and she blinked up at him. "You . . . do?"

Jonathan nodded slowly. Reaching out, he stroked a thumb across the tender curve of her cheek. "I've kissed you before. Is it so very hard to accept that a man might find you desirable?"

"I'm sure you believe that, Mr. Cartwick. But I do not pretend to understand the whims of men, and know that a kiss could simply be the result of an errant impulse."

He swiftly closed his hand over hers before she could yank it away. "*Caroline*," he whispered fiercely. "Clearly you don't know me at all. If you did, you would know that you are not the only one who has endured the changeable nature of love. You would know that my family was mercilessly ridiculed and disparaged by those very people who mock you now." His tone softened, his gaze dropping to her lips. "And you would know that I do not kiss women unless I find them desirable."

"Oh," was her stunned and barely audible reply.

Glancing aside, he took a breath before continuing in a low voice. "I think Lord Braxton was a fool."

"I'm assuming Lady Hedridge told you the particulars of how I left London," she said wearily.

"She did."

"And you still think him a fool?"

He realized he was still holding her hand, and against every instinct that demanded he get even closer, he released it and took a step back. "Her implications don't seem to match what I know of you so far."

"And just what do you know of me?"

Jonathan deliberated for a moment. "You are a loyal friend to Eliza. I believe this trait would carry over to your other relationships. So this leads me to believe that your need to leave London must have been founded in urgency— particularly because the cost was so high."

"The cost wasn't that high," she said with a stubborn tip of her chin.

"So, it did not trouble you when Lord Braxton chose another?" he asked. "It does not bother you that the *ton* now amuses themselves at your expense?"

"Fine, yes," she replied, glancing away sheepishly. "I was hurt when he moved on without a word, but perhaps it was understandable given the circumstances."

"It wasn't. If you had been mine, I would have sought answers."

Her shoulders hitched up into a tiny shrug. "Obviously he didn't think I was a question worth answering."

Cartwick supposed he had not gone to seek answers when Letitia had broken things off between them. But of course by that time, she'd been caught in the intimate company of one of his so-called friends. It had been all the answer he had required, and any affection he'd felt for her had dissolved in an instant. Perhaps it had been the same for Braxton, however unjustified.

Still, he felt that any man who knew Caroline at all would know to question such an occurrence.

"Like I said, my lady." He reached over to tuck an errant lock behind her ear. "Lord Braxton was a fool."

Her lips twisted and she backed away. "It costs you nothing to say that."

"I disagree." Only he knew how much it cost to lay his heart open for her.

"Regardless, I had no choice," she said with a small shake of her head. "I had to leave, and I needed help to do it. At least I discovered his real worth *before* agreeing to marry him."

And then it struck him with the force of a hammer. Here she stood before him in his study, beseeching him for help with her aunt, frantically trying to keep the unhappy truth about Frances's condition concealed from everyone . . . and he realized the truth. That she hadn't fled the season alone with the viscount, intent on debauching herself with a licentious rake . . .

She had fled with Lady Frances. And the viscount had helped her.

Jonathan stared at her, the wheels turning in his mind. "Was it your aunt?" he asked softly.

"I—" She blinked at him, hesitating for a moment before clearing her throat and folding her hands before her. "Yes, it was. She declined considerably during our time in London."

His next question was difficult, but he needed to know. "And enlisting his help did not bind you to the viscount in any way?"

Caroline's eyebrows shot up. "So you do believe the rumors," she snapped, turning on her heel. Her fingers wrenched at the doorknob, but she paused when his hands slid gently over her upper arms. She was unyielding beneath his touch.

"Not at all, my lady. I only wish to ascertain whether Lord Evanston is a problem. I would help you, if he is."

Her reaction was immediate, and he could feel it in the way her flesh softened and relaxed beneath his hands. She said nothing for a moment, and his hands moved away as she turned around to regard him.

"Thanks to Eliza, it did not," she replied, facing him now with the door at her back. "He made the bargain with her instead."

The thought of a man striking deals with a widow to secure his assistance caused his blood to heat. "And you let her?" he asked incredulously.

"The deal was initially made without my knowledge or consent. I advised against it when I found out, but she insisted. You should quit acting so outraged," she added. "I'll remind you that you were the one who originally displaced her."

"And I will remind you that this is how entailment works. It is neither personal nor malicious . . . it is simply family business."

"Business," she mused, staring up at him. "Then tell me, if everything is business to you, then what do you hope to gain by helping me with my aunt?"

You in my arms.

The whisper of truth that echoed in his mind shook him like a clap of thunder on a quiet night. So did the hypocrisy.

He could hardly criticize the viscount for striking a love deal when he might be doing the same thing himself.

Caroline looked up at him in expectation of an answer—eyes bright with ire, lips clamped together impatiently—but he wasn't sure she was ready to hear the truth. Hell, he wasn't even sure he was ready to say it. But perhaps he could own up to part of it, at least.

"You are my neighbor," he answered, his heart pounding in his ears. "Whatever our disputes may be, I will provide my services to both you and Lady Frances."

"And I am a close friend of the woman Evanston loved. He assisted me much in the same way and I was thankful for it then, as I am grateful to you now."

His fingers stretched out to skim against the length of satin ribbon that hung down from the bow beneath her chin. "Forgive me, my lady. I had to hear the truth from you, because I find myself unable to believe that any man, let alone the viscount, would have been able to resist your charms for long."

Her lips parted, and she stared at him in stunned silence before huffing awkwardly and glancing away. "Our kiss was my first, Mr. Cartwick, so we can lay to rest any thoughts you have of me being some kind of temptress," she said, a slight tremor marring her voice. "All of London knows I am not."

Caroline blushed fiercely, her cheeks turning a color only slightly lighter than the red highlights of her hair, while he heard her words ring once more in his head.

Our kiss was my first.

It seemed impossible. She had returned his attentions with such energy . . . such fervor . . . with a desire that had easily matched his own . . .

Her eyes flicked self-consciously over to meet his, as if hoping to assess the current turn of his thoughts. Would she welcome another kiss from him? He supposed he would earn another slap if she did not.

Slowly, he tugged on the ribbon, sliding it free of its knot.

"Yet here I am, standing with you," he whispered. The bonnet came loose and he gripped the edge, gently lifting it from her head before tossing it back onto the chair. "And I am tempted."

CHAPTER ELEVEN

Caroline leaned against the door for support. Somehow, she had allowed this to happen again, and Jonathan Cartwick was standing so close, looking so incredibly dashing and every bit as if he wanted to devour her. But she couldn't deny that she had wanted this too. That she had found herself lamenting every second away from this man.

Still, she needed to resist . . . for her sake and for Eliza.

Laughing weakly, her eyes flicked over to the bonnet he'd just deftly removed from her head, and she swallowed. "If you find yourself tempted, sir, then I should probably remind you of my abundance of displeasing qualities."

His mouth twitched in amusement and his eyes dropped to her lips. "Such as?"

"I can be disagreeable, for one."

"As can I," he conceded with a nod.

"And argumentative."

"To be sure."

She wracked her brain for something else, searching for something that would drive him away. "And," she said triumphantly, "despite my parents' thoughts on marriage, I have no intention of even being courted."

Caroline immediately winced at the implication. He'd already laid to rest her concerns about his thoughts on marrying her. The setdown still stung. But rather than scoffing at her assertion, this time he only shook his head, his gaze raising to lock on to hers.

"Such a waste," he said, in a low, sultry voice that caused her toes to curl. He reached out to stroke her cheek with his work-roughened hand. "I'll take care not to court you, then."

The idea was almost laughable; that he could find something worth wanting in her. She hadn't even managed that kind of success with Lord Braxton, and he had supposedly been about to propose.

But as the flame inside of her fanned hotter with Cartwick's gentle caress upon her cheek, she had to ask the question: Why him?

Oh, God . . . *why him?*

His fingers slid around the curve of her jaw and she could feel her resistance crumbling. She stood looking up at him, paralyzed in anticipation, and he leaned down to take her mouth in a slow and sensuous search that sent heat licking through every wanton corner of her soul. Warm and supple, soft yet demanding, his lips claimed hers in a way that was markedly different from their kiss in the hallway. There was no frenzied eruption of lust, no loss of control; this was a statement of his longing for her, eloquent and effective, the tip of his tongue teasing her full lower lip in a beckoning plea. Calling out to her own instinctual needs . . . stirring her desire . . . making her want to beg him for more.

Her mind rallied valiantly even as she accepted the invitation, parting her lips to open for him.

I'll not give him the satisfaction. I can just pull away and—

With a muted groan, he invaded her mouth in one luscious stroke, and all her best intentions were cast aside. There was no opposing the hot pulsing need that flowed through her veins, nor could she deny the call of those dormant places that his kiss was awakening. Places that ached to be touched by his strong competent hands . . . or kissed with the same wicked mouth. The mere thought of such a thing caused her body to respond in new ways, excited and more keenly aware of the intimate potential of this man who, until recently, had been her adversary. Distantly, she reminded herself that he still was.

A greedy flood of heat saturated her through to her core, and Caroline moaned softly. She suddenly felt confined beneath the tight press of her blue muslin bodice, and she longed for nothing more than for Cartwick to tear the meddlesome fabric away. Rising high on her toes, eager and full of longing, she wound her hands around the strong column of his neck and tugged him closer to deepen the kiss.

To her shock, his grip loosened nearly as quickly as hers had tightened. She could hear him issue a low noise as he pulled just far enough away to foil her attempt, breaking their kiss in the process.

"If I'd have known before that you had never been kissed, I would have been gentler in the hallway," he said, his hands trailing down the length of her arms in an unhurried way that caused her to shudder in delight. His voice was controlled, but it was the harshness of his breathing that betrayed his own struggle.

She was momentarily dazzled by his eyes, heavy and lidded with desire, golden and glowing. Her lips still tingled from his kiss, her body was primed for his touch, and she was in no mood to be shoved aside. Caroline stared up at him in defiance.

"Maybe I don't want you to be gentle," she said, privately shocked at her own audacity. Judging from the surprise on his face, he was more than a little taken aback himself. "Maybe I liked the way you kissed me."

He reached out beside her face, his fingers sliding along an errant lock of auburn hair. "On both sides of the ocean, I've never seen a woman as beautiful as you."

Caroline felt her lungs spasm in her chest. Surely, he didn't mean that. He couldn't possibly be sincere. She turned away.

"You don't have to say that."

He cocked his head to the side, perhaps seeing for the first time the extent of her insecurity. "But it's true. I wouldn't lie to you."

"What about my freckles?" Perhaps he hadn't noticed those yet. She would gladly point them out to find something, *anything*, to put more space between them. "They were always my worst feature. My mother never let me play outside for fear of them darkening in the sun."

His gaze grew serious. "What a notion. Your little freckles are one of my favorite things. In fact, I'd like to kiss each one . . ."

Jonathan's head lowered, and his lips briefly touched the sloped tip of her nose before drifting over to her cheek, then sweeping across to the other side. She stood there, rendered immobile by her own surprise as he worshipped each exposed place that was marked by the pinpoint spots.

"Oh," she breathed softly, knowing she should push him away but so very unwilling to do so. Her temperature increased with the thought of the freckles that were scattered haphazardly all across her body, her brain conjuring visions of Cartwick's simmering investigation of them all. Caroline slid her hands over the smooth linen that covered the broad expanse of his chest, luxuriating in the hard layer of muscle just beneath. "We mustn't—"

Jonathan claimed her mouth once more. She could envision him kissing her in every one of her soft places . . . across the curves of her breasts, between her eagerly parted thighs . . . and although she attempted to resist, the scorching heat of her arousal quickly spread. It had been a foolish supposition to think she could have somehow defied it in the first place.

Caroline's hands slid upwards to frame his face, and she flicked the tip of her tongue inside his mouth in a coquettish invitation to continue. He gladly accepted and wrapped his arms around her to pull her even closer. At last, she was pressed fully against him, only somewhat sated by the contact with him, separated as they were by their clothing. She wanted so much more . . .

Jonathan jerked away once again. "Forgive me," he said, the deep timbre of his voice and the breadth of his accent cutting through the hollow loss of his kiss. "You came here to ask for my help. You did not ask for this."

Caroline allowed her trembling fingers to drift down, testing the feel of him through the thin fabric of his shirt, traveling further down to his abdomen, then wrapping around his rib cage to splay across the tense muscles of his back. His body straightened and stiffened in her arms. It seemed to be a concerted effort not to touch her, but she understood his hesitation. Submitting to this overwhelming need would only complicate things between them, but she couldn't seem to help herself.

"I will ask for it, if that is what you require," she said, unable to meet his eyes.

"With all due respect, my lady, I don't think you know what you are asking for." His gaze lowered to the swells of her breasts, compressed by her bodice, and when his eyes raised back up to meet hers there was an undeniable shimmer of heat.

Perhaps she didn't. She'd never managed to elicit a reaction, noteworthy or otherwise, from men during the season . . . but the way this man was staring at her now was most *definitely* a first. An illicit thrill raced inside her.

"Mr. Cartwick," she whispered. "I wish you would stop talking." Caroline leaned in to melt against him, the softness of her breasts serving as an erotic counterpoint to the sculpted muscles beneath his clothes. She heard his breath catch and hoped his gentlemanly battle was nearing an end.

I am definitely *a wicked girl.*

How she had tried to talk herself into hating him. To talk herself into believing how singularly one-dimensional such a man must be. She'd been profoundly captivated by him instead. Now every thought was one of being possessed by him.

Moving her hands around to the hard span of his chest, Caroline could feel the palpable tension under her fingers. She continued the steady course up his neck, not stopping until she sank her fingers into the thick, bronze waves of his hair to pull a troubled sigh from his lips. His countenance visibly wavered—eyelids dropping, gaze turning hazy for just a moment, before fixating on her once again.

His fingers crept around the indent of her waist to settle over the small of her back, and she angled her face upwards to seek his mouth. But still, he shook his head and defied her by pulling away before she could catch his lips. She moaned plaintively in frustration.

"My lady," he murmured, his rapid breaths striking her cheek. "Surely you know there is no endgame here."

"I—" She paused, trying to think and failing miserably. "What do you mean?"

"I mean," he said, one hand straying dangerously over her hip, "you've no plans to marry—"

She stared at him as if in a daze. It was true, after all.

"No. Never."

"—won't even let anyone court you," he admonished softly, his other hand rising up to brush against the curve of her breast.

"Oh, yes," she breathed, the thread of their conversation momentarily forgotten as she arched into his caress.

"So what would be the point of any of . . . this?" he asked, his own breathing growing labored as he leaned down to press a kiss against the soft skin just beneath her earlobe.

Tipping her head to the side, she let out another moan. God, he was right. But it didn't change what was happening. It couldn't prevent her from trembling with desire; from needing to join with him in a way she'd never thought to explore with anyone else. Her body knew just what it wanted to do, especially when one of his hands was roaming so fiendishly close to her bottom, and the other was teasing her aching breast with strokes that were purely diabolical.

Enough.

Lunging upwards, she gripped great fistfuls of his shirt in her hands and kissed him hard. Jonathan's hands clamped securely around her as the sudden movement upset their balance to send him stumbling backwards. Only his agile recovery ensured they landed safely, and he let out a soft grunt when the backs of his legs slammed against the solid edge of his desk. Still, he did not break the kiss, taking care to widen his stance before shifting his grip to her hips and tugging her tightly against him. The hard feel of his arousal through her skirts was a surprise, as was the warm jolt of dizzying pleasure that it caused. She tore her mouth away to let out a gasp.

"I, oh—Jonathan . . ."

"Don't," he groaned in admonishment. In this instance, she knew for him to hear it might rob him of whatever restraint he still had.

Cartwick slid a hand up the length of her ribs to find her breast, his fingers closing around her swiftly, possessively. With a tiny intake of breath, she watched while he squeezed and kneaded, the sight of his hand on her unbearably exciting. Still, her clothing ruined the sensation of skin-to-skin contact that she so desperately craved, and she arched into his caress in silent supplication.

"Please—" she whispered against his ear, hoping he would know what she needed. She'd told him she would ask, but she would beg for it if she had to . . .

He took her lips once more, his fingertips gliding under the lace neckline of her dress to find the flesh that lay hidden beneath. She froze against his mouth, immobile with anticipation, and knowing what she was waiting for, he slowly stroked one fingertip against a tightly budded nipple. Pleasure rocked through her again as he teased her into unbearable sensitivity, then with a quick tug on the fabric he freed her breast from its blue muslin imprisonment. She bit her lip awkwardly and a hot wash of mortification flooded her cheeks, but his quiet laugh brought her gaze back to his in disbelief.

"I didn't take you for being shy." His voice was amused but his eyes were nearly glowing with unadulterated lust.

Her mouth fell open. "And I didn't take you for—"

Cartwick immediately silenced her with another vertigo-inducing kiss. Caroline did not think twice, or even at all, before receiving him, meeting his tongue with her own in what soon became a sensual duel that erased any last vestige of his amusement. Catching at her nipple, he squeezed it gently between his fingertips, causing the breath she'd been holding to release all at once, punctuated by a whimper of pleasure against his mouth.

"God, I would give anything to have you," he whispered, a note of mournful longing unmistakable in his voice.

His gaze trapped hers, and she was astonished by the level of regret she saw there.

Caroline had repelled him at every turn, for each wrong he had committed and even a few he had not. But now in the arms of this American invader, he was starting to feel like the only man who could help her put her life back together again.

She squeezed her eyes shut against the thought, only to have them fly open again when he bent down and drew her nipple into the searing liquid suction of his mouth. Delight shot through her amidst the soft chaos of her own cries, and she greedily sank her fingers into his hair to pull him closer. His tongue teased at the rosy tip, and he planted a soft kiss there before pulling away to cup her breast with a warm squeeze of his hand. She could only stare at him mutely as his thumb traced erotic circles around the swollen peak.

"Caroline, you should leave. Before I—"

Cartwick broke off, shaking his head and leaving the sentence unfinished. The rough surface of his fingertips scraped deliciously against her flesh, and she covered his hand with her own. His eyes lifted to meet hers, the pupils blown wide and dark.

"Before you what?" she asked, wanting to hear his answer in the worst possible way.

Jonathan's answer remained unspoken, but he pulled away to gently shake her off, winding his hands tightly around her waist to walk her backwards. Caroline's eyes darted anxiously, unable to see behind her, but in just a few moments he had pressed her back up against the oaken door where their lovemaking had begun. Hooking his fingers beneath her skirt-wrapped thigh, he raised her leg and urged his hips against hers, allowing her to feel him once again, watching as she writhed against the door with a gasp. His head lowered and he whispered roughly in her ear.

"Before I take you, here, right now."

Any retort she may have had to hearing his astonishing words was stolen away by the eager slide of his mouth. She wasn't certain what she would have said, but soon it didn't matter. Caroline gripped his arms and moved her hips against his in a motion that set off brightly kindling blooms of ecstasy.

"No."

His objection could barely be understood through the tangle of their kisses, which did not slow down or stop.

Mystified and driven wild by the pleasure that rose steadily where their bodies met, she was unwilling to heed him. Caroline rocked against him again with a soft cry, her head careening amidst another warm wash of bliss, and Cartwick muttered an oath as his grip tightened around her leg, straining forwards now to meet her. She tore her mouth away from his.

"Mr. Cartwick, I—oh—"

Too late she'd realized the perilous territory she'd strayed into, and all at once it became too much. The rhythmic press of his body, the sound of his labored breathing beside her ear and the knowledge that he *wanted* to give her pleasure helped her to quickly find it. Her surprised cry of release was hurriedly muffled by another kiss from Cartwick as she surrendered, surging inside his arms, each voluptuous wave enveloping her until she exhausted herself to slump against the door in a daze.

It didn't take long for his demeanor to shift into guilty acknowledgment of his own part in what had just happened, and his head lowered when it did. Slowly, gradually, he extricated himself from their embrace.

Her cheeks turned hot. She would have felt even more foolish, but Jonathan showed a little compassion by moving the neckline of her bodice, adjusting the cornflower muslin back into place over her breasts. Caroline could feel her lips shaking as she fumbled to find the right words . . . any words, really. In all her life, she'd never experienced such awkwardness.

"I–I'm sorry. I'll just . . ." Failing miserably, she scowled down at her hands then pivoted on her heel, making her way on wobbly legs to fumble at the cool handle of the doorknob. "Good-bye, Mr. Cartwick––-"

The flat of his palm pushed against the door, preventing her departure, and she turned to glance at him over her shoulder.

"As much as it pains me, you and I both know we cannot be lovers," he said in a gravelly voice.

Lovers. The word sparked another wave of desire and Caroline sighed in anxiety. She tried tugging on the knob again but his grip held fast.

"Must you?" she asked. Really, she just needed to leave before doing anything else she'd regret today.

But his large masculine presence was palpable behind her. Heat radiated outwards like the rays of some brilliant sun, and she longed to sink back into him; to let him warm her through from the inside. His next words were spoken beside her ear, closer than she'd expected, and she couldn't help but shiver in response.

"Perhaps, though," he continued, "you could treat me more as a partner, with our mutual interest focused primarily on your aunt's well-being? It *is* why you came here today, after all."

"Partners may be taking it a bit too far. Unless you don't mind my holding a meeting with your land agent to discuss Windham Hill?"

Cartwick stepped forwards to lean a broad shoulder against the doorjamb. He eyed her curiously. "In an effort to . . . what? Prevent the acquisition of property I already own?"

Caroline stared at him with surly insistence, knowing there was nothing she could really say to that. "Perhaps," she finally replied, struggling in vain to prevent a smile from forming. She valiantly forced her expression back into something more aloof. "Fine. It was a silly idea. Now let me out."

A grin flashed across his face, sending a thrill spiraling through her chest, and she narrowed her eyes at him even further. He straightened with a bow, then extended his hand in her direction.

"Right after we shake hands," he said, "just as I would with any other business associate."

This spelled trouble, especially when every place he had touched was still tingling and yearning for more. Even so, she stared disbelievingly at her own hand as she reached out to take his, desperate to be done with the silly gesture and out into the comparative safety of her awaiting carriage.

"Fine." Glowering, she completed the perfunctory handshake, trying not to notice the residual fire that burned beneath her skin at the merest contact with him. "Happy?"

Holding her gaze, he surprised her by turning her hand and smoothly raising it to his lips. Her whole body tensed in acknowledgment of the pleasure that suddenly flooded through her.

"Yes," he replied, his breath warm and lush upon her skin.

She very much doubted that he concluded normal

business conversations in such a way, but he had finally relinquished her hand and she needed to leave before she pleaded with him to finish what they'd started earlier. Caroline dipped her chin into a hasty nod and yanked the door open to bolt gracelessly from the room.

It was only after the carriage door had slammed safely behind her that she realized she'd forgotten her blasted bonnet in his study.

CHAPTER TWELVE

Caroline woke from a light and dreamless sleep, eyelids fluttering open amidst the gloom inside Frances's bedchamber. Her weary eyes moved across the dim shapes of the bureau at the far end of the room and the shadowy outlines of porcelain figurines on the small table nearby, before a shooting pain down her right arm indicated she had lain in one position for too long. She shifted her weight, tugging at the nightgown that had become trapped beneath her body, and rolled onto her back to massage the painful limb. As the circulation returned, she rolled over to her left side to find Frances lying beside her awake and wide-eyed.

Caroline stopped all movement, trying in vain to guess her aunt's current state of awareness. Normally she would have been out of the bedroom before being found out by her aunt, since she was generally more like herself in the mornings. But last night had been difficult—not just because

Frances had felt scared and unsure, but because Caroline herself was so very troubled over the way things had changed between her and Jonathan. She had not been able to find sleep until the small hours of the morning.

They stared at each other for a minute before Caroline gathered enough courage to break the silence.

"Auntie, it's Caroline."

Frances's slack expression of dread transformed into something resembling aggravation, the fine, gray wings of her brows drawing down in displeasure. "I know who you are, for goodness' sake. What are you doing in my bed?"

"You asked me to stay last night, so I did," she replied simply, hoping Frances wouldn't be too alarmed at her lack of remembrance.

But the alarm was plain to see. Her aunt's expression didn't change, but Caroline could see the wheels turning behind her eyes; could only imagine the terror she must be feeling.

Facts were facts. Frances needed more help. *Caroline* needed more help. And she had finally gone to find it. But no matter what choice she made, she ran the risk of losing someone she cared about . . . and unfortunately, she knew she had made the mistake of allowing herself to care about Mr. Cartwick. If Eliza were to find out she'd grown close to him, she might lose her respect and friendship. If she refused Jonathan's assistance out of spite, she might place her beloved aunt in more danger. Her stomach churned.

Caroline was starting to feel like a lobster in a copper pot.

She could jump out to escape the boiling water, but chances were she would meet the chef's cleaver anyway.

Caroline wrenched her attention back to the gray halo of hair that surrounded Frances's pale and timeworn features. Her aunt had always plaited her own hair before bedtime, but it was a habit that was becoming less and less common. The messy state of Frances's hair was one outwards sign of the inner deterioration that was occurring. Steeling herself against the sight, she pushed herself up into a seated position.

"I'll go and find Meggie, if you are ready for breakfast."

Frances remained where she was, laying on her side with wrinkled hands tucked under her chin, eyes unblinking. "I'm not ready."

"Would you like me to have a tray sent up?" she offered.

Her aunt only shook her head.

Reaching across the blankets, Caroline squeezed Frances's shoulder, feeling the impossibly frail and small form beneath the drape of her nightgown. "Some tea then, perhaps." It wasn't a question; she was truly growing worried and hoped a warm drink might help her aunt's mood. To her dismay, Frances closed her eyes with a bitter sigh.

"I . . . hate . . . this," she whispered, almost unintelligibly, through clenched teeth.

It took a moment to fully comprehend Frances's words, but Caroline's chin quivered when she did. Crawling back up the bed to wrap Frances in her arms, she rocked the only mother she'd ever known like she was her own child.

"I know it's hard, Auntie," she said, hugging her tight. "But I'm here to help."

"You have a life to live, dear," she said, her voice muffled against Caroline's shoulder. "Don't waste it on the last years of mine."

Caroline swallowed against the lump that had suddenly risen in her throat. "If it brings you cheer, you should know we will be receiving visitors soon. Today, in fact."

Frances scoffed. "Who will be here today? Your parents?"

"No, but Mr. Cartwick will be here." She couldn't bear to divulge the true purpose behind his call. Not now, anyway. There was very little way to predict how her aunt would react to the addition of staff to the household and the new servants meant to assist in keeping her safe.

Frances pulled away from Caroline's embrace. "The American?" she asked, her eyes widening.

Caroline glanced away with a smile. "Tell me, how is it you always remember *him* with such absolute precision?"

Tossing off the covers, Frances swung her legs over the side of the bed and tugged on the bellpull. She directed a critical look over her shoulder at Caroline. "If you don't know that by now, my dear, then it's no wonder you're still unmarried."

Caroline gaped at her. "You're still unmarried!" she exclaimed.

"That's only because I was proud and foolish in my younger years," she said, pulling on her wrapper and turning to kiss the top of Caroline's head. "My most fervent wish is that you not strive to emulate me. I'll see you downstairs for breakfast."

And without waiting for Meggie or anyone else, Frances threw open the door and charged into the hallway. From the sounds of it, she managed to startle the maid on her way downstairs, and Caroline felt the corner of her mouth quirk upwards into a little smile.

Say what you would about Jonathan Cartwick—and there was certainly plenty to say—he did seem to have a miraculously restorative effect upon her aunt.

Not an hour after rising, Caroline had both the pleasure and the distress of receiving two letters at the same time. They arrived on her doorstep after their journey from Kent, courtesy of her friends, Eliza and Clara, and she immediately rushed upstairs to her bedchamber to examine them in private.

The coincidence smacked of a coordinated effort between the two women, and Caroline took a moment to kick herself for possibly sharing too much in her latest letters to them. Upon reading the contents of Eliza's letter, she set to kicking herself a bit harder.

Dearest Caroline,

 I must admit to being concerned about your latest letter, and the upsetting news regarding Lady Frances. I know how very strong you are, but still can't bear to think of you struggling through this by yourself, alone in the country.

 Thomas and I would like to join you at Willowford House as soon as possible to help secure capable assistance and ease the transition for you and your aunt. We are aware

of your parents' impending arrival and would be glad to
stand by your side on that front as well. Please write back
with your thoughts as soon as you can.

    With love to you and Frances,
    Eliza

Her stomach plummeted. Eliza was an intelligent woman. If she ventured here to Hampshire, she would most certainly end up meeting the new owner of the Cartwick estate, and it would take only seconds for either her or Thomas to detect that her relationship with Cartwick was anything but benign. Likewise, Caroline had already accepted his offer of help so their assistance was not entirely necessary. While she loathed the idea of withholding information from her best friend, she worried that Eliza would question Caroline's willingness to involve her new neighbor in this very personal facet of her life. She knew *she* would question it, were the roles reversed.

Setting the parchment aside, she braced herself for Clara's letter. The lady was equal parts formidable and friendly, and Caroline had grown to cherish her friendship too. It had been only lately that she'd enjoyed the luxury of having two close and trustworthy companions . . . and it was just her rotten luck that they both lived halfway across England.

Breaking the seal, she unfolded the letter then scanned it with a pensive sigh.

Dear Caroline,

    By now, you will have received Eliza's letter to you.
What you have probably not guessed, however, is that

regardless of your answer to her, Eliza and Thomas plan
on making the trip to Hampshire anyway. Sadly, I will
not be able to join them since I have grown to the size of
a house and travel is considered unsafe at this point. But
please know I would be there if I was able. It was not a risk
William was willing to allow for myself or the baby, and I
prefer to be careful at this point as well.

My hope is that once your parents arrive back home,
they will give your household—most particularly its
occupants—the attention it deserves. But until then, please
know that we are thinking of you and Frances. We will be
out to Hampshire at the first possible moment.

Much love,
Clara

Caroline flopped backwards onto her bed with a groan,
the letters scattering beside her upon the ivory coverlet. Why,
oh why, were her friends trying to be so helpful? It made the
fact that she'd basically thrown herself at Jonathan Cartwick
just that much more repugnant. *Good* friends helped each
other in times of trouble. *Bad* friends allowed themselves
to be beguiled by handsome American neighbors. Not only
had Caroline ignored Eliza's request to make things difficult
for him, her propensity to find herself wrapped in the man's
arms showed both a lack of judgment and a serious deficiency
of character.

The sick feeling in her gut reminded her that it could
not happen again, and especially not now that she knew her
friends were on their way. But the thought of seeing him

again this afternoon still managed to fill her with a hot undercurrent of anticipation, her pulse singing faster at the remembrance of his tongue sliding against hers. At the feel of his fingers tugging at her bodice. The pleasure that had exploded between them, his deep groan reverberating against her flesh—

With a cry of frustration, she rolled off the bed and gathered her letters, taking a moment to wrest her thoughts away from where they had inadvertently wandered. It was the same place they'd been straying since fleeing yesterday in her carriage, and she was beginning to think that any interaction with him from now on would threaten the already tenuous state of her self-control. Unfortunately for her, there was no respite in sight. He would be arriving this afternoon and it was much too soon for her to pretend all was well, but do it she must.

If she knew what was good for her, she'd keep pretending until it became the truth.

Right now, she needed to concentrate . . . think about what on earth she was going to say to Eliza. How much should she confess before her friend's return to Hampshire? It wouldn't do to have Eliza show up at the estate—Frances surrounded by Cartwick's servants—with no warning. She would need to admit to some of this now.

Gripping the letters tightly in a trembling fist, Caroline threw open the door and headed down the stairs to the library. Frances was napping and Meggie was watching over her, so she had a bit of time to finish her task uninterrupted before Cartwick arrived to make a mess of her head again. The heavy door closed behind her with a loud *click* but her slippers made no sound on the thick patterned carpet as she hurried across the large room, gathering her parchment and pen before seating herself at the desk. Caroline closed her eyes for a moment, knowing what she was about to tell Eliza could not be taken back and praying for some sort of divine guidance to help her friend understand. When she felt she was finally ready, she dipped her pen in the inkwell and began.

> *My dear friend Eliza,*
>
>   *It brings me joy to think of seeing you and Thomas again, even if this situation is anything but joyful. Soon this house will be full of friends and familiar faces. Although I wish I could see Clara too, I understand why it would be difficult when one is "the size of a house."*
>
>   *Since you will be here soon, I should inform you that I have been in contact with the Cartwick heir. We have sufficiently squabbled over the boundary line near Windham Hill (a battle I've yet to concede, although I realize my efforts are wasted), and I've told him what I think of him (he took it better than expected). He's also had the dubious honor of seeing Frances at her worst, an event that prompted him to offer two of his servants to me.*
>
>   *I hope you may receive this news without any of the emotion that could be attached to my associating with a man whose presence here has brought you pain. My circumstances are such that it did not make sense to reject*

the arrangement, and I hope you would know me well
enough to remember where my loyalties lie. They will always
be with my friend, whom I love like a sister.

     Yours always,
     Caroline

She leaned back in the ornate wooden chair to read it over, and the butterflies soaring inside her stomach did a little flip for good measure. This probably wasn't going to be an easy letter for Eliza to read, but she could only hope that her friend's belief in Caroline's innate goodness would prevail in the end. With any luck, when Eliza finally came to Willowford House, she might miss entirely the charged undercurrent of attraction that flowed between Caroline and the man who had sent her packing.

The late morning air was brisk and refreshing, and Jonathan inhaled deeply as he tucked the box under his arm and stepped out of the carriage. His eyes automatically went to the small group that had gathered at the bottom of the steps of Willowford House, but he could not allow them to linger, tipping a brief nod instead before turning around to hand down the rest of the vehicle's occupants. The flash of a salmon pink dress and the chestnut hair of the woman who wore it had not escaped his notice, however, and he could feel himself tense as his body set to burning. It was necessary to behave normally for this visit here today, but he was not encouraged by the way things had already started.

His mother smiled, first at him, then at the two women who had alighted beside her, their crisp, white caps glowing brightly under the cloudy haze of the sky. Minnie and Beatrice had served their family well for many years, and he trusted them not just to keep a watchful eye over Lady Frances, but to keep their own counsel. Thankfully, they had agreed to the assignment, as he didn't feel it could be reasonably commanded for domestic servants to serve a mistress they did not know.

A delicate hint of rosewater reached him across a gust of spring wind. Unable to resist, his gaze shifted to Caroline, who looked sheepish and glanced away, almost as if she'd been caught staring. The rush of knowing he retained some kind of hold over her nearly caused him to charge over and seize her in his arms. Frances, beside her, looking every bit the refined lady in layers of skirts in a soft jade green, smiled broadly and hooked her arm through Caroline's to approach the group.

"Mr. Cartwick, and your lovely mother, Mrs. Cartwick—it's been too long since we saw you last."

It hadn't been that long, he recalled, but still he frowned slightly while feeling a well-earned twinge of guilt. Just yesterday at this time, he'd been ravishing this woman's niece in his own study, and here they were today doing their best to act as if nothing had happened. Caroline was failing prettily, he could see, as a charming blush spread across her décolletage and up the length of her neck. The sight of her struggle worked to challenge his own sense of restraint, especially when the feel of her soft curves was still burned into his flesh, and the taste of her skin lingered on his tongue.

Caroline had become exceptionally interested in the passing of some robins overhead. Unaware of the discomfort between Cartwick and her niece, Frances extended her hand to him and he clasped it in warm greeting, bowing over it in a show of politeness.

"I agree, my lady. It's been much too long." His eyes flicked over to Caroline, who was looking painfully awkward, and when Frances withdrew her fingers, he reached for hers next. "Lady Caroline," he said with a soft press of her hand. "A pleasure to see you again."

He thought he'd behaved admirably, even preventing himself from kissing her knuckles, and yet she managed to flush even deeper. Realizing his error too late, it seemed that perhaps *pleasure* was a word best avoided from now on.

His mother was the next recipient of Lady Frances's warm regard, with the elderly woman grasping both of Mrs. Cartwick's hands in imitation of her own unfashionable friendliness.

"So good to see you," she effused, then blinked in the sunlight at the two unfamiliar women standing nearby. Mrs. Cartwick smiled in return.

"And you, Lady Frances," she said with a squeeze of her fingers. "I hope you will permit me to introduce Beatrice and Minnie, two dear members of our household staff."

The two maids dipped into low curtsies, then smiled kindly at Frances. "Pleased to meet you, my lady," they said in a respectful echo of one another.

Beatrice was older than some of the other maids, solidly

in her thirties, with light brown, frizzy hair that had been brushed into unyielding submission beneath her bright white cap. Her cohort, Minnie, was at least a decade younger, and her slight build almost made it seem as if you could break her in half. But she possessed an air of maturity well beyond her years, and her light blue eyes shone clearly with intelligence. Both maids had always shown just the right balance of understanding and kindness, two things Lady Frances would certainly need in the trying times to come.

Frances's eyes grew round at the sound of their voices. "American as well?"

"Yes, Auntie. They crossed the Atlantic with them from New England, and now the Cartwicks wish to share their services with us—at least for a time. Isn't that kind?"

"Well, yes," she replied. "But why?"

At this query, Jonathan watched Caroline's body turn rigid. "Well, we're horridly short-staffed at the moment, and I'm afraid we will be for a while." Caroline wisely left out any reference to her parents and their part in the situation, at least in front of company.

Frances still appeared confused. "But aren't the duke and duchess taking care of all of that?"

Jonathan was sure that in the recent past, Frances would have known the answer to that question; that the Duke of Pemberton and his wife were far too busy off gallivanting about to bother with the mundane obligations of things like retaining staff for the family left behind. Caroline's frantic eyes locked with Jonathan's, beseeching him to say something, but his mother stepped in before he had the chance, looping her arm through Frances's and starting the walk to the house. Her onyx earrings dangled merrily.

"I'm certain it will be the first thing they take care of upon their return. In the meantime, however, I hope you will do us the honor of accepting Minnie and Beatrice into your home, where they will assist your staff as best they can. Lady Caroline believed you might be open to the idea."

Frances stopped abruptly, her shoes making a harsh scuffing sound on the gravel drive. She glanced back at her niece.

"She did?"

Caroline nodded, looking hopeful. "I hope you don't mind."

"No—not at all, dear," she said faintly, shaking her head. "Whatever you think is best."

Her aunt turned back around and he could see Caroline's shoulders drop with relief.

Frances smiled at his mother. "I know we're supposed to invite you in for tea, or some such thing, but I would love to walk through the gardens before the weather takes a turn," she said, casting a wary eye at the azure sky that was heavily dappled with suspicious-looking clouds. "Perhaps you will indulge me?"

"I'd be delighted," she replied, casting a questioning look back at Jonathan and Caroline. "And you two will help Beatrice and Minnie get settled?"

Caroline gestured to her own maid, who had been waiting patiently for acknowledgment and came forwards to dip into a curtsy. "Meggie will be happy to get them introduced and moved into their rooms." She tipped her a meaningful nod. "Thank you, Mrs. Cartwick."

With that, the two ladies ambled around to the side of the house, disappearing beneath the gentle green sway of a willow tree. And once the maids had bid their temporary farewell to their master, they ventured to the service entrance on the other side of the house, following Meggie's lead. The driver pulled the carriage down the drive, and with a jolt of realization, Jonathan saw that he and Caroline were alone again. She must have noticed too for she froze like a startled fawn, eyes darting about, then recovering as best she could. Clasping her hands before the low, pointed waist of her dress, she let out a laugh that he guessed was supposed to sound casual but didn't quite hit the mark.

"What's in the box?" she asked awkwardly.

He'd almost forgotten he'd been holding it. It was unsettling how her presence affected him. With a grin, he held it out in her direction.

"Care to hazard a guess?"

The wind teased a lock from her mass of upswept hair, and he stared as the reddish-brown strands gleamed in the sun, wrapping in front of her neck to trace along her collarbone. Her hair almost had a life of its own—wavy, touched by fire, and always seeming to be one hairpin away from breaking free of its styled imprisonment. Mesmerized, Jonathan envisioned his fingertips taking the same lazy route, and called to memory the impossibly soft feel of that skin against his lips. He would sell his own soul to have her in his arms again, her bodice tugged out of place, perfect breasts only partially concealed by the fall of her dark ruby hair. But with a stern shake of his head, he admonished himself. Not only was it not meant to be, but thinking of her in that way was the surest path to insanity.

Desire must have been plainly readable in his eyes, but thankfully she was oblivious, her gaze directed to his hands while she attempted to speculate at the contents of the box. Realization dawned at last and she leveled him with a wry expression.

"The bonnet."

Jonathan's eyebrows raised in faux surprise and he lifted the lid to reveal said bonnet. "Congratulations. You've just earned yourself this, er—" He tipped his head at the collection of garish ribbons and feathers. "—rather festive headpiece."

Caroline tried to keep a straight face, but her dark eyes grew unaccountably bright a split second before she broke into laughter. He watched her as she claimed the box, utterly charmed at the purity of her amusement. It was a side of her he'd never seen.

Her show of mirth came to an abrupt stop, almost as if some internal governess had just given her a sharp rebuke for the outwards display. Or perhaps it was more because she remembered the circumstances in which the bonnet came to be in his possession. She cleared her throat and started for the front steps of the house.

"I appreciate you returning this, I'll just—oh. Thank you, Taylor."

The butler had appeared in the front door as if he owned some supernatural affinity for the needs of his mistress—or as if he could have been watching from one of the windows. The man received the box from Caroline with a dignified bow, but did not miss the chance to shoot a subtle warning look at Jonathan. He could respect that. Cartwick nodded to the gray-haired butler, and with a gruff nod in return, Taylor marched back inside the house with the bonnet.

Caroline glanced at him inquisitively. "Would you care for some tea?"

"Since landing on these shores, I think I've drunk more tea than I did throughout my lifetime in America." He shook his head. "Thank you, but no."

It appeared she was trying to decide whether or not to be offended by his answer. "Oh? And what is your highly refined American preference?" she asked, her tone light and flirtatious.

"Honestly, I prefer coffee in the morning. Whiskey or beer later in the day."

She wrinkled her nose. "Beer?"

"Lager is my preference, but I've had some passable ale down in the village," he said.

"It's not a very dignified drink, I don't believe," she teased, eyeing him with a raised brow. It made him want to show her how very undignified he could be, but instead he lifted his shoulders into a small shrug.

"How very British of you to say. Have you ever tried it?"

"What do you think?" she answered with a light scoff.

Jonathan approached and extended an elbow in her

direction. He didn't truly expect her to take it, but to his surprise, her graceful arm looped through his in acceptance and they started down the steps. He thought remaining in the fresh air would be a good change, and perhaps just the thing necessary to keep her at ease in his presence.

"I think you shouldn't formulate an opinion until you've tried it."

"And just when am I supposed to try it?" she asked, gazing up at him incredulously while they crossed the drive.

"We could walk into the village now, if you like."

A flicker of excitement came to life behind her eyes; those shining pools that entranced him with their changeable nature. Right now they were the color of tumbled river rock, but he had seen them ignite with curious dark fire many times. Much as he didn't care to admit it, he found her unpredictable moods both confounding and thrilling. She was—as he'd once accused her of being—an enigma. Although unlike before, he no longer believed it was something she could help.

To his dismay, her expression closed and she pulled her arm free.

"That's not a good idea," she said hoarsely. "I can't be seen in the village drinking ale with . . . with . . ."

"A man?" he offered.

"Yes," she said flatly. "But more specifically, with you."

Hurt sliced through his chest, and he couldn't prevent himself from delivering an answering glare. "May I ask why, *specifically*, you find me so offensive? Have I not tried to be a gentleman?"

"Yes, certainly you have—" she said, recoiling at his reaction.

"And just today, did I not bring two servants to help ease your strain?"

She wound her fingers together anxiously. "You did, sir, and I am in your debt—"

"There is no debt. You owe me nothing . . . not even a drink in the village. But I would appreciate an explanation for why—"

Stepping forwards, she shocked the offense right out of him by placing one small palm on his chest. They stared at one another in silence for a moment, then she cleared her throat.

"Eliza and her husband are on their way to Hampshire," she whispered.

And that was all the explanation he required.

CHAPTER THIRTEEN

Jonathan stared bleakly out the window as the carriage swayed and bounced along the uneven country road. After spending most of his life in the busy shipyards of Massachusetts, he could grudgingly admit to appreciating the rural scenery of Hampshire. At this moment though, the sight of leafy hedgerows and passing birch groves did nothing to improve the state of his mood, and he was no good at hiding it. With a sigh, his mother threw her hands up in frustration and stared at him plaintively.

"My goodness. I've no idea what Lady Caroline could have said to upset you. I know she can be a bit brusque at times, but you haven't said more than two words since we left Willowford House. What happened?"

Releasing a breath, he ran a hand through his hair and shook his head. "It's nothing."

"Was she rude to you?" she asked anyway.

"Not particularly."

Dorothea's eyes remained steady on him. "Then what is it?"

Taking a moment to mentally debate the wisdom of imparting the true source of his troubles, he went ahead and said it anyway with a low growl of discontent. "She told me that Reginald Cartwick's widow would be arriving soon with her new husband." He shrugged and glanced away. "I suppose I just wasn't expecting it."

She pursed her lips in thought, her eyes evaluating him carefully in the shadowy interior of the carriage. "Fine. I can see how news of Lady Evanston's arrival might cause you to feel a bit uncomfortable. You received the estate she was living in and there is bound to be some awkwardness. But it still doesn't explain the reaction I'm seeing—"

"And what are you seeing, Mother? How am I supposed to react to this?"

With a gruff noise of irritation, he returned his gaze back to the window while she sat across from him in silence. He knew full well she was busy mulling over the possibilities in her mind, and that his uncharacteristic loss of temper had given her plenty to consider. He also knew that it was very likely that she would reach the correct conclusion: that he had scrapped his better judgment and fallen for Lady Caroline—an *aristocrat*, for God's sake—who would never consent to being his, with parents who would never agree to the match anyway. Eliza's arrival would serve as the first of many nails in the coffin of a relationship that had been doomed from the start. He knew it, Caroline knew it and now his mother probably knew it too.

He reached up to massage his temples. They had started to throb with an annoying ache.

Rather than continue to pursue what was obviously a touchy subject, she simply made a tiny noise of acknowledgment then directed her eyes out her own window. "I certainly don't have all the answers, dear. Although Lady Frances did tell me something rather interesting today." She reached up to adjust the hat that sat upon her thick, black curls with wisps of silver woven throughout. "I thought you might want to hear it, but it seems you're not in the mood for conversation."

Her head stayed where it was, but her dark eyes shifted to the side, viewing him in amusement. She was baiting him, and despite the bleak state of his disposition, he couldn't help the soft chuckle that escaped.

"Tell me. What interesting information did Frances impart to you?"

She clasped her hands eagerly in her lap. "Well, you remember hearing how Lady Caroline was close to Reginald's parents when she was young?"

"Of course, I remember," he replied. "Nicholas Cartwick gifted her a piano that matches the one at Greystone Hall."

His mother nodded. "Indeed. Well it turns out, Caroline would often climb the fence between estates to visit Windham Hill. But one time, when she was just five years old, she took a fall doing it and broke her arm."

"Five years old?" he asked, wide-eyed and incredulous. "But how could she have possibly climbed over the fence to reach Windham Hill, when it would have already been on her side of the fence?"

"Exactly," replied Dorothea with a satisfied smile. "It appears the fences were changed at some point during her lifetime, which makes me wonder how much she truly knows about the change."

Jonathan sat, lost in thought. His mouth was still wide in astonishment and he snapped it shut. "You don't think Lady Caroline is concealing something about it, do you?"

"I was rather pondering whether her accident may have been the *cause* of such a change, not that she had some underhanded involvement in it," his mother said quietly. At Jonathan's wide-eyed silence, she arranged her skirts around her lap and gave a small shrug. "It's hard to say for sure. But if Nicholas and Isabelle were indeed close to Caroline, is it entirely unthinkable that they moved the fence to accommodate her?"

"Yes!" he replied with a short bark of laughter. "It's absolutely astonishing if it's true. And of course, it would only make my insistence on correcting the border seem malicious in comparison," he added with a wry twist of his mouth.

"That wouldn't have bothered you before, I don't think," she observed, her dark eyes piercing him with a knowing look.

He glanced at her sharply, then looked away. Ignoring that pointed comment would be his wisest move. "We don't even know if this story is true, by the way."

"Why wouldn't it be?" his mother asked in confusion.

Jonathan hesitated for a moment. "Because Lady Frances has had an episode where she's even forgotten her own niece.

It's what prompted Caroline to change her mind about accepting our help."

Now it was his mother's turn to look incredulous. "She did? Why didn't you tell me this?"

Jonathan reached up to loosen his cravat, which had started to feel as if it might strangle him. "Caroline was very anxious about it. She made me promise not to tell you unless absolutely necessary." If he were being honest, that was only part of the truth. The other part was that revisiting their torrid meeting in his mind was something he tried very hard not to do. *Lady Caroline has changed her mind* was simple, to the point and didn't run the risk of him divulging any other details that were best kept unsaid and unthought.

His mother's thunderous frown, however, was a clear indication that she disagreed. "After crossing the Atlantic to be here with you—at least for a while—I must say that I don't like being kept in the dark."

Well, she was in the dark on much more than that. He swallowed back the guilt that had risen in his throat, knowing the extent of her displeasure would be large indeed had she known every intricacy of his dealings with the duke's daughter.

"My apologies," he said with a dip of his chin. "It didn't seem like essential information until now."

Dorothea Cartwick stared at him then, her unhappiness lessening by visible degrees, expression gradually turning thoughtful. With a sigh, she gazed out the window again, setting her palm on the door to brace herself against an especially sharp turn.

"Do you know if Eliza is set to arrive before Caroline's parents?"

"I believe so," he answered. "Why?"

She gave a small shrug. "I imagine Lady Caroline will act differently depending on who is nearby."

Yes, he thought with a pang. *Caroline won't want anything else to do with me, for one.*

"Most likely," was all he said.

"And Lady Frances probably can't be trusted to attend public functions any longer."

"I'm assuming that trust may have been broken sometime during last year's season, although Caroline did take the chance on bringing her here to dine with us," he mused out loud.

"It's something I've noticed about her," she replied. Her eyes lingered on the gardens that lined their drive, full of plants that would soon be in colorful bloom. "For as much as she's been through, and as pessimistic as she tries to be, she still nurtures an awful lot of hope."

His heart lurched painfully at hearing that word. *Hope.* He didn't disagree with the statement but found himself shaking his head anyway. Perhaps because everything felt useless now with the arrival of Eliza.

"I suppose she does, beneath it all."

His mother straightened as the carriage came to a stop in front of their house and gave him a tiny smile. "We should help her with that, don't you think? She's going to need all the hope she can get."

Caroline carefully tucked her needle into the linen edge of her embroidery and set it aside on the table beside her. With a sigh, she reached a hand up to shade her eyes against the sunlight. Needlepoint on the terrace was an unusual practice even for her, but she was determined to finish her project and Frances had wanted to venture outside. When Beatrice offered to accompany her aunt, the warm call of the afternoon sun had been too delightful to resist and Caroline had joined them, watching from her seat near the house and smiling at Frances's occasional exclamations as she came across various plants that were starting to bud now that the warmth of spring had started to take hold.

Her aunt pointed at a nearby bush. "Caroline!" she called loudly. "The rosemary smells divine."

"Won't you pick me a sprig, Auntie?"

At the ready, Beatrice nodded and stepped forwards to snip a tiny bit of the bushy green shrub with a pair of tiny scissors. She deposited the rosemary into Frances's waiting hands, who raised it aloft and smiled at Caroline before moving along to the rosebushes.

She appreciated the chance for this rare moment of contentment. Minnie and Beatrice had proven themselves capable and caring over the past few days, establishing a routine with Meggie that ensured Frances was always under close watch. This could have easily caused problems, for her aunt would detect and rebel against any attempt to smother her or minimize her privacy. Yet, the two women had assimilated into the household with an ease that was pleasantly surprising. There had been a couple initial hiccups, of course. Minnie had made the mistake of rearranging the pillows in the bedchamber, and Beatrice had accidentally offered to keep her company on that first night. Some of these adjustments would take more time than others and Caroline felt as if it could still take weeks before she was able to sleep in her own bed again. But Frances still seemed to appreciate their direct manners and no-nonsense personalities, and was all but willing to ignore the fact that they were clearly here to assist with her mounting difficulties, perhaps knowing in her heart that it was for the best.

Caroline also couldn't help but be amused at her aunt's apparent partiality for Americans. In that, it seemed the two of them shared that in common, although Caroline was still surprised at the unexpected way her neighbor had worked his way into her heart, almost without trying. She knew things would have been considerably less troublesome had she not grown so very fond of him, and part of her wished for the uncomplicated rancor the pair had shared between them at the start. This friendship, this affection that existed now was unsettling and frightening in its potency. Every day she worried how on earth she was going to be able to conceal it from Eliza and Evanston.

Still, she couldn't deny that she was eternally grateful for his help. There was only so much time, energy and patience that Caroline could humanly devote to caring for Frances in a day, and after a long time of sleepless nights and uncertain days, it was a blessing for both her and Meggie to have more assistance. In fact, poor Meggie was probably collapsed in a

corner somewhere, exhausted. Caroline was only shocked
the poor woman hadn't sought new employment long ago.
Many months had passed since she'd spoken to the housekeeper about an increase in pay for the maid, but these things
took time, especially when the duke and duchess were so difficult to reach.

The arrival of Taylor next to her wrought-iron chair caused
her to shift in her seat, and she squinted up at the butler.

"Yes, Taylor?"

He bowed to her, his silvery hair nearly glowing in the
afternoon sun, then straightened. "Pardon the interruption,
my lady, but Mrs. Cartwick is calling. Shall I tell her you are
at home?"

A surge of adrenaline caused her to stare blankly at him
while she struggled to gather her wits. She managed to formulate a question before it was necessary for Taylor to ask
her again.

"Is it only Mrs. Cartwick?"

The butler tipped his chin into a succinct nod. "Yes, my
lady. She visits alone."

Caroline felt a wash of relief, followed by a rising tide of
curiosity. She didn't feel prepared to encounter Jonathan at
the moment, especially knowing how awkward things had
become after the news of Eliza's upcoming visit. But it was
interesting that Dorothea Cartwick was choosing to visit
here by herself.

"I see. Well then, could you show her outside to the terrace?"

"Tea?"

She smiled at him. "Tea would be lovely. Thank you."

Taylor bowed once more before disappearing into the house. Caroline set to smoothing her skirts and ensuring her hair was in place, then rose to greet Mrs. Cartwick as she was ushered outside, her cheerful face a welcome sight despite Caroline's nervousness.

"Mrs. Cartwick," she said, coming closer to kiss the woman on both cheeks. Jonathan's mother looked resplendent in a cobalt dress, and Caroline noticed the always present touch of mourning in the jet pendant that hung from around her neck. "I hope you don't mind the show of familiarity, but I feel we are friends enough to warrant it by now." Her eyes strayed to the garden, where Frances and Beatrice could be seen weaving through the plants, examining each one with studious care.

Jonathan's mother issued a friendly cluck of her tongue. "My lady, I hope you will call me Dorothea from now on. And, oh. Will you look at that?" she breathed softly, her gaze traveling to settle on Frances and Beatrice as they continued their exploration. "It seems your aunt has taken to Beatrice."

Caroline gestured to the chair beside her own, and both ladies sank down into their seats. "You could say that," she replied with a fond glance at the pair, her eyes returning meaningfully to her guest. "Truly, I am grateful for your assistance. And I'd like you to know that I am still inquiring for help in the village. My hope is to be able to return Beatrice and Minnie to you as soon as possible."

"That is absolutely not necessary," Dorothea answered with a small smile. "Jonathan was just happy you allowed him to help, and it will make him even happier to know that Frances is doing well. But I can't help notice the dark smudges persist beneath your eyes." She paused. "Have your nights not been made any easier through this arrangement?"

Caroline waved away the question in nonchalant fashion. "I'm afraid it will take more than a few days for everyone to settle into the new routine, but there have already been improvements. Not the least of which is the security of knowing that Frances will always have someone with her to make sure she stays safe."

"Yes, that is certainly important . . ." A worried crease deepened between Mrs. Cartwick's brows.

The butler arrived with the tea set and Caroline realized she'd left her embroidery in plain view. Cursing her carelessness, she hurried to scoop it up from the table.

"Oh, what are you working on? Are you embroidering a handkerchief?"

Drat. It was too late. Taking advantage of Taylor's interruption with rattling teacups and clinking silver spoons, Caroline shrugged and stowed it safely away in the side of her chair.

"It's nothing. Just some old slip of fabric to help me pass the time."

"Ah," said Mrs. Cartwick, a hint of a smile tugging at the corner of her mouth. "I also enjoy needlework every now and then."

Thankfully, it didn't seem as if she had seen the monogram on her son's own handkerchief. Thinking on it now, Caroline wasn't sure what she would have done if she had. Melting into her chair in a puddle of humiliation was the only realistic reaction she could possibly envision. She added some sugar to her tea and gave the drink a stir with an unsteady hand, her anxiety building again.

"I'm sure you are much more adept at it than I am," said Caroline with a shaky laugh. "You can ask your son for his thoughts on my feeble attempts."

"He told me you were working on a rather lovely piece for your aunt," Dorothea said questioningly. "A rose, he said."

Her eyes lowered and she flushed. "I believe Mr. Cartwick must be exaggerating."

"I'm sure he isn't," her guest replied succinctly, taking a sip of her steaming beverage before setting it back down upon its white china saucer. "But you may be prone to an overabundance of modesty."

Caroline stared, then broke out into amused laughter. "You know, I don't believe anyone has ever accused me of being too modest." She knew that wasn't exactly true. Eliza had made that claim to her before. And speaking of Eliza, she needed to address the news of her upcoming visit. It would only be anticipation and nervousness for her until she did.

Heat bloomed in her cheeks and her fingertips plucked at the corner of the iron table. "I suppose you may have heard about Lady Evanston?" Avoiding the inquiring face of her guest, she cast her gaze out to Frances and Beatrice instead, who had worked their way to the far end of the flower beds.

"I have," Dorothea said quietly. "I understand she and the viscount will be arriving in Hampshire soon."

Raising her teacup to her lips, Caroline only nodded in silence. It sounded as if Jonathan had been talking to his mother. Unable to prevent the turn of her thoughts, she wondered how much he had told her about . . . them.

"And your parents will be here soon after that."

"Yes, they will," she said with another nod, glancing at Mrs. Cartwick over the rim over her cup.

Dorothea toyed with the porcelain loop of her teacup handle. "I understand that, perhaps, things might prove a bit . . . uncomfortable . . . once they arrive. And while Jon and I are grateful for the friendship that has developed between our families, we realize this is a possibility."

Jon. Hearing him referred to in such an informal way set loose a chain of heated recollections that threatened to ruin her composure. Memories of the way he'd torn that awful bonnet from her head and tossed it across the room . . . and of what had followed after . . .

She straightened her spine in horror. There was no good reason to indulge her fantasies, and especially not in front of the man's own mother. Not now, and not any other day. In fact, Eliza's arrival meant she would never have the chance to be alone with Jonathan again, so lingering too long on what had passed between them was pointless. The risk of discovery was too great, the danger of losing her friend even greater. Her sense of determination grew even as the hollow ache in her chest thudded insistently.

"Yes," Caroline muttered, her guilt prompting her to divert her gaze elsewhere. She'd lost sight of Frances and Beatrice, the women having made their way further into the thick of the gardens. "It could make things difficult for certain."

"Well, difficult for you, but also difficult for Lady Frances," Dorothea said quietly. "I suppose she might be confined to her room for any gathering, if she were to have an episode?"

A tremor of realization sliced through Caroline with the delicacy of a dull, rusted knife, and her troubled gaze moved back to meet Mrs. Cartwick's eyes. "Eliza would never insist on such a thing. But my father—"

Her guest interrupted with a barely perceptible nod. "Which is why Jonathan and I thought it might be nice to host a little party before things change . . . a party for Lady Frances."

Caroline said nothing. She sat there, unmoving, her stillness a stark contrast to the roiling waves of emotion that churned inside her now. The kindness in Dorothea's gaze only increased the damnable pressure that was rising and expanding inside, but years of practice allowed Caroline to sufficiently stomp down the feelings. She would not lose control as she had that day in the hallway when Jonathan had discovered her sobbing against the wall.

Even so, one scalding tear managed to escape down her cheek. Cursing herself, she hurriedly swiped it away with the back of a trembling hand just as her aunt came into view, face alight with happiness, gray hair flying in the wind and wrinkled fingers tightly grasping a colorful assortment of plants. Tipping her chin upwards, she could feel her mouth curving into an irrepressible grin.

"I think that would be delightful, Mrs. Cartwick."

Jonathan paced the floorboards in the drawing room, tugging at his white cloth cravat while his mother viewed him with amusement from the couch.

"For heaven's sake, dear, why don't you have a glass of brandy? You'll wear your boots out before they arrive and you're making me nervous."

His boots paused and he turned to regard her with a tug on his long black tailcoat. Normally, he abhorred tiresome attentions to formality, but tonight had found himself riveted on adhering to the details, even if the gathering today would be of the unconventional sort.

"I'm fine," he declared. "Besides, I've already had three."

Dorothea's eyebrows shot up and she shifted noisily in her taffeta skirts, which gleamed a warm pewter color beneath the light from the sconces. "Three brandies? Surely, that's two brandies too many."

"Or too few," he muttered beneath his breath with a wipe of his brow.

His mother *tsked*. "You act as if we don't know these people, Jonathan. We've seen Lady Frances and Lady Caroline on multiple occasions—"

Yes, he thought wearily. But the thought of feeling the soft curve of her waist beneath his hands again caused his pulse to increase to an unbearable degree. Hadn't he imagined and reimagined such a thing countless times? They had shared much intimacy between them—too much, if he were being honest—but there was something about the notion of dancing with the woman in front of others that worried him.

Was it the idea that he might not be able to conceal his growing tenderness for her in front of others? Possibly. Although, he also couldn't discount the likelihood of her infuriating him to the point of dragging her away to silence the sharp-tongued beauty with his mouth . . .

Heaving a disgusted sigh at himself, he raked a hand through his hair and glanced over at the sideboard. "Perhaps it's the fact that I will be the sole male in attendance. Compared to the varied offerings in London, I am sure they will find me quite insufficient once the first dance is finished."

Dorothea uttered a tiny snort, and his head snapped over to her just as her gloved fingers flew up to conceal her mouth.

"Forgive me," she said, stifling her laughter, "but neither of those ladies consider you insufficient in the least. And don't think I can't see you eyeing the brandy again."

If the alcohol he'd already consumed had not worked to soothe his nerves, Jonathan knew another glass would only impair his abilities to approach Caroline with the cool detachment that was necessary. "Don't worry yourself. Since the burden of keeping everyone entertained must fall to me this evening, I wouldn't dream of overindulging." Privately, he reserved the right to overindulge to his heart's content after the night had concluded, knowing full well that after spending an evening with Caroline, determined to be on his best behavior, he would likely need to.

The rattle of carriage wheels upon the gravel drive caused both of them to glance towards the windows, and he strode over to steal a glimpse before stepping away, a crease between his brows.

"They're here," he said, anxiously adjusting his cuff links.

"And thank goodness for that," his mother replied with a smirk. "With all your pacing, I was becoming worried for the state of the floors."

Jonathan shot her a look of wry disapproval before offering his arm, and once she'd risen from her seat they advanced through the hallway, out the open front doors into the brisk late afternoon air, and down the curved stone stairway to meet their guests. Dorothea released his arm as they came nearer, and he increased his pace in order to assist the ladies in alighting from their vehicle. Lady Frances was her usual charming self and not the least bit confused, accepting his proffered hand with a grin that belied her age before proceeding to his mother with outstretched hands. But when he caught sight of Caroline . . . that was when his breath stopped in his throat.

Wrapped in a silk gown the color of raw emeralds, she hesitantly emerged from the dim interior of the carriage to take his hand. In a considerable breach of tradition, her reddish-brown tresses fanned over her shoulders and back, very nearly down to her waist, with artful pieces braided and woven into the stylish fall. Her color heightened as their eyes met, and he attempted to neutralize his expression, for he could only imagine the shock she had already registered there.

Both the long-sleeved cut and the color of her dress would have been considered unusual fashion choices for tonight's festivities; the style of her hair, even more so. But Aphrodite herself couldn't have affected him in such a way, and he would have spurned that goddess in a blink for the one standing before him now.

The fine arch of her brows furrowed slightly, and he realized that he was staring, his jaw hanging open in astonishment.

With a jerk of his head, he came nearer to assist, wishing with every fiber of his being that there was a way to avoid touching her. Close proximity seemed a perilous venture when all he could think about was how to steal her away from the party so he could have her all to himself. She touched him anyway, the slide of her slender fingers around his arm enflaming his already impassioned state.

"My lady," he said in his most carefully controlled voice. "You look . . ."

"Ridiculous," she whispered, turning her head away, abashed. "But my aunt insisted on all of it."

Sparing a grateful look at the relative in question, Jonathan then raised his eyebrows at Caroline in censure.

"That was *not* the word I was going to use."

She finally raised her head as she alighted next to him, a ghost of a smile forming on her flawless, strawberry lips. "Well, you have quite the selection of words to choose from, Mr. Cartwick. *Outlandish . . . absurd . . .*"

He pulled tightly on the arm that was looped around his, and she collided with his side, turning to stare up at him in breathless surprise.

"Consider yourself admonished, Lady Caroline," he murmured as they approached the other women. "And if you wish to discover which words *I* would have chosen, you'll need to behave yourself from now on."

She was discomfited, for certain. Then he flashed her a smile and watched the tension dissolve into something . . . warmer.

"I'll only need to behave tonight?" she asked.

He laughed quietly. It felt low . . . deep and satisfying and woefully unfamiliar. "It would be an unreasonable request to ask it for any longer. I wouldn't wish for you to strain yourself unnecessarily."

The answering tinkle of her laugh was mesmerizing. And as they joined the others, Jonathan Cartwick thought that this night had gotten off to an amazing start for two people who would be forced to part ways, perhaps forever, at its conclusion.

CHAPTER FOURTEEN

"Champagne?"

Caroline nodded at the footman before lifting a gleaming flute off the silver tray he had extended in her direction. He bowed, retreating backwards, and she resumed her quiet observation of the dance floor. Jonathan Cartwick was waltzing with Lady Frances at the moment, and while it was nearly impossible not to stare in appreciation of his gentlemanly attention to her aunt, a tiny laugh reminded Caroline that the man's mother was standing beside her. Turning, she faced the woman in polite inquiry.

"Poor Jon," said Dorothea, shaking her head with an amused smile. "How he hates being a spectacle, and yet here he is . . . the only man in attendance with each of us waiting to dance."

She took a long sip of her drink, the bubbly liquid searing

a pleasant path down her throat before returning Dorothea's smile with what she hoped was cheerful indifference. "He seems to be enduring rather well, given that my aunt has not yet relinquished him after three dances, and you danced with him before that. I imagine a lesser man would be sweating by now."

His mother surveyed him proudly, her fingertips lingering on the black lace that edged the satin collar at her throat. "Yes, well he has something that most aristocrats do not—an upbringing that included both education and physical labor, not to mention the running of a successful business. It would take a great deal more than dancing with a few ladies to make him perspire."

Caroline glanced across the room at him, intrigued. "And yet he had to give all that up to claim this estate on the other side of the Atlantic." The echo of Frances's laughter rang through the ballroom as Jonathan whirled her around with an athletic grace that nearly stole Caroline's breath. She looked away before his mother could detect her obvious admiration. "I've often wondered why he would do such a thing," she said, tipping her glass up for another drink.

"Have you?" Dorothea's mouth compressed in thought before she raised her eyebrows and sighed. "I suppose he felt a sense of duty to his father; to explore his birthright in a way my Robert never could. And . . ." She paused before continuing hesitantly, "It may have had something to do with his broken engagement."

Caroline sputtered and lowered her champagne. "His broken engagement?"

"Why yes," his mother answered, her face suddenly serious. "She never deserved him, in my opinion, although he doesn't like to speak of it."

But remembering now, Caroline thought back to a time when he *had* spoken of it. The two of them had been alone in his study, just mere moments before he'd kissed the sense right out of her . . .

Clearly you don't know me at all. If you did, you would know that you are not the only one who has endured the changeable nature of love.

She felt the blood drain from her face. Perhaps she'd been too distracted with his closeness to really hear what he'd been saying, or she'd been too busy complaining about her treatment at Lord Braxton's hands. Jonathan, as it turned out, had actually been engaged—

Her gaze darted across the floor as the musicians played the final strains of their song. Frances's cheeks were flushed with happy color, and Jonathan played the gentleman to her debutante, leading Caroline's aunt back to the group. It was impossible to reconcile what Mrs. Cartwick had just told her with the charming vitality that shone from him now, but she couldn't deny that knowing of his past heartache affected how she saw him. This man had wounds she hadn't known about, and he hadn't wanted to bother her with them either. Her chest tightened at the newfound knowledge.

Pasting a smile on her face, she came forwards to wrap an arm around Frances's shoulders, feeling the unwelcome fragility of her aunt's frame.

"What is this?" she asked lightly, avoiding the amber evaluation of Jonathan's gaze. "Are you allowing Mr. Cartwick a chance to rest at last?"

Frances laughed wryly and swatted at her arm. "I'm only giving him a chance to recuperate so he will be able to properly dance with you, my dear."

Caroline's eyes caught Jonathan's, her face growing unaccountably warm. "I am certain he must need at least a few moments of rest," she replied, her heartbeat thundering oddly inside her chest. To her surprise he reached out smoothly in her direction.

"I'll dance with you this moment, if you are ready."

The velvety richness of his voice with that curious blend of accents—a lilting softness tempered by sharpened *r*'s—caused her knees to weaken beneath her skirts. How had she ever loathed the things that had made him different? Now she found herself admiring those same qualities. Here he stood, looming large before her while Caroline stared mutely at his gloved hand. She knew the feel of the skin underneath, grown coarse from his time as a shipbuilder's apprentice. It was all too easy to remember the rousing scrape of his hands as they had passed over her flesh to touch her, to torment . . .

The subtle jab of an elbow caused her to turn and blink at Lady Frances, who had delivered it.

"I, oh," she stammered, eyes darting to each inquisitive face while panic raced through her. "I suppose we could, although—"

The thought of dancing together—the emotions between them still so raw and absolutely forbidden—seemed like the surest pathway to disaster. She was certain it would take only a moment of being in his arms for Frances and Dorothea to glean that they had lost themselves in each other's arms before, however ludicrous that might seem.

"Perhaps you might care to see the greenhouse instead?" he asked, deftly sidestepping her discomfort. "I've made some changes that I'd like to show you."

She dreaded being alone with him, but before she could make herself seem like any more of a fool, she set her glass down on a nearby table and looped her hand around the hard curve of his bicep. "Yes, Mr. Cartwick. I would like that," she replied breathlessly, willing herself to ignore the way her body sang at the contact.

With a polite nod to the other ladies, he guided her across the floor and into the foyer. Despite the absence of dancers, the orchestra began its next piece in a flourish of stringed harmony. Caroline retrieved her hand once they had rounded the corner into the hallway, where they paused to face one another.

"Forgive me," she started awkwardly. "I'm sure you've heard by now that I am wretched at social engagements." *Especially when I am terrified that I will throw myself into your arms at the least provocation.*

Jonathan evaluated her with a small smile. A knowing smile. "I would qualify that as an inaccuracy." Narrowing his eyes, his gaze slid curiously over her features as she worked to seem impassive. "Truth be told, I wasn't looking forwards to dancing with you either."

Her gasp caused him to smile wider, and she realized he wasn't being serious. Still the comment made old wounds seem fresh, even if that had not been his intent.

"I see. Well then, it seems I am equally repulsive to both British and American men," she quipped, casting her burning eyes over the familiar oil paintings that spanned the walls.

He shook his head slowly. "I don't believe you have a proper notion of yourself at all."

"I can tell you how my parents would describe me. Although they'll tell you themselves very soon, I'm sure."

"I have no interest in hearing their thoughts on the matter," he said, his voice suddenly serious.

"It won't be terribly shocking," she said with a shrug. "Likely just a variation of what I said earlier. A spoiled and selfish girl who looks ridiculous, outlandish, absurd . . ."

Caroline heard the breath hiss out through his teeth, and his brows lowered in irritation. Wordlessly, he slid a hand around her wrist and she felt a sudden flurry of excitement. Had she annoyed him on purpose? She couldn't say, but all she knew was that the last time she'd uttered those words out on the drive, he had jerked her bodily against him . . .

He tugged her through the maze of hallways and just like that, Caroline felt like a very willing sheep being led off by a just as hungry wolf. Her thoughts were pleasantly fuzzy—

probably from the champagne—and his strong clasp was a bit too authoritative for her liking.

"You don't have to tow me along. I know my way well enough."

He spared her an annoyed glance as he kept going, his pace and his hold on her unrelenting. "If only you knew when to stop talking," he grumbled.

"And just a few moments ago you were taking me to task for not speaking enough," she said drily, yanking at her hand. "Besides, why you are so upset is beyond me—"

"Is it?" he demanded, releasing her to whirl around and pin her with a stare. "Has the disappointment of your family brought you so low that you cannot see your own virtues? Did your experience with Lord Braxton make it impossible for you to tell when a man wishes to pay you a compliment?"

"I—" Caroline struggled to make sense of his words, blinking as she focused on the impressive breadth of his chest, the way his waistcoat was molded to the muscles beneath. "Of course I can tell when a man is spouting flattery, although whether or not he means it is another thing altogether. And I couldn't care less about Lord Braxton," she added acidly. "Or my family."

"That's not true."

"It is," she replied with a sniff.

His expression gentled. "Fine. But at the very least, I wish you would allow my opinions more credence than those of some unworthy suitor."

She raised her gaze to meet his, seeing hurt, frustration

and longing in equal and disconcerting measures. "I thought
we had established that you weren't courting me," she said
quietly. "What difference could your opinion make?"

He ran his fingers through the short cut of his hair. She
could feel his heat . . . could smell the pressed fabric of his
shirt mingling with his own scent . . . slightly sweet and absolutely irresistible.

"It makes no difference, Caroline," he murmured. "None at
all. Unless you'd like to hear it anyway."

Saying no and pivoting on her heel to flee back to the
drawing room would save her countless hours of heartache
later. But oh, it was so tempting to know the turn of his
thoughts, which was why she could never ask him.

"I think that is an exceptionally bad idea, Mr. Cartwick.
And you should address me as *lady*."

A hint of a smile passed over the tempting, full shape of
his mouth, its presence fleeting and gone all too soon. "I'll
call you *lady* if you'll call me Jon."

Caroline viewed him in something close to astonishment,
heat spreading through every cell at the thought. "You know
I can't do that."

"We'll see," he replied. Then changing the subject, he inclined his head towards the end of the hallway. "Follow me."

He led her to the greenhouse, holding the door open as
she approached. The heated air struck her face as she entered, laden with moisture. Caroline inhaled deeply. It was
a place she was very familiar with, having spent many a fond
afternoon running along the narrow pathways as a child

under the smiling gazes of Nicholas and Isabelle Cartwick. Taking tea with Eliza and helping Rosa toddle between the bushy green plants and towering palms made up some of her more recent memories, and her heart throbbed at the recollection.

"It's strange to be in here again," she said, weaving between the rows of lilies, the air heavy with their aroma. Her gaze lifted hesitantly to find his. "I'd never thought to return after Eliza's departure."

Jonathan viewed her in silence before replying. "Did you not?"

Caroline shook her head and stepped past him, taking another breath. His enticing scent was more alluring by far than anything else in this shining glass room, and she took care to avoid him while surveying the selection of plants. They were strategically arranged, but there was a haphazard method that contributed to the garden's charming layout. Large spiky palms rose above them, tall and mighty, framed down below by a riotous collection of carefully cultivated flowers that she could not name. She trailed her fingertips over the dark waxen leaves of a shrub adorned with lovely white blooms tinged with pink.

"I'd like to thank you for hosting this gathering for Frances," she said softly, still avoiding his gaze. "And for accommodating us with the unconventional hour."

"You are most welcome," he answered with an incline of his head. "I would not wish to tax your aunt's endurance during the evening." His eyes slid over the emerald silk of her dress, and she felt her cheeks warm in response. "I have to say that all seems well with her so far. And while I appreciate the daring of your dress and coiffure, I am a little confused as to why she would choose it since . . . well, since—"

"Since she is not actively experiencing an episode?" finished Caroline, meeting his eyes finally. "That is a good question, and one I asked myself as we rode over in the carriage. Also, I'm not certain this style truly constitutes a *coiffure*."

Her embarrassment rising, she swept the loose hair over her shoulder in an effort to contain what felt like an intolerable mess. Too late did she realize that by doing so, she had exposed the naked length of her back to view, the bold cut of her dress further illustrating the strangeness of Frances's choice. Caroline threw her hair back down to conceal her mistake, but not before noticing how his topaz eyes had widened at the sight. He glanced away.

"Surely, you could have refused her requests, had you wished to do so?"

Caroline leaned down to inhale the scent of the flower, trying desperately to act normal. "I could have, I suppose. But she has so very little control of her life now. If seeing me in an outrageous dress with wild hair—or in a ludicrous bonnet, for that matter—gives her any comfort at all, why would I not acquiesce? Besides," she added, throwing a deliberate look over her shoulder, "it's not as if I am trying to impress anyone."

Lies, lies, lies. Regardless of whether she wished to impress him or not, there was a stubborn part of her that hoped she did. But the dimple that appeared in his cheek told her he could have already deduced the truth of things.

"No?"

She laughed weakly. "Be serious."

He reached in front of her to pluck a pale pink bloom from the plant she'd been admiring, his solid chest grazing her shoulder as he did. Caroline felt the room tilt when his arms raised up to tuck the stem into one of the braids at the crown of her head.

"As you know by now, I am always serious," he said in a husky tone that triggered a rolling wave of delight throughout her body. "And I think this camellia would suit you well. It is a variety called 'Lady Hume's Blush.'"

As if summoned by the words, Caroline's face grew warm. She looked away, but not before Jonathan lowered his hand, allowing his fingers to graze her cheek.

"I-I thank you," she forced out. "It's lovely."

Cartwick's eyes dipped briefly to her lips, venturing down her shoulders, continuing over the front of her green bodice and layered skirts. When he met her gaze again, she saw his color had heightened too.

"Yes," he said in a rusty sounding voice. "Lovely."

Caroline's lips parted in astonishment, and perhaps sensing that he had shocked her, he cleared his throat and turned the other way, leaving her to trail numbly behind him.

"I have arranged a meeting with my land agent," he mentioned, almost offhandedly, over his shoulder. "But before

I see him, I have some questions for both you and Lady Frances. Perhaps we can put this matter of fence lines and boundaries to rest once and for all."

She let out a tiny groan. "Why not just dig up the fence and be done with it? Surely that will be the end result anyway."

Now it was his turn to be surprised, and he stopped to pivot suddenly in front of her.

"I'm certain I have no idea what the result will be." His brow furrowed in thought. "May I ask why, after all your letters and arguments, you have suddenly chosen to give up?"

She felt her mouth twist into a grimace. "I think I am simply tired of fighting."

The truth she could not bring herself to confess was that he'd not turned out to be the heartless monster she'd believed him to be. The thought of losing Windham Hill to a cruel and reckless American had been intolerable, but the reality of the Cartwick heir was profoundly more disturbing. He was intelligent and thoughtful in ways she'd never thought to expect from a man—and she was being forced to accept that she may have fallen for him, at the likely expense of her friendship with Eliza.

The knowledge placed a strain on her already weary heart.

"Really?" he asked.

"Yes. Don't tell me that comes as a surprise."

His boots sounded on the stone pathway as he approached and she felt every muscle tighten in anticipation. "But I am surprised. This is not what I've come to expect from you."

The distant melody of the orchestra floated into the greenhouse. She had not heard it upon first entering, and wondered if perhaps the musicians had been asked to play louder in an attempt to lure her and Jonathan back to the party.

"I see you are still quite free with your opinions, Mr. Cartwick, even to a lady."

He pursed his lips in thought, which had the decidedly distracting effect of bringing her attention to his mouth. "I'm not usually," he admitted. "but I'm also not used to British sensibilities. American ladies are—in my own experience—a different breed of woman."

She bristled, a prickle of jealousy making itself known. "A better breed of woman?"

Instantly, she regretted saying it. Her heart started to hammer as he took another step, closing any remaining distance between them.

"That's not even close to what I said. Why do you ask?"

Her foot slipped off the pathway and she stumbled slightly, realizing she'd been backing away. "I may have heard that you were once engaged," she confessed sheepishly, her eyes darting about the room to avoid the fiery inquiry of his gaze. "To an American woman."

Jonathan's body went rigid in surprise, then he let out a sigh and his eyes fell closed. Reaching up, he pinched the bridge of his nose as if to stave off a sudden headache.

"Dear God, why would she tell you that?" he muttered.

"I'm sorry. I shouldn't have mentioned it."

His hand fell away and he stared at her for a long moment. Finally, he shrugged. "I just . . . don't like to talk about it. It's not important."

"It sounds more important than whatever I had with Lord Braxton," she said, her voice barely above a whisper.

Cartwick shook his head. "My relationship didn't play itself out in front of every rumormonger in London. It's not the same situation at all."

An intoxicating warmth expanded inside her chest at his acknowledgment. In that moment, Caroline wanted nothing more than to wrap her arms around his torso and squeeze tightly. Hold him until the pain they both felt ebbed gradually away, leaving a light-filled space for something better. Something more.

Something impossible.

Her stomach felt hollow. "If you have found me to be more insufferable than—"

"I've never compared you to her," he interrupted. "If I have found you insufferable, it's been on your merit alone."

Caroline laughed shakily. "I'm not certain if you are paying me a compliment, or chiding me for being misbehaved. Either way, we should rejoin the party before—" Glancing behind him, she broke off her words, her brows lowering into a frown. "Did you remove the pineapple plants?"

"I—" He swiveled to follow the direction of her perturbed gaze. "Well, yes."

Caroline regarded him in horror. "But think of your guests. Many would be eager to sample such an exotic offering."

"I was under the impression that they were used for display purposes, but were otherwise rather useless," he answered slowly. "I can't say I've ever actually tried one before."

"Useless?" Her lips pursed forwards in a barely subdued pout. "Not at all. Pineapples are delicious."

"You are fond of them?"

"Very much so," she replied, walking to the corner where a selection of the spiky plants had once been, only to let out a surprised gasp at the shallow pond that had been put in its place. The water shimmered its way between an intricately arranged rockery, while tiny orange-and-white fish scattered into the depths at her approach, seeking refuge beneath the shelter of jade green lily pads. "Oh—"

A delightful wooden bench had been thoughtfully placed just to the side of the little pond, and Caroline thought it looked like the perfect place to sink down and gather one's thoughts, or to perhaps read a favorite book with a steaming cup of tea. Jonathan came to stand behind her. She stared at the scene in wonder.

"And are you fond of this?"

"Yes," she breathed, the pineapple plants all but forgotten.

"Not as delicious as a pineapple, perhaps. But charming in its own way," he teased.

His eyes caught hers and the music echoed lightly through their surroundings, loud enough to distinguish from any other ambient noise but still understated. It provided a dreamy musical landscape one would not find in a ballroom. Her breath quickened when Cartwick extended his hand, much like he had earlier.

"Perhaps now, away from the others, you will allow me the honor of a dance." The softness of his voice couldn't quite disguise the hint of hope beneath it.

She opened her mouth to tell him *no* as she knew she should, then gave up trying to pretend—at least for a little while. She slipped her fingers inside his instead, the squeeze of his hand warm and thrilling.

Jonathan led her farther onto the stone pathway to a small clearing, his other hand lowering to press against her back. "Shall we . . ."

The thought remained unfinished. The length of his fingers brushed against her bare skin due to the low cut of the back of her dress, and they both froze at the unexpected sensation of contact. His hand jerked but did not raise from its position.

"Forgive me, I—"

Had she been offended at the impropriety of his touch, she might have demanded that he remove his hand. But she hadn't been thinking that at all. Instead she'd thought about how intimate it was to feel the glide of his fingers upon the exposed length of her back, and almost as if reading her thoughts, he flattened his palm against her skin again.

How lovely it would be to just allow it . . . to let her eyes fall closed as he touched her in whatever way he wished . . . to rise up on her toes, body leaning into his, so they could kiss just one more time . . .

Jonathan's breathing halted. Illicit hope raced through her as the heat from his fingers sank into her back, holding their position low against her spine in an unflinching declaration.

Surely you know there is no endgame here.

Oh, she knew. The words he'd spoken to her that day

in his study had never been truer. And while it should have brought her a measure of comfort, especially with Eliza and Evanston arriving within days, she found the thought of losing that closeness with Cartwick to be troubling.

Before she could think of a way to respond, his hand shifted to a much safer position on her waist and he moved her around in preparation to begin. The music could barely be discerned but he counted them in regardless, leading her into the swooping steps of the waltz with gentle restraint. Shortened steps were necessary within the tight confines of the garden and was an adjustment that he easily made, and his capable lead stirred the butterflies inside her stomach to flight. For once, she permitted herself to enjoy the feeling, eyes drifting closed in wonder. He leaned closer, his breath tickling her neck in the most inappropriate way.

"Beautiful," he whispered. "Intelligent. Capable. Lovely." His lips brushed against the ridge of her ear. "Overwhelming."

Her eyelids flew open. She'd earned the words he'd promised her earlier; the words he would use to describe her.

Shock paralyzed her expression, but he did not intrude on her moment. He merely pulled back and continued their dance. And suddenly she wished that he would never let her go.

But they had started late, and all too soon the song was finished. Her heart ached when the last strains were heard, the sound subdued through the greenhouse door, and when she stepped away he immediately pulled her closer. She made a tiny noise of surprise as she bumped softly against his chest.

"Lady Caroline, thank you for this dance."

A sad smile tugged downwards at the corner of his mouth, and she knew he was speaking of much more than sharing a waltz in the greenhouse. And rather than raging against the unfairness of it all, Caroline turned her head against his shoulder in an unspoken gesture of mourning, the veil of her hair concealing the traitorous rise of tears that pricked at her eyes.

CHAPTER FIFTEEN

Caroline squeezed her aunt's hand as Eliza's carriage pulled forwards on the drive. The previous evening had not gone smoothly for Frances. But even with the setback, Beatrice and Caroline had calmed her sufficiently enough to lie down, while Minnie had fetched her aunt a steaming cup of tea. Once the worst of it had passed and Frances had settled in beneath her blankets, the women had shooed Caroline off to her own bed.

It was gratifying to see the compassion with which the women treated her aunt, and when Caroline had finally crept off to her room, she'd seen Frances relaxed, with eyes closed peacefully and mouth softened, lost to the respite of sleep. Soon she'd found herself asleep too—her own exhaustion taking over—and when Meggie had tugged the curtains aside the next morning, she'd felt refreshed in a way she had not for months.

The thinned ranks at Willowford House stood silently in line, ready to greet their arriving guests, and she cast a quick glance at Cartwick's servants, standing among the others. Their presence there was more than reassuring—it was a relief. Although the persistent whisper of conscience reminded her who was ultimately responsible for providing them and lightening her burden.

How had Eliza taken the news of Cartwick's assistance? There had not been a reply so there was no real way of telling. She supposed if her friend were *very* displeased, she would not be arriving here today, and decided to take comfort in that thought since she desperately needed comfort anyway. The trembling that shook her entire frame was not due to the temperature.

The carriage door snapped open and roused Caroline from her melancholy reflections. A cloud-filtered ray of sunlight slid off the ebony hair of Lord Evanston a moment before he glanced up, viewing her with eyes that were impossibly blue before stepping down to extend a hand to the lady who still waited to descend. Within moments, Eliza was on the ground and rushing to wrap Caroline in her arms.

"Sweetest Caroline," she whispered. Eliza gave her a last squeeze before pushing away to arm's length so she could evaluate her. "You look well! I am so pleased to see it."

Caroline let out a breathless laugh. "As do you," she answered, feeling more than a little bit giddy at the warm reception. "I've missed you unbearably these past few months."

With a cheerful glance that promised more conversation to come, Eliza turned her attention to Frances, pulling her close to plant a kiss on both cheeks. Her aunt's eyes fell closed at the embrace, a smile rising to her lips.

"And Lady Frances—"

"Lady *Evanston*," Frances replied with a raised eyebrow, looking past Eliza's bonnet to spy her husband, who tipped her a wink. The older woman laughed, almost girlishly. "Congratulations again on marrying that exceedingly handsome man."

Eliza glanced over her shoulder at the man in question. A happy smile tugged at her lips. "I think I'll keep him," she replied, eyeing him appraisingly.

Thomas stepped closer to place his hands over Eliza's shoulders. "What's this I hear about a handsome man?" he asked in a feigned show of ignorance.

"Don't get too excited," Caroline replied dryly. "You know Lady Frances has always gone aflutter in your presence."

Her aunt grinned and motioned for the footmen to come unload the trunks from the carriage.

"Indeed," she agreed. "But you should know there is a bit of competition here in our little corner of the country."

Caroline froze, the smile dropping from her lips. Cartwick would be the only attractive man Frances could be referring to.

She's going to tell them about Jonathan before we've even made it inside the house.

Evanston's brows raised in good-natured challenge at the same moment that the icy impetus of dread prompted Caroline to lunge forwards.

"Did Rosa choose to stay in Kent?" she asked, perhaps more loudly than she had intended.

Eliza chuckled in reply, but not before casting the tiniest glance in Thomas's direction. "Why, yes. There was no way to tear her away from Clara. She gets such satisfaction from being of use to her pregnant aunt."

Caroline began walking up the front steps, the rest of the group falling into step behind. "Does she enjoy fetching her slippers? Or bringing the newspaper?"

"It's probably more along the lines of tea and baked treats, but yes that's close. Clara always finds useful tasks that Rosa will enjoy too," Eliza added with a fond smile.

Thankful for the safer shift in conversation, Caroline looked over at Thomas. "And William?"

"Another handsome man . . ." Frances muttered under her breath.

Thomas shook his head with a grin. "Well I've never seen *that* man so excited in all my life. And I daresay Rosa is educating him in the ways of fatherhood as we speak."

"She can be rather high-spirited sometimes," said Caroline with a laugh. "But I am sure William is more than capable of meeting the challenge."

Their footsteps echoed in the spaciousness of the foyer and the air, fresh with an undertone of new leaves and emerging flowers from the mild spring day, swirled around them as they entered the house. Lord Evanston turned at the foot of the stairs to regard the women with smiling eyes, reaching a hand out to his wife.

"Shall we get settled, my love?"

Eliza smiled, and a hint of color passed over her cheeks as

she reached out to clasp his hand in return, her feet staying firmly planted where they were.

"I'd like to speak with Caroline before joining you, my lord."

Bending his sleek black head over her hand, the viscount placed a soft kiss upon her knuckles then straightened to regard his wife. "As you wish," he replied amiably, performing a polite bow to the group before vaulting up the stairs. But his sultry parting glance at Eliza nearly caused Caroline to blush as well.

Now there was no doubt what would be waiting for her friend in their chamber when she was finished downstairs, and Caroline couldn't help feeling a swift pang of remorse. Not because Evanston loved Eliza . . . nothing could have pleased her more. But because Caroline had become increasingly convinced that she would never experience such a fulfilling relationship with a man. Especially now.

That blaze of passion in Evanston's eyes when he sought Eliza? She'd seen that same fire lurking behind Jonathan's gaze more than once. The joy had seeped out of every day that had passed since the party at Greystone Hall, each moment a little bleaker than the last. And although her conscience had quieted considerably since their final meeting, her lonely heart had only increased its volume. Now it spoke loudly . . . achingly . . . painfully.

"Well!" exclaimed Lady Frances, "I do believe I'll let you two catch up. Perhaps I will work on my needlework . . . in the library this time. Why don't we all meet in the drawing

room in an hour?" She threw a mischievous glance at Eliza. "I
do hope that will allow you enough time to settle in."

Caroline clapped a hand over her mouth to keep from
laughing, and didn't miss how Eliza's eyes had grown bright
with her own efforts. "Thank you, Auntie," she said. "We won't
keep you waiting for tea."

Frances nodded to Minnie and Beatrice who came forwards with polite curtsies. She smiled at Eliza, placed an
affectionate kiss upon Caroline's cheek, then made her way
towards the rear of the house. The two women watched in
quiet solemnity, and when the last servant had disappeared
around the corner, Eliza turned to her.

"Lady Frances seems well today," she said with a chuckle.
"I see her powers of observation remain intact."

"Oh yes, she is still highly perceptive. Last night was difficult for her, however. She is acting better now than I might
have expected."

Eliza's brow furrowed, and her eyes filled with concern.
"I am sorry to hear that." A slight pause. "And are those the
Cartwick servants you spoke of in your letter?"

Caroline knew the question had been coming, but still
felt herself begin to sweat beneath the layers of her dress.
"Yes. Minnie and Beatrice are with us for the time being,"
she replied, working to keep the nervous tremor from her
voice.

"That seems . . . rather kind."

She shrugged, unwilling to let on how kind it truly was.
"I suppose so. But after what Mr. Cartwick witnessed, with
Frances wandering outside in little more than her night-

clothes, it would have perhaps been more ungentlemanly for him to do nothing."

Eliza's peridot eyes grew huge. "Caroline . . ."

Shaking her head, Caroline turned away and began walking to the drawing room. "It hasn't been easy—for me, for Meggie and least of all for Frances. She made it out to the meadows that day."

"*To the meadows?*" Eliza asked, incredulous, walking beside her. "How on earth was she found? And how did Mr. Cartwick bear witness to such an event?"

"I, well . . . he was with me. I mean—we met by chance at Windham Hill." The words tumbled clumsily from her lips. "I had walked there by myself and discovered both Cartwick and his land agent. It was quite by accident. We both rushed to the meadows when I spotted Frances."

"By foot?" Eliza asked, the amazement creeping back into her voice.

Caroline felt a bead of sweat finally give way to roll down her back. "Not exactly," she confessed. "He allowed me the use of his horse."

"So he joined you later by foot?"

"Well, no. He was, er, on the horse too."

Realization dawned on Eliza's face and she stopped in the middle of the hallway. Caroline stopped too, dreading her friend's reaction to what she'd just said . . . which was why she was utterly confounded when Eliza burst out laughing.

"Caroline, for goodness' sake. You're acting ashamed, but it's not as if you kissed the man," she teased gently.

She couldn't even make a reply, but felt the telltale warmth of mortification spreading across her chest, up her neck, to suffuse her cheeks with obvious color.

But oh, I've done much more than kiss him.

"I—"

Shaking her head, Eliza linked an arm through Caroline's and resumed walking. "You were a lady in need. Frances was a lady in need. It sounds like he was actually being a gentleman, despite his contention over the property lines."

"Property lines that are still the subject of vigorous debate," Caroline replied, thankful to shift the topic away from such a revealing turn of events. "Nothing can be resolved until he has met with Father, of course, and that is a conversation I won't be a part of so all of my bluster is useless."

Eliza's head swiveled to stare at her. "Did Cartwick actually *say* that to you?"

"No," she admitted. But he had said other things to her since that first time they'd met.

On both sides of the ocean, I've never seen a woman as beautiful as you.

Panic seized in her chest. Within those thoughts lay danger.

"Well obviously he has some rough edges," Eliza said slowly, "but that was to be expected given the circumstances of the entailment. I have to wonder, though, at his readiness to help with Frances. Do you think he can be trusted not to speak of her condition?"

She was certain he could, but took care not to seem so sure. "Only time will tell."

The pair of them entered the drawing room, a shaft of

sunlight streaming in through the windows to gleam across her friend's golden curls, artfully pinned into place.

"What about other family in the house? Can they be trusted?" asked Eliza. "Is there a brother, a mother, a wife . . ."

"He is a bachelor. But his mother did accompany him from America." Glancing down, she toyed with the row of tiny ribbons that decorated the front of her bodice. "Apparently she plans on returning once Jonathan is settled. His younger brother has taken over the shipbuilding business in New England."

Eliza released her arm to close the doors behind them with a soft *click* before regarding her with a curious stare.

"Jonathan?"

Caroline spun around, then froze.

She'd actually uttered his given name to Eliza. Casually. As if she and the Cartwick heir—the same man who had ejected Eliza and Rosa from Greystone Hall—were the closest of friends. Or perhaps even lovers . . .

Squeezing her eyes shut, an awkward laugh escaped her lips before she could prevent it. "My goodness, what was I thinking? I'm surprised I even remembered his first name at all."

Eliza's neutral expression gave nothing away. "An innocent enough mistake."

But it wasn't and Caroline knew it. She was certain Eliza knew it too, but thankfully her friend did not belabor the point.

"Well if he can be trusted to stay silent, we can only hope his mother follows suit. And what of Meggie?" Eliza inquired, coming closer to Caroline. "How has she been holding up through all of this?"

"Meggie is doing well. She still helps with Frances on occasion, but she's returned belowstairs now for the most part." Caroline sighed. "It's a relief she was willing to stay on at all. These past few months have not been easy for her."

"It doesn't sound as if they've been easy for anyone, really," Eliza replied, pulling her in for a tight hug.

Tears threatened, stinging her eyes, and Caroline blinked furiously to dispel them.

"It really hasn't," she said with a scowl. "I couldn't even arrange an increase in pay for Meggie's trouble without approval from my parents. They were impossible to reach, as they always are."

Eliza scoffed and pulled back to view her in sympathy. "Soon, your complaint will be very much the opposite. When do they arrive?"

"Within the next few days. The servants have been working themselves to the bone preparing the house."

"They must have been enraged when you refused to go to London," Eliza said with a quirk of her eyebrows. "I can't imagine anything but fury motivating them to rush back to Hampshire on such short notice."

"Oh, they were. Enough that they interrupted their happy life just so they could force the issue in person." She grinned, unable to help it. "I won't deny that I take great satisfaction in inconveniencing them. And I plan to annoy them a good deal more once they arrive."

"Take care, friend," Eliza warned, "I wouldn't harass

them overmuch or you might end up married to some tooth-
less old baron who smells like fish."

Caroline wrinkled her nose. "Oh, I know of the risks. But
I could probably manage to accept such a husband as long as
he ignores me most of the time, which he probably would. I
also know that it's useless to worry about who they pair me
up with. I won't have a choice when the time comes."

"You really believe that?" Eliza asked sadly.

She shrugged. "I really do . . . but no matter. I'll happily
annoy them all. What other joy will I have left at that point?"

"Is there a man who might meet their requirements
and please you too? Have you met anyone since our time in
London?"

Caroline's lungs spasmed in agony at the question.

Jonathan was off-limits in more ways than one, but as
luck would have it, was the only man she wanted. Shaking
her head, she averted her eyes.

"No."

Eliza crossed to the sideboard to lift a glittering crystal
decanter, the caramel-colored liquor catching the light from
the windows. Removing the stopper, she leaned her nose
over the container and sniffed experimentally. "No one?"
she asked, tugging over two glasses with her free hand.
"Not even the man Lady Frances seemed to think was so
very handsome?"

Caroline winced. Privately, she wished Lady Frances
hadn't been so quick to sing his praises to her friends. She
needed to convince them that nothing existed between her
and Cartwick. That would be a great deal more difficult if

Frances could not keep her mouth closed when it came to their troublesome neighbor.

"I'm not sure who she was talking about, exactly," she replied, sinking down into her seat, taking a moment to arrange her skirts deliberately across the golden velvet settee. "I've started to think that perhaps she is not as selective as she once was."

Eliza's brows shot up as the liquor flowed into the tumblers. "I've never known your aunt's tastes to be anything but precise . . . especially when it comes to attractive men," she added with a snicker.

Caroline laughed too, but hers was a weak and uneasy attempt at sounding normal. "A lot has changed in the past few months, Eliza," she said, joining her friend at the sideboard with an amused smile. "Have you adopted a drinking habit?" she teased. "Perhaps Lord Evanston really has been a bad influence on you."

"Oh, he has," Eliza answered, waggling her eyebrows comically. "But I figured you could probably use this." She extended a glass in her direction.

"Why?" asked Caroline warily, accepting the offering.

Her friend clinked her glass against Caroline's and raised it up in a mock toast. "Because if you are truly at the mercy of your parents, something tells me this is going to get worse for you before it gets better. But you need to know that Thomas and I will be here . . . and we will defend you to your parents, and to American neighbors, if need be." Tipping her glass back, she took a long swallow of the amber liquid.

Caroline glanced away. Sadness and guilt warred relentlessly within her.

"Thank you," she whispered.

"Don't be silly . . . thanks are never necessary. Now drink up," Eliza demanded with a grin. "In case you've forgotten, I've got a viscount waiting for me upstairs."

"Yes, right over here will do. I need room for five clay pots."

Jonathan hooked his fingers beneath the large stone planter, and with a grunt, he and his head gardener moved it to the side of the pathway. The man shook his head and eyed Cartwick in befuddlement.

"For pineapples?"

"That's right," Cartwick answered, brushing a sweaty lock of hair away from his forehead. Too late, he decided to strip off his jacket and drape it over a nearby bench. His shirt was already damp and clinging to his back.

"The pineapples we just removed?"

"Yes," he replied with some effort, dragging another container out of the way while his gardener viewed him skeptically.

"I thought you said they were ugly plants that served no purpose."

Cartwick thought he could detect some lingering resentment. After all, the man had argued against their removal quite vehemently. Tossing his head back, Jonathan shot him a humorous scowl as best he could manage, hunched over as he was.

"I'm starting to wonder what purpose you serve, Campbell," he said, his breathing labored now with another heave of a large pot. "Now stop talking and help me make room—"

A brilliant square of light danced across the greenhouse as the door opened, and he raised a hand to shade his eyes, blinking into the reflected morning sun. His mother's pale face stared back, and he released the pot to stand upright.

"Is something wrong?"

Dorothea's hands were clenched tightly together and she turned to look behind her before responding, almost as if she was worried they would be overheard. "Not exactly. We have a visitor, dear."

A tremor of excitement raced through him and he cleared his throat. "Do we?" he asked. "Who is it?"

"Well that's the thing I don't quite understand," she said, the dark wings of her brow lowering in confusion. "It's Baroness Hedridge."

The thrill he'd experienced just a moment before transformed into a cool rush of displeasure—something not easily achieved in the steamy warmth of the greenhouse. He frowned, slapping his trousers to free the dust from his hands, then reached over to retrieve the jacket he'd just discarded.

"Baroness Hedridge?" he murmured, shaking his head. "Why would she be calling?"

His mother frowned dismally. "That's a good question. I suppose I shall have to find out."

"No. I wouldn't force you to endure such a trial on your own. Let us go and meet her together."

After shrugging on his jacket, he and Dorothea entered the parlor to greet their unexpected guest who—to his consternation—viewed him in poorly concealed delight. He could only speculate as to why she might take such joy in seeing him here today. The knowledge that Lady Hedridge gossiped at Caroline's expense rankled him greatly. Still, it would do no good to pick an argument with the woman now, especially since he believed she probably possessed information he might find important.

"My lady," he said with a bow, choking on the deference required. "I must admit to being surprised by your visit—"

"Pleasantly, of course," supplied his conscientious mother.

He smiled thinly. "Of course."

"Would you care for some tea?"

The blue eyes of the baroness bounced back and forth between them, growing brighter in her amusement. "Why yes," she replied in a too-cultured voice, sinking down onto the couch amidst the surrounding puff of her mustard-yellow skirts. "I would love to stay for tea."

His mother rang for tea while Jonathan clenched his teeth in an effort to keep from groaning out loud. The notion of entertaining this woman for any longer than absolutely necessary needled at his already frayed nerves, but he came to stand near the mantel with an expression of absolute politeness.

"What can we do for you, my lady?" asked Dorothea, seating herself in a chair. The question prompted the baroness to sigh in a show of faux distress.

"My goodness, thank you for asking. I actually just came

by to bend your ear about a recent development with an acquaintance of yours." Her glance shifted over to catch Jonathan's from beneath the dark fringe of her lashes. "Although I suppose Mr. Cartwick may also be interested?"

His insides clenched in anticipation. All he could do was pray that news of Frances's illness had not been made public . . . for both her and for Caroline's sake.

He shrugged and laced his fingers together before him. "I suppose we'll know in a moment."

Taking his comment as encouragement, she leaned forwards on the couch, the fullness of her skirts rustling with the motion.

"Well," she said, lowering her voice conspiratorially, "it seems the Duke of Pemberton has taken the matter of his daughter's marriage into his own hands by enlisting the help of a certain personage and her connections." She smiled in false modesty and cast her eyes to the ceiling. "And I've succeeded in putting together a list of three titled suitors who would serve quite well. They have been invited to a special dinner with the duke."

Dorothea's mouth actually fell open, while Jonathan somehow managed to retain what he hoped was a neutral facade. She was the first to speak.

"I'm not certain why you would think we'd be interested—"

"Wouldn't the duke's daughter be the best judge of which suitors would *serve quite well*?" he interrupted with an edge to his voice that he couldn't quite disguise.

The lady's smile widened and she surveyed their reactions with wolfish eagerness. "She has been afforded multiple opportunities to select a husband over the past few years, and at considerable expense to her parents. But each time she has behaved rather unpredictably, even going so far as to swear off marriage altogether." She clucked her tongue in censure.

"And why exactly is your help required in such a personal matter?" he asked with a scowl. "Didn't Lady Caroline endure enough hardship during last year's season?"

Blast. That final sentence would surely reveal his allegiance, were Lady Hedridge perceptive enough to see it. And she was. He saw the way her eyes had narrowed briefly in that moment. He'd also seen the way his mother's eyes had flashed over to him in warning.

"Oh, she did," said the baroness, nodding solemnly. "One could hardly blame her for not wishing to return to London again this year. Still . . . the girl must marry. And since she refuses to make the choice for herself—"

"The girl . . ." Jonathan stared down at the floor, contemplating the amount of disrespect contained in that single phrase. "Is she not the daughter of a duke?"

"The tea is here," his mother declared in relief, pushing up from her seat to meet the butler as he wheeled in the cart. "That's fine, Shaw, I have it from here. Do you take sugar, my lady? Cream?"

The butler departed and Dorothea busied herself asking questions and pouring tea, doing her best to keep tensions from boiling over. Oddly, Lady Hedridge was not offended after his terse correction of her. Instead, she stared at him with something like fascination. It was almost as if he was an exotic specimen she'd spied in the depths of an aquarium tank.

You know better. Keep your mouth shut around this woman.

In an effort to do just that, he crossed his arms and strode casually over to the windows, pretending to gaze outside. It wasn't proper behavior when receiving a guest, he knew, but it was preferable to what he wished he could do. Kicking her out of his house, for starters.

"So," his mother said, lowering cautiously back down into her chair, "these men will be attending a dinner . . . by special invitation?"

Jonathan could hear Lady Hedridge stirring her tea, the spoon making numerous noisy revolutions around her china cup before finally clinking to a rest on the saucer. "Yes. The three men will be summoned by very special invitation. I have already ascertained their—in some cases, *reluctant*—willingness to acquiesce to the match. But each man sees the obvious benefit in aligning with the Duke of Pemberton, even if his daughter would not be what most men would consider an ideal wife."

His back was still turned but he sensed this woman took great satisfaction at seeing Caroline brought so low, and she was desperately trying to elicit some kind of reaction from him. At the sound of the baroness slurping her tea in what had to be a subversive attempt to annoy the holy hell out of him, Jonathan decided he'd finally heard enough.

"It appears you were wrong, my lady," he said, abruptly turning from the windows and crossing over to the door. "I don't find this conversation diverting in the slightest. Allow me to leave so you two may continue your discussion in peace."

He issued a perfunctory bow in her direction then tossed a sideways glance of apology at his mother, who nodded in both understanding and gratitude. Even if Dorothea had not been aware of his feelings for Lady Caroline—which he was almost certain she was—she knew better than to argue if he felt the sudden need to excuse himself.

In this case, it might be the only thing keeping him from throttling the snake in the mustard-yellow dress whose eyes were following him with nauseating glee.

Chapter Sixteen

A knock at the study door roused Jonathan from his ledgers and he glanced up, thankful for the interruption. The past few days had been nothing but an endless chain of headaches and no manner of distraction, exciting or dull, could assuage the uneasiness Lady Hedridge's visit had produced.

"Enter," he called, rubbing a palm restlessly across the back of his neck.

The door opened to reveal his butler, Shaw, a shining salver in his hand. "Pardon the interruption, sir." He came closer and with a polite incline of his head, extended the tray in his direction. "You have a letter from America."

Jonathan's eyebrows raised, and the dull pounding at his temples lessened by an infinitesimal degree. "Do I?"

Retrieving the envelope, he excused Shaw with a brisk nod. Once the door had closed, he sighed and leaned back in his chair, turning over the letter and leaning his elbows upon the polished wooden surface.

Smiling fondly at the familiar handwriting on the envelope, he tore into the worn and battered parchment that had traveled to him all the way across the Atlantic. He raised the leaves up into the golden afternoon light.

Jonathan,

I hope this letter finds both you and Mother well and increasingly at home in your new English estate. It is still difficult to believe that you agreed to all of it—any of it, really—and yet I am surrounded by mounting evidence of your absence each day. Perhaps you will find the chance to voyage back to America, if for no other reason than to share a pint with your brother on occasion.

At any rate, the shipyard is much as you left it. This is due in large part to your fastidious preparations, but I like to think that I've done a worthy job of keeping things running smoothly. Graham is still as bullheaded as ever and quick to temper, but he knows how to talk to the builders and I appreciate his passion for the job, even if we don't always see eye to eye.

Contracts are up and business is good. The only thing missing is you. Father would have been proud to see the shipyard continuing on, and he would have been prouder still that you set out to carve your own way in life, even if you had to return to England to do it.

Speaking of, I can only imagine how it must irk you to

deal with all of those highfalutin society types, especially that one who was such an irritation from the start. Lady Caroline, the spinster daughter of a duke . . . and it's no wonder she hasn't married if her initial letters are to be believed. It sounds as if you put her neatly in her place, and I look forwards to hearing about your meeting with the duke. It should nearly be happening by the time you receive this.

I debated whether or not to tell you, but Letitia visited the shipyard last week. She had a ring on her finger but, of course, we'd been expecting that. Although for as happy as she professed to be, she was equally perplexed at finding me in your place, and I've never seen someone so shocked as she was when I informed her you now lived halfway around the world. It seems she would have much preferred to rub your nose in her deceit at close range. I am glad you did not give her the chance.

In conclusion, I am well. Damned busy, but otherwise good. I would ask about Mother, but something tells me she is enjoying this little adventure of yours. Her cheerful attitude is an example for us all, but don't tell her I said that. She might start expecting more of me.

　　　Fond regards,
　　　James

Jonathan ran a finger contemplatively across his lips, then set the letter aside and buried his fingers into his hair. The news of Letitia's marriage did not bother him, as her initial betrayal had effectively neutralized any of his softer feelings for her. He couldn't deny the whole sordid affair still smarted, but it was mainly due to pride.

And now that he thought about it, what *really* bothered him was that his brother believed Jonathan had accepted the entailed estate as a means of escaping his faithless bride-to-be. In actuality, his own reasons for leaving America had not been obvious, even to him. Not at first. But it was a truth that was becoming increasingly clear, like when you squinted to see the landscape once the morning fog had lifted.

He was here to reclaim his family's rightful place in the world. And now through his father's initiative and hard work, their branch of the Cartwick family had two rightful seats, an ocean apart.

Shoving his chair away from his desk, he stood and crossed to the window. This was the truth, but something had been noticeably wrong since the last time he'd ridden away from Willowford House. Since saying good-bye to Caroline one final time. His happiness had now become indelibly tied to her. It was the only logical explanation for why he felt as if he'd left half of his heart behind that day. Not in America with the faithless Letitia, but here in Hampshire with the surprising, beautiful and vexing Lady Caroline.

A sheen of perspiration prickled across his forehead, and he lowered himself onto the soft leather couch at the far end of his study. Right this minute, Lord and Lady Evanston were guests in her home, likely poisoning her against him, undoing hard-won familiarity and shared affection. He was the one to blame for Eliza's removal from Greystone Hall.

And yet if he hadn't ventured to England at all, he and Caroline would never have met, and he would not be yearning for her now.

His eyes wandered over to the door where he had kissed the duke's daughter, and Jonathan's body came alive in remembrance. It didn't seem possible that the highborn woman he'd once viewed as a nuisance could so thoroughly haunt his thoughts, yet here he was, grasping after that lingering apparition.

Had he ever truly loved Letitia? He'd thought so until he'd fallen in love with Caroline.

Jonathan sighed before propelling himself off the couch and to the door. He threw it open and stopped in place at the sight of his butler standing there with a silver tray, knuckles raised in the air. Light blue eyes regarded him in surprise.

"I beg your pardon, sir, but it appears this was somehow mixed in with the rest of the house correspondence. My apologies for the delay."

The man bowed over the salver and Cartwick smiled, bemused. "The delay was negligible, Shaw. It couldn't have been more than a few minutes." Jonathan plucked the folded parchment off the tray, his movements slowing at the decorative script on the front. "I appreciate your diligence, though," he added absently, turning to close the door behind him.

It was a missive from Willowford House.

He slid his finger beneath the wax seal to break it. And Jonathan's eyes widened as he scanned the pages, looking for evidence of some kind of mistake. His anxiety only increased when he could find none, for it appeared that—despite

having been at war with the man's daughter and being a shipbuilder to boot—he held in his hands an invitation to the
Duke of Pemberton's private dinner.

Caroline slid further down in her wingback chair and stared
sullenly at her father.

Upon his arrival, and after greeting the rest of the group
with a hastily sketched bow, he'd deftly gripped her by the
arm and hauled her up the front steps. Frances's face had
remained impassive during the spectacle, but she had followed them closely as they'd made their way into the house,
not stopping until they were all safely concealed within his
study. Likewise, Thomas and Eliza had given her a serious
and supportive nod as she'd been ushered away, and she
knew that, for her sake, they would try to soften his temper
in the days that followed. But she also knew there was only
so much they could do or say in her defense. He was her
father, and he was the Duke of Pemberton.

He was much as she remembered him; still the same
stick-thin, upright sort of man from her childhood, even if
his black hair had now faded to white at the temples and
wrinkles framed his eyes at the corners. She imagined he'd
gained those creases by smiling. But there was no smile to be
found now as those eyes pinned her to her chair, thunderous
in their anger. Her mother, Eugenia, stood close at hand, her
own gray gaze filled with disappointment and reprobation.
Frances sat in the chair next to Caroline's with her hands
folded in her lap, docile and polite. There was comfort in

having her aunt there with her, but there was fear as well. She prayed Frances would not expose her own condition . . . not now, when Caroline was not in the best position to defend her. In their current rage at Caroline, they would give her words no weight at all.

"To think that my daughter would have the *gall* to defy me," he ranted. "How *dare* you refuse to return to London when I *expressly*—"

He spoke with emphasis, with at least one especially important word scattered in the midst of each sentence. She stared at him in taut recognition, but let the cadence of his lecture lull her into a sort of waking sleep. Speaking of gall, she wondered at his. Yes, of course she knew he provided for her—although it was from hundreds of miles away and came without the gift of familial affection. But being the Duke of Pemberton, the man was quite used to getting what he wanted without any resistance, even if it came from a willful daughter who did not appreciate being tucked away in the country to be forgotten.

There was a break in his cadence and she jerked herself into awareness, raising her eyes to meet his. It was a tactical mistake.

"What do you have to say for yourself?" he demanded, leaning forwards across his desk.

She cleared her throat and folded her hands upon her lap. "Father, it was not my intent to displease you. But I can hardly see how my marriage can be of much importance when you are so often away—"

"You question my authority in this?" he bellowed. Not for

the first time, she wondered how such a tall, yet slightly built man could be so surprisingly loud.

"I would never question your authority," Caroline replied quietly, hating how she could already feel herself shrinking under his scrutiny, noticing how suddenly small and less like herself she was. "I merely question whether or not marriage is absolutely necessary. I live a peaceable existence here with Aunt Frances, a respectable life—"

"There is no respect to be had as a spinster," he spat.

Caroline flinched and glanced sideways at her aunt, who either had not heard her brother's insult or had, in fact, heard it so many times before that she no longer felt its effect. Frances seemed more concerned about her, and Caroline gladly accepted the warm clasp of her wrinkled hand as she reached across the gap between their chairs to give her a reassuring squeeze.

She tipped her chin up at her father. "I disagree."

His expression was a stormy range of emotion, fury crossing his face with uneven and disconcerting tics. She didn't think she'd ever seen her father so angry, and while her parents had often wounded her by being absent, they had rarely resorted to such displays of emotion.

He shook his head bitterly. "Tell me then. What respect is there to be had in your existence? Stubborn child that you are."

Hot tears willed themselves to pour forth, but she fought them back. She thought of Nicholas and Isabelle Cartwick, neighbors who had treated her well. She thought of Frances, whose loving care and sound advice had carried Caroline through some of her darkest times. Even Dorothea Cartwick had shown her a maternal sort of kindness. And not one of them would have asked her to justify her own existence, even if they saw marriage as her best course of action.

Frances's voice cut through the tense silence, and her cloudy gaze was the clearest it had been in weeks. "Caroline tried her best in London. I was there."

"Oh?" Her mother had chosen to speak at last—the silent shade hovering near the bookshelf, her face gently twisted into a moue of disapproval. Her upswept hair shone in the light, as dark as the coffee Jonathan claimed to prefer over tea. "Then what of the rumors? How is it she came to leave London in the presence of a known rake, when she should have been nurturing the affections of Lord Braxton?"

Frances released Caroline's hand to sit up straighter in her seat. "Viscount Evanston accompanied both of us back to Hampshire at my request. I was not feeling . . . myself."

Caroline jerked in alarm.

No . . .

She would not have her aunt endanger her own situation merely to appease her parents. "Auntie took ill near the end of the season. Her stomach . . . all the rich food . . ." she blurted out. "Lord Evanston was kind enough to see us safely back home, and if the *ton* wishes to concoct their own version of events, we can hardly be held responsible." Caroline slid a look of reprimand in Frances's direction, willing her to stay quiet, then shuddered in relief at her tiny nod of acknowledgment.

The duke tilted his head. "Why did you not write of this, sister?"

"I have not written of a great many things these past few years, Alexander," she said defensively. "Perhaps I didn't think you would care for the details of my digestive difficulties."

"Point taken," he answered with a sigh. "However, I still think if Caroline had truly been committed to finding a husband, Lord Braxton would have continued his pursuit after her departure . . . not offer for the first pretty face in a ballroom."

There was a twinge of hurt at the remembrance of her humiliation, but no feelings of a stronger nature. It only caused her to think of Jonathan. Of how Caroline wished she could wrap herself around him and keep him from leaving her now.

But he's already gone, she thought bleakly.

"Please tell me how exactly you find me lacking, Father," she forced out. "Because if it is because I am a woman, I can assure you I had no choice in the matter."

"No, of course you didn't. And had your birth not been so very difficult, your mother might have been able to produce an heir," he said. Caroline supposed he held her accountable for this crime as well, but the duke continued before she could dwell for too long. "That doesn't change the fact that this dukedom will never pass to a child of mine. Instead, it will go to our distant cousin, Marcus in Sussex, an unworthy lad."

Caroline uttered a harsh laugh. It was only slightly gratifying to see that his tendency towards strict censure did not apply exclusively to her.

"Cousin Marcus is but two years old, is he not? It seems he could use a bit more time to establish his worth."

His eyes narrowed beneath the dark furrow of his brows while Caroline stared at him in silence. "Your mother and I

have discussed things at length. Even though Frances failed
in her duty to facilitate you finding a marriageable suitor—"

"Aunt Frances failed at nothing," she snapped, shooting up
from her seat to stare down at him for once. Her hands curled
tightly at her sides. "She is the only relation of mine who sees
me as a human being rather than some nuisance that must be
sold off—"

"If your cousin's family had agreed to the match, you
would have accepted your role and fallen in line," he said,
rising to glower darkly at her.

"Pemberton—"

Her mother's lilting voice cut quietly through the air,
giving him a necessary moment of pause. The duke's shoulders
dropped almost imperceptibly and Caroline's eyes darted between them in resentful intrigue. The graceful Eugenia had
always possessed a way with her father . . . a manner of language and movement that put him at ease and ushered him in
a certain direction. In this instance . . . calm.

Why couldn't you have convinced him to come home, Mother?

The answer to that, of course, was that Eugenia had not
cared overly much about coming home, or about the people
waiting for her there.

He tipped his head in warning, and his next words were
spoken through gritted teeth. "Your days of living like a hel-
lion are over. I've already written to Lord and Lady Hedridge,
and they were able to make inquiries for us while we were en
route—"

"No." Caroline backed away, her face suddenly numb with
panic. The thought of Lord and Lady Hedridge scrounging

together a few passable suitors who might consent to marry her was beyond mortifying. "Not them, Father . . . please. They do not like me." She gazed down at Frances in panic, who seemed strangely unsurprised.

He silenced her with a slash of his hand. "They are well connected. I'm even going to be generous and give you a choice between three men who have already indicated their openness to the pairing. You will have a chance to meet each of them—Frances sent out the invitations earlier this week."

Icy fingers trailed over Caroline from head to toe, and she struggled to speak. Her aunt's eyes shifted guiltily up to meet hers.

"Aunt F-Frances?" she stammered.

Betrayal . . .

Her heart writhed helplessly inside her ribs. She wouldn't . . . *she couldn't* . . . believe her aunt would have participated in such an orchestration of events on purpose, but there was no way to be absolutely certain without speaking to her in private.

Frances reached out to her once more, but she tugged her hand out of reach and looked away, unable to grasp the situation quite yet.

"You will meet the suitors that evening. A decision can be made afterwards."

She felt the bitter rise of nausea. Caroline would end up marrying a man chosen for her by an enemy, approved by her loveless father and invited into their home by the aunt she'd tried so hard to protect. Would still protect, no matter what the cost.

Then she paused in wide-eyed contemplation. The American had socialized with Lord and Lady Hedridge. One might even consider him an acquaintance of theirs, however remote.

Her father continued. "They are . . ."

A spark of hope flared to life.

Jonathan Cartwick.

"Viscount Bryant . . ."

Caroline, felt the keen slice of disappointment, knowing that to even wish for such a thing made her the worst sort of person. That were she ever to admit to loving him, she stood to lose the dearest friend she'd ever had. Yet strangely enough, in this moment she couldn't bring herself to resist the idea as she knew she should. Right here, right now, there were still two names left, and the hope was still burning.

Jonathan Cartwick.

"The Earl of Davenport, and . . ."

Caroline winced. A widower, old and grizzled and set in his ways. She kept her attention turned to her father. There was one name left. She held her breath. In her heart, there was only one name that would do.

Jonathan Cartwick.

"—Baron Horne."

The hopeful spark winked out of existence.

Caroline tried to speak and she couldn't. Swallowing hard, her throat issued a dry click, and she tried again as she backed away from them and towards the door, feeling blindly behind her with trembling fingertips.

Frances rose from her chair. "Caroline—"

A taut shake of her head silenced her aunt, then she returned her gaze, wide-eyed and accusing, to the illustrious Duke and Duchess of Pemberton.

"When I was a little girl," she said hoarsely, "I used to dream about you and Mama coming back home for me."

Both parents blinked at her, as if waiting for her to finish her sentence. But she already had. And the tears she'd been holding at bay fell at last when she twisted the knob, escaping the study to run down the hallway and out the front door.

Chapter Seventeen

Despite the sunshine that peeked stubbornly from behind the clouds, this particular spring day was a cool one. Jonathan raised the collar of his coat then snapped the reins, urging his horse faster out of town.

His head was pounding. This morning, the discomfort had increased with every hoofbeat that brought him closer to Willowford House, and his brain had throbbed mightily by the time he'd actually passed the place. And as he passed it again this afternoon on his return home, he caught the unwelcome sight of the ducal carriage parked in front of the grand estate.

Although he resisted, he couldn't help but wonder about Caroline and how she was faring. Her friend might be willing to forgive a little assistance from a well-intended neighbor, but a personal visit from that same man would most certainly push the limits of what she was willing to believe about their relationship.

What is our relationship, anyway?

The question darkened his mood and he couldn't help but deliver an irritated jab of his heels into the horse's muscular flanks. The bay tossed its mane, letting out a loud snort of protest before complying to the demand, and Jonathan reached forwards to pat its neck soothingly.

The rooftops in town became visible just as he noticed his jaw beginning to ache, and he forced himself to unclench his teeth. If only she'd been the vapid and pampered princess he'd thought her to be instead of the intriguingly complicated and challenging little minx she was—how this all could have turned out so differently. But here he was, he thought grimly . . .

And . . . there she was?

With a soft *whoa*, he tugged on the reins and leaned in the saddle to squint up ahead. At first he thought his mind might have conjured her up, as if he could call her into being using only his thoughts. But raising a gloved hand to shade his eyes, he saw that it really was Caroline, her slim figure and the chestnut gleam of her hair impossible to miss as she walked, head cast down unhappily.

She stepped along quickly beside the overgrown grass at the side of the road, her slender arms wrapped around her torso in what appeared to be an effort to keep warm. The need to be out of doors must have taken her by surprise, and he fondly recalled a similar instance on the back lawn of

Willowford House that had included archery and a hot cup of tea. He also remembered the first time they'd met, with her walking on this very same road while dutifully toting Frances's hatboxes.

But what was she doing here by herself with no coat or chaperone to speak of? The ruffled muslin dress she was wearing, while charming, would not protect her from the chill.

With a quick flick of his reins, he brought his horse closer before swinging his leg to dismount, his boots landing solidly on the packed dirt. Caroline's gaze, previously fixed upon the ground in front of her, snapped over to him in astonishment and she stopped in mid-stride.

"Jonathan?"

His heart gave a peculiar little lurch at hearing her call him by name, but he could not allow himself the same kind of familiarity. Not when that same heart trembled in expectation of her rejection.

"My lady," he replied, towing his horse behind him as he approached slowly, cautiously. "Where are you going?"

Caroline's eyes of cool polished gray stared at him in confusion, then her gaze shifted to the road behind him.

"Going? I—" She moistened her lips before pressing them together and shaking her head. "I don't know."

Something was wrong—he could see it in the way her eyes darted wildly. He slid his hands over her shoulders to steady the tremors that visibly shook her.

"Tell me what's happened," he said softly. "Is it Frances?"

Her bottom lip trembled and she nodded. "Yes, it's Frances." A glassy tear tumbled down her cheek.

Christ. Ignoring the fact that they were standing on a public road, he pulled her into his arms, feeling a pervasive spread of satisfaction as she submitted to the embrace. His hands trailed across the graceful length of her spine.

"Is she all right?"

Her ribs hitched beneath his touch, and burying her face against his jacket, she nodded again.

"My parents wish to marry me off . . . and Aunt Frances . . . she helped them." The moisture from her tears absorbed through to his shirt, warm and wet and devastating. "She invited three lords herself."

His fingertips paused on her back, as did his breath, but not for the reason she was probably expecting.

"Lords, you say?"

"Y-yes," she said with watery sniff.

Jonathan wanted to reassure her, but he stood frozen as his thoughts had suddenly become a whirl of uncertainty. Her words echoed in his head.

Aunt Frances . . . she helped them.

Could it be that Frances had tried to help him as well?

His train of thought was derailed when she gripped his lapels and sank against his chest with an agonized sigh. "That's not all. Lady Hedridge selected my suitors. She made inquiries to see who might be able to t-tolerate having me as their wife."

He'd known this already. But hearing the truth stumbling from her lips, her voice tainted by a shame she didn't deserve to feel, brought every emotion he'd struggled to contain these past months rushing heedlessly to the surface.

He pulled her tighter against him, lacing one of his hands through the upswept mass of her dark ruby hair.

"Any one of those men would be damned lucky to have you for a wife," he ground out, savoring the feel of her in his arms and the scent of rosewater that suddenly seemed to be everywhere. He inhaled hungrily, then checked himself and the passion that could quickly overthrow his better judgment. Releasing her, he stripped off his coat, and the unexpected heat in her gaze as he removed the garment nearly caused him to ravish her right there.

Christ, you're not undressing for her . . . just give her the coat.

Averting his eyes, he wrapped the black broadcloth coat gently around her shoulders, not missing her tiny shiver of relief. Her moonstone eyes trapped his.

"Do you really think that?" she asked softly.

It was impossible to miss the hopeful tone in her voice. And it made him question what he had done to earn that hope. Displaced her best friend? Argued back and forth over a blasted boundary line?

No wonder she hadn't liked him. No wonder Eliza disliked him still. He was just thankful he'd finally managed to come to his senses—not that it would help him in the least. Not even Frances could help him at this point.

Trapping an errant lock of auburn hair between his fingers, he tucked it softly behind her ear with a chiding glance. "Do you really believe I would say such a thing without meaning it?"

A tiny crease formed between her elegant arched brows and he longed to soothe it away with his fingertips, or perhaps with a kiss. Her only reply was a reluctant shake of her head.

"You should join me at Greystone Hall. Warm yourself with some tea before returning home," he said, extending a hand out to her. At least it would get them off the road and out of plain sight, should the duke come looking.

She stared at his gloved hand in silence, probably contemplating whether such a thing would be wise. Then she slid her bare fingers inside his before accepting his assistance up onto the bay.

The ride home was thankfully short, as the saddle did not properly accommodate two riders. The press of her lush bottom against his hips would have been enough to test any man, but they soon arrived. He dismounted swiftly, reaching up to assist her in similar fashion before handing the reins to a footman and leading her up the curved stone steps at the front of his house. Shaw greeted him at the door with a polite incline of his head, then his eyes widened at the unexpected sight of Lady Caroline, still enfolded in Jonathan's coat. He delivered a deeper bow in her direction then straightened to regard them both with a neutral countenance.

"Welcome home, Mr. Cartwick. And welcome to Greystone Hall, my lady."

"Thank you, Shaw," he replied, continuing past his butler to usher Caroline inside. "Is my mother at home? As you can see, we have a guest."

The man blinked and shook his head. "I'm sorry, sir. Mrs. Cartwick left an hour ago for town."

Jonathan halted in the foyer, suddenly remembering.

Yes, she'd had an appointment with the tailor, and he'd left before her to attend a meeting with his land agent. How he'd forgotten that little detail, he couldn't say.

"No matter," he said dismissively. His manner belied his sudden awareness that he and Caroline would be here together . . . alone. "Tea in the drawing room, if you please."

Shaw hurried off to fulfill his request, and once the drawing room door had closed behind them, Caroline turned to lance him with an accusatory gaze.

"You'd forgotten that your mother would not be here?"

He gave a shrug of apology and crossed the room to stand by the fire. "Actually, I did. I suppose my mind was more occupied with my own meeting today and by finding you alone on the side of the road." Eyeing her in amusement, he continued, "It's much warmer over here, I assure you."

Likely realizing he was correct and that she was still freezing, she ambled closer to him and gave a grateful little shiver at the warmth that flowed forth from the fire. Best intentions aside, he couldn't help but imagine her shivering beneath the eager heat of his mouth. But the truth was, he didn't have to imagine it at all. He could still recall—all too well—her cries of pleasure as he had tasted her flesh.

The soft rap on the door snapped him out of his trance, and he took a step back as if the fire rather than mere closeness with her had scorched him.

"Enter," he said tersely.

Shaw wheeled the tray into the drawing room and poured two steaming cups of tea before departing with a bow. Striding to the cart, he glanced at her in inquiry.

"How do you take your tea, my lady?"

She stayed facing the fire, the feminine angles of her face alight with flickering golden light. "No cream. One lump on the side, please."

Jonathan uttered a laugh. "One lump on the side?"

Caroline turned her head and said nothing, her expression one of cool defiance. Clearly, she had been challenged on this before. He raised his hands in capitulation and grinned before grasping the tongs to remove one sugar cube from its china container, placing it with more care than was required upon the side of her saucer. By the time he'd reached her with the tea, her eyes had narrowed.

"Thank you," she said. Skirting around him, she lowered herself onto the settee with her drink, still swathed in the coat that was much too large for her. He watched in wonder as she simply raised the cup to her lips, leaving the sugar cube where it lay. "So, you had a meeting today?" she asked.

"I did. With my land agent. It was in preparation for meeting with your father."

Her eyes lifted to meet his, their granite smoothness a perfect complement to the sumptuous red hue of her mouth and the fiery shade of her hair.

"When is your meeting with my father?" she asked, taking another sip of tea. A hint of annoyance had crept into her voice.

Jonathan found himself still staring, bound by suspense, at the glittering sugar cube that seemed to hold no purpose. "He'd like to discuss the issue with the fence lines just before the start of dinner." He paused before adding, "And I'd like to have both you and Lady Frances present."

Caroline's eyes widened and her arms fell, the saucer lowering to rest upon her lap. Distractedly, she plucked the sugar cube up between her fingers and brought it to her mouth, nibbling a bit off the corner before replacing it beside her cup.

There it was . . . the most adorable use of a sugar cube he'd ever witnessed. A little treat when times were tough. And now he found himself damnably obsessed with the idea of tasting her sugar-sweetened lips for himself.

"Why?" she asked at last. "You've waited all this time to speak exclusively with my father."

He shrugged and sank down onto the opposite side of the settee, watching her carefully. "Perhaps now I think you ought to have a voice in the matter."

With a shake of her head, she took another sip of her tea. "I appreciate the gesture, Mr. Cartwick, but it won't make a difference. He won't even allow us through the door."

"Back to Mr. Cartwick, am I?"

Caroline evaluated him in shock. "You've always been Mr. Cartwick."

"No, not always," he corrected, glancing down at his hands. "Not when I kissed you in my study, and not on the road earlier today."

"I—" Her gaze fell to the floor. "Well, I apologize. That was improper."

Change the subject.

Jonathan welcomed the barely detectable whisper of conscience, especially when his mind was overwhelmed with all the improper things that might cause her to say his name.

He reached up to tug at his cravat. It suddenly seemed

much tighter than before . . . or he was warmer, one of the two. "With regards to the meeting, I think I might be able to bring the duke around to my line of thinking. Also, I feel your aunt may be able to shed some light on the matter."

Her lips were worrying at the sugar cube again, lost in thought, and he could actually feel his temperature increasing now. Catching herself, she placed it back onto the saucer and cleared her throat.

"You think Frances knows something that I do not?"

"I think it's possible," he conceded reluctantly.

"Why? Did your land agent say something?"

Jonathan twitched his head in negation. "My land agent has not been able to produce any official documents that reflect the change in boundary. Everything we've found so far show the fence lines as they should be. I don't suppose—" He hesitated. "I don't suppose you've any idea why or when the fence would have been moved?"

"Me?" Her cheeks paled. "Do you think I would conceal that kind of information?"

"No, I don't. Not intentionally. But—"

Setting her tea aside, she rose from the settee, her slim torso dwarfed by the oversize drape of his coat. "I wish I could help you, Mr. Cartwick, but I can't. And it seems like you might not believe what I say anyway."

His brow lowered into a frown. "That wasn't what I intended to—"

"I really should be leaving anyway, Mr. Cartwick."

Caroline's eyes had taken on a glassy sheen, and he inwardly cursed himself for adding to her woes. She shrugged out of his coat and tossed it onto the settee with a noise of frustration, and in doing so, loosed a neatly folded handkerchief that had been hastily tucked into her skirt pocket. The square of cloth fell to the carpet and before she could trouble herself, he knelt down to retrieve it.

"Thank you, sir. I'll take that now—"

The words tumbled out of her mouth rapidly, unnaturally. Which only further drew his attention to the linen he now held in his outstretched hands. There was a brief moment when he did not realize what he was holding. Then he unfolded it, and the world seemed to rotate on its axis.

A square of white, meticulously pressed, the initials *JRC* monogrammed at the corner . . . a cluster of bluebells painstakingly stitched onto the linen . . .

JRC.

Jonathan Robert Cartwick.

His handkerchief. The bluebells embroidered by her. Tucked away in her pocket for God knew how long, almost as if it held some kind of sentiment.

Jonathan stood slowly, raising his eyes in amazement, and saw that her expression had already changed. Regret colored her features, quite literally, with the pink blush that crept over every inch of visible skin. He swallowed hard, raising the handkerchief up in the air.

"I don't understand . . ."

"It's nothing," she said, her face now bordering on crimson. "Simply something to pass the time—"

"As I recall, needlework was not your preferred method of passing time," he pressed.

She still couldn't meet his gaze. "You're right, and it's nothing. I should have just returned the handkerchief. And now I should be heading back home—"

He came closer, the fabric clutched tightly in his fingers. She stood her ground but he observed her own fingers tighten over the polished mahogany trim of the settee.

"No. This is something, Caroline," he said quietly. "I want you to tell me what it is."

"Please, don't call me that."

It was more of a plea than a demand, but he was unwilling to let her off the hook quite yet. He shook his head. "We've engaged in more scandalous behavior than the simple use of first names, or have you forgotten?" The way her teeth closed over her full bottom lip told him she had not.

"It's useless to speak about any of that now," she replied, her nostrils flaring. "I'd take it all back if I could."

His chest tightened at her words. "Would you, really?" he asked.

"I would," she choked. "Those moments have brought me nothing but pain. And now I will marry some withered old man with a title, tortured by memories of you . . . and wish none of it had ever happened."

Sensing that any pressure from him would cause her to flee, he took another slow step in her direction, like a snake charmer wooing a rebellious cobra.

"For my sake, I hope that isn't true," he said. "Even if the rest of my days are lived out in solitude, I'll remember our times together fondly."

Sparks shot from her eyes. "Maybe that's because you'd

be living a life of solitude by choice. *I don't get that choice,*
Mr. Cartwick. It seems I owe my family a great debt for not
being born a man."

Jonathan's mouth twisted. "Caroline—"

"Don't . . . call me that," she sputtered, charging forwards
to jab an accusing finger at him.

Seizing her wrist, he tugged her until she fell against his
chest, speechless and disarmed. She stared dazedly into his
eyes, then her lashes closed as he lowered his face to within
inches of hers. Her flawless lips were trembling, and now he
knew he was going to kiss them before she left this room.

"My handkerchief . . . why did you keep it?" he rasped. "I
need to know."

But in his heart, he thought he already might. The notion
that she truly cared for him was enough to rock him in dizzying waves.

Caroline uttered a little sigh, her eyes rolling in frustration beneath the pale satin of her lids. Staring in awe, he
could see that even her eyelashes were the same rich, reddish-
brown hue of her magnificent hair.

"I just—" Shaking her head, she paused to consider her
words, then started again. "I suppose I thought—"

A sharp rap on the door caused those lashes to fly open
in astonishment, and she turned to the sound, twisting in
his arms. The movement, and the enticing friction of her
body against his, pushed his already taxed resistance past
its breaking point. Rather than answer the servant, he sank
his fingers into her hair and brought her head back around
as he lowered his own. She made a small noise when their

lips met, and her familiar, sweet softness set him instantly on fire.

Her initial shock briefly rendered her motionless, but soon his lips had teased hers open and he gladly delved inside her mouth, his body thrumming in excitement at how she submitted to him. The sugary sweetness of her kiss nearly caused him to take things further, but before he could, another knock sounded at the door. He groaned in agony before tearing himself away.

"What is it, Shaw?" he snapped, frantically willing his blood to cool. Caroline raised her fingers to her lips and stared down at the floor. The door opened to reveal the butler.

"I beg your pardon, sir," he stated with a bow, "but Lord Evanston is waiting to speak to you on the drive."

Jonathan eyed the man in shock. "Is he?"

And not a moment too soon.

"Fine," he relented with a sideways glance at Caroline who looked ready to hide behind the curtains. She shook her head but he held out a staying hand in reply. "We'll be right out."

The moment the door closed behind the butler, Caroline set to pacing, tidying her appearance with smoothing hands and crisp tugs on her dress as she strode across the carpet in a panic.

"What were you thinking? He can't find me here . . . like this . . ."

"He must find you here," Jonathan said, reaching out to catch at her arm when she passed. "Otherwise, you risk the duke sending out a search party to the village and beyond. Better to just deal with the viscount, don't you think?"

Her face had gone ashen, but she nodded and wrapped her arms around herself to steady her shaking limbs. More than anything, he longed to go to her and promise that all would be well, but he couldn't do that. There was no guarantee that it would be. Instead, he simply came closer and tucked his handkerchief between her fingers.

"Take it. It's yours."

Her head raised, brows furrowed in wordless inquiry.

"Consider it a gift," he insisted on his way to the door. "And if I were you, I'd hide it before we greet Lord Evanston."

He continued on his course to the foyer, and Caroline's light steps quickened behind him. Glancing her way, he spotted her shoving the fabric back into her skirt pocket. There was a peculiar sense of satisfaction at the sight, which was quickly erased when he saw her change of expression. It was cool. Detached. Almost as if he'd disappeared entirely . . . or as if the incendiary moment they'd just shared in his drawing room hadn't even occurred.

Ah.

Trying not to be offended at the abrupt change in her demeanor, he descended the front stairs to square his shoulders at the rider who was waiting for him below, eyeing him critically.

"Greetings," called the man before swinging down from the saddle of a lithe and muscled chestnut horse. He strode forwards to shake hands after shooting a curious glance at Caroline. "I am Lord Evanston."

The infamous Lord Evanston, come to claim the Duke of Pemberton's daughter from her ill-advised outing. With his sleek black locks and powerful frame, Jonathan had to admit the man possessed quite a presence. He squeezed his hand strongly in return.

"Jonathan Cartwick."

The viscount released his hand, stepping back to survey him with bright blue eyes that were now alight with equal parts intrigue and realization. "I see," he said, placing his hands on his hips. "And it seems you are already well acquainted with our Lady Caroline." Evanston's gaze slid over to Caroline, who stared back at him uneasily.

"Yes, of course we are acquainted," Jonathan replied with an annoyed jerk on his sleeve. "I'm sure you've heard about the current boundary dispute."

"I have." The corner of Evanston's mouth hitched up in a smile, but there was no humor behind it. "Forgive me for not being clear. My confusion stems not from the fact that you two might happen to know each other, but more that I might find her here at your estate. By herself."

Caroline stepped closer to the viscount. "Thomas—"

"If you are insinuating something inappropriate about finding Lady Caroline at my home," Jonathan said sharply, cutting her off, "then you should know I encountered her on the road. We returned here so she could warm up near the fire with some tea."

Evanston scoffed. "Could she not be warmed in her own drawing room just as well?"

"Perhaps she wasn't ready to return home quite yet," he replied, narrowing his eyes.

"*Perhaps* she is standing right here, and doesn't wish to be spoken of as if she is not!"

Both men paused, realizing that their introduction had been derailed, then glanced her way. Caroline stared at them and Jonathan thought there was nothing lovelier. Her lips were still slightly reddened from their kiss, chest heaving as if she'd like nothing more than to strangle them both.

The viscount fell silent and bowed his head, but Jonathan steadily, and stubbornly, maintained eye contact. Her eyes brightened at his show of defiance, then she glanced quickly away.

"Let's try this again, shall we?" she said.

"I've no need to prolong this debate," Jonathan growled, pinning the viscount with a stare. "If you've come to collect Lady Caroline then by all means, do so. My only question would be why you came here to look for her in the first place."

Evanston shrugged. "It seemed like a good place to start. Better, anyway, than scouring the entire village."

Even Caroline seemed flummoxed by his leap of logic, but reluctant to explore it further, given the circumstances. Before any more could be said, Jonathan caught the gaze of his butler, waiting patiently at the top of the stone staircase.

"Bring my carriage around for Lady Caroline."

Shaw hurried off while Caroline looked around in panic. "But, I-I can't be seen in your carriage."

"Why not?"

"Well, because I . . ."

"The alternative, you realize, is riding on horseback with Lord Evanston," he pointed out. Jonathan had enjoyed the exhilarating, tight press of her body not an hour before on his own saddle, but the thought of watching her ride off like that with another man caused every muscle in his body to coil in unspent tension. "You can say that I saw you on the road and sent my carriage."

"While we're making up stories, why don't we just tell everyone that none of this even happened?" snorted the viscount.

Jonathan stepped closer and lowered his voice. "Tell them whatever you like, my lord. But her reputation has very nearly been ruined by you once, however inadvertently. I will not have it happen again."

"Mr. Cartwick!" Caroline exclaimed. "Please——"

But Evanston's amusement had already vanished from his face, and he also took a step closer in challenge. "Forgive me. I'd no idea what a staunch defender of women you are." He winced and tipped his head. "Yes, you removed a widow and her young daughter from the only home they had, but——"

"I had every right to claim this estate, as I've explained to Lady Caroline *many* times before. Although after so much trouble, I am starting to wonder if I wouldn't have been better off staying in America."

The comment had been tossed out carelessly, but it hit a mark he hadn't even known to aim for. Pain flickered across Caroline's face, almost as if she'd been physically attacked.

"I see," she said in a small voice. "Well then, I wouldn't wish to take up any more of your time. Thank you for your assistance this afternoon. Good day."

She curtsied then turned away to the sound of horses rounding the drive, growing louder on his carriage's approach. It took every bit of restraint he had to stop from going after her, but he could only watch helplessly as she accepted a hand from his coachman and disappeared into the vehicle. Jonathan sighed and massaged his temple as it departed briskly for Willowford House, then realized that the viscount was still standing beside him. Lowering his hand, he cast a weary glance in the man's direction.

"Shouldn't you be leaving too?" he asked.

Evanston gave him a baleful stare before slipping his gleaming black boot into his stirrup and swinging up onto his horse. The chestnut stomped restlessly upon the gravel.

"Listen, Cartwick," he said, tugging his kid gloves more tightly over his fingers. "Our differences aside, I expect we'll be seeing you again. I also expect that you'll refrain from ravishing the duke's daughter in the future. In fact, I insist upon it."

Jonathan worked to conceal his surprise by smoothing a hand over his linen shirtfront. He cleared his throat.

"I beg your pardon?"

"Come now," said Evanston, jerking on the reins. "I know what a woman looks like when she's been kissed. More importantly, I know what she acts like."

And with a jab of his heels, the viscount left Jonathan alone on the drive, standing in slack-jawed contemplation of what else the viscount might know.

CHAPTER EIGHTEEN

Caroline sighed and leaned against the windowpane, her eyes fluttering in nervous anticipation. This evening the guests would be arriving, and with them would be her suitors: Viscount Bryant, the Earl of Davenport and Baron Horne. And of course, Jonathan Cartwick would be present earlier in the afternoon for his long-awaited meeting with her father, although the thought of seeing him after their last uncomfortable parting was nearly too much to bear.

Rubbing her hands over the gooseflesh that had suddenly raised across her arms, she came away from the window and stood before the looking glass. Impossible to miss was the waxen curve of her cheek and sunken hollows beneath her eyes. The past few days had taken their toll, and she'd spent most of her time trying to avoid nearly everyone in the house, save Eliza—who had not yet mentioned anything about Thomas finding her with Jonathan. She thanked God for that small favor, as she knew concealing any awkwardness over that encounter would be incredibly difficult.

Frances was being dutifully cared for by Jonathan's servants, and as far as Caroline knew, her behavior since the duke's arrival had been close to normal. Grappling with the notion of her aunt's betrayal was still difficult and, at times, overwhelming. She wanted to believe the best, but found herself fearing the worst: that Frances had acquiesced with her brother's demands because her allegiance to him was stronger than the affection she held for her niece.

Even so, there had still been one night . . . just one . . . when she had knocked softly at her aunt's door and crawled into bed beside her.

Frances had been fast asleep—both a blessing and a testament to the nurturing efforts of her caregivers. Beatrice had nodded with solemn brown eyes and slipped into the darkened corner of the room to allow her some privacy. And it was there, in the warm and blanket-cocooned softness of her aunt's slumbering embrace, that she squeezed her eyes shut and sobbed wretchedly into the pillow.

She'd meant to be gone in the morning. Instead, she'd awoken to cloudy gray eyes and the soft stroking of a hand upon her tangled hair.

"He'll be here, little Caro," Frances had whispered. "I made sure of it."

But she'd spoken no more after the one curious admission, and Caroline had no clue what to make of those few nonsensical words.

Now she stared at herself in the mirror, the sage-green

dress she was wearing a lovely complement to the chestnut sheen of her hair, which had been artfully arranged into a decadent mass of braids and curls. She had not chosen the dress, and she had not instructed the maid on how to style her hair. It was safe to assume that her mother had played some part in their selection, and the salmon-colored evening gown that was hanging from the front of her armoire had also likely been chosen by her. The Duchess of Pemberton did not know her daughter well, but she knew enough to know that Caroline would do nothing to further her own marriage ambitions . . . including but not limited to, dressing to impress her suitors.

The one man she cared about would be meeting with her father today about the property lines, but he would not be calling on her. He'd all but admitted that his time in England thus far had been a disappointment, and this just mere moments after kissing her. And after accusing her of withholding information about Windham Hill.

Her attachment to Jonathan had not lessened, no matter what she'd told herself. And she'd told herself many things. That he was an opportunistic American who would probably sell off parts of the Cartwick estate for a tidy sum. That his kindness towards her was offset by the way Eliza had been turned out of Greystone Hall. That his attention to fence lines would far outweigh any attention he would pay to her. Little matter that she believed none of these things anymore.

The soft knock at her door interrupted her bleak reverie, and she opened it to find Eliza waiting for her, seeming a little anxious herself.

"You're being summoned downstairs," her friend said, leaning in to whisper conspiratorially. "Mr. Cartwick is set to arrive at any moment."

"Right," she replied anxiously. "I'll be right down."

"Surely it's a formality, but one we must observe." Eliza cast her green eyes to the ceiling. "You can hold my hand, if you think it will help."

She stepped out into the hallway, closing the door behind her. "Thank you, but if I haven't wilted by now, I think I'll be fine."

"I was rather hoping you'd hold my hand anyway," Eliza admitted with a laugh. "For my sake, perhaps?"

Caroline stopped in mid-step to regard her friend, her own cares momentarily forgotten.

"How thoughtless of me. Are you very anxious to meet him?"

"I'm not sure anxious is the right word, but I'm certainly something," Eliza replied with a wan smile. "Thomas said he was rather unpleasant."

"Oh, no—not at all. I mean, well, *yes* . . . he was unpleasant to Thomas, but Thomas was interrogating him. I think he felt cornered."

Caroline realized she was talking about that day with Jonathan—something she'd managed to neatly avoid until now. Eliza hadn't pried or pressed her with questions, seeming content in the fact that Caroline had been found and safely returned. But here in this hallway, her gaze was alight with newfound interest. It could be because she was trying to reassure herself before meeting the man.

Or it could be because she suspected something.

Eliza nodded. "You've found he can be reasonable?"

"I suppose any man can be reasonable, if given half the chance," Caroline said. Her heart started to pound and she renewed their course through the hallway. "He's been sympathetic about Frances, anyway."

Her friend clasped her arm tightly and leaned closer with a smile. "So, does that mean you'll hold my hand?"

"You know I will."

When the Cartwick carriage pulled up before Willow-ford House minutes later, they were doing just that. Caroline couldn't think about what Jonathan might think to see her fingers linked with Eliza's, but figured there was a chance he'd see it as a show of unity against him. For her part, it was not. She couldn't speak to Eliza's intentions.

Frances stood near her brother and his wife. Her complexion was unusually pale today, and with a start Caroline realized that Minnie and Beatrice were not in attendance. She spun in place and searched the servants gathered in vain.

"What is it?" Eliza breathed under her voice.

"I-I can't find my aunt's helpers . . . can you?"

Eliza's eyes widened and she also attempted to glance around without catching notice. Thomas bowed his head in surreptitious inquiry, and at his wife's whisper, he straightened and scanned the drive, then looked over at Caroline with a small shake of his head.

Perhaps futilely, she hoped that they'd been asked to remain inside. But still, she couldn't help the nagging feeling that something was wrong. Cartwick's perturbed expression as he disembarked from his carriage only cemented that notion, but the duke was oblivious to it.

"I am pleased to meet you at last, Mr. Cartwick," her father declared with a nod. He gestured to the duchess. "This is my wife, the Duchess of Pemberton."

Eugenia performed a tiny curtsy, and Jonathan obligingly took her hand, lowering into a deep bow. "Your Grace."

Caroline glanced at Eliza from the corner of her eye, hoping to ascertain what her friend could possibly be thinking. As usual, Jonathan looked resplendently handsome, his golden eyes gleaming in the afternoon sun. Eliza's gaze was fixed on him and although she could surely see these things for herself, her face was as unreadable as a sphinx. Thomas scowled discreetly from beside her. There was no mystery there.

"And I believe you already know my sister, Lady Frances—"

Caroline watched her aunt perk up at mention of her name, and Jonathan came to a stop before Frances, his amber gaze holding hers meaningfully as he grasped her hand and bowed deeply.

"My lady," he said. "I hope you are well."

Her aunt's hand shook slightly as she reached out to pat the side of his face.

Nobody was quite expecting such an interaction, not even Caroline, who knew of the mutual respect between the pair. Eliza's lips were parted in astonishment.

"And here, of course, is Viscount Evanston," her father continued, "with his viscountess, the former Lady Eliza Cartwick."

Caroline inhaled sharply through her nose and tightened her hold on Eliza's fingers. How could her father introduce her in such a way? But Thomas was clearly used to dealing with aristocrats who often spoke with little thought for others. He slid an arm around Eliza's shoulders as if to shield her from any other words.

"This is my wife, Mr. Cartwick. Lady Evanston."

With a nod to Thomas, Jonathan came to a stop before Eliza, and he held out his hand.

"I can't say I ever thought the two of us would meet, my lady."

Eliza didn't say anything at first, seeming nonplussed. Then slowly reached out to place her fingers inside his awaiting clasp. "No, I suppose you didn't."

"I hope you'll forgive me for any awkwardness," he replied, bowing politely over her hand.

"You'll need forgiveness for a lot more than that," muttered Thomas under his breath.

"I'll do my best, Mr. Cartwick," she replied with a small smile, acting as if she hadn't heard her husband.

Jonathan released Eliza's hand and his eyes flicked cautiously in Caroline's direction. She was sure to receive the tamest version of a sanitized bow after their last meeting. But the duke's words cut across the stillness of the crowd.

"And my daughter, of course."

Of course. Why would she require an actual introduction? Even Jonathan frowned at the slight, and she could feel her cheeks growing warm as Eliza squeezed her hand then let go, perhaps so she could offer them to him in greeting.

But all she wanted to do was escape up the stairs to disappear into the safety of her bedchamber. All she wanted was a little respect . . . to feel like she had some *control* . . .

Smoothly, as if it was the most normal thing in the world, Jonathan reached down and took her hand from its stubborn place near her side. He bowed over it, and to her surprise he did not stop until he had pressed the enticing warmth of his lips upon her skin. By the time he straightened to regard her, she could feel her face flaming.

"Lady Caroline, I am pleased to see you again."

She stared at him mutely, then reminded herself to speak. "I—Thank you."

His hand gripped hers for perhaps a second too long, but with a nod he released it and her father's voice asserted itself once more.

"Mr. Cartwick, it is a busy morning and there is much to do." The duke squinted in the sunlight and started walking to the house. "Join me in the library and let's get this little meeting underway."

"Yes of course, Your Grace," Jonathan replied, turning to face his host. "And with your permission, I'd like it if Lady Caroline and Lady Frances could join us as well."

The scuff of her father's boots as he came to a sudden stop caused Caroline to flinch.

"I can't see why that would be necessary," he said. Annoyed, he motioned for the servants to file back inside.

"And I can understand your reservations. But I believe they both have valuable insight into the situation. Insight that cannot be gleaned from the documents we have already found."

Frances was watching the discussion with great interest, while her mother's frown indicated her stern disapproval.

"He's a brave sort, isn't he?" Eliza whispered in awe.

The duke approached Jonathan with predatory finesse. "Perhaps your time across the Atlantic has caused you to forget yourself. I couldn't care less about a boundary line near a house I rarely visit, particularly if the discrepancy is in my favor. I only agreed to this meeting because you had written to me requesting it—"

"And I am grateful for that. So if I can have no objection to whatever information the ladies may impart, surely you might be willing to allow it?"

Caroline could hardly believe it, and indeed the entire group appeared to have stopped breathing, waiting in anticipation of whether the duke would relent . . . or kick the audacious American off his estate.

Her father's expression was one of pure distaste. "And if I don't?"

"Then we forego the meeting," Jonathan replied with a shrug. "Although that would not be my preference."

Thomas let out a huff of amusement. "You know," he whispered, "I may grow to like him after all."

Rather than delivering a reply, her father pivoted swiftly on his heel and marched into the house. Jonathan did not question the reaction, but simply removed his hat and gestured for both Frances and Caroline to follow, and the tremulous wave of encouragement from Eliza did very little to soothe her nerves.

When the library door had closed behind them, the

Duke of Pemberton sank down into a leather armchair with
a long-suffering sigh.

"You, Mr. Cartwick, are going to tell me what the hell is
going on. And if I don't like what you have to say, then this
meeting will be brief."

"We will get to that, Your Grace, but first I'd like you to
reconsider your decision to send back my servants."

The duke waved the idea away with the back of his hand.
"I am perfectly capable of securing my own staff, Mr. Cartwick." His dark brow lowered into a frown. "I'm not certain
what gave you the impression there was ever such a need, but
I've set things to rights now that I'm home."

Jonathan's eyes darted over to catch her gaze, and Caroline
heard Frances sigh beside her. She smoothed a remorseful hand
across her back. It was only a matter of time now before the
truth of her condition came out, and she gave him a silent nod
of gratitude for his efforts. The muscle jumped in his jaw but
he added nothing more. Her father's mind had been made up.

"Now," the duke said, tapping an impatient finger upon
the arm of his chair, "tell me about this debacle with the
property lines."

Jonathan cleared his throat and leaned against the wall,
folding his arms across his chest. "Actually, I think it is Lady
Frances who will be able to explain this situation better than I."

Frances, who had sat and was busily straightening her
skirts around her on the couch, glanced up. "Oh?" She smiled
and folded her hands in her lap. "Please remind me of the
situation."

"The fence line, Auntie." Caroline lowered down beside her, looking up at Jonathan in confusion. "Do you know anything about it?"

"Should I?" she asked.

"Not unless you have knowledge of why it may have been changed," Jonathan replied, his gaze shifting back to Caroline. "And I suspect the circumstances had something to do with your niece."

She froze. Was this another accusation?

"I beg your pardon, Mr. Cartwick, but I—"

"Yes," Frances interrupted, blinking up at him with newfound clarity. "It did."

Caroline fell back against the couch cushions, feeling sick to her stomach. Her eyes darted furiously between them. "What are you talking about?" she whispered hoarsely.

Her father had shifted in his seat to lean forwards, elbows resting upon his knees. She was sure he'd love to have one more reason to despise her.

"What happened?" he demanded.

Frances resumed the attention to her skirts, her eyebrows raised in judgment. "It happened while you were away, Alexander. Which, let's face it, you often are. Except your daughter was five instead of twenty, and she ran away to her favorite place. Windham Hill."

"I'm surprised at your tone," the duke said tautly, a warning gleam in his eyes. "It is my kindness that has allowed you to live here all these years."

"And it is because of me that you were able to live as you

wished," she replied. "I've often wondered at my own role in enabling you and Eugenia to neglect your own child, but that discussion is for another day perhaps." She reached over to take Caroline's hand. "You broke your arm when you fell, dear—when you climbed over the fence."

"I . . . think I remember. But what does that have to do with . . ."

Her voice trailed off as the pieces suddenly snapped into place. With a gasp, she straightened and covered her mouth. Jonathan watched silently from his position across the room, but his eyes were dark and full of emotion.

"The Cartwicks . . . moved the fence?" She turned away to conceal the scorching tears that had filled her eyes, swiping them away when they spilled over anyway. "Oh, but why did you not tell me? Why did *they* not tell me?"

Frances shook her head and squeezed her fingers in sympathy. "They didn't want you to question it. I think they simply hoped you'd feel as if that place had always been yours."

"Fine," the duke said, looking uncomfortable. "But why keep quiet about it until now?"

Frances tipped a blithe smile at her brother. "I suppose nobody thought to ask me."

Caroline eyed her aunt with some skepticism. Frances's recollections had grown unreliable since the start of her memory troubles, but she was still as sly as a fox. The bigger question, she supposed, was what purpose could it have served to conceal the truth?

"Well, you weren't entirely silent on the matter," Jonathan corrected. "It was only after you told my mother about Caroline's broken arm that we made sense of things."

"How long have you known?" Caroline asked him, suddenly needing the answer.

His eyes held hers in their singular warm glow. "For a while."

Her breath hitched. Nicholas and Isabelle had loved her. She'd known it before, but this was beyond any of her feeble imaginings. They'd given her a gift she'd never been able to thank them for.

Frances had loved her enough to keep it a secret.

Did Jonathan love her? She hesitated to believe it.

But the handkerchief safely hiding in her pocket—the one he'd insisted she keep—made her want to believe it was possible.

Her father rose from his seat and placed his hands on his hips. "I have to admit, Cartwick, I'm confused. I thought this meeting was about restoring the original boundary . . . not solving old family mysteries."

"It started that way, Your Grace," Jonathan admitted, staring down at the carpet. "But now I propose we leave them as they are."

The duke's hands fell from his hips. Not even he knew what to say to that.

"You do?"

"No," said Caroline, sitting upright in alarm. "Please, don't."

Jonathan pushed away from the wall to regard her with a frown. "Why not? It's my land."

She stood and crossed to the library door. She hoped to preserve her dignity if possible, and the longer this discussion went on, the more likely it was that she would lose it.

"Because I have prevailed upon the charity of others for far too long, even unknowingly, it would seem. And I appreciate your offer, Mr. Cartwick . . . please know that I do. But—"

"But nothing. The fence stays where it is."

Frances looked delighted at the turn of events while the duke had ambled to the sideboard to fetch himself a brandy. Before the argument could go any further in front of mixed company, Caroline threw the door open. She tipped her head at Jonathan.

"Could we have a word in private?"

Her father threw back his drink and tossed the tumbler back onto the sideboard. "Excuse me?"

"The pair of them have been conversing without you for months," Frances pointed out. "I don't think a brief chat with a neighbor will ruin her, for goodness' sake. Besides, it would give us a chance to discuss preparations for tonight's dinner."

The duke eyed Cartwick in careful contemplation, then gave a gruff nod of permission. Caroline spun on her heel and walked briskly out of the room and down the hall, her pulse hastening at the knowledge that Jonathan was following. Taking a quick glance at her surroundings to ensure they would not be seen, she then slipped inside the music room. Caroline crossed over to the piano, turning to meet his eyes as he entered behind her and closed the door. The way his gaze drifted appreciatively over her caused her heart to beat faster, but she had been weak too often with him before; she could not allow it to happen again.

"Why?" she asked, leaning back against the rosewood piano case. "Why did you wait to tell me?"

Jonathan approached her dubiously. His hands were shoved into his pockets and that was good. Perhaps he was also trying not to be weak with her.

"It needed to happen a certain way."

"Why?" she repeated.

"Does it matter?"

"It does to me," she answered sadly. "At least it does right now. In a few hours at dinner, I'll be meeting my future husband, and then it won't."

He looked away. "I wanted your father to see the great lengths people had gone to . . . for you."

"Now you want to go to even greater lengths by letting me keep Windham Hill." She said, scoffing lightly, "I cannot allow it."

"Consider it a gift."

"I will not. This—" she said, digging into her pocket to retrieve his handkerchief, "this is a gift. *That* is not the same thing at all—"

"If we were married, it wouldn't matter."

Silence . . . in the room. In her head . . . chaos.

Caroline felt her lips moving, but the words were shapeless, airless. Briefly, she wondered if he had uttered the words on accident.

Jonathan slid both hands out of his pockets and placed them on the piano on either side of her. He was suddenly so large, and so close . . . the heat of his body scorched right through her dress.

"But, we can't," she breathed. "You know we can't—"

"I'd move that boundary back if that's what you want," he whispered near her ear. She squirmed as her body responded to his voice and to the desire that had thickened it. "But you'd need to be living on my side of the fence when it happens," he added, his lips brushing against the teardrop-shaped pearl that dangled from her earlobe.

"But why?" she asked, hating herself even as she leaned her head to the side to offer him the vulnerable skin of her neck. His lips hovered there in what she was sure was a deliberate attempt to torture her. "What have I done to—"

"What haven't you done?" he asked, raising a hand to gently trail it down her cheek. "You've fought me on almost everything."

His delightfully roughened fingers were sending sparks of sensation everywhere, while his words brought the reality of her actions crashing home. Yes, she had resisted him. But she'd had her reasons. Good reasons. And she couldn't just run off and marry the man who had hurt Eliza . . . a man her father would laugh out of his house for even suggesting such a union . . .

Could she?

"So why suggest marriage at all?" she asked, her fingers clutching tighter at the piano case as his hand now strayed down the length of her collarbone. "If you feel that way?"

"Because I don't feel that way. I don't think you do either." He straightened, replacing his hand on the piano behind her. A light waft of his sandalwood scent caused her pulse to rocket in helpless reply, the need for more nearness with him clawing its way through her. "And I wasn't asking you to marry me."

Caroline went still, and then she went cold. "You weren't?"

He shook his head thoughtfully, like a man who'd just discovered the solution at the end of a long and difficult mathematical equation. His gaze dipped to her lips, and he leaned in for just a moment before seeming to think better of it.

"You almost sound disappointed, but you and I both know what would happen if I asked."

She blinked up at him, knowing she should end the conversation right here but unable to keep herself from taking it just a tiny bit further. Oh, how she ached to touch him . . . her body longed to feel his skin—

"What would happen?" she breathed.

He inched a bit closer, setting off alarm bells in her head. "You would say no."

The truth of his statement was an unwelcome reminder of how closely they were treading forbidden territory. Of course she would say no. She had no choice—not when her father had locked her into marriage with one of the three lords who would be arriving tonight, and not when accepting Jonathan would mean being disloyal to Eliza.

"I-I suppose that's true . . . but—"

"You seem uncertain," he murmured. His accent, that delightful blend of both America and England, sent a cascade of shivers all the way down to her toes. "Shall we test it?"

She stood there, paralyzed, as Jonathan reached up to softly brush the curls away from the side of her face, then leaned down to whisper his request.

"Will you marry me, Caroline?"

His lips brushed against the delicate edge of her ear when he said it, and she squirmed as a warm tide of pleasure flooded through her veins. She could so easily imagine being this man's wife. Had envisioned giving herself to him countless times already.

And knew, after she had married another—as she must—that she would always think of him . . . always want him . . . never stop loving him.

Cartwick pulled away to gauge her reaction, and when she finally managed to meet his eyes, a single tear had already slipped down her cheek.

"I was wrong, then. You can't bring yourself to say no. But you will also never be able to say yes." He pushed away from her, but not before she saw the hollow look behind his eyes.

"Jonathan," she choked, her throat tightening around his name, "I can't—"

He took her hand and pressed a light kiss against her skin. "I know."

And that was the last thing he said to her before walking out of the music room and, most likely, the rest of her life.

CHAPTER NINETEEN

Caroline stared dismally at the men who had arrived to court her, her stomach heavy and laden with remorse. Old men, all of them, but she'd known they would be. They were busy posturing and preening before the duke, and as she fought against the stinging tears that threatened just behind her eyes, her mother leaned close to whisper in her ear.

"You should have worn the lovely pink gown I chose for you," the duchess admonished quietly. "It would have brought a little more life to your face."

But Caroline had no interest in appearing lively for these men, and the cornflower blue dress she had chosen instead had suited her mood much better. She twisted her lips together, catching sight of Frances from across the foyer. Her aunt's gaze swam with compassion, and Caroline glanced away quickly. Right now, she'd rather stare at a thousand annoyed relatives than a single well-intended loved one. Any softness directed at her would only make tonight's task more difficult, and it was difficult enough already. Impossible, really. Tonight she would be expected to promise herself to one of these simpering lords, when all she wanted was to see Jonathan once more . . . to go back in time to the music room and beg him to stay. To tell him she loved him.

The realization had come too late. For all her efforts to remain loyal to her friend, Eliza stared at her now as if she were in mourning again—except this time it was Caroline's happiness she grieved for. Distantly . . . pointlessly . . . she wondered how Eliza might have reacted if Caroline had been truthful from the start. If she had confessed her feelings for Cartwick and let the cards fall where they may?

Her struggles against loving Jonathan had been for naught, and she could see now with wretched clarity that despite his flaws or mistakes, he'd had enough perfection in him to carry them both. That life with him could have been the fulfillment of a dream, had she worried less about what everyone else would think and more about the call of her agonized heart. Jonathan Cartwick had asked her to be his, she'd had her chance, and then he'd walked out of her life for good. Now she was going to pay the price, and that price was steep.

"My lady."

Baron Horne was standing before her, his bare pate gleaming in the light of the chandelier above. As she lowered into a listless curtsy, she saw a tiny drop of candle wax fall down to splatter the fabric on his sleeve.

"My lord," she said in greeting, suddenly fixated by the

spot. At her mother's pointed stare, she offered her hand, and was immediately repulsed by the baby-soft smoothness of his skin as he claimed it. Jonathan's hands were large and strong, roughened by work, with long fingers that were graceful enough to either play a tune on the piano, or coax her body into finding such pleasure—

Her heart seized at the memory of him and she twitched her head to forcefully dispel it, which startled the baron into releasing her hand. Caroline heard a cross sigh from her mother, and it only goaded her into vexation.

"Forgive me, my lord, but you have a bit of wax on your coat." She eyed him in faux concern, unable to help herself.

You would have thought the man had lost a limb given his reaction. Even Caroline was surprised when he whirled around in a frenzy, and soon the footmen were off to fetch his valet in an effort to remedy the great injustice that had been committed to his formal attire. The duke shook his head in disgust, some of which was most definitely directed at her.

"I beg your pardon, Lady Caroline," said Viscount Bryant, hurrying closer to take advantage of Horne's predicament to ingratiate himself to her. "I very much look forwards to getting to know you better."

He was the youngest of the group, which might normally have lent him a competitive edge had not his fetid breath nearly knocked her over. Not even her mother could withstand the onslaught, leaning back with a visible wince, and she heard an irreverent snicker of amusement from somewhere over near Thomas.

"Looking forwards to it," she wheezed.

Both she and the duchess dismissed the viscount with a curtsy, who thankfully subsided to reveal the final man who had come to curry her favor, the Earl of Davenport. But it quickly became apparent that there would be no fawning or flattery from this particular man. He approached seriously, almost angrily, with bushy brows that could not quite conceal the reddened eyes beneath them, and graying mutton chops that were surprisingly large.

"This is all very irregular, my lady," he groused to her, "but I am here at your behest."

Now that was categorically untrue. "At *my* behest?" she inquired.

"*Thank you*, gentlemen," barked the duke, his patience clearly at an end. "Let us make our way into the dining room."

Caroline's motion was stayed by her mother's viselike grip on her wrist.

"We'll join you in a moment, if you don't mind?" she called to her husband.

He gave his wife a curt nod of approval before ushering the men through the hallway, and Caroline steeled herself for the unpleasant lecture that was to come, noting in gratitude that Frances, Thomas and Eliza had chosen to linger behind.

"You will not embarrass this family, Caroline," her mother spat. "Do you understand me?"

Caroline couldn't help but feel that any embarrassment served her parents right for placing their trust in the likes of Lord and Lady Hedridge. Sadly, her lack of good luck meant that she would be the one to pay for it.

"Honestly, Mother . . . have our standards sunk so low that only a baby or a doddering old man will do?" she asked, her desperation rising. "What can be the harm in giving me a little more time?" *Enough time for you to leave again and forget about your spinster daughter.*

"You've had plenty of time. And you speak your mind altogether too easily for a woman who has contributed so little to this family."

Caroline rocked backwards as if she'd been slapped. "Does my existence count in any way as a contribution?"

"There now," said Eliza, coming forwards, her eyes shining with concern. "The situation is already emotional. Perhaps we should join the rest of the guests for dinner?"

"But we're still missing one."

Frances's strange, soft declaration caused the entire group to turn, but she didn't seem to notice as she was focused almost exclusively upon the front doors. With a jolt of dread, Caroline glanced at her mother. More than anything, she couldn't let things go wrong with Frances. Not here . . . not this way.

She rushed over and hooked a protective arm around her aunt's arm. "Here, Auntie. We'll go into dinner together."

Still Frances resisted.

"Come, Frances," said the duchess with a quick glance at Thomas. "We're going in to dinner now."

Stepping near, Thomas extended an elbow and flashed her aunt a charming smile.

"Join me, my lady?"

Frances blinked up at him first, then slowly curled her

hand around his arm, allowing him to lead her to the dining room. Her mother followed with a twitch of her head and a sweep of her vast skirts, and Caroline breathed a sigh of relief. They would likely not permit her to sit next to Frances during dinner, especially since she was supposed to be familiarizing herself with her suitors. But as she passed the grand staircase that led upstairs, the impulse to bolt and shut herself away in her bedchamber was nearly overwhelming. Eliza slid an arm around her shoulders.

"I know what you're thinking," she said, her eyes gleaming with sadness.

I'm thinking that I will be unhappy for the rest of my days.

I'm wondering how everyone would react if I went to Jonathan now and pleaded with him to give me another chance.

But the time for all that had passed. Come and gone.

Swallowing down her anxiety, she shook her head with a bitter smile. She couldn't tell Eliza the truth, but the time for pretending was over.

"No, you don't," she whispered.

A notch formed between Eliza's brows, but before she could say anything more, Caroline looped her arm through her friend's and started the walk to the dining room, where her fate awaited her—whether she was ready for it or not.

Jonathan stepped out of his carriage onto the dimly lit drive, the torches nearby bathing the landscape in flickering hues of yellow and gold. Glancing up at the stately stone facade of Willowford House, he thought it was strange how the house he'd visited many times before now seemed somehow more imposing . . . looming and massive, as if he was no longer welcome. He supposed he wasn't. And if his hunch was correct, the invitation that was tucked away safely inside his coat pocket was the result of some unofficial interference on Frances's part and would provide no guarantee that he would be met with civility. He expected to be turned away. But he could not sit idly by while Caroline was promised to another.

After their conversation in the music room, he knew she would be surprised, and that was as he'd intended. She'd been comfortable keeping him at arm's length for all the reasons she felt were so important—not the least of which was her loyalty to her friend. But after her refusal, he *needed* her to feel the sting of his loss in the hopes that when the time came to offer for her, she would know exactly what was at stake. But she was a stubborn little minx. He could just as easily see her tossing him out herself. And while his mother fully supported his plan to ask for Lady Caroline's hand, she couldn't quite hide her nervousness at how this would play out here tonight. It was highly likely, after all, that the duke would be expecting him. Jonathan hoped his late entrance would be enough to catch the man slightly off guard.

Smoothing his hands over the front of his tailcoat, he took an unsteady breath and vaulted up the steps. Rapping loudly at the door with the brass knocker, he waited, squinting slightly as the door was opened to reveal the brightly lit interior of the house and the hawkish face of the butler who stared at him in increasing confusion.

"Mr. Cartwick?" he asked, forming the words slowly as

if attempting to solve some kind of puzzle. His gaze took in Jonathan's formal coat and breeches, and the man frowned. "Can I help you? The duke is indisposed this evening."

Jonathan smoothly withdrew the invitation and extended it in his direction. "Yes, I am aware. My apologies for being late."

The butler unfolded the parchment in an obvious show of shock, raising his hand to cover his mouth at what appeared to be a colossal blunder. "I—Oh. This is most upsetting. The duke was only expecting three guests tonight, and yet . . ." His voice trailed off, then he lifted his chin and snapped into action. "Please wait in the foyer, sir, while I make inquiries."

He nodded. "I appreciate it."

His footsteps echoed on the marble floor as he paced restlessly. At last, the butler reappeared after what felt like a lifetime but was likely only five minutes, and the duke was following behind him with the invitation tightly clenched inside his fist. He did not look happy.

"What is this about, Cartwick?" he demanded. Unfolding the paper, he held it out to view the lettering again, raising it to the light, almost as if he suspected Jonathan of committing forgery.

"I received that invitation, Your Grace, and have merely shown as requested."

The man's eyes narrowed. "Merely showing is one thing. Offering for my daughter's hand is quite another, and that is the purpose of tonight's gathering."

Jonathan bowed deeply. "I am prepared to request her hand."

The butler looked as if he was about to fall over, while the duke's look of bewilderment quickly transformed into one of outrage.

"Absolutely not—"

The sound of light steps approaching from the hallway caused both men to turn, and after the duke's surly greeting, seeing the smiling eyes of Frances was a relief.

"Mr. Cartwick," she exclaimed, "I'm so glad you could make it." Placing her hand on his back, she exerted a small amount of pressure to begin ushering him along. "Forgive the error—I've had the footmen add a place setting for you."

Her brother pivoted to pin her with an icy stare. "*Absolutely not.*"

"Why not?" she replied with a coolness of her own. "You tasked me with issuing the invitations for tonight, and I have done so."

"To the suitors I had approved!"

Frances leveled the duke with a critical glance. "And we can see how well that turned out. Did you ever stop to think that perhaps Lady Hedridge was so eager to humiliate your daughter by her choices, that she would end up embarrassing this family as well?"

"I don't require those men to be anything other than what they are," he said with a sniff.

"If money is what you're after, Mr. Cartwick has more than enough."

"Mr. Cartwick," he said through gritted teeth, "is not titled. And Caroline might be used to getting her way with you, Frances, but that is not going to happen with me."

"Exactly how has she gotten her way, Your Grace?" Jonathan asked, unable to stay silent any longer.

The duke turned to stare at him in disdain. "Lady Caroline has had her chances before, and she chose to leave the season last year while she was being courted by Lord Braxton."

Frances sighed. "Oh, for heaven's sake. She didn't do it to upset you, she did it to help me. And if you'd been at home a little more, you might know how much I needed the help."

Jonathan's heart sank at her admission.

The Duke of Pemberton tipped his head. "What are you talking about?" he asked quietly.

Rather than answer his question, she nodded in Cartwick's direction instead, sending the silver curls bobbing alongside her face. "Will you tell him for me? Please?"

He paused. "Is that entirely necessary—"

"He needs to know."

Lady Frances was ready to risk her future for Caroline. The realization caused Jonathan's chest to squeeze tightly in emotion, and he cleared his throat before speaking.

"Senile dementia, Your Grace," he muttered reluctantly. "Lady Caroline fled London to protect her aunt, and keep your family safe from the scandal that could possibly ensue."

The duke opened his mouth to reply, then closed it, his eyes darting between the two of them in an attempt to either understand the truth of things, or deny it altogether. Finally, he shook his head.

"I'm sure that's not right. Have you been seen by a physician—"

"No," Frances replied, "but I *have* been seen cavorting

around outside in my underthings, as Mr. Cartwick here can personally attest to."

The duke's mouth gaped in disbelief, and Frances took advantage of his surprised state to slide her hand around Jonathan's arm. "Let's go into the dining room, shall we?" she whispered.

Figuring the duke might need a moment to himself anyway, Cartwick inclined into a bow then proceeded down the hallway with Frances on his arm. He moved his gloved hand over hers and squeezed it.

"I wish you hadn't done that, my lady."

She *tsked* at him as if there wasn't a care in the world, but her cloudy eyes had acquired a look of distress that he did not like. "It's nothing Caroline wouldn't do for me, and surely you knew I was prepared to do whatever it took to get you into that dining room. He knows now that you're aware of the family secret, and that might just be enough to keep him from being unreasonable." Frances tugged on his arm to pull him closer. "Now do me a favor and rescue my poor niece from these buffoons."

Caroline sat perfectly straight in her chair and stared at the door in something akin to dread. She was surrounded on either side by Baron Horne and the Earl of Davenport, while the disgruntled Viscount Bryant and his breath had been seated across the table. Eliza was the unfortunate soul who'd been assigned to sit next to him, and she also kept glancing at the doorway, perhaps for an excuse to flee.

It was unclear what could have called her father's attention away from such an occasion, but she could only surmise that it was important. She wouldn't have put it past Lord and Lady Hedridge to scrape up one last, lowly suitor from the dregs of the *ton*. The abrupt addition of a place setting did not reassure her in the slightest, nor did her aunt's disappearance.

Then the door opened and her world came to a spectacular and stunning halt.

Lady Frances entered the room escorted by none other than Jonathan Cartwick—who was absolutely dressed for the occasion, looking dashing in black and white.

Eyes huge, she bolted up to her feet and sent the chair scraping gracelessly behind her. A million emotions roiled through her all at once. Surprise, elation and even anger caused her stomach to lurch in equal measures. Hadn't she already given up on the notion of a happy life? Hadn't an afternoon full of tears been required to kill any lingering fight left in her?

Yet here he was, his eyes warm and golden, gazing at her as if she were the only thing worth seeing.

Caroline forced herself to look over at Eliza, who was clearly taken aback by Jonathan's appearance. Her friend stared at Cartwick in blank amazement then rose from her seat too.

"Mr. Cartwick, I wasn't aware you had been invited." Her eyes darted back over to Caroline, who felt herself flush under her friend's scrutiny. "Or that you and Lady Caroline were so well acquainted."

He pressed his lips together and tipped her a nod. "Understandable, my lady. Although I daresay any level of familiarity, either distant or close, would far outweigh what the men here can rightly claim."

"Now, see here," blustered Viscount Bryant in a show of personal affront. "I was told there would be *three* suitors in attendance—"

Frances lowered down into the chair Jonathan had pulled out for her, and hitched her frail shoulders into a shrug. "There must have been some mistake, my lords, but I did send out four invitations." Her eyes met Caroline's and her lips quirked into a smile. "My apologies."

A single sob escaped Caroline before she clapped a hand over her mouth and sat back down. Mortified, she risked a glance at Eliza, who had also lowered into her chair and was staring over at Thomas who looked surprisingly . . . unsurprised. Come to think of it, Eliza didn't seem nearly as shocked as Caroline would have expected.

Jonathan bowed politely to the duchess, whose silence spoke volumes about the state of her confusion, before taking his seat next to Frances.

"Thank you for having me, Your Grace."

Unable to even form a sensible reply, Caroline's mother simply nodded. When her husband finally appeared at the door, he beckoned to her. Placing her napkin on the table, she rose to a stand and left the room with the duke.

The ill-tempered Earl of Davenport must have decided he was finished playing second, third and fourth fiddle to the rest of the men, for he suddenly tossed his napkin aside and stood to survey those gathered in abhorrence.

"I have never . . ." he sputtered, jowls trembling as he foundered for words and came up short. "In all my days!"

The earl stalked from the dining room in a huff just seconds before the footmen entered with the first course. Their shock at finding that nearly half of the guests were no longer at the table was almost comical, and after a few uneasy glances between them, went ahead with service anyway. Caroline stared down at her plate, desperate to avoid the curious stares. Then she made the mistake of allowing herself to look at Jonathan. His wavy hair gleamed like polished bronze beneath the yellow glow of the candles, and it was clear from the intensity of his expression that he had no desire to eat dinner. In fact, it seemed that he'd much prefer to devour her.

Her heart hammered in a series of poorly timed thumps.

"So tell me, Cartwick," said Thomas in an obvious attempt to break the tension. "Do you plan on returning to America or have you decided to settle in the English countryside?"

Jonathan's gaze shifted to the viscount.

"Moving back to America was never an option for me, given the conditions of my entailment."

Eliza stared. "But wouldn't that mean leaving the shipbuilding empire your family worked so hard to build?"

"Yes, but my brother has things well in hand. Soon my mother will rejoin him and I will be left here to carry on alone." His eyes flicked over to Caroline. "Or not alone."

He wanted her to join him. Her heart fluttered painfully at the thought.

With a little help from Frances, Jonathan had decided to take matters into his own hands. She couldn't deny that his willingness to pursue her was not just unexpected, it was thrilling as well.

Baron Horne chimed in from beside her. "Wait. Are you telling me that Viscount Bryant and I are to be considered alongside a man *in trade?*"

"I believe one would now refer to me as landed gentry," Cartwick replied sardonically. "But I would not be averse to finding new opportunities here in England."

Thomas appraised him thoughtfully from his side of the table. "How do you feel about cotton mills?"

The idea of Evanston teaming up with the same man who'd been instrumental in displacing his wife seemed nothing short of traitorous. Luckily, Jonathan laughed at the notion.

"Don't patronize me, Lord Evanston."

The corners of the viscount's eyes crinkled with mirth. "Stand down, Mr. Cartwick . . . I've been thinking about it, and you and I have no quarrel. In fact, without you here to claim the estate, I may have never tempted my fair wife into matrimony."

Eliza rolled her eyes heavenward. "I think you would have probably found a way."

"Yes," Jonathan replied. "Surely you give me altogether too much credit for that."

Caroline frowned in dismay, her eyes darting frantically between each of them. She would have definitely expected more of a reaction from Eliza, but she'd greeted her husband's casual discussion of the entailment with nothing more than a little sarcasm.

She couldn't stand it any longer. Everyone at the table focused on her when she stood once more, nearly knocking her chair over in the process, but it was Eliza's gaze that she sought.

"I am confused," she said, her eyes pleading for answers.

Eliza rose as well, but any reply she might have made was cut off by the angry suitors.

"As am I!" Lord Bryant raged, banging his fist upon the table and sending the oysters jumping on his plate.

"And I!" added Baron Horne.

Now it was Caroline who rolled her eyes. Her dress rustled loudly as she made her way around the end of the table to reach for Eliza's outstretched hands, and her friend tugged her away for a bit of privacy near the edge of the room.

"It's obvious you love him, and he's fighting for you, Caroline," Eliza whispered in a gently scolding tone. "Why aren't you fighting for him?"

She stared at her best friend, the blood draining from her face in a cool rush.

"I—what?"

Eliza pulled her closer with considerably more urgency. "Oh, for heaven's sake. I knew something had changed from the moment you called him *Jonathan*. Thomas could see it too." Her peridot eyes shifted past Caroline's shoulder to glance at Cartwick. "Whatever is stopping you right now, don't let it. If you're worried about me, you shouldn't be. Everything has worked out for the best—surely you can see that. And if you're worried about him loving you in return, then let me put you at ease . . . the man is completely enamored."

Caroline turned slowly to follow her gaze. "He is?"

"Do you think Lord Braxton ever would have stormed in here and taken on the Duke of Pemberton for a chance at winning your hand?"

The raised voices in the dining room were growing louder, as her two titled suitors were now shouting across the table. Thomas could be heard chuckling at the errant barbs that were occasionally directed at Cartwick, who was much too preoccupied by Caroline's secretive conversation to be bothered by the animosity. His serious gaze caught hers for a brief moment and she glanced away with a blush.

Eliza winced. "This is getting out of hand."

"It's hopeless," Caroline cried. "I don't know what I could possibly do to convince my parents to let me marry him."

Lips pursed in thought, her friend considered the options. When her eyes came alive with the light of an idea, Caroline thought she might kiss the woman.

"Yes?" she pressed.

The doors flew open with a bang and Caroline and Eliza both jumped.

"What on earth is going on in here?" raged the duke. The room lapsed into silence as his gaze passed over each person accusingly, and it was no surprise when it settled on Caroline last with an irritated gleam.

"Take your seat," he said in a deadly tone.

She felt that old, but familiar, quake of fear after having displeased her father, and her first inclination was to hurry back to her chair. But Eliza's fingers caught at her wrist.

"What would your Aunt Frances do?" she asked softly. "If she could have it to do over again, what would she do?"

Stunned, Caroline contemplated the question.

Her father took another step in her direction. "Take your seat. Now."

She heard Jonathan rise from his chair, and knew he would defend her if need be.

What would Aunt Frances do? She cast her gaze in her aunt's direction, then paused in horror. Frances's plate was nowhere to be seen, and the lady was kneeling on the floor—half tucked beneath the tablecloth—whispering fervently. Caroline strained to hear her.

"Tipper, you leave some for the rest," her aunt admonished quietly. "You greedy thing."

The duke and duchess stared with widened eyes, and a crease formed between Cartwick's brows as he turned, realizing something was amiss. Moving to assist Frances, he leaned over and gently gripped her around the shoulders.

"Forgive me, my lady. Allow me to assist you with your dropped plate."

Her aunt could be wildly unpredictable at times like these, and Caroline held her breath as Frances whirled around sharply.

"Don't, I—"

The protest died in her throat. Caroline couldn't say with certainty whether she recognized Jonathan, but a small smile appeared nonetheless. She allowed him to retrieve the plate and replace it upon the table before accepting his help in standing.

"Frances, you should retire to your room," said the duke solemnly.

Her aunt's head swiveled to stare at her brother, chin jutted out in defiance.

"*No.*"

Baron Horne pushed himself away from the table. "Well, Your Grace, I think I've seen enough. I'll be on my way, if you please—"

"And me, as well," agreed Viscount Bryant.

"*Everyone* take your seats," demanded the duke. "Except for Mr. Cartwick. The duchess and I would like a word with you in the foyer."

"My apologies, but I'm not leaving this room," he replied. His eyes flicked over to meet Caroline's and he nodded in her direction. "Unless she desires it."

That was about the farthest thing from what she desired as far as Jonathan Cartwick was concerned. She held his gaze and shook her head slowly, and if the heat in those amber eyes was any indication, he was of a similar mind.

The duke glowered at him. "Let me be clear, Mr. Cartwick. My daughter will not be marrying you." He gestured to the unhappy suitors at the table. "She will be marrying one of these . . . What the devil . . . Where has Lord Davenport run off to?"

"Oh, he left fairly early on, Your Grace," Thomas supplied helpfully.

"Mr. Cartwick would be an excellent husband," Caroline said, ignoring her father's edicts to try and reason with him. "He's from a respectable family—"

"The wrong side of it. And I don't care what family he's from. He is not suitable, and if he doesn't leave on his own power, I'll be forced to have my footmen remove him."

Jonathan scoffed. "I'd like to see them try."

"But, Father, won't you even listen—"

He silenced her with a glare that told her, in no uncertain terms, that he was not willing to budge where her marriage prospects were concerned.

The room was an immediate cacophony of noise. There were shouts and various threats from the suitors. Eliza and Thomas argued her case to the group. The Duke and Duchess of Pemberton railed at everyone in offense.

Caroline's breathing turned shallow and quick. Try as they may, there wasn't anything else her friends could do to help her now. She would have to help herself. Frances had already done more than her part. Eliza had released her from the shackles of betrayal that, as it turned out, had ceased to exist. Jonathan had fought—first to earn her regard, and then to win her hand—but it was all to no avail if she didn't do something, and fast.

What would your Aunt Frances do?

She glanced over at the gutsy woman who had raised her. Frances had become increasingly confused, yes, but she was still as fearless as ever. Her aunt had even managed to put one over on the duke just to give Caroline a final chance to make her own choice . . .

And the answer came to her in a sudden flash of insight. *Aunt Frances would do whatever she damn well pleased, and* there was only one thing that was going to send these suitors packing . . .

Amidst the chaos and noise of the acrimonious gathering, Caroline strode with purpose towards Jonathan. She heard the din that had surrounded them fall almost completely silent as his eyes widened in realization.

"Caroline!" yelled her mother.

But it was too late. The stubborn, self-declared spinster daughter of the Duke of Pemberton had already risen up on her tiptoes to kiss the very willing Cartwick heir, and she'd managed to do it before anyone could stop her.

Scandal and ruination had never tasted so sweet.

CHAPTER TWENTY

Jonathan glanced out the window at the first weak, gray light of dawn. He had been dressed for half an hour already, impatiently considering how best to go about seeing Caroline. Their time had been cut short the previous evening after her shocking, but incredibly effective way of asserting her own choice of husband, and he still couldn't help but marvel at her audacity. He ran a finger across his lips and smiled. She was every inch a duke's daughter . . . much to the chagrin of the duke himself.

Tomorrow, she had breathed as their fingers had touched one last time. But when? He knew her night had surely been filled with all sorts of commotion and turmoil, and he longed to ease her burden in any way she wished, although he definitely had his own rather heated thoughts on how best to go about it. But more than anything, he simply wished to revel in the victory of this battle that had been hard-fought, and most certainly hard-won. He wanted to stroke the dark ruby gleam of her hair with his fingers, enfold her protectively in his arms and brush his lips against her forehead while he watched her sleep. Had dreamed of such a thing since first laying eyes on her.

Lady Caroline Cartwick.

He couldn't deny that the thought of her being his at last sent thrills of desire coursing through him. The knowledge that she would soon be his in name—and in every way that mattered—caused his carefully crafted control to slip ever so slightly.

Jonathan sighed, willing his passions to cool. He briefly considered donning his black morning coat, then decided against it given the warmth of the morning and quietly exited his bedchamber. Casting a look down the long hallway in the direction of his mother's room, he knew it would still be hours before she rose from bed. It was the perfect time to seek out his bride-to-be; he only hoped he wouldn't have to gain admittance to Willowford House in order to find her. Something told him that, at least for a while, his presence there would be frowned upon.

Once he'd retrieved his bay from the stables, he set off across the drive and turned out onto the road. The air was still brisk due to the early morning hour, but the gently slanting rays of sun had already warmed the landscape, and Jonathan breathed in the scents of the English countryside.

He broke off to frown at a figure in the distance, his heart galvanizing its pace at the mere suggestion of her, although he knew it wasn't entirely realistic to expect her on the road at this time of day. But as he neared, he could see it was merely a merchant ambling slowly along with a pony towing an equally diminutive cart behind it. Stowing his disappointment, he moved past, giving his horse's flanks a jab to spur it faster until the wind was whipping through his hair. So it was only the purest irony when he almost didn't see her a half mile later. With a sharp yank on the reins, he managed to correct course before passing her entirely.

There was no doubt it was her, though. She had a way about her, a lithe athleticism tempered with unpretentious feminine appeal. It was what had drawn his eye that first time they'd met on the road. Caroline was a beauty, and he used to think she flaunted it. It was only over time that he came to realize she was not even aware of her splendor. Jonathan looked so very forwards to changing that.

This morning she was achingly pretty in a peach-colored walking dress, her burnished chestnut locks mostly hidden beneath a bonnet. Her lovely gray eyes grew bright in both surprise and recognition, and bringing his horse around to a stop, he swung off the saddle to land in the road.

"Caroline," he said in a rush, coming close to take her chilled fingers in his own gloved ones. "What are you doing alone on the road?"

"I could ask you the same thing," she said with a smile and a mischievous quirk of her eyebrow.

Pulling her to him with one hand and sliding the other greedily around her waist, he searched for the rosewater aroma he hungered for—the same smell that would now forever be tied to his craving for her.

"Why, I was looking for you, my lady," he said huskily with a light kiss on her neck, his body growing warmer at the way she writhed in his arms. "Although I must say, I'm rather disappointed at this understated headgear you're wearing."

She laughed breathlessly, her usually stormy gray eyes turning brilliant. It was perhaps the first truly carefree laugh he'd heard from her during their acquaintance. "Now that I've managed to secure you, Mr. Cartwick, there's no longer a need to astonish you with my aunt's tremendous bonnets."

Jonathan pulled back to gaze at her and trailed a finger down the length of her simple ivory ribbon. "There was never a need. From the first moment I saw you, there was never a need."

"Even after I insulted you to your face?"

"*Especially* after you insulted me to my face," he said with a smothered laugh. "Much to my dismay."

With a little sigh, she slid her hands up to frame his face and met his awaiting mouth with her impossibly soft lips. In an instant, he was lost. The kiss they'd shared last night had been satisfying in a different way—it had been Caroline declaring her love for him publicly, and choosing him above all others. He would always remember that kiss fondly. That kiss was important. But this kiss was private. It was between them. And as she rose up to deepen it by sliding her fingers into his hair, he knew with certainty that she had no regrets. He would spend the rest of his life making sure it stayed that way.

He toyed playfully with her tongue, his darting slyly with hers amidst a series of soul-stealing kisses. Gripping her waist, he pulled her flush against his body. He wanted her to feel what she did to him . . . how hot he was . . . how incredibly ready for her . . .

"Oh—" she cried softly against his lips. Wrenching away from the kiss, she stared at him in something nearing desperation. "Jonathan . . . take me home, please."

God, yes, he would take her home. And then he would take her straight into his bed.

Once she was nestled into the saddle with her legs draped over to one side, he swung up behind her and immediately stifled a groan, his teeth clenching with the effort. She turned to survey the way his eyes had squeezed shut.

"What is the matter?" she asked innocently. A little too innocently.

His eyes flew open to stare at her, his need only increasing at the impish gleam in her eyes. He reached around her to grab hold of the reins and gave her a very serious look indeed.

"You are about to find out, my lady."

With a jab of his heels, the horse lurched forwards, right as the amusement on her face was replaced with something much, much warmer. *Christ.* It would take all the restraint he possessed—and even some he did not—to make it back to the house without compromising her on the way.

They passed the merchant he'd seen earlier, and the old man tipped a knowing glance up at them as they flew by. Jonathan couldn't bring himself to care. It hadn't been long ago since he had ridden together with her like this, but he had been on his best behavior that day. Now he had earned the love of his moody little aristocrat, and they burned to be joined at last. The only solution was to ride quickly, and he hooked an arm around her waist to keep her safe as he did just that. But by God, the soft bouncing motion of her lovely derrière would likely kill him before they got there.

Riding into the stables, he dismounted before the horse had even fully stopped. Tearing off his gloves, he reached up to help ease her off as expeditiously as possible, then tossed the reins to his stableboy and tugged her behind him. They went through the back door and swiftly up a darkened staircase normally reserved for servants. Halfway up, he heard the tinkle of her laughter.

"I'm flattered by your impatience, Mr. Cartwick," she said with a cheeky grin.

Even in the dimly lighted stairwell, he could see the color that had risen to her cheeks. He also vaguely noted that at some point along their journey, she had lost her bonnet. But that quick glance at her had been a mistake, and the frayed cord that had been holding him together snapped. He released her hand and press her up against the cool surface of the wall. Her eyes widened in surprise, then fell closed as he inserted one of his legs between the folds of her skirts.

"What will it take, I wonder, for you to call me Jon?" he asked hoarsely, slowly moving his thigh higher until it came to rest against her sex. The layers of fabric maintained a slim element of separation between them, but he could hear from her soft whimper that the contact was definitely having an effect. "Will it take this?"

Caroline wasn't about to give in so easily . . . it was one of the many things he loved about her. She clenched her fists against the sensations and licked her lips before speaking.

"I'm sure I don't know what it will take—"

He lunged down to claim those wet, luscious lips with a kiss, and when he finally raised his head, she was gasping.

"Do you think that it would take this?" he asked, pulling down the neckline of her dress to reveal the petite, perfect shapes of her breasts. His shaft, swollen and rigid with arousal, twitched eagerly at the sight, straining to be freed from beneath the tight confines of his waistband.

Sweet Jesus, he needed to stop before he took her here on the stairs. But his impetuous fiancée only arched her back in a silent plea for him to take it farther, the rosy circles of her areolas tipping up into the air while she moved against his thigh.

"I think . . . it might take a bit more than that," she struggled to reply.

Absolutely intent now on helping her find her pleasure, he cupped one breast with his hand and squeezed, finding the tight bud of her nipple with his fingertips. The other hand followed the line of her thigh, searching through seemingly endless layers of peach muslin until reaching the linen-covered shape of her mound through her drawers. He used his leg to open her wider to him.

"And this?" he ground out, his breathing labored with the effort to keep himself in check. She was warm and damp against his fingertips, and that thin layer of fabric had become his lifeline. It was absolutely essential. Without it, he was a hairsbreadth away from simply undoing his trousers and plunging into her.

His fingertips began a cycle of slow revolutions on top of that tiny reclusive bud that would usher her into ecstasy, and her head fell back against the wall.

"Oh, *Jon*."

"There it is, my love," he growled in approval. "I thought I'd never hear it."

And now that she was in his arms, submitting willingly to his touch, he had no idea how he'd ever held back for as long as he had. His fingers kept working, the initial slow circular motion giving way to swift beats, and her breaths started coming in fits and starts.

"I, Jonathan—You should stop, I—"

But he didn't, and when she climaxed against him, he could feel the luxurious spasms coursing through her, bringing every ounce of pleasure coalescing into that single place. Her cries echoed loudly through the deserted staircase, and he thought he'd never seen anything so beautiful in all his life. Although he had yet to see her sprawled naked upon his bed—something he was reminded of with another aching strain against his trousers.

Sliding his leg from between hers, he gave her breasts a last caress, feeling the scrape of his callouses against her soft skin. Caroline gave another sharp gasp then slumped back to lean against the wall, her energy sapped for the moment.

Drawing her bodice back up to cover her, he leaned forwards and gathered her in his arms. She gave him a hazy smile of assent and he swept her up the rest of the way, her head leaning languidly against his shoulder while they exited into the hallway near his bedchamber. It was but a matter of seconds before he had the door closed behind them, and by the time he set her carefully upon his bed, his heart was pounding in anticipation.

"I never knew it could feel that way until our day in the study. How I thought of you . . . so often," she added sheepishly.

"It can feel a great deal better than that, my love," he said hoarsely, gazing down at her from beside the bed. He beckoned to her with a hand.

Despite the obvious heaviness in her limbs, her eyes were still bright with desire. Her body knew there was more, even if she was uncertain what that might involve, and he was going to be the one showing her. And he thanked God for that as she slid towards him on the counterpane, her skirts gathering around her to reveal a pair of very shapely calves.

"I must say, I'm sorry we don't have your bonnet," he said, shaking his head regretfully as he pulled off her walking boots and rolled down her stockings. "I think it has become a new fascination of mine."

She pushed up on her elbows to glare at him. "You cannot be serious."

Leaning down, he reached under her skirts to untie her drawers. He slid them off too, then tossed them heedlessly behind him. "Perhaps you're right. But I *do* have a new fascination with your hair."

Caroline sat up to touch the bun that was messily affixed

on her head, and made a face. "My hair? How my mother hated my hair."

"I've met your mother," he murmured, reaching around her to release the buttons on her dress. "She's not nearly as smart as she thinks she is. I've never seen such a lovely shade." He swept a hand across the bare length of back that he'd just revealed, and she gave a tiny shiver. "Or such a lovely woman."

She glanced up at him self-consciously. "You've said that before. Do you really mean it?"

Jonathan took her hand and backed up, pulling her into a stand next to the bed. With a little shrug, her peach dress fell in waves around her feet, and the creamy skin he'd longed for was almost fully revealed to him. His body struggled with the Herculean effort to be patient as he started unhooking her corset, when she was so close already . . . so nearly undressed. But no, he would not rush this. He wanted her totally at ease.

"You didn't know me very well before, so I'll forgive the question this time," he said with a wry smile, freeing her at last to reveal her crumpled chemise. "But now that you know me better, my lady, I expect you to also know that I don't say things unless I mean them."

The corset joined her other undergarments on the floor and he turned to fold her into his arms, one hand seeking her lush bottom, and one hand closing around the enticing weight of her breast. Her eyes drifted closed as she gripped his shirt, becoming enslaved to his movements once more. Jonathan caught at the point of her breast, giving it a gentle squeeze. Gripping her tighter, he pulled her hips forwards to meet his, letting her feel the ridge of his arousal through the gauzy fabric.

"You have no idea how badly I want to be inside you," he said in barely more than a croak.

Eyes fluttering open, she stared at him in anticipation. "What are you waiting for?"

He turned serious as he realized what she was saying, but before he could say anything else, Caroline reached down to undo his trousers. Knowing that she was inexperienced with men, he placed his hand over hers and tried to issue a warning.

"You should, perhaps, allow me—"

But she let the last button loose then, and he uttered a groan when he sprang free into her hands, long and thick and so very ready for her. Once her initial shock had passed, she stared down at him with a mixture of excitement and curiosity, and wrapped her hand carefully around him.

"I think I have a new fascination," she breathed, moving her hand over his length.

Jonathan's eyes rolled into the back of his head while she teased him with experimental degrees of pressure. His hands shot out to grip her waist, helpless to do much else with her touching him like that. "God, Caroline," he gasped. "You should stop—"

She must not have heard him, because her hand kept moving, up and down. Slowly. Methodically. The pleasure built until his knees were ready to buckle, and beads of sweat formed over his brow.

"Do you like this?" she asked, shining gray eyes gazing up at him curiously.

"Yes," he managed shakily. "But you should stop—"

"Why?" she asked, a wicked glint in her eye. "You didn't stop for me earlier when I asked you to."

Oh, the little hellcat was going to end this too soon, and he'd waited long enough for her already. Seizing her wrist, he halted her motion and gave her a deadly serious look.

"Because my lady, I want you on the bed. Right now."

Caroline's wide-eyed expression told him she took his meaning, and with a long-held sigh of relief, he felt her fingers uncurl. Before he could exact a carnal punishment of some sort for her misbehavior, she stepped back and hopped onto the mattress, kicking her way into the middle while keeping an eye on him as he joined her.

"You're not even going to take off your—"

No. He wasn't going to take off his clothes. There was no more time for anything except silencing her with the fevered press of his mouth, while his hands shoved at her chemise. Her body squirmed in delight as he jerked it up and over her head, taking most of her hairpins with it to send her hair cascading down her back in a chestnut wave.

And just like that, she was naked beneath him, glorious and perfect in every way. In a show of shyness, her hands flew up to cover herself, but he intercepted her attempts and swatted them away.

"No, Caroline. I need to see you," he pleaded.

His eyes roamed eagerly across the charming constellations of tiny freckles, and the skin of pale ivory that perfectly complemented her enchanting hair. He would never forget what a lucky, lucky man he was.

"One day, my love, I'll kiss every last one of those," he promised as she laid flat, bracing himself above her while settling his hips between her legs. "One day—"

Jonathan guided his shaft to her, throbbing in anticipation. She grabbed fistfuls of the counterpane as he entered her slowly, sliding inside, giving her time to adjust, then giving her another inch. Then another. And another. Her breath hitched and she writhed as her body was filled and stretched in a new way, and although he wanted nothing more than to plunder her, he forced himself to pause, brushing a kiss against her forehead instead.

"Is this all right?" he asked huskily.

Caroline's hands moved to his rear and tipped her hips up higher.

"More," she begged in a quivering whisper.

He could hear the strain in her voice. Rather than sink any further, he withdrew slightly—which earned him a hiss—and started a series of shallow thrusts. Her ire cooled, though, as her pleasure increased, and as *his* pleasure increased, he wondered how he was going to last long enough to make this worthwhile.

"Jonathan . . ." she whispered, her grip on him increasing. "I said *more*."

Sinking deeper, he growled at the way her body squeezed him. She was so warm, and so unbelievably *tight*. And there was something almost forbidden about the way he was taking her . . . a fully clothed gentleman laying claim to his lady, naked and willing beneath him. A rush of unspent lust caused him to rear back and drive into her with a loud groan of relief.

Her pained gasp stilled him immediately. He counted backwards from ten to distract himself from the pleasure that had him so close to finding his release, until her glassy eyes fluttered open at last.

"Forgive me, my love," he said, knowing his moment of mindlessness had caused her pain. The last thing he'd ever want was to hurt her.

He wasn't certain if he'd been expecting tears, but Caroline shook her head instead, the russet waves of her hair shimmering across the bed behind her.

"It's fine," she choked out. "Please, Jon—"

And his body followed her request before he could think any better of it, with deep-seated thrusts that started making her moan. Jonathan wasn't sure if she would be able to join him, but there was no stopping now in his quest to reach that shining pinnacle, their bodies moving in perfect timing, joining together in just the right way.

Dear God, yes—

Caroline was overtaken once more, and he drove even faster as he felt it. Her head tipped back, moistened lips parted in a silent plea, and his entire body went rigid with an ecstasy that flowed like honey through his veins. He shouted an oath and surged into her once, twice, three times more, then held there for her until he was certain that every well-earned tremor of bliss was over. With shaky arms, he sank to one elbow with a gasp, utterly and totally spent.

Head hanging and eyes closed, Jonathan fought to catch his breath. He'd been used to physical labor back in America, but this was something different. Caroline could cause his heart to race with simply a look or the lingering scent of her perfume.

Gradually, his heavy lids raised to see her covering a yawn demurely with a hand, stretching beneath him like a cat. In true Caroline fashion, she made everything seem effortless, although he knew how very hard she tried to make it appear so.

"You never even removed your clothes, Mr. Cartwick."

He glanced down at his attire in amusement. "I was much too busy removing yours, my lady."

"Well that's hardly fair," she said with a tired pout.

Jonathan couldn't disagree. Rolling over to stand next to the bed, he stripped his linen shirt swiftly over his head, with trousers following after, then pulled down the counterpane so they could both crawl under. Once he'd rejoined her in bed, she sat up with a strange look on her face.

"You are . . ." she said, staring at his chest ". . . magnificent."

His cheeks grew warm. "I-I don't believe I've ever been called that before."

"Oh, but you are," she breathed, laying back down beside him to press her naked body against him. Her hands delved reverently into the light brown hair that covered his chest, grazing a nipple with a fingertip, then roaming to the place where his shoulder met his bicep. "Just look at you."

Jonathan swallowed a gasp. It felt incredible. He tugged her upwards for a scorching, searching kiss, and when he pulled back, she was breathless again.

"Speaking of magnificent," he said with a smirk, "now that I've seen your parents, I have to wonder where your lovely hair is from."

"Well, you wouldn't know it now that she is older, but Aunt Frances and I have more in common than just the gift of saucy retorts."

He smiled at first, then felt himself instantly sober. "You should know that Lady Frances told your father about her condition," he said, plucking a lock of auburn hair away from her neck and smoothing it aside. "I think it's probably why she had trouble in the dining room; it had to be upsetting for her, even if she used the information to good purpose."

"She had trouble last night too, and of course Father sent Beatrice and Minnie back here, but at least I still have Meggie." Caroline gazed at him in heartfelt gratitude. "I can't tell you how much your help meant to me, Jonathan. And to my aunt."

"Then put your mind at ease a little more, my darling. Lady Frances is welcome to come live at Greystone Hall, if it is what she wishes."

Her eyes shone with a gleam of happy tears. "Really?" she whispered.

"I wouldn't have it any other way," he replied, placing a kiss on the tip of her nose. "Although, I'm still puzzled at why she kept the truth about the boundary lines a secret. This entire battle between you and me could have been avoided."

"Are you puzzled?" she said, nestling with him under the covers. She sighed happily against his chest. "I'd have thought you might have figured it out by now."

Jonathan froze, glanced down at the way they were entwined around each other, then broke out into laughter.

Caroline ran a finger over his cheek, probably tracing along the dimple that sometimes appeared.

"You know, you really are a lovely man, despite what I've said before." At his soft chuckle, she added, "But you'll have to be the one to tell her that she's moving in with us."

"Why?" he asked, arching a brow.

"Because after all her efforts to bring us together, I think she'd like to hear it from you."

He pulled her tighter against him, and his body stirred for her once again. "I'll do whatever you ask of me."

She tipped him an eager, but skeptical glance. "*Whatever* I ask?"

"That is what I said," he clarified.

And that morning, he discovered that the duke's daughter had an exceedingly long list of requests.

Caroline had waited for what felt like forever. But here at last, she and Jonathan stood atop Windham Hill, together. Holding hands, surrounded by a summer wind that smelled of lush, green grasses and wildflowers, they had been married.

This stretch of land that had served as their initial battleground had not only become the perfect place to celebrate their love, it was a fond reminder of how far they had come. And despite her resistance to marriage, there had been no hesitation when she'd said *I do*. Beneath the beaming smiles of devoted friends and family, the two of them had made their vows, and Caroline knew her life would be so very different in a million wonderful ways from this day forwards.

Daily meetings at Windham Hill had become their routine during those months of hard-fought patience. Her private escape became their refuge instead, and riding out to spend long, lazy afternoons wrapped in the arms of the

American, her preferred way of passing time. Jonathan Cart-wick wasn't just the man she was destined to be with, he was as essential to her as the air she breathed. As necessary as life itself.

Much less necessary, she'd found, was the presence of her parents. In a move that had surprised absolutely no one, they'd packed up and left shortly after she'd claimed her husband with an illicit kiss. But it was all for the best.

"Good," Frances had said upon being told of their latest departure, and Caroline couldn't have agreed with her more. It was good. She was more than ready to throw off the pall of their Pemberton expectations to move on in a new and better direction.

And today, when Jonathan had brushed aside the ivory lace veil concealing her face, they had kissed for the first time as husband and wife. That was *more* than good.

"Do you like the wedding cake, my darling?"

Roused from her thoughts, Caroline paused in mid-bite of the pineapple confection to slant her husband a droll look.

"You know I do," she replied with a laugh, leaning in to plant a kiss on his cheek. "And I'm not the only one," she said, tipping her head at Eliza's daughter, Rosa, who was crowing in delight at having made off with two pieces instead of one.

Thomas caught sight of her and gave chase, but she managed to land squarely at the side of her uncle William, Lord Ashworth, who slid a protective arm around her shoulders and leveled his brother-in-law with a mock glare.

"Help, Uncah!" she giggled, burrowing under his jacket.

He puffed his chest out. "Not to worry. I'll save you."

Of course, she was now a bit older now than when she'd initially had trouble saying *Uncle*, but still the name had stuck and Caroline grinned to hear it. She noticed William did not care to correct her either.

Thomas continued towards Rosa—her squeals growing louder—until he reached her and William . . . then dropped to one knee.

"I only wanted to see if you might share with me, little one," he pleaded.

Rosa did not hesitate to extend her plate, and Thomas winked at William as he claimed the extra piece of cake. It never failed to surprise Caroline at just how easily Lord Evanston had become a loving father to Rosa. It was not a role in which he'd ever professed any interest. That was, until he had fallen in love with the widowed Eliza Cartwick. His devotion to her daughter was then a natural progression of things, and was absolutely reciprocated. Rosa loved him fiercely, and the two made for a mischievous pair when at play—something that amused Eliza to no end.

"Yes, the cake does seem rather popular," Jonathan admitted. "Although it was the least I could do for you after you finally agreed to drink ale with me down in the village."

Caroline laughed softly. "Well, by my second mug, I found it had quite grown on me."

"A lot like how an opinionated little aristocrat grew on me, no doubt?"

"Did you just compare me to a mug of ale?" she asked, jabbing an elbow into his ribs.

He tugged her closer to brush his lips across her forehead.

"Yes, and I know you will take it as the compliment it was intended to be."

His nearness stirred her, as it always had—even when she'd worked so tirelessly to fight against it—and she leaned up to sigh against the strong column of his neck. Her heart picked up its speed, as did his pulse beneath the gentle pressure of her mouth.

"Stop trying to entice me with your American ways, Mr. Cartwick," she whispered.

"But why?" he asked, tightening his hold, "when it has worked so spectacularly for me thus far?"

"Because it makes me wonder if anyone would notice if we just happened to slip away . . ."

Jonathan chuckled. It was a warm sound, but she heard the unmistakable edge of hunger in it.

"My lady, I think—"

"Goodness!" exclaimed Frances.

Frances and Dorothea were suddenly before them. Sheepishly, Caroline realized that she and Jonathan had not only neglected their guests, at least for a moment, but they'd been carrying on in front of them, no less. Dorothea's lips were clamped shut in what was obviously an effort not to laugh.

"Apologies, Auntie. Mrs. Cartwick," she said, her face a mask of contrition as she eased away from her husband. She wasn't truly ashamed, though, knowing that nothing made her aunt happier than seeing the two of them married and together at last. And her aunt's happiness was one of the best wedding gifts she could have ever asked for.

"Heavens, no. Don't stop on our account," Mrs. Cartwick

replied quickly. "Lady Frances and I were just observing the irony in how after resisting each other for so long, it seems that now you can't bear to be kept apart."

Jonathan laughed. "Well, Mother, I'll have you know we did a terrible job of resisting each other before."

The two ladies exchanged a knowing look.

"Tell us something we didn't know," his mother said with a laugh.

"It was obvious," Frances added at their scandalized expressions. "We're just not precisely certain when it started. My guess was somewhere around the time I was caught running through the meadows in the altogether."

She and Jonathan stared at each other for a moment before he cleared his throat.

"A gentleman does not kiss and tell," he said in wary disapproval.

The two women swapped another glance. Dorothea nodded. Frances grinned.

"That's when it happened," they declared in unison.

His mother stepped forwards to place a reassuring hand on the arm of his formal black coat. "Regardless, your father would be so grateful to know that you have found your own way in life, and with the one woman who truly deserves you."

She saw the muscle in his jaw tighten upon hearing his mother's words, and he gazed down at Caroline with eyes that had grown bright with emotion. "I can only hope to deserve her too."

And without any of the modesty he'd attempted to affect before, he kissed her.

When at last he pulled away, she was certain her cheeks were crimson. But thankfully a tiny gurgle caught everyone's attention, and they turned to find Eliza standing nearby while Clara adjusted her hold on the newest, tiniest member of their group. Jonathan squeezed her hand.

"You should go to them."

She pressed a kiss to the back of his hand. "Then we should go home, don't you think?"

He said nothing, but his eyes spoke for him. They told of tangled bedsheets and sweat-slickened skin. Her heart fluttered inside her chest.

Soon, she mouthed.

He nodded moments before being accosted by William and Thomas, who were no doubt eager to put Jonathan's business acumen to good use as a new partner in the development and expansion of their northern cotton mills. His rocky start with Evanston notwithstanding, the three men had grown close over the summer and Jonathan was ready to embark on this new venture. Caroline couldn't wait to see what the trio could accomplish.

Clara and Eliza glanced up on her approach, and Caroline's own happiness was mirrored in the smiles that greeted her.

"How is the little darling?" she asked in a hushed voice.

"She's sleepy," said Clara, gazing down adoringly at her daughter. Little Maria Halstead had been born just a few days after Caroline and Jonathan were engaged. "But I think she appreciates the fresh air. You were right," she added, surveying the natural splendor all around them. "Windham Hill is a lovely place."

"And your dear husband even relocated the fence to accommodate you upon your move," teased Eliza.

"And Aunt Frances has already settled in nicely, with Beatrice and Minnie close at hand."

Eliza touched her shoulder. "What a lovely man. I'm sorry I ever doubted him."

Caroline shook her head in wonder. "No matter where I live, I am grateful to have had at least one Cartwick looking out for me," she said with a soft smile at her friend. After all, she had once been one of those Cartwicks too.

An excited shriek interrupted their musings and Caroline barely caught sight of Rosa's golden curls as she dashed off into the sunlit birch grove. Eliza turned her eyes heavenward.

"A squirrel no doubt."

"Some things never change," Clara murmured, her mouth quirking upwards into a smile.

But some things did, Caroline realized. Each of them had started their journeys in different places . . . one a runaway, the other a widow and Caroline all but a spinster. They'd faced their own unique challenges in their own ways, but they'd all had one distinct trait in common . . . *reluctance.*

And now being here together with them, she could see that it wasn't just she and Jonathan who had come so very far. Clara's life had been transformed when she'd captured the heart of an earl. Eliza had lost nearly everything, only to find it again with her viscount. And it had taken this headstrong American to help Caroline see that worthy men still did exist, and that they could love her utterly. Completely.

She raised her hand, admiring how her wedding ring glittered in the brilliant sunshine. Topaz. Like the eyes of the man she loved.

Stepping closer, Caroline slid an arm around both her friends. She wasn't surprised to hear them join her in breathing a hard-won sigh of relief.

They were reluctant brides, no longer.

ACKNOWLEDGMENTS

I'll be honest—it's tough to say goodbye to these ladies, and I had no idea how much they would end up changing my life. Thank you for being part of it.

As ever, my family and friends have been there for me—especially when the stress was high and deadlines were looming. Thank you to my dear mother, Dorinda, for her valuable reads of my work and for her support in countless other ways (seriously, she sings my praises to just about everyone she knows). To my father, Dave, thank you so much for being a fan and for the encouragement. Thanks to my brother, Adam, who always has a minute to listen, and to his son, Connor, who is simply the best. You guys mean the world to me.

To my husband, Gary, a heartfelt thank you for helping me get the guts up enough to try writing my own books. Thank you to my own children, Elise and Reid, who make me proud every day and who are the most wonderful people.

And to Pat, thanks for always being there. I couldn't do this without any of you.

Every day I feel lucky to have Kevan Lyon as my agent. Thank you for supporting both me and my work and for helping me navigate all things literary. Thanks to Taryn Fagerness, who does a wonderful job on the international side of things. To my editor, Elle Keck, many thanks for helping me polish my stories and for being a truly great person to work with. Thank you to Pam Jaffee, Kayleigh Webb, Jes Lyons, Michelle Forde, Gena Lanzi, Angela Craft, Erika Tsang, May Chen, Nicole Fischer, and everyone at Avon/HarperCollins who is so excellent at what they do.

To my friend and fellow writer, Erika Bigelow, for helping me get off the ground and for keeping me aloft, I am thankful. To my Eastside Romance Writers chapter and the GSRWA, thank you for helping me to grow and for teaching me so much. Thank you to L.E. Wilson, Samantha Saxon, Alexandra Sipe, Christy Carlyle, Lenora Bell, Nisha Sharma, Lorraine Heath, Lori Foster, Cathy Maxwell, Christina Britton, Eliana West, Charis Michaels, Vivienne Lorret and Eloisa James. And many thanks to Julia Quinn, who helped me when she didn't have to and is a constant source of inspiration. I am in awe of every last one of you.

Thank you to Shannon Sullivan and Heather Bottomley (and the power of the Tres). Thanks to Kristi Beckley and Eryn Frank, who have been with me since the "olden" days. To Rachel Whitaker, Anna Waller, Sakura Sutter, David O'Connell, Mary Murphy, Haley Ostrander and to all my friends who have read my book and cheered me on, thank you. You'll never know how much it means to me.

And finally, to my readers—thank you for opening this book and giving me a chance to try and make life a little bit more romantic.

Yours always,
Marie Tremayne

**Want to know where it all started?
Turn the page to read the first
installment in Marie Tremayne's
sparkling Reluctant Brides series,**

LADY IN WAITING

She wants to escape her present . . .

When Clara Mayfield helps her sister elope, she's prepared for the scandal to seal her fate as a spinster. What she doesn't expect is to find herself engaged to the vile Baron Rutherford as a means of salvaging her family's reputation. Determined not to be chained to a man she loathes, Clara slips out of Essex and sheds her identity: she becomes Helen, maid at the Earl of Ashworth's country estate. After all, belowstairs is the last place anyone would think to look for an heiress . . .

He wants to forget his past . . .

William, Lord Ashworth, is attempting to rebuild his life after the devastating accident that claimed the lives of his entire family, save his beloved sister and niece. Haunted by memories of what was and determined to live up to the title he never expected to inherit, William doesn't have time for love. What he needs is a noble and accomplished wife, one who can further the Ashworth line and keep the family name untarnished . . .

Together, can they find the perfect future?

From their first encounter, the attraction between them is undeniable. But Clara knows William is falling for Helen, a woman who doesn't even exist. The question is, if she reveals the truth about her identity, can she trust the broken William to forgive her lie and stand by her side when scandal—and the baron—inevitably follow her to his door?

Available now from Avon Impulse!

CHAPTER ONE

The End of the Season
London, England
August 1845

William, Lord Ashworth, was not going to the ball tonight.

Having finally made the decision, he reached up to loosen his white cravat with a sigh of relief. He strode to the sideboard to pour himself a brandy, seeking to numb himself from this acceptance of his failure. It was a pity. After all, he had endured the carriage ride from his country estate in Kent to make an appearance at one of the final and most fashionable events of the season. Were he actually to attend, it would have served to satisfy the *ton's* annoying demand to see the new Earl of Ashworth in the flesh, and perhaps quieted their rumormongering for a time. On the other hand, it could just have easily stirred the flames of gossip to unbearable heights. The *ton* was an unpredictable lot.

Sweat broke out upon his brow, and he unfastened the top button of his linen shirt before gripping the tumbler with shaking fingers and throwing back the drink, sending fire cascading down his throat. He uttered a groan, then slammed down the glass and only the sudden appearance of his friend, Viscount Evanston, stayed his hand from pouring another. In contrast to William's own state, Thomas looked crisp and perfectly at ease in his formal black-and-white attire. He glanced first at the decanter in William's hand, then with a raise of his brow, cast a critical eye at the state of his clothing.

"I wouldn't normally recommend attending a ball with your shirt open and cravat untied, but no doubt the ladies will approve," he said lightly, crossing the study to join him. The viscount's tone was teasing, but William did not miss the note of concern that was also present.

"I am staying home tonight," he said stonily.

His friend paused, then slipped the crystal container from his hands and replaced the stopper. "Come now, Ashworth," he chided gently. "Don't force me to be the responsible one. We waited until the end of the season, as you requested. You went through the motions. Accepted the invitation, traveled to London—"

William shot Evanston a leaden stare, silencing him immediately. "Yes, I went through the motions. As it turns out, that is all I can offer."

The disappointment that briefly flickered across his friend's face set William's teeth on edge. Inevitably, people would be upset by his inability to come out in society, especially after he'd finally relented for the event in Mayfair tonight. But even if he were to show up, there was no guarantee that the *ton* could be appeased. Any answer to their questions would be ruthlessly scrutinized for a sign that he was failing in some regard. A moment's hesitation could be the difference between projecting an air of self-assuredness and creating more fuel for their stories.

William knew there were fewer things more fascinating than an eligible lord who had suffered a calamitous loss, and for the past eighteen months he'd given them very little in the way of entertainment. Instead he'd shut himself away in the country, spending the time mourning three loved ones while recuperating from his own injuries, physical and otherwise. They would not take kindly to his absence tonight.

He closed his eyes wearily. They could all go to hell.

"Look, I don't care what you do," said Thomas, although the statement rang untrue. "And I certainly wouldn't bother yourself with what the *ton* thinks at any given point in time. But might I remind you that this was something *you* wanted to do . . . both for yourself and for your sister?"

Yes, William could admit that Eliza had probably been his most important consideration. Especially now that her house had been entailed to the next male in line for her late husband's estate. He needed to smooth their way back into society to make things easier for her, should she choose to remarry. And he needed to represent the earldom in a way that would have made his father proud, and his older brother, too—though they were no longer of this world.

He swallowed hard against the inevitable memories that always lurked, ready to invade his consciousness. They were actually less like memories, and more like the reliving of a horrid tale that often insisted upon its own retelling.

The sickening tilt of the vehicle . . . the screeching of the horses . . . the last time he'd seen them alive, eyes pale in the gloom and wide with terror. His father reaching for him from across the carriage—

"*William!*"

William blinked to stave off the nightmarish recollection, and he could feel the blood draining from his face. Evanston must have noticed, for his gaze dropped down to the sideboard. Going against his earlier censure of William's drinking, the viscount removed the stopper to pour another drink while waiting for his reply.

"I would do anything in my power to make things easier for her," William managed at last.

His friend cocked his head. "Is this not in your power tonight?"

He seriously considered the question, then shook his head gruffly and looked away.

Evanston surveyed him calmly, then heaved a large sigh.

"I know you don't think I understand, but I do," he said, sliding the tumbler towards William, then retrieving a glass for himself. "But rather than viewing this as the aristocracy cornering you in a ballroom, you need to see it as a strategic move on your part, designed to—"

"I can tell myself anything I like," he said sharply, cutting him off, "and don't think I haven't tried. But I was *in the carriage* too, Thomas. My scars are not visible, but still they show. This isn't simply a matter of losing family and moving on. It's a matter of losing control, and of those selfish bastards finding any sign of my struggle so *vastly* entertaining!"

Throwing his glass down, it shattered loudly despite the carpet on the floor. The amber contents splashed out unceremoniously to soak the ground, and silence hung heavy in the air as he and Evanston stared down at the messy aftermath of his temper. William ran a hand impatiently over his face.

"Christ."

Thomas leaned casually towards the wall to tug on the bellpull. Then he came close again to grip William's shoulder.

"You will not be able to exert perfect control over every situation. This is a truth you need to accept."

William rolled his eyes. "Says the man who can command a room, and everyone in it, simply by entering." He sighed. "Besides, you know this is different."

"Not true," Thomas corrected. "It is more similar than you know. My success in navigating society comes from being adaptable. By changing course to suit what the situation demands, not the other way around."

"And given the reality of what this situation demands of me and my inability to provide it, I am changing course by *not going to this ball*."

Even as he spoke, he knew his friend was right. But being out among society was not the effortless exercise of his past. With no notice at all, he could get pulled back into the carriage to relive his family's final moments. It was a risk he was, quite simply, unwilling to take.

Evanston squeezed his shoulder, bringing him back to the present. A crooked smile brightened his face.

"Fine. Perhaps it is best for you to skip the ball tonight."

William laughed weakly in spite of himself. "I believe I already knew that."

"Not a word more," said Thomas with a shake of his head. "Only come with me to Brooks's. You can distract yourself at the card tables."

He scoffed at his friend's suggestion. "Surely you must be joking. To roam about London after declining to show at the ball? That would not help matters in the least."

"No, I suppose not." Evanston's grin lingered. "What about a woman? They can sometimes be the most effective kind of distraction."

William shrugged out of his black tailcoat, ready to make a biting retort, when his footman Matthew appeared in the doorway.

"You rang, my lord?"

He gestured to the crystal shards surrounded by a pool of liquor, now almost completely absorbed into the dark cerulean carpet. "I have made a mess, Matthew. Please have it cleaned up immediately. Also, please have Lord Evanston's carriage brought back around as he'll be leaving shortly."

The viscount's eyebrows shot up. "Have I done something to offend you?" he asked with a laugh, although clearly worried.

"Not at all, but it's obvious you've got other places you'd rather be," William answered heavily, "and I am suddenly very tired."

The two friends shook hands firmly. Evanston lowered his voice.

"Shall we return to Kent tomorrow?"

William hung his head in silence, his teeth clenched.

Thomas nodded succinctly. "Tomorrow it is, then. There will be other balls, William," he added reassuringly. "You'll see, all will be well."

And while he nodded in agreement, the Earl of Ashworth did not feel overly optimistic.

Clara sighed and folded her gloved hands carefully upon her lap while gazing longingly at the couples waltzing by on the dance floor. After her failure of a season, she had no delusions of actually securing a suitor, but what she wouldn't do for just a *dance* . . . she loved to dance.

As she had expected, the disgrace of Lucy's elopement had made association with the Mayfield family not only undesirable, but unthinkable. Dressed in all her finery, Clara had spent the duration of her season in the stuffy drawing rooms and ballrooms of London ignored, relegated to standing alone in corners or seated against various walls.

Well, not quite alone. Because of Lucy's chance meeting with her lowborn beau, her father was taking no risks. The constant watchful eye of her mother ensured there would not be a repeat of the scandal that had claimed her older sister, and this last great ball in Mayfair was certainly no exception.

It wasn't that Clara didn't have anything to offer as a prospective bride. She certainly had wealth as the heiress to the Mayfield banking fortune, and knew her looks were tolerable. So it had stung all the more when invitations to balls and soirées had dwindled, her letters received fewer replies, and more women went out of their way to avoid calling on her socially. Friends she'd known for years had turned their backs on her, even going so far as to shun her in public. She longed to rage at them for their bad manners and fickle ways, but sternly forced herself to smile instead, unwilling to expose her family to the additional ridicule that an outburst would bring.

The lack of gentleman callers was also not a surprise, but she hadn't grasped the dire truth of her situation until recently. By then, her parents had been left to calculate their mounting losses on this massive waste of a season, and Clara could finally envision the stark reality of her future—living as a spinster, alone and childless, with not even her sister to confide in.

Her head began to ache, and she stole a covert glance at her mother. Like Clara, Mrs. Mayfield was fair skinned with dark hair. They even shared the same dark eyes, and right now those eyes were staring unseeingly at the lavish gala before them. Not for the last time, guilt wracked through Clara. Her parents were good people. The *ton* was cruel and took an almost gleeful satisfaction in the Mayfield's misfortune, but she knew they were not selective. Any ill-fated family would have been shunned just the same, though this did not lessen the sting of it.

In fact, another target had emerged during the course of the evening. Clara had overheard a barrage of offended whispers between the lords and ladies in attendance, relating that the Earl of Ashworth had chosen not to attend tonight despite accepting the initial invitation. Aside from what they considered to be his unforgivable rudeness was their peevish discontent at being denied the opportunity to view the man, who had recently suffered an awful family tragedy.

It was mentioned too—by more than a few disgruntled women—that he was rather attractive, although Clara did not see these people as true authorities on the matter. Often enough, even if a titled bachelor was old and portly but still possessed all his natural teeth, they would consider him to be exceptionally handsome. Still, she did feel a sense of gratitude to the man for allowing her to share the hateful spotlight for a change.

Tired of overthinking the *ton* and their ways, Clara turned to her mother. "Would you like something at the refreshments table, Mama?" she asked, touching her arm lightly.

Her mother jerked, as if suddenly awoken, then smiled feebly at her. "Yes, that would be lovely. It is rather hot in here."

The pair rose to stand, and made their way into the refreshment room, which was currently empty, save one older gentleman, who was standing nearby with a steaming cup of negus. Clara couldn't bear the potent smell of the spiced port drink, and quickly directed her mother towards the lemonade and ices at the far end of the table. Glancing furtively in the man's direction, she realized she knew him. Gray head, no whiskers, slightly rotund physique. A widower. She had

seen him often during the course of the season—he tended
to leer at her when he thought her attention was occupied
elsewhere. However, despite his seeming fixation on her, he
had followed suit with the *ton* and remained distant, never
once condescending to ask Clara for a dance. Yet his presence
now put her on edge, the fine hairs on the back of her neck
lifting as they might in the oppressive quiet before a thun-
derstorm.

Her mother leaned over. "Baron Rutherford," she whispered.

Clara nodded in confirmation and a shudder passed
through her. His eyes alighted with recognition and he began
walking towards them. She tensed her shoulders; there was
nothing to be done except endure the uncomfortable exchange as best she could. Resolute, she pasted a waxen smile
on her face and curtsied politely beside her mother.

He bowed. "Mrs. Mayfield, what a delight . . . and Miss
Mayfield." He focused his attention on Clara, and she noticed an almost predatory gleam in his eyes. It was as if he
were hunting in the woods rather than seeking a bride in a
civilized London ballroom. "Why, you haven't been dancing.
I won't stand to see you tucked away in the refreshment room
during the final ball of the season. Allow me the honor." He
extended a mottled hand.

It wasn't a request so much as a command. Clara could
feel her eyes narrowing at his show of superiority, made
worse by the indelicate reference to her lack of dance partners. Mrs. Mayfield flushed, but stood silently by, waiting
for her daughter's reaction to this rare invitation to dance.

While Clara longed to refuse the baron, it could not reasonably be done without fear of mortifying her mother, and her mother had been through enough this year already.

She tipped an icy smile in his direction. "If it pleases you, my lord," she forced out.

Accepting his proffered arm, they approached the dance floor. Clara glanced over her shoulder to her mother, who waved in encouragement, although the confusion in her eyes was somewhat less encouraging. She was probably trying to understand why a titled gentleman would now show interest in her daughter after a long season of snubbing her.

Rutherford led her out onto the floor, ignoring the flurry of disbelieving looks from those nearby, and launched into a waltz upon the first notes from the orchestra. His clasp on her waist was noticeably tight, as was his grip on her hand. Surprised, Clara glanced upwards to find him smiling hungrily down at her. The sight was disconcerting to say the least.

"My lord, is it absolutely necessary to—"

His hands tightened further, shocking her into silence in mid-sentence.

"Perhaps you are wondering why I might wish to dance with you now," he offered. "Particularly when an association with your family is considered so highly undesirable."

Clara's mouth fell open in offense. "I wouldn't want you to blacken your good name on my account. Pray, let me relieve you from such a *trying* act of generosity . . ."

She did not wish to create a scene, but her own sense of self-worth prevented her from blithely accepting his insults.

She pushed against him again and he retaliated by jerking her closer. The cloyingly sweet smell of negus on his breath engulfed her and she turned her head to the side, gasping for air while trying to create more distance between them. All efforts were futile, though, and he continued forcing her to dance while leaning down to whisper in her ear.

"I have watched you these many months, Miss Mayfield. And I have waited. Tomorrow I will pay a visit to your beleaguered parents to make an offer for your hand. It is an offer they will accept, for the season has ended and your prospects are dire."

The baron whirled her around into a dizzying turn before she could respond, and her stomach lurched. Her eyes searched desperately for her mother, who was craning her neck to find them through the mass of dancing couples and frothy skirts. Clara knew that she was likely not able to see Rutherford's behavior from where she stood. She glared angrily up at him.

"Even were it so, I will never accept you as my husband."

He smiled. "Oh, you will accept me, my dove. Perhaps in time you will come to realize how very little control you have over the situation. It is of no importance, either way. In fact," he added, his voice lowering, "a little resistance might make things more enjoyable, if I may be so bold."

Shocked beyond belief, Clara wrestled out of his grip.

"You've had months to pay your courtesies, and this is how you choose to make overtures? With insults and threats and . . . detestable imaginings?"

The ladies and gentlemen surrounding them began to

slow the pace of their dancing, immediately drawn to the commotion. Her cheeks burned at the unwanted attention, but it was minimal when compared to the fire of her sudden hatred for the baron. He took a step towards her. She immediately took a step back.

"I am not interested in making overtures, Miss Mayfield. You will consent to being my wife or your family will be ruined."

She scoffed. "I will consent to nothing of the sort."

The baron simply chuckled. As the music came to an end, he sketched a bow in her direction, and Clara spun on her heel, rushing off the floor into the relative safety of her mother's arms.

Clara paced fretfully in the parlor of the Mayfields' country home in Essex. Six weeks had passed since the night the baron had made his insulting offer—and yet the time since had been more awful still, something she wouldn't have thought possible.

Of course, she also wouldn't have thought it possible for her father to actually agree to marry her off to the baron, yet here she was on the eve of their wedding, the preparations having been hastened along by her husband-to-be. He was in the drawing room this very moment, preening and posturing before her parents in his penultimate moment of victory. As much as she loathed to admit it, he'd been right about everything. The state of her family's reputation being what it was, there had been no true alternative in the end.

Rutherford had easily been able to force her father's hand, for denying the baron what he wanted could only damage the family further, while her marriage to him could repair it.

Her father chose to view the situation in a more optimistic light than Clara could, entreating her to give the baron a chance to prove himself a worthy husband. However, the season had afforded him many chances already, and he had shown plainly what kind of man he was.

Absently, she swiped at her cheek, then gazed down at the moisture on her hand. She hadn't been aware that she was crying. She'd shed enough tears to last a lifetime these past months, first with the loss of her sister, and now with the loss of her own free will. At least Lucy had found love— she reminded herself of that. But oh, the cost . . .

There was a discreet tap on the door. She rushed over to crack open the portal to reveal the white-capped head of her lady's maid, Abigail, holding a cup of coffee. Clara admitted her inside the parlor before they could be seen, then closed the door securely behind. Abigail set the steaming beverage down on a table and reached out to clutch Clara's shaking hands tightly in her own.

"The preparations have been made. My sister, Amelia, has agreed to provide a reference to the housekeeper at Lawton Park, although I did not give her the particulars of your identity. I only told her you were a capable housemaid from the Mayfield estate in search of work in Kent."

Clara regarded her anxiously. "And if they should turn me away?"

"I don't think they will," replied Abigail with a thoughtful shake of her head. "Amelia has commented on the understaffed conditions there for quite some time."

She chewed on her lip. "And the master there is kind?"

"From what I have heard, the Earl of Ashworth is . . . a bit of a recluse," Abigail replied. "But I believe him to be fair."

Clara nodded, but she had known this already. She had remembered the rage of his fellow aristocrats when he had backed out of the ball in Mayfair. His solitary ways were one of the reasons she'd even considered fleeing to his estate. Without the constant risk of having a master who enjoyed entertaining and throwing balls, safeguarding her secrecy would be easier.

Abigail paused in conflicted silence. "You'll tell me if you change your mind?"

Clara pulled her close in a familial embrace. Over the years, Abigail had become so much more than just a maid. She had become a close friend, and Clara would miss her almost as much as she missed Lucy. She hugged her tightly. "There's no chance of that," she whispered.

Another knock sounded on the door, causing the two women to spring apart. Clara smoothed her skirts and cast a nervous glance at Abigail.

"Yes?" she called out.

Mrs. Mayfield appeared. She gave a brief nod to the maid, and with a last departing glance at Clara, Abigail left the room. Her mother stared after her curiously.

"What was Abigail doing in here?"

Clara froze in panic for just a moment, before remembering her coffee. She strode to the table to retrieve the cup and saucer.

"She brought me coffee while I waited, Mama." She took a sip of the warm, lightly sweet drink. Clara had always preferred coffee, and this was perfect, just the way she liked it. Cream with two lumps of sugar. It reminded her of how comfortable her home—her life—had been. Her heart clenched at the thought of leaving it.

She returned the cup to its saucer, the china rattling noisily in response to the trembling of her fingers. "Do you have news?" she asked, attempting nonchalance but feeling the full burden of her guilt.

"Yes, my dear," Mrs. Mayfield answered lightly. "They are ready for you in the drawing room."

Her heart began to race and her stomach roiled. It didn't matter that she had no intention of marrying the vile Lord Rutherford. Just the thought of seeing him, smirking and self-congratulatory, was enough to cause an adverse physical reaction.

She set her drink down on the table again. Otherwise, she might have been tempted to toss it in the baron's face. Extending her hand, she tried to smile at her mother.

"Shall we go in together?"

Moments later, they entered the drawing room. Both Mr. Mayfield and Rutherford stood to greet the ladies, although Clara did not approach the man or even look at him, electing instead to seat herself on the farthest edge of the settee across from his chair. She stared stubbornly down at her hands and an awkward silence ensued, which was finally broken by her father's rumbling baritone.

"Lord Rutherford," said Mr. Mayfield. "I am very pleased we could come to a mutually beneficial arrangement. Very pleased . . ." His great moustache absorbed any final murmurs on the subject.

Clara's fingers tightly gripped the dark emerald velvet upholstery as she listened silently, finally raising her gaze to evaluate the situation. Her fiancé sat opposite her, triumphant in his crisp attire that did nothing to conceal his bloated form. Mutually beneficial, Clara understood, was a relative term, one that excluded her entirely.

Baron Rutherford flicked an invisible speck off his perfectly pressed pants. "It seems we have, Mr. Mayfield," he drawled. "Your daughter will make me the happiest of men, I'm sure."

"Yes, my lord—such a handsome match," said Mrs. Mayfield. "It will inevitably be the talk of *le bon ton* . . ."

If there was to be any talk within high society about their match, it would likely not be flattering. Another titled old widower, his estate destitute after years of improvident financial decisions, finds a wealthy young wife to refill his family's coffers—almost certainly to drain them again.

What a tale for the ages, thought Clara.

It was strange to feel so helpless. Clara ached to confide in her sister, but the last thing she wanted to do was give Lucy any reason to worry on her account.

As if sensing Clara's despair, Abigail skirted by the door,

giving Clara a nod of support as she passed. If their plans succeeded, it might allow Clara to live life on her own terms versus getting crushed beneath the baron's bootheel. It would also mean hiding in service until Lord Rutherford either remarried or died, but under these dire circumstances, she was determined to be eternally patient. Although if this scheme failed, which was a distinct possibility, it could mean a life of ill-repute—further ill-repute, rather—and destitution.

Or worse, returning home to be claimed by her enraged fiancé.

She sank lower into the cushions, wishing she could disappear. Every second felt more suffocating than the last, and while the men discussed the particulars of the arrangement, Clara passed time by studying the gleaming hardwood floor and the ornate golden rug that lay upon it. She knew her parents wished only for their remaining daughter to make an uneventful, but advantageous, marriage, to dispel the smoke of Lucy's scandal and return their lives to normal.

Rutherford had laid his trap well, silently waiting for its jaws to spring closed around Clara as if she were some unfortunate animal.

The baron's gravelly voice grew louder, disrupting her melancholy train of thought.

"You look lovely today, Miss Mayfield."

Before thinking better of it, she glanced up to see his mouth curved upwards in what could only be described as a leer. It did not surprise her that he was enjoying her discomfort. Clara merely disregarded his compliment with a dismissive raise of her brows. His steely gray gaze sharpened.

"So, my lord, the arrangements are all in place for the wedding," said her mother abruptly in an awkward attempt at conversation. "We've hired an orchestra, and the weather should be fine, so we will have tables and chairs on the back lawn—"

"That sounds delightful, Mrs. Mayfield," interrupted the baron without taking his eyes off his betrothed.

Clara's mother could certainly detect the simmering hostility, but persevered anyway. "Clara's dress is beautiful and just arrived yesterday. I had it made in Paris at this wonderful little shop . . . they even rushed to finish it in time. No expense spared," she said proudly. "White satin and lace, with tiny pearls . . ."

Mrs. Mayfield trailed off as she observed her daughter's increased pallor. Clara squirmed uncomfortably, aware that she had begun to sweat. She tried to discreetly wipe her palms on the couch. What would happen if she jumped up and started yelling gibberish while waving her hands about? Would they care that she had been driven to such madness? Even better, would it end this farce of an engagement?

"And what of you, Miss Mayfield? Are you *prepared*?" He was no longer even trying to sound friendly. Clara knew he wanted to intimidate her, but it was shocking that he was doing it openly in front of her parents.

"I prefer not to think about it," she snapped, and was rewarded with her father's sharp intake of breath, but she refused to feel badly for being impolite. Her only regret in all this was that her behavior vexed her parents, although they would be more than vexed by tomorrow morning for sure . . .

Suddenly Clara felt ill. She stood abruptly.

"May I be excused?" she asked, hoping not to cast her crumpets in front of the baron. He'd be certain to take that a sign that he'd won.

Her mother's brow wrinkled in a flash of concern before arching once more with a forced smile. "No, my darling," she replied in a soothing tone. "You must stay until we are finished speaking with Lord Rutherford."

Slowly, Clara sat back down on the couch and smoothed her skirts, trying to hide her trembling hands. She looked up and caught the baron watching her every movement. It made her shudder.

"Forgive her, my lord. Clara has always been an unconventional girl," her father excused. "She takes great interest in matters of the estate. Why, I've often discovered her making rounds with my land steward, much to my dismay," he admitted with a chuckle. "But she does enjoy getting her hands dirty every now and then."

Rutherford scoffed. "She is a girl no longer, and will certainly not be getting her hands dirty on my estate. I expect her to behave as a baroness should."

Clara's eyes narrowed to slits. He would seek to control everything about her, she was sure.

Mr. Mayfield blinked, then continued. "Certainly, my lord. You will find Clara to be a cheerful and complacent bride despite the quirks of her personality. It may take time, but love so often does."

The thought of *love* with such a man made her skin crawl.

"She can be willful, but indeed wouldn't you say that is part of her charm, my lord?" added her mother.

Clara glanced at the baron, who trapped her gaze.

"Indeed," he said with a mirthless smile that shook her to her core. He rose abruptly, and Mr. and Mrs. Mayfield struggled to stand quickly as well. Clara stood hopefully, ready to dash out the door, but her fiancé stayed her with a look. "I'd like to have a word alone with my bride now, if you please."

Her father nodded and bowed, quickly escorting Mrs. Mayfield towards the door. "Certainly, my lord."

Clara shot a pleading look at her mother, whose brow furrowed slightly just as the door closed between them. She didn't think her mother fully grasped her abhorrence of this man. Attempting a brave countenance, she cleared her throat and faced Rutherford, who stared at her in barely concealed rancor. A jolt of alarm shook her already unsteady frame.

Perhaps a little politeness might hasten this meeting along. She attempted to switch tactics.

"Would you like a drink?" she asked lightly, approaching the sideboard.

His expression remained unchanged. "No. I would not." She did not hear him step across the carpet, but suddenly his voice was right near her ear. "I want my wits about me when you finally submit."

Immediately, all thoughts of politeness vanished. She whirled around. "Well then, I suppose you're giving up drinking altogether?"

His teeth clenched noticeably, but he only smiled. "It will

take far less time than you think, pet. And I will enjoy every second." He regarded her. "Tell me, how does it feel to know you are already mine? Is it upsetting to see how eagerly your father accepted my proposal, as I'd told you he would?"

"I am not yours," Clara seethed, her fingers curling into fists. "And as for my father, I think he ended up having very little choice in the matter."

"By design. While you waited on the edges, hoping for someone, *anyone*, to court you during the season, I was watching in anticipation. Reveling in your every rejection." He closed the final distance between them and seized her shoulders in a punishing grip. "You will learn to yield. You will learn to be grateful. Especially in my bed—"

Before she could even flinch, he crushed his mouth against hers. Clara cried in revulsion and raised her fists against his chest, and once again she was surprised at the strength a man of his age could possess. She struggled to twist her face away, but he followed each way she turned. At last, he released her, and she took a step backwards to slap him soundly across the face. He instantly countered by grabbing her throat and squeezing tightly.

"You will learn to yield," he repeated slowly.

She clawed at his hand, struggling to breathe and eyes blown wide with panic.

"Stop," she rasped. "Please—"

The vice-like pressure around her neck was removed, and she fell against the wall, gulping in huge breaths of air.

"See?" he spat, tugging on his jacket. "You're learning already."

He proceeded across the room to throw open the door without giving her another glance. Clara massaged her neck, her thoughts hurtling wildly. She was supposed to be safe here. This was her family's drawing room, her home, where she and Lucy had played as children, and had grown into womanhood.

Her gaze flitted across the familiar paintings, her favorite green settee, the heavy patterned draperies beside the windows. It all felt wrong now, somehow. As if his violation of her here had challenged her very notion of home.

It needed to be safe. *She* needed to be safe.

Clara's resolve to flee grew stronger. Seeing what he was truly like, she couldn't help but wonder if Rutherford's previous wife had exited this world in an effort to escape his cruelty—or if he had sent her packing early.

She would not be lingering to discover the truth of it for herself.

Clara felt nearly blind in the darkness, but could see the soft rays of moonlight illuminate the gleaming satin of her wedding dress. It hung silently in the corner of her room like the hovering wraith of the bride she was to become.

She sat perched on the edge of her bed, had sat there for many hours, listening to the sound of crickets chirping outside. She had once thought the crickets' song sweet, but after listening tonight it somehow sounded sad; like the end of summer, like a hundred tiny good-byes.

Clara was wearing one of Abigail's dresses. Definitely not

normal nighttime attire, but this was not a normal night. It was the end of a long struggle for her. The struggle of wanting to do right by her family, but incapable of sacrificing herself to the baron to do it.

She wished he'd been a different man. Maybe then she could have made peace with her fate. Remorse coursed through her. Standing, she went to her desk. She opened a drawer with unsteady hands and unfolded the letter inside.

> *I cannot do this. I'm sorry. I love you.*
> —*Clara*

The room became blurry with fresh tears as she refolded the note and pinned it to her wedding dress for her mother to find. She was careful not to damage the delicate fabric, for despite her complaints against the groom, the gown really was beautiful.

Clara loved her parents, and knew they had been devastated by Lucy's marriage. What was more, she knew they missed her, and longed to see the daughter they had lost. Their world would shatter one more time tomorrow morning upon discovering Clara's own flight from home, and while she wished to avoid causing them more pain and humiliation, she could not see how.

Leaning over, she retrieved a small satchel and her coin purse of saved funds. As she did, she caught sight of herself in her looking glass. Haunted eyes, her mother's eyes, admonished her in the gloom. Surely she didn't have the strength to break from the only family she'd known and loved. There was no guarantee that the strange world outside would have any more love for her, after all . . .

She touched the faint bruise the baron had left on her throat and turned abruptly.

She did not have the luxury, or the time, for second thoughts.

Shaking her head to clear it, she strode swiftly across her room and threw open the windows. The fragrant breeze of late summer engulfed her as she leaned out, one of her tears making the jump before she did to the carefully sculpted greenery below.

ABOUT THE AUTHOR

MARIE TREMAYNE graduated from the University of Washington with a B.A. in English Language and Literature. While there, a copy of *Pride and Prejudice* ended up changing her life. She decided to study the great books of the Regency and Victorian eras, and now enjoys writing her own tales set in the historical period she loves. Marie lives with her family in the beautiful Pacific Northwest.

www.marietremayne.com
www.facebook.com/MarieTremayneRomance
www.facebook.com/avonromance